Austea E. Kette

Before She Remembers

Remember Me, SQ
#1

Before She Remembers
Remember Me, SQ
by Austea E. Kette

Copyright © 2024 Austea E. Kette

This is a work of fiction. Names, places, characters and incidents are the product of the author's imagination and are fictitious. Any resemblance to actual persons, living or dead, events or establishments is solely coincidental.

Couple and background design by Kondrat
ISBN: 978-609-08-0616-6

Bibliographic information is available on the Lithuanian Integral Library Information System (LIBIS) portal

All rights reserved. No part of this book may be reproduced, stored in or introduced into a retrieval system, or transmitted, in any form, or by any means (electronic, mechanical, photocopying, recording, or otherwise) without the prior written permission of the author.

CONTENT GUIDANCE: This novel contains mentions of sexual assault, suicide and depictions of violence. Please read with care.

To my readers, who sometimes just want
to forget and wake up to a hot, caring
book boyfriend claiming to be their husband

And to my partner . . .
Please, read chapter 34

The Fire

"**YOU CAN'T DO THIS TO ME!**" Teodora shouted as she pulled the handle down and pushed the door with her shoulder. "Hey! You can't leave me here!"

Despite Teodora's attempts, the reality was undeniable: she was stuck, and there was nothing she could do. Yet, she clenched her hands in frustration and pounded on the door. "Open the door! Please!"

No one answered.

Tears pooled in her eyes as she slid down to the floor, her determination slipping. "Please," she whispered hopelessly.

Teodora hadn't expected the day she had been waiting for a year to end like this. When she woke up this morning, nervous and excited, she didn't think she would be kidnapped. Lost in her own world, she hadn't seen it coming, even though she'd been working with Steven and Robin almost every day for the past year. She thought of them as her unassuming, quiet coworkers, but in reality, they were quite the opposite.

Just five minutes ago, when Teodora stepped into the abandoned Hôtel du Passé, Steven and Robin greeted her, saying they wanted to show her something. Without thinking much, she followed them to the fifth floor and into a room. As she turned to ask what they wanted to show her, the door closed and locked with a click.

The shock rendered Teodora immobile, preventing any response. As it eased, she tried to open the door, unable to believe they had trapped her inside. These were the men she saw almost every day, her most trusted partners, who had betrayed her on her most awaited day.

Since arriving in Monte Carlo, Teodora had anticipated that day to be the highlight of her career. She couldn't let them take it away from her. She couldn't give up. If she did, Steven and Robin would steal the accomplishment she had been working on for a year. That was why they had tricked her, right? She saw no other reason.

With renewed determination, Teodora stood up. "Please! Someone!" she shouted in the hope that someone would walk by, hear her, and help her. But time passed, and no one came.

Everyone must be on the first floor, gathered in the hall for the announcement. When they revealed the creators of the alternate Cure, Teodora wouldn't be among them. Only Steven and Robin would step onto the stage, claiming all her work for themselves. Their names, not hers, would go down in history as the saviours from the evil organisation in Monaco.

Teodora hit the door so hard that pain shot through her fist. Hissing, she clutched it with the other hand.

No, she couldn't take all the credit. She wasn't the sole creator; her kidnappers had helped her. But she deserved her moment to shine on that stage tonight. Even if Steven and Robin had assisted her, she knew they wouldn't have created the drug without her. She could have done it alone if necessary. All they did was make the process easier and possibly faster.

Teodora looked back at the door, realising she was being stupid. Who would come to the fifth floor when the event was on the first one? Steven and Robin might be thieves and kidnappers, but they weren't stupid. They must have planned this, making sure no one would show up on this floor. Her only shot was to rescue herself, not wait for someone else.

She looked around the room with no bed, only an empty desk, a chair, and two windows. Jumping out of a window wasn't an option since it could leave her paralysed for life. Still, she hoped she could figure something out.

She threw open the drawers, finding nothing but useless papers, markers, paper clasps, clips—

Paperclips!

Teodora knelt in front of the lock, unfolded the paperclip, and inserted one end into the hole. A feeling of déjà vu came over her, followed by unwelcoming memories, but she pushed them away.

She hadn't done anything like this in years, but she hoped she was still capable.

While Teodora focused on unlocking the door, she had no idea a hooded woman was pouring gasoline in the basement. Every drop fell on the floor that Teodora had walked on almost every day for the past year. The flasks and beakers watched as the evildoer casually whistled her favourite tune while covering their home in the highly flammable liquid.

The woman was on the first step of the stairs when she ran out of gasoline. Done whistling, she tossed the jerry can away and pulled out a pack of matches. She struck one against the side and raised it, her eyes glued to the flame.

A wicked smile curled at the corner of her mouth, and she dropped the match.

02:59

Flames immediately shot up across the floor of the secret laboratory.

In three minutes, the fire would advance to the first floor where people were gathered. Satisfied with her work, the woman turned and rushed up the stairs.

Upstairs, Teodora wrestled with the lock, while the woman hurried down the hallway. She passed the large room where 'Boléro' by Maurice Ravel filled the air and people in elegant clothes had gathered to learn about the life-changing creation.

At last, the lock yielded with a satisfying click. Teodora stood up, eagerly pulling down the handle and swinging the door open, but her excitement quickly turned into shock.

Teodora's entire body froze, from her toes to her neck, as all thoughts of what to do next fled her mind.

A woman stood before her, with the same hazel eyes and freckles across her nose and cheeks, staring back at her. They looked alike, except for their clothing. Teodora wore an emerald-green dress with a lab coat over it, while the woman was dressed entirely in black.

The stranger smiled and waved at her innocently.

Teodora didn't question her presence. She had things to do.

She tried to move past her. "Excuse—"

But the woman pushed her further into the room. "You're not going anywhere."

She pulled out a gun.

Teodora's heart stuttered.

The woman closed the door behind her and pointed the gun at Teodora. "Take off your clothes. *Now*."

She didn't know the woman's name, but it was clear as day where she was from. A member of Monaco's infamous criminal organisation, Sanctus Quinque, had a gun aimed at her, and she might know why.

SQ found out she had created something that could destroy

them.

But why would the woman order her to undress?

02:28

The fire engulfed the expensive equipment, touching the flammable substances, triggering the explosions.

"I don't have all day," the woman gritted her teeth, clearly losing her patience. "Take off your damn clothes!"

Teodora snapped out of her haze. She didn't need to be told three times. She wanted to live. If it meant dancing to the woman's flute, she would happily do so. Even add a somersault if it would make the woman leave her alone sooner.

She removed her lab coat first, and the woman snatched it away before she could hand it over. As she undid her dress, the woman unzipped her jacket. She pushed back her hood, revealing her fiery hair pulled into a tight ponytail.

"W-Why," Teodora stuttered. "You look just like—"

"If I shoot your leg, will you be faster?"

Saying nothing anymore, Teodora slipped out of her dress as the woman, too, took off her clothes. Teodora couldn't understand why she was also removing her clothes and struggled to come up with a single plausible reason.

The woman stood there, unabashedly naked. Teodora quickly averted her gaze, using her dress to cover herself, but the woman snatched that away as well.

She threw her own clothes at her. "Dress up. Fast."

02:03

Everything melted, smoke filled the room . . .

As they exchanged and put on each other's clothes, their similarity struck Teodora more than before. The woman could pretend to be her, and nobody would bat an eye.

Was it her plan to pose as Teodora? But why?

Aiming the gun in her direction, the woman pointed towards the door. "Go."

01:34

The smoke consumed the basement.

Teodora obeyed, walking out of the room. She sensed the gun on her back as she walked to the stairs. She was about to descend when she felt a push and tripped, falling down the stairs.

She hit her head against the wall. As she reached to touch the throbbing area, the woman grabbed her hand and forcefully pulled her to her feet.

"Keep walking," she ordered.

01:21

The first tendrils of smoke slipped through the cracks and gaps into the first floor.

If the woman didn't have a gun, Teodora would have given her a nasty look. She pushed *her*! What was she up to?

Teodora heard a crackling sound coming from the woman, who then pulled out a walkie-talkie that was smaller than usual from her lab coat. A male voice then came through the device. "Are you leaving the building? Over."

"Yes," she replied, her eyes fixed on Teodora. "Over." She put the walkie-talkie back in her pocket.

The rumours are true, Teodora thought. *SQ has more advanced technology than people are aware of.*

The woman gestured for her to keep walking. Teodora stepped closer to another flight of stairs, her heart pounding. She put her hand on the railing to steady herself and avoid being pushed again, but her palms were sweaty—

Teodora felt a forceful hand on her back, sending her tumbling down the stairs. When her body crashed against the wall on the bottom floor, her vision blurred and then everything went black.

01:04

The smoke crept into the hallway.

The red-haired woman knelt in front of her and tapped her cheek, looking for any sign of consciousness. Nothing. She pressed her fingers to the side of her neck, feeling the steady pulse beneath them.

She grabbed Teodora's ankles and carelessly dragged her down the rest of the stairs, leaving bruises and scratches on her back. The fire was seconds away from reaching the first floor. People would soon panic and rush to the exits, only to find all but one locked.

For now.

00:24

People went quiet for the host on the stage, and the smell of smoke tickled a woman's nose.

The woman dragged Teodora towards the exit in the back and lowered her legs on the floor before opening the door.

00:20

The mayhem erupted.

Ignoring distant shouts, the woman held the hotel door partly open with her shoulder, lifted Teodora's legs, and pulled her outside. After dropping them, she hurried to lock the door. Just as she turned the key, she heard the first pound on the door.

The woman returned to Teodora and, crouching in front of her, pulled out a syringe from her bag. She injected the clear liquid into the vein in Teodora's inner elbow, pressing the plunger until the syringe was empty. Then she set her bag and the walkie-talkie next to her.

00:04

People rushed around the building, seeking an exit. But every door and window was blocked and barricaded as black smoke swallowed the first floor.

The woman pulled out a flask and unscrewed it, taking a heavy sip before pouring it around Teodora's body. She pushed the empty flask back in her pocket and took out the box of matches. As she struck one and dropped it, the flame sparked to life around Teodora.

She turned away and proceeded to leave.

00:00

A woman fainted.

01
Who Are You?

Teodora

MY FIRST MOMENTS WERE UNCLEAR.

I forced my eyes open, only to be met with a haze. The shift from darkness to light pierced my brain, but eventually, the pain eased. My eyes adjusted, and the fog cleared, revealing my surroundings.

A white ceiling stared back at me, as if asking what was so interesting about it. My mind raced, grappling for anything familiar, but there was nothing. Nothing until . . .

Where am I?

Panic shot through me, and I looked away from the ceiling. With my heart pounding, I pushed myself up with trembling hands, my muscles straining as if they had barely been used. An unpleasant pressure below my belly appeared, growing with each movement until it became impossible to ignore. Despite the sweat on my forehead and back from the effort, I managed to get into a half-sitting position, resting on my elbows. Gasping for air, I darted my eyes around the room, hoping to find something familiar.

But the room was a stranger. Dim light seeped in through a narrow gap in the heavy maroon curtains, casting ghostly shadows on the grey walls. The red artwork on the walls reminded me of blood, making me wince. Purple flowers in vases were scattered around—one on the table with a mirror, another on a bedside table . . .

The flowers had a name, I was sure. Yet, as I racked my brain for one, I found nothing.

The tightness in my chest grew, along with a frantic beat inside.

Where am I?

Feeling a sudden heat, I kicked off the blanket. I tried to sit up straighter, but something tugged at my arm, stopping me cold.

My eyes snapped down to a small tube coming out of my arm, connected to a bag of clear liquid hanging from a metal pole beside the bed. It looked vaguely familiar, but I had no idea what it was or why it was there.

I pinched the tube with my fingers, ready to yank it out—

"What are you doing?"

A voice shattered the silence, and I flinched. I looked at the stranger in the doorway, holding a vase of the same purple flowers. As he came closer, I instinctively recoiled, watching him grow taller with each step. I didn't know him, didn't recognise the softness in his eyes or the concerned lines on his face.

He placed the vase on the bedside table, his movements slow

and deliberate, as if he didn't want to scare me more. His hands reached out and touched my bare arms. I jolted at the contact, a shiver of fear and electricity shooting through me, adding to my bewilderment. My mind screamed at me to pull away, but my body refused to move. I didn't even notice when he gently pushed me back to the bed.

It wasn't until he withdrew his hands to scratch at his stubbly jaw that I realised what he had done. I didn't think he had any clue about the fear and confusion fighting inside me.

"You're not supposed to do that," he said, but his words went in one ear and out the other. I was too focused on his face, alarmed yet entranced by his husky voice and . . . him.

A mop of brown curls draped over the stranger's forehead, and I felt an inexplicable urge to fix his hair. It was weird. It unsettled me.

A white shirt clung to his lean, toned physique, and he carried an air of refinement, which made me wonder why. Was it his defined face, his beautiful yet weary brown eyes, or his mere presence?

"Are you scared?" he asked, his voice tinged with something darker, something that made the hair on the back of my neck prickle. "Don't be. It's alright. You're awake now." A faint smile tugged at his lips, but it did little to ease my panic. "I didn't think you would wake up. Not after all this time," he added, disbelief evident in his tone.

My heart stuttered. *After all this time?* I stared at him, alarmed, my mind spiralling. *Am I supposed to know this man?*

He reached for my hands, taking them without permission.

I watched him with alarm, my pulse roaring in my ears. His touch was warm—perhaps too warm—and gentle, which only intensified my fear. He was too close, and I had no memory of him at all.

His eyes searched mine, as if expecting something—something I couldn't give. My heartbeat quickened, each beat a desperate plea for understanding, for escape. Should I say something? Do something?

"Speak to me," he urged softly. "Say something so I know it's real."

I stared intensely at the stranger, trying to recognise him, but I couldn't. I didn't know him. How did he know *me*?

His expectant stare and the pleading look in his eyes pressured me into forcing my lips apart. I tried to make a sound, but my vocal cords failed me.

"It's okay," he reassured, and to my relief, I didn't detect any disappointment in his words. "Don't move while I fetch Dr Zunino, okay?"

I nodded my head without thought, even if I didn't fully understand what he meant. He smiled—warm, almost tender—and headed for the door.

But as he turned away, a new wave of panic surged through me. What if he didn't come back? What if I was left alone, trapped in this nightmare with no answers and no idea who he was?

I tried to summon my voice again, and a faint sound came out. He stopped, turning back to me. "Did you say something?"

I swallowed hard, trying again, but despite having the question in my brain, I couldn't voice it.

Why can't I speak?

"Hold on a moment." He approached a small gilded table by the chair and picked up a cup. He returned and held it out to me. "Drink."

I peered suspiciously into the cup. It was half-filled with clear liquid. I brought it to my nose and sniffed it, not sure why. I didn't know what I was expecting, but it had no smell.

"It's water," he said with a small smile. "I'm not giving you vodka right after you woke up."

His playful tone brought a smile to my face and eased my tension. *Maybe there's nothing to be scared of after all.* The water was cool and soothing, and as I swallowed, something in my mind clicked.

Water.

I knew that. I remembered it now.

I drained the cup in one go, the relief short-lived as the anxiety crashed back in. "What—" I sighed as my voice faltered. "What is your name, sir?" The words came out as a rasp, but they were out, hanging in the air between us.

He turned slightly, pushing his hair away from his ear to unveil a small device. "Can you repeat that a bit louder and clearer?"

I went still, studying the device until it occurred to me it must be some kind of hearing aid. That was why he wanted me to repeat my question louder.

I wondered why he would need that, especially since he didn't look older than twenty-five.

When I repeated my question slower and louder, his playful expression vanished, replaced by complete shock.

My smile faded, and my heart beat faster at his silence, drowning out everything else—

"You don't remember me?" he finally asked, his voice tight with disbelief.

I managed a shaky laugh, thinking he was joking. But his face stayed serious, with no trace of humour. My smile vanished, replaced by a growing dread. "S-should I?"

"No shit." He frowned, a mix of annoyance and confusion crossing his face. "I'm Ettore. Your husband."

02

Secret Activities

Ettore

VITTORIA'S FACE BETRAYED NO RECOGNITION. The hope that she was playing tricks on me, as she normally did, vanished.

She didn't know me.

To her eyes, I was a stranger.

Some people would celebrate that. They would instantly start coming up with ways to mess with her. But I didn't feel like throwing a party.

Why didn't I?

"You don't recognise me?" I inspected her clueless face for a lie. "For real?"

She simply shook her head.

If she didn't recognise me, did that mean she didn't know who she was either?

"Do you know *your* name?" I asked.

Her eyes went distant, as if she was searching for it in her mind, until she said sadly, "No, I'm sorry."

I couldn't fully trust her. If anyone could trick me into believing Vittoria couldn't remember a thing, it was Vittoria. I didn't deem myself a gullible person because no one could ever tell when Vittoria was lying or telling the truth. She was a notorious master of lies.

But there was only one way to find out if she was lying now.

I turned to the door and approached it. Before opening it, I paused, glancing at her over my shoulder. "Stay in bed," I ordered. "I'm going to get you a doctor."

Vittoria didn't listen, her focus locked on the tube coming from her inner elbow. Realising she might attempt to pull it out again, I hurried back to her bed. As I touched her arm, an electric jolt shot through me, causing me to jerk my hand away. It was unlike any spark I had ever felt. It wasn't the kind of shock that came from objects. This was . . . a very different feeling.

Did she also feel it?

"Don't do it," I said quietly.

I didn't mean to whisper, but I had never felt such a spark with Vittoria before. Why now?

"Don't do what?" she asked, her subtle French accent catching me off guard. Before the Fire, she had always spoken with an Italian accent. But I didn't give it much thought. My attention was fixed on studying her face for any sign that she had felt the spark too. I found nothing.

A sense of disappointment descended upon me, perplexing me more than the spark itself. Quickly, I brushed it aside and withdrew my hands. "Don't touch the tube."

"Why?"

"Because this," I said, pointing at the bag with liquid, "keeps you hydrated. I know you're awake and can drink on your own, but I wouldn't remove it without the help of a doctor if I were you."

"Okay."

I stared at her, naively hoping she would think twice before trying to pull it out anyway. It wouldn't affect her if she did, but I wanted everything to stay the same when Dr Zunino arrived.

Again, I turned to leave.

"W-wait," she stammered, then cleared her throat. "Where am I?"

I stopped. She didn't even recognise her own bedroom? It shouldn't surprise me since she barely spent time here before the Fire, but it was hard to believe.

"You're in your bedroom." I glanced back at her. "In our villa."

She nodded, but the lost look in her eyes showed she either didn't understand or didn't fully grasp what I was saying.

I needed to call Dr Zunino as soon as possible.

"Please, stay here," I said, moving towards the door. As I opened it, a blinding light from the hallway poured in, coming as a shock after being used to the dimness of Vittoria's bedroom. Squinting against the sudden glare, I hesitated before stepping out and closing the door behind me.

Instead of heading straight to the living room where the phone was, I lingered outside her door, confused and unsure. *How? Why? What happened?* Questions swirled in my mind but provided no answers.

I shook my head and hurried down the hallway, passing open French windows that welcomed a refreshing breeze. The creamy walls with intricate crown moulding and the polished floor felt overly bright compared to the gloomy atmosphere of Vittoria's bedroom. The short hallway seemed never-ending.

Lost in thought, I almost missed my white cat sitting on a windowsill, hidden by silk curtains. She was sniffing the fresh air drifting in from the garden and the sea.

I stopped, and she lazily turned her head to look at me.

I smiled. "Hi, Regina."

She merely squinted at me before returning her blue gaze to the view outside, more interested in the bushes I had trimmed last week.

Remembering I needed to call Dr Zunino, I turned away and continued down the hallway. As I rounded the corner, Sofia appeared unexpectedly, like a gust of wind carrying the scent of rosemary, giving my heart a jolt.

By now, I should have been used to my housekeeper's sudden

appearances. How she managed to rush around so silently every time was beyond my understanding.

She stopped when she saw me. "Good afternoon, Ettore. Natalie asked if you're going to eat dinner with her tonight. What should I tell her?"

Had it really been five days since Natalie left for Morocco and had now returned?

"Uh . . ." Caught off guard by the question, I didn't know what to say. Since Vittoria was awake now, it didn't feel right to dine with my sister. But I had been turning down Natalie's invitations to eat or go out for almost two months. Guilt weighed heavily on me. I couldn't leave Vittoria either, confused and alone, especially when she couldn't remember a thing. Who knew what could pop up in her unpredictable mind.

Natalie would understand, right?

"Tell her no, okay?"

Sofia hummed in agreement, but I could see the look of disapproval in her brown eyes.

Guilt should have suffocated me long ago for always finding excuses to avoid people. But I had to keep an eye on Vittoria.

Sofia turned around to leave, prompting me to ask, "Are you busy right now?"

She paused, huffing out a laugh. "There's always something to do around this estate." She tossed me a glance. "But I can do those things later if there's something more urgent."

Of course, I knew Sofia was always on her feet, whether she was cleaning rooms, preparing meals, or handling other tasks around the house. I wouldn't have bothered her with anything beyond her contract, but she was the only person in the villa besides me. And I was afraid Vittoria wouldn't listen to me and try to pull out the IV again.

"Could you be with Vittoria while I ring Dr Zunino?"

I could have asked Sofia to do it while I stayed with Vittoria instead. But I needed some time alone to process everything that had happened since I entered her room.

The lines under her eyes deepened. "Why? Did something happen to her?"

"Everything is fine," I said to calm her down, realising I was lying. Something *was* wrong with her, and I needed a doctor's help to identify what it was. "She's awake."

Her eyes widened. "She's awake?"

"Yes," I confirmed, "she is."

"Why didn't you tell me sooner, *ragazzo*!" She playfully slapped my arm, and I forced a smile. "That's great news! I'm going to see her."

As she was about to step towards Vittoria's room, I said hastily, "Before you go, there's something you need to know."

Concern replaced her excitement. "What is it?"

Before She Remembers

I drew in a breath before I delivered the news. "She might not remember you."

After calling Dr Zunino I should have gone straight back to Vittoria, but my feet carried me to my office. As I opened the door to the veranda, the sound of chirping birds greeted me. Stepping outside, I pulled out a pack of cigarettes and a lighter. I took a cigarette, placed it between my teeth, and lit it, shielding the flame with my hand.

I took my first inhale of the day, adding another taint to my lungs, but I needed it.

I'd been telling that to myself for the past eight months.

Holding the railing, I watched the sea fifteen steps away.

I don't deserve this, I thought. I didn't deserve to live near such a stunning view of the sea, where I could enjoy it anytime by just stepping outside. All I had to do was cross my yard, go down the rocky steps, and my feet would touch the pebbles bathed by the azure waters. I had lived by the Mediterranean Sea my whole life, and its beauty never ceased to amaze me.

With a puff of smoke, I tilted my head, enjoying the warm promise of the morning sun, hinting at another hot July day.

"Are you here?"

I snapped my head towards Natalie. She was standing behind

me, sporting a white hat. Her hair was cut short. When I saw her a week ago, her hair fell down to her waist, but now it barely touched her shoulders. Despite her recent trip to sunny Morocco, her skin remained pale, showing no signs of a tan.

Natalie frowned. "You look horrible."

"And you look pale. Have you even seen the sun this year?"

"Ha ha." She stepped closer and tilted her head, inspecting my face. "When was the last time you slept?"

"A few hours ago."

"Doesn't look like it."

Maybe because I barely did, haunted by nightmares almost every day.

She extended her hand, fingers subtly gesturing towards the cigarette in my mouth. "May I?"

"Should have brought them yourself," I remarked, despite already pulling out a cigarette for her.

"What lady carries a pack of cigarettes with her?" she quipped. "It's a man's job."

"Ah, yes, men are the providers," I shot back sarcastically as I handed her the lighter.

She rolled her eyes, placed the cigarette between her lips, lit it and then passed the lighter back. I slipped it back into my pocket.

She puffed out a cloud of smoke. "Have you finally become bored waiting for her to wake up?"

I exhaled the last smoke and mashed the cigarette in the ashtray. "She *is* awake."

There was a moment of silence before Natalie asked, "That's great, no?"

I didn't answer.

She grimaced. "Why so grumpy? Your wife is awake after you spent two months stuck in this house, waiting for her to open her eyes again. You can finally come back to work."

Work.

Anxiety gripped my chest, twisting my stomach into a knot.

I knew the day would come when Vittoria woke up and I would no longer have an excuse to avoid my duties. Although two months might seem like a long time, it had passed quickly—much faster than I had anticipated.

She grimaced slightly. "Why did your face suddenly change once I mentioned work?"

Stupid idiot.

I should have controlled my facial expression in front of her. Perhaps avoiding people and social environments for so long weakened my ability to keep up my inscrutable façade.

"I'm just tired."

Natalie watched me suspiciously. "Are you happy she's awake or

. . . ?"

I hesitated to answer. Yes. No? Saying *no* felt wrong. Perhaps it *was* wrong to hope that Vittoria wouldn't wake up. But with her unconscious, I could keep using her as an excuse to immerse myself in my hobbies instead of dealing with work. I didn't have to worry every day about whose life I would be responsible for if I found them.

But that was about to end.

"She doesn't remember me."

"What?"

"She doesn't remember me."

"I heard you, but . . ." She gave her head a slight shake. "It can't be right."

"I wish."

"Are you sure?"

I was not.

It was Vittoria. She could be playing games with me. I would only be certain when Dr Zunino confirmed it.

"She asked for my name," I explained. "I asked her if she remembered me, and she answered with no."

Natalie laughed. "Oh, I'm sure she's joking."

"Could be, but what if she's not?"

She paused, the amusement draining from her face. "Maybe it's nothing to worry about," she said, but the uncertainty in her voice belied her words. "She has just woken up after two months. Could be a post-coma thing."

Could be.

Maybe Vittoria would remember soon. Our best doctors performed many surgeries to speed up her recovery and bring back her beauty as much as possible. Without our advanced technology and science, Vittoria would have woken up swathed in bandages. Her skin would have still been healing after the Fire, leaving her forever covered in burn scars.

I rubbed my face with my hands, then stood tall, meeting my sister's blue eyes. "What if it's not a post coma-thing? What if she never remembers?"

But I already had the answer. Natalie didn't have to say anything, as we both read it in each other's eyes.

I could only hope Sanctus Quinque would consider that Vittoria was young and the daughter of a superior. I hoped they wouldn't cast her out simply because she couldn't remember everything she had been taught by her parents and SQ since birth. Sanctus Quinque was unpredictable—one could always expect the worst from them.

"What did Dr Zunino say?" Natalie asked.

I shrugged.

A puzzled frown marred her expression. "What do you mean by

that, Ettore? Didn't you discuss your wife's condition with her?"

I should have. I could still go back to her room and find out Dr Zunino's diagnosis, but . . .

"Not yet," I murmured. "But I called her and told her to come."

She stared at me as if I was the stupidest person alive. "Ettore Cosette Morrano," she said in a strict tone, sounding like our mother, which unsettled me. "You're a smart man, but sometimes you act like an absolute idiot." She crushed her barely touched cigarette in the ashtray. "We're going there together."

She grasped my arm and pulled me, but I didn't move. "What the hell?" She frowned. "Were you working out while sitting in her room day and night?"

Guilt gnawed at me. Unlike I had claimed, I hadn't been exercising or staying in Vittoria's room. Natalie was better off not knowing what I had really been up to.

I cracked a smile as I brushed past her. "What if I told you I was preparing to fight Raff?"

Natalie's laughter sounded behind me. "I'd say you're aiming for the same fate as your wife, minus the burning part."

My smile dwindled as the thought that had been pestering me for a long time returned in full force.

What if I wanted the same fate as Vittoria? Not the same, but similar: what if I would never wake up?

03
The Blonde Woman

Teodora

"**HOW ARE YOU FEELING, VITTORIA?**"

Next to my bed stood a woman with one blue eye and one brown eye. When she entered the room, she appeared intimidating with her towering height and a striking scar cutting across her eye. But when she saw me, a kind smile softened her serious features. I felt myself relax as she introduced herself as Dr Zunino.

"Umm, good?"

Sofia, the dark-haired woman with curls who kept me company when Ettore left, wordlessly made her way to the door and exited.

Dr Zunino inserted two earpieces of a Y-shaped tube in her ears. The device looked familiar, but like many other things, I couldn't recall its name. She then pressed a metal, oval-shaped piece against my chest. I flinched slightly at how unexpectedly cold it felt.

"It's okay," Dr Zunino reassured me. "It's just a stethoscope."

I nodded, even though the name didn't tell me anything.

"What does it do?" I asked.

She adjusted its position on my chest. "It's a medical device that listens to the sounds inside your body, like your heart and lungs."

That made sense.

When Dr Zunino finished examining me with the stethoscope, she went to her bag. She pulled out a notebook and wrote something down. "Your husband said you don't remember him?"

After he left, I tried my best to recall anything about him. The confusion in his eyes made me feel awful, but trying to remember only gave me a headache.

"No," I replied sadly. "I'm sorry."

"Don't be. It's not your fault you don't remember." Dr Zunino offered me a smile, making me feel a little better. "How about your head? Does it hurt?"

"It starts to hurt when I try to remember."

She puckered her lips, tapping the pen against the paper in thought. "Do you think you will be able to urinate on your own?"

Warmth spread across my face as I felt a blush coming on. "I . . . I think so."

"Great." She put her notebook on the small table by the chair and pulled out a pair of white gloves. "I'll remove your catheter. It shouldn't take long. If you feel uncomfortable or experience any pain, don't hesitate to tell me."

I tensed as she approached the foot of the bed and removed the blanket, instructing me to bend my legs. She slipped on her gloves, while I stared at the ceiling, afraid to breathe and disrupt her job. It felt like an eternity, but it couldn't have been more than a few moments before she said, "All done."

She tossed the blanket back over my legs, and I lowered them. "Any urge to pee?"

I swallowed uncomfortably. "No."

She returned to her stuff with a bag of my urine, and I felt my blush intensify.

"I'll draw some blood for tests, but I'll need to see you at the hospital for a better analysis," she informed, searching for the equipment in her bag. "I had expected Ettore to be here to schedule your appointment, but it looks like I'll have to find him myself."

My heart stuttered at the now-familiar name, but then I frowned. "Why do you need Ettore to schedule my appointment?" I realised my question might have sounded harsh, so I quickly added, "I mean, can't you schedule it with me?"

She inserted the needle into my arm, and I felt a slight prick. "I could, but your brain might have experienced something we don't know about. It's safer if your husband is available to take you to the hospital." She pulled out the needle and pressed a wet cotton ball to my inner elbow. "Keep this pressed for a while, and you're all set." She gave me a reassuring smile and went to her bag.

A knock sounded on the door, startling me. As it opened, the man I now recognised as my husband walked in, accompanied by a blonde woman in a short black dress, high neckline, and short sleeves. I tensed at the sight of another new face, guessing it was someone else I was supposed to remember but couldn't.

I still tried.

With her short hair falling in soft waves, a white hat perched on her head, and cherry-red lips popping out against her porcelain skin, she reminded me of a doll. She smiled at me as she lifted her hand in a wave. I looked down.

No, I couldn't remember her at all.

"We were just talking about you, Mr Morrano," Dr Zunino said.

Ettore came closer to my bed. The blonde woman stayed by the door, watching me closely, as if inspecting me. No, my face.

Was something wrong with it?

I refrained from touching it, but I wished she would stop staring at me. I felt like I was naked.

"Is she okay?" he asked.

Dr Zunino raised her eyebrow. "You can ask her yourself."

"I meant her memory," he clarified. "Is this memory lapse temporary?"

"To be able to tell, I'll have to do a proper check-up in the hospital."

"But didn't you just do that?" His voice now carried an edge of tension, and his entire body seemed to stiffen with impatience.

I tensed at the sudden shift in the atmosphere. The blonde

woman walked over and put a hand on his shoulder. His shoulders visibly relaxed. "I'm sorry." He cleared his throat. "I'm not myself at the moment."

It felt like someone was squeezing my stomach. What was wrong with him? Was it because I couldn't remember him, or was there something else bothering him?

"It's understandable." Dr Zunino took a step closer to him. "I would like to schedule her appointment for next Thursday. Is that okay with you?"

Thursday? What day was it today? What month? Did I have no say in this?

Ettore hesitated, and the blonde woman gave his shoulder an encouraging squeeze. "No, of course," he blurted out. "The sooner, the better."

Dr Zunino turned to me. "The appointment is in seven days. Do you think that's too soon for you?"

Finally.

I shook my head. "No, seven days are fine."

"That's settled then." Dr Zunino marked something in her notebook and closed it with a clap. "I think the IV has fed her enough." She giggled, but no one laughed. She paused briefly before continuing, "Vittoria should be ready to get some real food in her stomach."

She placed her notebook back in the bag and pulled out a leather case before coming over to me.

But wasn't she done and ready to leave?

She unzipped the bag and placed it on the bedside table. Then, she slipped on a new pair of white gloves, took a bottle, uncorked it, and poured it onto a piece of cotton. "You can hand me that."

"What?" I asked, confused. Then I followed her gaze to the cotton I was still pressing against my other arm. "Oh, right."

I gave it to her, and she tucked it into the pocket of her pants.

She slowly pulled out the tube and pressed the cotton to my inner elbow, securing it with tape. "Since she's been lying in bed for two months, she may have difficulty walking."

Wait, two months? I have been lying here for two—

"My advice is to get her used to it slowly," Dr Zunino informed, tidying up and putting her tools in the bag. "But bring her meals in bed for another week or until she's able to walk on her own again. If you want, you can get her a wheelchair, but I don't think it's necessary. I'd say that's about it." Her lips rose into a soft smile. "May I talk to you in private, Mr Morrano?"

"By all means." He turned his head to the blonde woman. "Will you stay with Vittoria while I'm gone?"

"Just go." She gave him a friendly push towards the door.

When Ettore and Dr Zunino left, the woman came closer to me, smiling. "Natalie Cosette Morrano, Ettore's younger sister. Pleased to meet you, Vittoria." She curtsied, and I felt my cheeks heating up again.

I understood she was playing around with her introduction, but I wished she hadn't done the curtsy. "I am indeed Vittoria, apparently."

I am indeed Vittoria, apparently? Who talks like that?

Natalie issued a short laugh. "You are." Her gaze swept across the room. "I have never seen so many irises in a room before."

"Irises?"

She gestured at the purple flowers. "The flowers?"

So that's what they're called! But why irises? Were they my favourite?

"Ettore must really care about you," she said, a tinge of doubt in her words.

Why wouldn't he? I was his wife. Shouldn't a husband care for his wife, decorate her room with flowers while waiting for her to wake up . . .

Why had I been asleep in the first place?

Natalie moved towards the chair, sat down on it, and stretched out her legs. A moan of delight escaped her as she sank deeper into the seat. "This chaise lounge is surprisingly comfortable. I think I need one of these in my future home."

"Yes, I think you should have one too."

I had no idea how the so-called chaise lounge felt, yet I spoke anyway. It was better than saying nothing and facing the uncomfortable silence that would have inevitably followed her words.

She hummed thoughtfully. "I need to own a house first before that can happen." A dreamy smile graced her lips. "But you're awake!" She extended both of her hands to me. "We're throwing a party to celebrate your recovery, that's for certain. Maybe it'll help you remember something. We'll invite all your friends and acquaintances. Maybe enemies, too? For the sake of your memory." She winked at me as though we shared a secret. "What do you think?"

Natalie's energetic nature was draining me, though it wasn't her fault. Maybe it was because I had only woken up an hour ago and was still trying to remember people I couldn't.

I wished I could match Natalie's excitement at the thought of meeting more people I was supposed to know but didn't. I wished I could remember. Then I wouldn't have to tread so carefully around people to avoid hurting their feelings.

"Dr Zunino said I should rest," I said gently.

Natalie only laughed. "I'm not saying we should throw a party tomorrow," she said. "We can do it next month, even a year from now, whatever works for you. Or we don't need to do it at all. I suggested it only because the old Vittoria . . . Okay, maybe not *old*, but the one before the Fire, liked celebrations."

"Before the Fire?"

Natalie's good spirits vanished as if someone snapped their fingers and said *disappear*. She stood up and brushed her skirt, avoiding my eyes. "I don't think I should—"

The door opened, and Ettore stepped inside. "You can go, Nat. Vittoria needs some rest from the guests."

"If that's so . . ." She walked over to the door and patted his shoulder, whispering something to him that I couldn't catch. "Goodbye, Vittoria." She waved at me happily, and I raised my hand awkwardly in response. "I'll see you someday again. Hopefully, very soon."

As Natalie left, Ettore approached the chair and slowly sat down, dropping his face into his hands.

"Are you okay?" I asked, sensing that something was wrong.

"Yeah." He brushed his hair out of the way as he straightened. Seconds later, a short laugh escaped him. "No." He shook his head, confusing me even more. "I think? I don't know."

"You don't know?"

He shrugged, offering no verbal explanation. Whatever was wrong with him, I didn't want to press, but I had questions. One question in particular. "Have I been lying here for two months?"

He hesitated, then nodded slowly.

"Why? What happened?"

"I think today has been eventful enough for you." He stood up. "You should rest."

He moved towards the door.

"B-but—" My voice trembled with frustration.

"You should sleep." He gave me a weak smile that only fuelled my annoyance. "I'll see you when you wake up."

I didn't want him to leave. I needed answers. I needed to know why I had been confined to this bed for so long, and why I couldn't remember. But he left me alone, shutting the door behind him.

I wanted to cry, but no tears came.

Frustrated, I slid down the bed, resting my head on the pillow. Ettore was right. I needed some rest. Meeting new people and the pressure to remember had drained me. But . . . what had happened to me?

Knowing there was nothing I could do to force my memory back, I closed my eyes. Despite the boiling anger and confusion, sleep eventually took control.

04
Brown Like Chocolate

Teodora

I WOKE UP TO FIND ETTORE SLEEPING, SLUMPED IN THE CHAIR. *He came back.* I couldn't help but smile.

With nothing else to do, I watched him, not wanting to disturb his sleep.

His chin rested on his hand, his chest rising in rhythm. An open book was lying upside down on him. Messy curls fell over his forehead, tempting me to stand up, walk over, and push them away. I wanted to see his face better.

Some might find it dull to watch someone sleep, but not when it was Ettore, my husband whom I couldn't remember.

I could see why I had married him. He was attractive, brought me flowers, and cared for me. He felt like a dream come true.

My stomach growled.

I had heard Dr Zunino's advice not to walk alone. But if something happened, Ettore would wake up and help me, right?

I lifted the blanket and tossed it aside. Carefully, I pushed myself up on my elbows and attempted to move my legs. They felt strange, but I was relieved to still be able to feel—

"It's all my fault," he whispered.

I froze, looking at Ettore. To my surprise, his eyes stayed closed. Was he dreaming?

"I'm sorry. I . . ." he trailed off, the rest of his sentence inaudible.

Should I wake him up?

He stopped talking, and I waited for him to say more, but nothing came. Slowly, I lowered my legs to the floor. With the help of my hands, I shifted myself off the bed, but my legs couldn't support my weight and gave out.

Strong arms caught me before I reached the floor. I looked up, meeting bleary brown eyes staring at me. Brown like . . . chocolate! His eyes were like dark chocolate.

The things I would do right now for a piece of dark chocolate . . .

"How many times will I have to find you putting your health at risk?" he asked. "Maybe I should tie you to the bed?"

My cheeks warmed. I wasn't sure if it was from his closeness or the suggestion he just made. I could smell a hint of sweat from him, but I didn't mind. "I don't think that's necessary."

"I beg to differ." His hand slid down my legs and lifted me up. "You shouldn't leave your bed without my help." He eased me back onto the bed and covered me with the blanket.

"I know, but I was bored."

He gave me a knowing look. "Being bored isn't an excuse."

I looked down, fidgeting with my fingers. "Why did you come back?"

"I couldn't risk you doing exactly what you just tried to do."

Fair point.

My stomach protested again, and I covered it with my hands as if it would make it less loud.

"I'll get you something to eat," he declared. "But only if you promise to stay in bed." He raised his little finger.

As I focused on it, I tried to understand its meaning, as it clearly meant something.

"It's called a pinky promise," he explained, noticing my curiosity. "You hook your finger when you promise something, and it's like a pact that ensures you'll keep your word."

His explanation sounded highly unrealistic. "That can't be real, can it?"

A soft chuckle escaped him. "Not that I know of, but it's a common tradition, especially among children. It adds a touch of magic to a promise, I guess."

The idea of a pinky promise felt familiar. As I was about to hook my finger over his just for the fun of it, a brilliant idea popped into my head, spreading a mischievous smile across my lips. "I'll promise to stay in bed, but only if you bring me some chocolate.

Dark, preferably."

He let out a snort, his eyes twinkling playfully. "Deal. I'll bring you *dark* chocolate."

I hooked my finger over his, unable to suppress a smile. "Then I promise to stay in bed."

Ettore chuckled softly, lingering for a moment before he left.

As promised, I remained still, waiting for him. Every time I checked the clock, time seemed to crawl. It was about twenty minutes before he returned with a tray of food and a newspaper tucked under his arm. He placed the tray over me with food, and I was pleased to recognise them quickly: two sandwiches, three pieces of dark chocolate, and a glass of red juice. Curious, I tried a sip of the juice, but the combination of sweetness, sourness, and saltiness made me wince.

"You don't like it?"

I swallowed it with effort and shook my head, setting the glass back.

"But it's your favourite."

I gave him a look of disbelief. He must be joking. "Is it?"

"Yes. I never understood why you like tomato juice so much. It disgusts me, but it's your favourite."

I raised the glass again, suspiciously eyeing its contents before trying another sip to confirm that the first taste hadn't deceived me.

Once it touched my tongue again, I cringed.

The flavours were a little overwhelming, and I didn't like the thickness. I preferred clear juice that ran down my throat like water.

I put it down, unable to understand how I could have liked it before. "Are sandwiches my favourite, too?"

"No. That's all I can make." He awkwardly scratched his temple. "It's too early for Sofia to make breakfast. I had to put something together myself."

Unease settled in my chest. I didn't want to be a burden. "You didn't have to do this."

"It's my duty as your husband." He smiled, but it failed to reach his eyes. "Now eat, please. You need your strength back."

I couldn't help but feel like a burden, but I said nothing, pushing aside my concerns. Saving the chocolate for dessert, I started eating one of the sandwiches. The sooner I could take care of myself, the less of a burden I would be. And for that, I needed nutrition.

The sandwich tasted much better than the tomato juice. While I was eating, Ettore relaxed in the chair and read the newspaper. Squinting, I tried to make out the text.

"Riviera hit by record heatwave," I read aloud. *"Temperatures soar across the French Riviera."*

"It's the worst heatwave yet in 1966," he remarked. "But it's typical around here. I don't get why people are still surprised. Is there nothing new to report? How about the US and their ridiculous nuclear arms race with the Soviet Union? That never makes the headlines. Apparently, a heatwave is more alarming than the possibility of nuclear war."

I wished I could understand what he was saying so I could empathise with his frustration. Instead, I ate quietly as he continued reading. But then a question occurred to me.

"Why would Sofia make breakfast?" I asked. "Is she your mother?"

A faint smile appeared at the corner of his lips. "No, she's a nice lady who works for us."

"Why?"

He laughed, confusing me more. "Why?" he asked incredulously.

I felt embarrassed to ask questions with obvious answers, but how else could I know if I couldn't remember a thing? "Why is someone catering to us? Aren't we capable of making food for ourselves?"

He laughed again, this time harder, as if my lack of knowledge amused him. Annoyance stirred within me.

What an insensitive—

I broke off a piece of the chocolate and tossed it in his direction. To my dismay, it didn't make it and landed on the floor. I sighed. *Well, there goes that piece.* At least it stopped his laughter.

"I'm sorry, but . . ." He closed the newspaper and laid it on the small table next to him. "I never thought I would hear something like that coming from your mouth, and in such an incredulous voice too."

"Why?"

He looked away. "You're a . . ." His Adam's apple bobbed up and down as he swallowed.

I leant forward, raising my eyebrows curiously. "I'm a . . . ?"

He chuckled uncomfortably. "Growing up, you were *a little bit* pampered."

"So I'm spoiled?"

He hesitated to admit it. My annoyance faded, replaced by curiosity about his reluctance to be honest. It was endearing, I had to admit, but . . . Was he trying to spare my feelings, or was he afraid of my reaction?

"Yes," he admitted at last, "You are. *Spoiled*." He dropped his hands on his knees in resignation, letting out a heavy sigh as if someone had lifted a weight from his shoulders.

Maybe I should feel offended for being called spoiled, but it didn't affect me. Then again, it was hard to take offence when I didn't even remember my life and who I used to be.

I giggled, picking up the sandwich again and sinking my teeth into it.

He stared at me with clear confusion. I could only assume it wasn't the reaction he had expected from me.

I swallowed, assuming a clueless expression. "What?"

"Are you not angry?"

"Angry?" My voice shot up in disbelief. "Why would I be angry?"

All he did was stare at me with a look someone would give a puzzle that was hard to solve. I patiently waited for his answer, but he stood up. "I'm going to take a shower. Don't go anywhere without me."

I watched him walk towards the door, wondering why he didn't answer. It couldn't be because he wanted to spare my feelings. Maybe he was afraid to voice the truth.

I opened my mouth, ready to stop him and demand an answer, but I changed my mind. I didn't want to push him, so instead, I said, "Okay, husband."

He paused by the door. I tensed, worried I had said something wrong. But seconds later, he opened the door, leaving me to enjoy the last bites of the cheese and ham sandwich he had made for me.

05

Unexpectedly Bold

Ettore

***O*KAY, HUSBAND.**

If I had a penny for every time Vittoria called me her husband without meaning it as a tease, I would have exactly one penny. It was one of the many puzzling words she uttered after the Fire, but I had to remind myself that she didn't remember. I shouldn't be overthinking this.

I was walking to my room when Sofia emerged. She jumped back, her hand flying to her chest. "Oh, my God."

"It's Ettore, actually," I said comically.

She playfully swatted my shoulder, and I shot her a rueful smile before opening the door to my bedroom.

"You've received another call," she said, just before I could enter.

My stomach twisted. Lately, I had been receiving many calls, and I ignored most of them because I had a feeling none of them would be pleasant.

Instead of surrendering to the instinct to flee and hide, I stayed. It took a lot of willpower to ask, "A call from whom?"

"Your mother," she voiced my worst fear. I had expected it, and still, hearing it disturbed me. "She insisted on bringing you to the phone."

I had been on my way to take a shower. It had been too long. I wanted to tell Sofia I'd call my mother back later, but putting it off would make me stressed while I showered. It would be better to talk with her first, so I could relax after.

"Thank you, Sofia."

I went to the living room, approaching the rotary phone reluctantly. Hesitating, I stared at it, plucking up the courage before I placed my finger on the first number. I wished I wouldn't have to do this, but I had been avoiding her for a long time. Sooner or later, I would have to face her, and it was better to do it through a phone call than in person. No reason to continue dragging out the inevitable.

It was time to rip off the bandage.

I spun the dial, the mechanical clicks echoing in the quiet room. Bringing the handset to my ear, I waited anxiously. Finally, the voice I dreaded answered, "Sybille Cosette speaking."

I closed my eyes for a second. "Good morning, Mother."

"Ettore." Her voice lacked warmth, as if she were addressing one of her subjects rather than her son, as usual. "After all those weeks of silence, surprisingly, I still recognise your voice."

I should not have called her, but it might have been worse if I hadn't.

"As always, it's a pleasure to hear your voice, Mother."

"Ettore, darling," she said, and I could imagine her rubbing her fingers against her temple, already annoyed with me. "Before you hang up, I would like to know why I had to hear the news from Natalie and not you."

"You called me because I failed to tell you Vittoria woke up from a coma?"

I didn't believe for a second that she called me because of Vittoria. Sybille Cosette never liked her, and her sudden interest in her sounded like a subterfuge.

Even when Vittoria was a little girl, my mother didn't care about her. I didn't like her either at first. She's always been mysterious, a bit scary, and thought everything was about her. Sometimes, when I talked with someone and she showed up, she would jokingly ask if we were talking about her. She did it so often, sometimes I doubted it was a joke.

When I nearly died in a car accident a year ago, it made me take life more seriously and changed my perspective on Vittoria. If she was going to be a significant part of my future, we had to stop disliking each other.

I tried to get to know her better while keeping an open mind, but Vittoria didn't make it easy. She didn't like being around me and often replied to my attempts at conversation with sarcasm or mockery.

Over time, my efforts to be friendly began to pay off. She softened her demeanour and became less defensive, though she still kept her distance. I sensed she might be hiding something or enjoyed giving the impression that she had secrets.

"You should have told me," she said. "I'm visiting today when I'm free."

"You're visiting Vittoria?"

"Both of you."

I had a bad feeling, but I couldn't stop her. If she wanted to visit Vittoria, she would. Sybille Cosette always got her way. "Okay."

"I have to go," she announced. "See you later, *mon fils*." She mimicked the sound of two kisses.

"Goodbye, Sy—"

She ended the call before I could finish. Classic mother, having no regard for people.

I returned the phone to its place and went to my room. Scrubbing my face, I stepped into the bathroom. I faced my reflection in the mirror and grimaced at the stubble on my chin. At least I didn't have to worry about growing a beard because it wasn't in my genes. My hair was falling into my eyes, so I pushed it back.

It was time to pull myself together.

For a minute I considered working out, but knowing it would take a long time, I pushed it until tomorrow.

You've been rescheduling your workout for two months now,

my voice of reason argued.

I promised myself I would get back to it as soon as I could.

I shaved the stubble, brushed my teeth, and jumped into the shower. Feeling a little better and more motivated to tackle the day, I walked out with a towel around my hips. As I was buttoning up my white shirt, I remembered my mother's visit.

My clothes would be too casual for her, and I wanted to avoid as many remarks about my appearance as possible. I was already bracing myself for her comments on my hair.

I found a grey waistcoat and a black tie. I hesitated before putting them on, and once I did, I felt restricted. It had been a while since I'd worn formal attire, but I could endure it until my mother left.

Thankfully, Vittoria was still in bed, not trying to get up like she did this morning when I woke up.

When she saw me, her eyes brightened and a happy smile graced her lips. My chest warmed, followed by a confusing twist.

No one has ever been this happy to see me walk into a room before.

I closed the door behind me. "Ready for a walk?"

"Yes, please." She attempted to sit up. "Get me out of this bed already."

Her enthusiasm brought a smile to my face. I walked over to her bed, removed the tray, and placed it on the floor, uncertain where else to put it. Each piece of furniture in the room had a vase of irises—flowers I had picked up for Vittoria out of guilt for using her as an excuse.

She had already pushed the blanket off herself. I took her hand and put my arm around her waist, providing support as she lowered her legs to the floor. I helped her stand.

"Do you feel any pain?" I asked.

"No, all good."

Slowly, we walked towards the door. But as we passed the dressing table, she whipped her head to the left, coming to an immediate stop. I followed her gaze to the mirror set atop it, reflecting her aghast expression.

"Where's my hair?!" she exclaimed.

I mentally face-palmed.

I should have covered the mirror earlier to avoid the shock, but I was too immersed in my own thoughts to think about it. *Stupid, stupid idiot.*

Vittoria's hand slipped from mine. She frantically patted her head, shocked to find it almost bare. The fire had taken most of it, but it was beginning to grow back. Panic flickered in her eyes, threatening to overwhelm her.

I reached out and gently brushed my free hand against her cheek. "Hey . . ." I guided her face away from the mirror to meet my gaze. As our eyes locked, I offered a reassuring smile. "The fire burned your hair, but it will grow back. If you're not comfortable without hair, you can wear a wig."

"I lost my hair in a fire?" She blinked incredulously. "How?"

"I found you unconscious outside a burning building." It still puzzled me why she was the only one burning outside, unless someone else had tried to harm her. Perhaps it was the same person who had left the note in my car and vanished into the night. "We extinguished your burning body, but you were barely recognisable."

She stared at me with a distant look, processing the news. "That's why I've been lying in bed for two months?"

"Yes, you were in a coma."

She pressed her lips together in thought. "How did you know it was me you saved and not someone else?"

"I . . ." I scratched my head, unsure how to explain the note to her. It would lead to more questions that I couldn't answer. Only she could when she remembered. "While we were waiting for you, someone dropped a note in my car. It said if we didn't want you to die, we would find you behind the building."

A gossamer-like line of worry appeared between her eyebrows. "Who's we?"

"Raff and I."

"Who's Raff?"

"Your brother."

She looked back at the mirror. I waited for her to ask more

questions, one question specifically.

"Aren't you going to ask who tried to take your life?"

"Will I get the answer if I do?

"No."

"So what's the point?"

I was speechless. If I found out someone tried to kill me, I would want to know who it was before they tried again.

"Someone tried to kill you, and you're not even a little bit worried?"

"If they wanted me dead, they wouldn't have left you that note."

"Your body was burning."

"But I'm alive. I lost my hair, but it will regrow, right?"

"Why are you so calm?"

"I can't worry about something I can't remember."

I opened my mouth, but realised I had nothing to say, so I closed it.

She might not believe me. She had no reason, really. As she said, she couldn't recall a thing. Why should she trust someone she couldn't remember?

She touched her face carefully. "If my body was burned and barely recognisable, why don't I have any burn marks?"

"I'm not an expert in science, but you've had many surgeries. Our doctors are absolute magicians. After they took care of you, you came out with no sign of the incident. Except for the hair, of course."

That earned a pointed look from her.

I might have stretched the truth a bit. She didn't look the same as before. Her freckles were gone and her eyes seemed bigger. The doctors had tried their best to bring back her original appearance, but they warned me that she might look different. At first glance, you might not even realise the changes.

I couldn't tear my gaze away from her eyes. Could they have really made them bigger? Was she still the same Vittoria?

I snorted inwardly.

Don't be absurd, I thought.

I realised I had been staring at her face for far too long, so I looked away, clearing my throat. "The wigs you liked to wear should be around here somewhere. You can try them on if you like."

She nodded eagerly. "Yes, please."

I brought her closer, her side bumping against mine more forcefully than I intended. She raised her head at me, her eyes wide and speechless.

"Sorry," I apologised. "Was I too rough?"

Her lips parted slightly as she spoke in a quiet, almost breathless voice, "No, I . . ." She looked down. "It's nothing."

I stared at her a moment longer before guiding her to the door on my left. With my hand on her waist, I opened it to her walk-in wardrobe. In the centre stood a table with bags, and shelves in front were filled with shoes. Clothes hung on hangers along the walls, with rows of black mannequin heads sporting wigs stacked above them.

Her eyes widened in disbelief. "This cannot be all mine . . ."

I smiled at that. The Vittoria before the Fire would have dismissed it as nothing. The difference between her then and now was striking, but her current version was incredibly cute.

"Here." I helped her to the scarlet-red sofa near the door. "Take a seat and have a look at all these wigs." I motioned towards the neatly arranged wigs on the top shelf.

She raised her head, and a gasp escaped her mouth. "I didn't even see them there!"

No wonder, given her diminutive height, but I refrained from teasing her about it. I would have joked around Vittoria before, but now I was careful not to offend her.

I helped her sit while she remained captivated by the wigs, taking in each one in awe before moving to the next.

"There are so many to choose from," she said. "They're all so different."

I also surveyed the wigs, amazed at the diversity of colours, length and shapes. It was my first time setting foot in her wardrobe. I had seen some of the wigs on Vittoria before, but most of them were new to me.

"Why did I need so many of them?" she asked.

I smiled, recalling having asked her the same question before. She had answered, 'To be someone else.' When I asked her why, she turned her head to the window without a reply.

"You can ask yourself when you remember," I said. "Which one do you like?"

Vittoria looked at me with confusion. "Why can't you tell me?"

"Is it that important?"

Her forehead furrowed, mild annoyance shining through. "It's not a matter of life and death, but I'd like an answer when I ask, no matter how trivial the question may seem."

"I don't want to interrupt the process of your memory coming back. I think it's better if you remember things on your own instead of me putting information in your head," I admitted. "I hope you can understand."

Her face clouded over. "But what if . . ." Her voice trailed off, quieter now, tears filling her eyes.

I turned my right ear towards her. "I'm sorry?"

She paused for a moment. As I waited for her to repeat her words, a dreaded question left her lips, "What happened to your hearing?"

The ringing in my ears. The shock. The pain . . .

"Ettore?"

I swallowed hard and opened my eyes. "I got into a car accident about a year ago."

"How?"

"Hit a tree," I said quickly, staring at the wigs. "Which wig would you like to wear?"

She ignored my question. "How did you hit it?" she pressed. "What ha—"

"I don't want to talk about it," I interrupted sharply.

She flinched, and guilt immediately washed over me. "I'm sorry," I whispered.

The disappointment deepened in her eyes. I wasn't sure why. Was it because of my sharp tone? Or because I didn't elaborate further? There was also a hint of sadness. Was she feeling sorry for me?

If she knew why I had got into the car accident, she wouldn't be.

Vittoria looked away, wiping her eyes.

I lowered myself in front of her, angling my head to make eye contact, but she purposely looked elsewhere. "What's wrong?"

She took a deep breath. "What if I don't remember? What happens then?"

I felt terrible because I couldn't answer that question either.

The situation was complicated, and I couldn't be sure. SQ could give much harsher punishments for smaller offences than forgetting your job. There were no limits to what they could do to her. And no matter how difficult Vittoria used to be, she was still my family. I didn't want her to suffer.

"Ettore?" she prompted, her voice on the verge of breaking.

I offered her my hands. She didn't take them, staring at me resolutely, waiting for my answer.

I put my hands on my knees instead. "I'll figure it out."

It was the best I could give her right now.

"Figure out what?"

Whether or not you will be cast out.

Instead of voicing that concern, I nodded towards the wigs. "So which one would you like to wear?"

A look of disappointment crossed her face, but she didn't push. Instead, she finally turned her attention to the wigs.

A faint, albeit forced, smile appeared on the edge of her lips. "I would like a red short one, please."

06

Doubts

..✤..

Teodora

I WENT LESS THAN FIVE STEPS OUTSIDE MY ROOM BEFORE I GAVE UP. "I can't do this anymore."

"Okay." Ettore lifted me, and I wrapped my arms around his neck. "We'll try again tomorrow."

He laid me on the bed carefully, but his movements seemed strangely tense. He pulled the blanket over me and tucked me in, his forehead creased with worry. I watched him, concerned.

"Are you okay?" I asked.

He gave me a smile, but it felt forced. "Of course. Why wouldn't I be?"

I hated that he was hiding things from me, especially things that worried him. I wanted to know what troubled him. He was my husband, after all.

But if he was my husband, why was I lying in a bed meant for two while he slept in the chair? We were married. Based on my limited knowledge, weren't we supposed to be sleeping together? If not, where was I getting that idea from?

"Why aren't we sharing a bed if we're married?"

"We agreed on this way," he said, offering no further explanation.

I understood he didn't like going into details, instead expecting me to remember them. But I wasn't willing to stay in the dark until then.

"Why?" I pressed.

He forced out a chuckle and started to pull a blanket over me, but I stopped him. "Don't. It's too hot."

He nodded and straightened, awkwardly scratching his temple.

"So why?" I repeated.

He dropped his hand. "Before we got married, we agreed to live in separate bedrooms."

I tried to make sense of it but failed. "I don't understand. Why get married if we don't sleep together?"

"Sleeping in the same room isn't what marriage is about," he said, but it sounded like he was convincing himself it was normal. "There are other benefits that come from being married."

I sat up straighter, eager to hear some examples. "Such as . . . ?"

He massaged the side of his head with his two fingers. His stomach growled, interrupting us.

"You haven't eaten yet?" I asked.

"Taking care of you isn't exactly luxury, Vittoria."

A ball of icy coldness contracted in my chest, and I turned my eyes away from him for the first time in a while.

"I'm sorry," he blurted out. "It didn't come out the way I intended."

Despite the tears stinging my eyes, I managed to say, "It's okay." The lie caught in my throat. "You're tired. You should go get something to eat. I should try to get some sleep, anyway."

I rolled on my side, turning my back to him, but he stayed, not saying a word. If he intended to stay silent, he should leave, as he only heightened the discomfort in the room.

Yet, I wanted his touch. I wanted him to make me meet his gaze and insist that he didn't mean his words.

"I'll be back in an hour," he said finally.

His footsteps faded, and the door opened and closed. I shut my eyes, disappointment flooding over me instead of relief.

I had lied to him. Instead of trying to sleep, I fought back tears. But crying because Ettore practically called me a burden would get me nowhere. I couldn't cry and feel sorry for myself. It was a waste of time.

I needed to put my energy into something more useful, like learning to walk again and stimulating my mind. I was determined to regain my memories. I couldn't rely on Ettore to tell me everything, and I was fed up with depending on him.

I put my feet on the floor and stood, hesitating before taking my first step towards the dressing table. After five determined steps, I dropped onto the stool and examined my face, which I hadn't had the chance to do before.

I lifted my hand, tracing my finger from temple to chin, amazed by the smoothness of my skin. I couldn't help but entertain doubts about the story of how I survived the fire. How could I have survived the flames, supposedly burned from head to toe, yet have no visible scars?

It couldn't be possible.

I poked my right auburn eyebrow, content I hadn't gone astray in choosing a red wig.

I rubbed it from side to side, smiling like a child discovering something fun for the first time.

As I gazed longer into the mirror, my smile faded until it vanished completely. Once, I easily brushed aside the faint voice of doubt, the thoughts that had seemed insignificant at first, but now, they had taken root and grown into a vine of fear, coiling tightly around my heart.

Who was it, staring back at me in the reflection? Was it truly me or a stranger? What was the truth, what were the lies? Did Ettore's secretive behaviour mean he was lying to me? If so, why was he hiding the truth from me?

But I would learn nothing if I let my thoughts consume me.

I stood and approached the last unopened door, which was

closer to my bed. Gripping the handle, I pushed it open to reveal a bathroom.

Shivers ran down my spine.

There was a small window on my left, but it provided little light to the room. It was black from the floor to the ceiling. I hesitated to go inside, but my bladder was about to burst and I didn't want to use the bucket next to my bed when the bathroom was just a few steps away. Summoning my courage, I put one foot forward, entering the ominous bathroom.

As I raised the toilet lid, a startled yelp escaped me.

A cat's skull stared right at me from the shelf above the toilet.

Why would I put a cat's skull in my bathroom? Didn't I like cats, or . . .

I shuddered to even think about what might follow after *or*.

After relieving myself, I hesitated to turn on the tap, fearing that blood might pour out instead of water. Thank God, it was only my imagination. I washed my hands and returned to the room, stopping at the sight of a woman in a white blouse and a brown midi skirt standing by my bed.

She turned her head, her luxurious blonde hair bouncing with her. As she stepped closer, a faint smile appeared on her lips, and I caught a whiff of her sweet perfume.

"Sybille Cosette." She stuck out her hand. "Ettore's mother."

I parted my lips to speak, but words failed me. My palms grew warmer than usual, and my attempt to smile must have appeared awkward. Her mere presence unsettled me, and I could speculate it was because I was alone with my mother-in-law.

I brushed my sweaty hand against my nightgown before I took her hand, surprised at its coldness. I thought I should introduce myself, but before I could, Ettore's mother asked, "How are you feeling?"

Nervous. Anxious. Uncomfortable . . .

"Great." I managed a tight smile.

She observed me closely, and a deeper discomfort settled into my bones. "Really?"

No. "Yes."

The lie slipped out before I could stop it. I wasn't sure why, but every instinct screamed at me not to show weakness to this woman. All I craved was a moment of peace, but fate had other plans in the form of another unexpected visitor I should remember, but didn't.

"I anticipated finding my son here." She looked around as if Ettore might suddenly pop up. "But oddly, he's not."

Earlier, I would have wondered why everyone expected Ettore to be here, but not after his biting words. All he did was take care of me. Still, I couldn't comprehend why he cared so much when we didn't even share the same bed.

"He told me he'd be back in an hour," I said.

"I haven't heard from him in a while." She walked over to the curtained windows, ignoring my words. "Why stay in such darkness?" With a swift motion, she drew the curtains apart, and sunlight flooded in, causing me to squint. Sybille's silhouette remained dark until my eyes adjusted to the light. "Afraid of burning to dust, like a vampire?"

I had no idea what she was talking about, and I chose not to ask. Despite the smile on her lips, she radiated coldness. She struck me as a formidable woman, compelling everyone to tread carefully around her.

Yet, I dared to ask. "I hope it's not impolite to ask, but what brings you here?"

She walked away from the window. "You don't remember me, do you?"

I shook my head with uncertainty. While I knew I didn't remember, her presence was sucking out my confidence.

She stepped closer. "You don't remember anything?"

Again, I shook my head.

Taking another step closer, she loomed over me, forcing me to lift my chin to maintain eye contact. "Absolutely nothing?"

I refrained from gulping. Why did she make me nervous? Was it because she was my mother-in-law, and I felt an unconscious need to impress her? Did I want her to think highly of me?

Sweat covered every inch of my body, but finally, I whispered, "I don't remember people."

"I'm sorry, dear, but I can't hear you."

"I don't remember people," I repeated louder this time.

"Is that everything?"

I hesitated before shaking my head.

"What else don't you remember?"

She was the first person to show such curiosity about what I remembered and what I didn't. It had always been brushed off, never delved into. I wasn't sure if I wanted to tell her more, but it seemed like she wasn't going to leave if I chose silence.

"I don't remember names," I said. "I don't even remember my own name. I don't remember what I like or . . . liked. I have to rely on others to fill in the gaps." My voice broke at the end, and I took a deep breath to collect myself.

Don't cry, don't cry, don't cry.

"How does it make you feel?" she asked gently.

Horrible, I wanted to say but instead managed, "Afraid."

"Why afraid?"

I could feel tears gathering in my eyes. Ettore's mother seemed the sort who always got her way. I had kept my feelings about my situation to myself, but no one had even asked before. She was the first, and while I felt grateful, I also felt pressured to share more.

"I'm afraid I will never remember," I admitted. "I'm afraid that people will share memories with me that I cannot recall. Yet, I remember things I must have learnt throughout my life. I have common sense, or at least I believe I do. I understand how certain things are supposed to work, and I have my own beliefs. But also, I'm afraid to remember."

"Why?"

My shoulders slumped. "I don't think I would like to remember the person I used to be."

Not after discovering the cat's skull.

"You're afraid you were a bad person before the Fire?"

I nodded.

"Worrying is your only problem," she stated. "Once you remember, which I am sure of, you will not concern yourself with whether you're a good or a bad person. Your concerns will be different. But until that day comes, let yourself breathe. Be open to learning new things, no matter how they might surprise you and challenge your beliefs. If things ever become overwhelming, talk to someone, whether it's Sofia, Ettore, me, or someone else. *Tu me comprends, chérie?*"

"Oui, je—"

I stopped myself, realizing I was speaking in French. I didn't even know I could.

I avoided looking at her. No one had ever spoken to me in French before. Why had she suddenly switched languages? Did it mean something?

"Do you understand me, dear?" she repeated in English.

Hadn't I just answered her? Maybe I was imagining things. But why would I hear her speaking French after she'd been talking in English? I decided not to ask.

I pulled myself together and forced myself to meet her eyes. "Yes."

She stepped back with a knowing smile on her lips. "Take care." She turned towards the door and made to leave, but paused. "Oh, and don't punish my son too much. He's been through a lot."

Punish him?

She exited the room before I could ask what she meant by that.

07
Familia. Officium. Honos.

Ettore

AS I ENTERED THE KITCHEN, I HEARD THE BEATLES' LATEST RELEASE 'PAPERBACK WRITER' PLAYING ON THE RADIO. Sofia was there, swinging her hips and singing along while rolling out dough.

I slumped into the chair at the table and closed my eyes, circling my throbbing temples with my fingers.

The sound of something heavy dropping on the table forced my eyes open. Sofia placed a plate of omelette and a glass of orange juice in front of me before going back to the counter.

"Thank you, Sofia," I said.

"I don't accept it."

"You don't accept it?"

She sprinkled the countertop with flour. "I'll accept your thanks when you finish every last crumb."

Famished and unable to think clearly, I had already planned on doing that. Still, her words evoked a smile and a warm feeling blossoming in my chest. Someone cared about my well-being, even if it was the hired help. Not once did my mother show she cared if I was eating well or taking care of myself.

My smile dropped.

She only cared about when I would come back to work.

"I would never dare to leave it unfinished," I promised.

Without another word, Sofia rolled the dough. Right . . . Actions spoke louder than words.

Fork and knife in hand, I started on the omelette. A smile formed on my lips after the first bite. The flavours melded perfectly—a testament to Sofia's culinary skills. Hiring her was undeniably one of the best decisions I'd ever made, and making good decisions felt rarer than encountering a unicorn these days. I could count them on one hand—actually, just two fingers would suffice.

Halfway through my breakfast, I asked, "What are you making, Sofia?"

"A galette."

I perked up. "Topped with . . . ?"

"Blueberries."

The thought of biting into the crust and tasting the sweet burst of blueberries made my mouth water.

"How is Miss Galletti?" she asked.

I swallowed the bite first before replying. "I'm helping her to walk." I raised the glass of orange juice and took a gulp. "Despite the nurse's efforts, it looks like it will take some time for her to walk on her own again. It's like her muscles have turned soft over the last two months."

I finished the omelette, and Sofia came to take the plate. I thanked her.

"She's lucky to have you." She gave me a knowing look as she put the plate in the sink.

I wanted to dig a hole, jump in it, and bury myself. Only Sofia knew what I had really been up to in the last two months, hiding behind the pretence of taking care of Vittoria. I trusted Sofia not to tell anyone, even though she was risking her life.

In my defence, I had been nearby when Vittoria was in a coma. Whenever the nurse visited, I would drop everything and stand outside her bedroom door.

Okay, I did that in case someone from SQ asked the nurse about my whereabouts. They couldn't know that instead of caring for my wife, I was tending to my flowers and building ship models.

But if the roles were switched, and I was in bed, Vittoria wouldn't have cared. She probably wouldn't have even hired someone to—

Sofia placed a coffee mug in front of me, and I thanked her.

I drank the coffee, trying to ignore my craving for a cigarette. I could have stepped outside for a smoke, but it felt rude. Sofia might work for me, but I appreciated her impeccable breakfast. The least I could do was keep her company.

Unless she didn't want any company.

I rose from the chair and walked to the window, gazing out at the garden with its freshly trimmed bushes and cut grass. The sight brought a smile to my face.

Before I took a break from work, the branches of the bushes stuck out haphazardly, and some flowers were wilting. Sofia had suggested hiring a gardener, but I couldn't stand the thought of a stranger taking care of something I loved in my territory.

"Hello, Ettore."

My smile dissolved as I flinched, and my untouched coffee spilled over the rim, splashing onto the floor. Sofia scurried over and started wiping it up with a rag.

I looked over at the woman standing in the doorway. "Mother."

She scanned me from head to toe, appraising my appearance. She did that with anyone, and discomfort only eluded a few. By now, I was used to it.

"When was the last time you went to a barber?" she asked.

No matter how much time had passed, my mother always had something to say about my appearance the moment she saw me. I had almost hoped she wouldn't this time.

"Didn't you say you were going to visit Vittoria?" I asked, pretending her biting question hadn't touched me. "I can escort you to her bedroom. Maybe she's awake now."

Her chin rose proudly. "I've already been there. She was leaving her bathroom when I saw her. Didn't Dr Zunino say she shouldn't be walking by herself?"

I thought she was joking, but Sybille Cosette didn't entertain humour.

Goddammit.

Mother shouldn't know that Vittoria wasn't under my control. But that concern was the least of my worries.

If Mother wasn't aware of Vittoria's amnesia before visiting her, she must be now. Vittoria's life might be in danger.

Despite my hopes that I was switched at birth, Sybille was my mother *and* one of the superiors. Yet she always prioritised her role as a superior over being a mother. I felt like I had to be careful with everything I did or said around her. It exhausted me, but if I wanted to stay safe and keep others safe, I had no choice.

"I'm aware of Dr Zunino's advice, but Vittoria has been making great progress," I explained. "If she wants to take care of her needs, we agreed she can go to the bathroom on her own."

She evaluated me again, reading my body language, but I stood determinedly.

Before the silence could go on for too long, I asked, "What did you two talk about?"

Was my mother aware of Vittoria's amnesia? I couldn't see how she wouldn't be, but I couldn't be one hundred percent sure.

"Oh, this and that." She toyed with the brooch on her shirt. "Girl talk."

I stifled a laugh.

Sybille Cosette capable of girl talk? She was a strict and sophisticated woman. Gossip and so-called girl talk were nothing but a waste of time to her. Some joked she was a man in the body of a smoking-hot woman. It always made me uncomfortable to hear my mother described that way. It wasn't exactly a child's dream.

"I hope you were nice to her," I said.

"Why wouldn't I be? She's my daughter-in-law."

"That didn't stop you from wearing a white dress at her wedding."

She chuckled, seemingly oblivious to the concept of being a decent human being. "I shine the brightest in white."

Right.

My mother thrived on being the centre of attention. Any shift of interest towards someone else would likely send her into a coma—how dare they pay attention to someone else?

I felt second-hand embarrassment as I recalled her showing up in a white dress at my own wedding. It shouldn't have surprised me, given her blatant disregard for the day that was supposed to be mine. Mine and Vittoria's. What saddened me most was the silence that followed. No one dared to confront her, simply because she was

Sybille Cosette, one of the superiors.

"Oh, darling . . ." She drew closer, causing my muscles to tense. "I see the look in your eyes . . ." Her cold hand pressed against my cheek. "You're worried, and I may know why. Vittoria . . . She doesn't remember a thing."

My arms went numb. Something I had expected shouldn't have surprised me, but here I was.

"I know you, Ettore. You think I don't, but I do." Her sweet voice, a tone that claimed she knew better, stirred something unpleasant. "You're afraid of what we might do with her if she doesn't remember. You would like to know that, wouldn't you?"

I remained silent. She slid her hand off my cheek. "Come for dinner sometime this month."

"How does that—"

"Bring Vittoria with you." She pressed my arm gently, a soft smile on her face. "I've missed you, *mon fils*. Don't be a stranger anymore. Remember, your father counts on you."

My father.

She always pretended as though my father expected things from me, when in reality, she was the one counting on me. My father? He was nothing more than her puppet.

"At least promise to consider it," she said.

She had never invited me for dinner before. Natalie usually took that initiative—the only person who cared enough to bring our family together. Sometimes even our father would offer an invitation, but our mother? She wouldn't invite me for dinner unless she had an ulterior motive. There was always a reason behind her—

It struck me, like the next step in a ship model suddenly making sense. Vittoria's memory loss and the dinner were distractions from the real reason she was here.

I was so naive to believe, even for a second, that she had visited Vittoria and me because deep down she cared.

Mother cared about no one but herself and her title.

Tired of her games, I decided to go for it. "When's the evaluation, Mom?"

She raised her fingers to her brooch, choosing silence.

"Isn't that why you're here?" I pushed. "To tell me the date when you'll punish me for abandoning my duties for two months?"

Why pretend? Knowing her, she'd casually drop a bomb right before leaving, saying something like, 'Oh, I almost forgot. There's an evaluation waiting for you next week, 9 o'clock sharp. Don't be late.'

"Okay." She dropped the pretence. "You're right. There is an evaluation, but you know that's not why I'm visiting you, right?"

I stared at her resolutely, not believing her one bit. "When is it?"

"Lorence is still on holiday with Marie, and Mia is undergoing nose surgery, so we've settled on the 31st of July."

Nine days from now.

"I'll be there." Not like I had a choice. They would track me down and punish me worse than they would during the evaluation.

"Will you promise to consider having dinner sometime?" she asked.

"I will."

My answer must have satisfied her, because she smiled and turned her attention to Sofia. "How are your children, Sofia?"

Sofia had placed the galette in the oven and was now washing her hands. "They're great. Thank you for asking, Miss Cosette." She wiped her hands on the towel. "But my sister has caught the Rash. Would I be able to get the Cure?"

"Why didn't you tell me?" I spoke before Mother could.

"You've been so busy, Mr Morrano . . ."

"Sofia," I said firmly, conscious of my mother's evaluating stare. I wasn't putting on a show for her. I did not want Sofia to hesitate to tell me if a member of her family got sick, even if I seemed unavailable or aloof. "If someone you care about gets sick, you tell me, okay? Don't worry if I seem busy. You're like family to me, and family always comes first."

"Familia. Officium. Honos," my mother whispered reverently, pressing a fist over her heart.

I mirrored her gesture without a second thought. "Familia. Officium. Honos."

Family. Duty. Honour.

08
Newfound Friendship

Teodora

ETTORE HAD LIED.
Instead of returning in an hour, he showed up the next day.

All day, I had hoped to see him entering my room, my excitement building every time the door opened. But whenever Sofia appeared with a tray of food, the anticipation faded. While I appreciated the food, it didn't compare to the excitement of seeing *him* walk in.

When Ettore finally returned, he helped me out of bed. I considered asking him if I could walk by myself, but the feeling of his hand around my waist and my arm on his shoulders held me back. I knew I should try walking on my own, but his proximity was addictive. If I didn't need his help, I worried he wouldn't touch me again, at least not so intimately.

We walked further outside my bedroom than yesterday.

"Have you rested well?" I asked, staring at him instead of watching my steps.

He lowered his head, his eyes fixating on my wig, much like

when he had entered the room. Panic gripped me. Did I look bad wearing it? If so, I had plenty to choose from in my wardrobe—an entire room filled with clothes. I still couldn't believe I had a room just for clothes and accessories. If I ever did believe it, it would be the day I remembered.

"Why?" He chuckled, surprised by the question. "Don't I look like I have?"

The corner of his lips quirked into a grin, and I clung to him, grateful for his embrace. The amusement danced in his eyes, sending a tingling sensation straight to my core—a feeling both warm and unfamiliar, yet undeniably enticing.

Snap out of your delusions, I told myself.

We might be married, but this marriage was as complex as everything else since I woke up.

"That wasn't my question," I pointed out.

He slipped his hand away from my waist and lifted my arm from his shoulder.

I watched in confusion. "What are you doing?"

"You walked to the bathroom yesterday," he shrugged. "You should be capable of walking on your own."

Before I could ask, "Who told you that?" I realised it was his mother. My heart raced until it occurred to me it didn't matter if she had told him. My ability to walk wasn't a secret, and there was no reason to treat it as one.

I put my hands on my hips and narrowed my eyes at him, trying to think of a clever response. But all I could muster was a defeated "Fine."

I turned my head away, preparing to take a determined step forward, but something jumped on the windowsill. A white cat stared at us with the brightest blue eyes, like the sea outside the window.

A smile gradually formed on my lips. "We have a cat?" I asked, trying my best to contain my excitement.

It could be a random cat, but what if—

"*I* have a cat," he clarified. "Her name is Regina."

I approached her with slow steps, avoiding direct eye contact to not scare her away. Placing my hands on either side of her, I trapped her and levelled our eyes. "You're the most magnificent creature I've ever seen." I offered her my fingers, and she sniffed them curiously. As she didn't leave, I laid my hand on her back, moving it down. She arched her back into my touch, issuing a contented purr.

If she knew about the cat's skull in my bathroom, she might not be so friendly.

"I thought you hated cats," Ettore said, his tone bewildered, drawing my attention back to him.

His words stung, but it would explain the skull. "I do?"

"Yes."

I scratched Regina's neck. She raised her head, offering better access, and closed her eyes in pure bliss.

"How could anyone hate such a cute creature?" I wondered aloud.

How could *I* hate her species? How could *I* hate *her*?

As I sat down next to Regina, she moved into my lap. By the surprise on Ettore's face, I gathered it was an uncommon sight. While Regina kneaded my legs, her nails sometimes poked through my trousers, scratching me. But I endured the pain, scratching the area near her tail.

"Regina hated you too," Ettore said in an incredulous tone.

I let out a short laugh. "If this is how she shows hate, she's a lovely kitty."

Regina relaxed in my lap. I wished I knew about her existence sooner. My time in my room would have been much less lonely.

"You can't move unless she does," Ettore warned. "It's the law."

"I don't see a problem with that."

He leant against the wall. "It seems like after the accident, your entire personality has changed."

"Was I that bad before?"

"Uh . . ." He pulled out his hand to scratch at his temple. "You weren't exactly everybody's favourite."

I wished I could deny his words. I felt he was wrong about me, but it was just a feeling. I didn't know who I was before the Fire, and I hated relying on others' judgement. They could be right about my character, but I should know myself better. Yet, I knew nothing. *Nothing* about myself.

I stared at Regina, forcing my tears away. "Why did you marry me if I was that horrible?"

"You weren't horrible."

I gave him a sceptical glance.

"Not *all* the time," he amended.

"You didn't answer my question," I reminded. "I may not remember a thing, but I have strong feelings about certain things. When I think of marriage, I imagine people joining their lives because they love each other and believe they're stronger together than apart. But it seems like it wasn't our case when we got married. Am I wrong?"

A moment of silence passed before he gave in. "No, you're not wrong."

"Can you tell me where we stand in our marriage instead of leaving me in the dark until I get my memory back, if I ever do?"

I gazed at him, hoping he would quit that mentality and explain it to me. Not knowing what I should and should not feel when I was around him was tearing me apart. Was it okay to be attracted to him, or should I stop those feelings before they grew stronger and led to heartbreak?

"I would prefer it if you remembered," he said.

Hiding my disappointment, I focused on Regina sleeping in my lap. "I would like to be alone now, please."

"Vittoria—"

"If you have nothing to share about our marriage," I interrupted, looking up at him with determination, "I want you to leave."

He didn't, nibbling at my nerves.

"Ettore—"

"What if I told you other people arranged our marriage?"

I raised my eyebrows curiously.

He continued. "I can't tell you who those people were, but picture a scenario where you have no say against most votes. They arranged our marriage before we were even born. I grew up knowing you would be my future, and over time, I learnt to like you, even though you made it hard to."

I swallowed, suddenly craving water. "But you don't love me."

"I respect you and care for you."

Respect you.

Care for you.

But no *I love you.*

"I didn't love you either?"

He pursed his lips thoughtfully. "Not that I know of. But if you did, I doubt you loved me the way you think."

"Did I respect you?"

"To some extent, but I respected you more than you respected me."

"We're not compatible, then?"

He smiled, finding the question amusing. "Not romantically. In work, we make a better team."

"We work together?"

He raised his hand to scratch at his temple again. "We do."

"I suppose I will not learn about the work we do?"

He gave me an apologetic look. "Not today, at least."

If he had married me out of obligation, and didn't even love me, yet stayed by my side while I was in a coma, then . . . "Am I a burden?" I asked.

Surprise crossed his face. "What? No, Vittoria. I can assure you that you're not. I like taking care of you and keeping you company."

I recalled Sybille's words. *Don't punish my son too much.* Was that what Sybille meant? Not to depend on him and let him focus on himself?

"I'm awake now." I forced a smile. "You should return to your life. As far as I know, I can take care of myself."

He stared at me sceptically. "What did Sybille want from you?"

"You mean your mother?"

"The one and only."

I found it weird that he referred to his mother by her first name, but it was one of many things that didn't make sense to me. I would have asked why if we hadn't already had an intense conversation about our marriage. "She asked about my well-being."

He lowered his head, his eyebrows furrowing. "That's . . . odd."

"What's odd?" A man echoed the question in my mind.

I tensed at the sight of another stranger—a strongly built blonde man. His hair matched the length of my wig, which I touched nervously.

"Artificial flowers," Ettore answered. "Are we, as a society, losing respect for real ones, replacing them with fake flowers because we're too lazy to take care of anything that is alive?"

The man stared at Ettore as if he were the strangest human alive, but I found it interesting. Why had Ettore lied? And why, of all things, did he settle on his dislike for artificial flowers?

As I realised a slight smile was tugging at my lips, I forced it away.

"You're right. That *is* odd." The man's eyes cut to the sleeping cat. "Since when does gorgeous Regina like *her*?" He put stress on *her* with disgust.

"*Vittoria* likes Regina, too," Ettore noted. "The end of the world might be near, so watch out."

The man came closer to touch Regina's head. As his fingers brushed against her fur, she stood and jumped off. Without my shield, I felt even more uncomfortable, wanting to leave.

"Relax, sis." He noticed my tension. "If one of us should be tense, it's me."

"She doesn't remember you," Ettore warned. "To her, you're a stranger."

"Right." He stuck out his tattooed hand, finally deigning to look me in the eye. "Raffaele."

I hesitated to take his hand.

"Your brother," Ettore clarified.

Brother or not, I still didn't take his hand.

Something about him felt off. Maybe it was because he was the first person who wasn't kind to me, or because Regina jumped off my lap when he touched her. Whatever the reason, I couldn't make myself like him, despite him being my brother.

A laugh came from Raffaele's mouth. "I see we're still on mutual terms."

Instead of accepting his hand, I clutched the hem of my nightgown. "What terms?"

"So she speaks." He cupped his hand around his mouth and whispered to Ettore loudly enough for me to hear, "Unfortunately."

Every instinct screamed at me to leave, and I wished I could just stand up and go without another word. But I didn't want to be as horrible as Ettore said I once was.

Ettore observed me, his gaze as analytical as Sybille's, as if he could sense my discomfort.

Then, his attention shifted back to Raffaele. "Why are you here?"

Raffaele pushed his thumbs into the pockets of his trousers. "For a very important reason, which we should discuss in private, my friend."

Tension entered Ettore's shoulders.

"Let's go," Raffaele urged. "I could use a drink."

"It's barely eleven."

"I know, right? I missed my morning drink."

Ettore looked at me. "You'll be okay if I leave you alone?"

"Weren't you listening to what I said before?" I asked.

"You can take care of yourself." He let out a sigh. "Whatever you do today, don't cause any trouble, okay?"

"Don't worry." I flashed him a fake smile. "You'll forget I even exist."

Raffaele leant towards Ettore's ear. "A man can only dream," he whispered, glancing at me from the corner of his eye.

Even if I was annoyed, it appeared that was Raffaele's intention. I refused to give him the satisfaction of knowing he had achieved his goal, so I sat there, staring at him blankly.

"You should apologise," Ettore told him.

Raffaele laughed, taking it as a joke despite Ettore's serious tone.

"Raff," Ettore pressed. "Apologise. Now."

His laughter died off. "Apologise for what?"

I slid to the floor. "It's okay," I said, looking at Ettore, hoping he could see in my eyes that I'd prefer he didn't make a scene. "I'm tired. I think I'll go to sleep."

A faint line creased his forehead as he discerned my lie.

I offered Raffaele a smile. "Goodbye, Raffaele."

Raffaele might have been mean to me, but it didn't mean I should reciprocate. He knew me as who I was before the accident, not who I was now. With time, he might grow to respect me, even if I didn't know why he had lost respect for me in the first place.

I walked towards my room and found Regina rubbing herself against the door. I smiled and opened it to let her in.

She walked inside hesitantly. As I settled in the chaise lounge, Regina's delicate paws padded softly against the floor. She sniffed every piece of furniture with curiosity, as if she was here for the first time.

At least I had closed the bathroom door.

Eventually, Regina hopped on the chaise lounge and curled up in my lap. I petted her, taking refuge in her calming purrs after the discomfort I had just experienced.

"If I was *that* horrible, you wouldn't be on my lap," I muttered.

Regina looked up at me with a loving look, bringing warmth to my heart.

"I'm not wrong. You like me, which means I'm not as bad as they say. At least not anymore."

Regina kneaded my legs with her paws, her nails pricking my skin once again. If it made an adorable creature happier, the pain was nothing I couldn't handle.

I relaxed into the chair. Ettore's sister was right. It was surprisingly comfortable.

Closing my eyes, I whispered, "I'm throwing out the skull before it harms our new friendship."

09
It's okay to ask for help
..✤..

Ettore

AS SOON AS WE STEPPED INTO THE OFFICE, RAFF GRABBED MY ARM AND PUSHED ME AGAINST THE WALL, HIS HAND PRESSING AGAINST MY THROAT.

"What are you thinking, man?" he demanded, as though I had committed some grave offence.

"Straight so far, but you're giving me ideas."

Raff smirked. "It would be a crime if I wasn't." His expression turned serious again. "Why are you skipping work? Are you trying to get yourself killed?"

"Can we talk without your hand against my throat?"

Reluctantly, he stepped back. I walked out onto the veranda, retrieving a cigarette and a lighter. I guided the flame to the tip of the cigarette before tucking the lighter back into my pocket.

Raff leant against the balustrade. "So?"

I took a drag and pulled the cigarette from my lips, exhaling a puff of smoke. "So nothing," I said. "I haven't been thinking much since the Fire."

"Haven't you thought about your life?"

"My life?"

"You have missed every meeting because of what?" He crossed his arms over his chest. "What have you been up to, by the way? Smoking a joint? Enjoying magic mushrooms?"

I frowned. "Taking care of Vittoria."

He threw his head back, laughing. "Taking care of Vittoria. That's the funniest thing I've heard in forever," he said. "Okay, let's say SQ believes you. Do you think they won't kill you anyway?"

I blew out a smoke. "Yes."

"I like your positivity, but you're using it in the wrong field, my friend."

"Superiors won't kill me for missing work. The worst they can do is cut off my income to add a bit of struggle. Did you forget who is the brains and who is the muscle in our group?"

Raff's jaw tightened. He didn't like it, but he knew it was the truth.

"You need to remember your place," I said. "Try not to forget it next time. Don't play a superior when you aren't one."

He mumbled something, but the words eluded me.

"What did you say?" I asked.

Once again, his lips moved incoherently. I turned my right ear toward him. "Can you—"

"You're not a superior either!"

I let out a heavy sigh. "Yelling was unnecessary."

"You didn't hear me."

"You see, I have a little problem." I tapped my finger against the hearing aid. "Instead of screaming, you could have spoken more clearly and *a little* louder."

Guilt cast a shadow over his face. "I'm sorry. Sometimes I forget about . . . *it*."

People always grew uncomfortable whenever I mentioned my partial deafness. Maybe it should make me uncomfortable, and I should want to hide my disability, but why would I? The hearing aid was a part of me now. Instead of regarding it as something that caused social discomfort, I took it as a helpful device. It was better to actually hear people than to pretend like I did. And if it made them uncomfortable, it wasn't my problem but theirs.

"I'm not acting to be a superior, *by the way*." I crushed the cigarette in the ashtray. "We're the puppets doing their bidding. They need us more than we need them. I'm not worried about my life."

I'm worried about Vittoria's.

But I couldn't share that with Raff because he wouldn't get it. I understood the complexity of sibling love, but Vittoria and Raff's relationship was beyond my understanding.

I always thought that one day, they might kill each other. They couldn't stand each other, constantly being mean and cruel. I never understood why they were that way. Perhaps it began in their childhood, when they were always competing for their father's attention.

"I guess you're right," Raff admitted.

I *was* right. Growing up in SQ with my mother as a superior, I knew SQ inside and out. My knowledge could lead to my demise if I wasn't careful.

"I don't understand why you've been taking care of her," he said. "She's terrible."

I couldn't disagree. Vittoria was hard to like, but she was my wife. I didn't love her, but it didn't mean I had to disrespect her like Raff did.

"I vowed to take care of her for the rest of my life."

"In sickness and in health?" He laughed. "That shit is as fake as your marriage."

Instead of showing him my annoyance, I looked out at the sea. "Vittoria is not the same anymore."

"I saw," he agreed. "If Regina likes her, something must have really changed."

"I'm not raising any hopes because if she regains her memory, she might return to her old self."

"What if she never gets her memory back?" His words exuded excitement.

I had, and it wasn't the excitement I felt but concern.

"Imagine if she's cast out," Raff continued, casually strolling along the veranda as if he were talking about paintings in an art gallery. "Imagine what your life could be like. You could go out with whoever you like, commit to whoever you like."

"Right . . ." I pretended to entertain the fantasy until I pinpointed him with a deadly serious look. "My life wouldn't be any different."

I could go out and commit to whoever I liked, sleep with whomever I wanted, all while being married to Vittoria or not. Committing to someone I loved instead of a duty sounded surreal. Impossible. Despite having crushes, I had never been in love or met someone I wanted to spend the rest of my life with.

Vittoria was never a burden. Even if she were, I could never consider her being cast out from SQ as a good thing.

"Still, you wouldn't have to live with her. You would be free from the witch for—"

"I understand you two are siblings," I interrupted, resisting the urge to push him against the wall. We weren't children anymore but adults. "You have your issues, but she's not the same now. She can't throw you a witty response. Can you promise me to be more considerate and not be rude to her next time?"

Raff's lip corners curled up in disgust. "I can't promise you that."

"Why not?"

"She's my sister." He shrugged. "I'm allowed to make the call."

"And she's *my wife*."

We locked eyes, tension stretching out between us. I stepped back. This was getting silly. "Can you be honest with me, Raff?"

He crossed his arms and drummed his fingers against his biceps. "I always am."

"Have you told anyone about the note?"

"Of course I—"

Someone knocked.

I turned my head, finding my father stepping out onto the veranda. He greeted me with a slight bow of his head, holding the tip of his hat. "Ettore. Raffaele."

I reciprocated the gesture. "Father."

"Good afternoon, Mr Morrano," Raff said.

"May I talk to my son alone?"

"I'll be out of your hair." Raff hurried out without hesitation.

Once he was gone, Father's serious and unwelcoming face morphed into a broad, friendly smile. He pulled me into his arms, patting my back. "How are you?"

I awkwardly hugged him back, mustering a small smile. "Fine."

He looked at me, reading the lie. "When I ask how are you, I don't want to hear *I'm fine*. I want to know exactly what's going on in my son's life."

My parents were like fire and ice. While his partner was controlling and cold, my father had an easygoing nature and a knack for finding humour in any situation, appropriate or not. His jokes, though sometimes groan-worthy, could make even the most uptight person smile. Everyone loved him.

But I never understood how he could love my mother. For the longest time, I was convinced he didn't. I had never even seen them kiss. It came as a shock when I learnt that every other kid's parents did. When I asked my dad why he didn't kiss mom, he told me he did, but they preferred to keep their love private, cherishing it just between the two of them.

Right.

"But I don't even know," I said. I wasn't lying. I couldn't pinpoint my emotions, and when something surfaced, I drowned it with a cigarette.

"Aren't you planning to return to work soon?"

The mere mention of work made me sick, conjuring the phantom sounds of screams and the smell of smoke. I gripped the balustrade with white-knuckled intensity. "I am, but . . ."

"But . . . ?"

"Vittoria," I said, ready to voice my fear for the first time to someone. "She's not herself. Before you say it's because she doesn't remember, I think it's more than that. Please don't tell Mother what I'm about to say, okay?"

As I looked over at him, I found him staring at my hand on the balustrade. I relaxed my grip.

"Okay." He met my eyes. "I won't tell."

I stared at him suspiciously. If he hadn't lied and he loved my mother, he would tell her. I should keep it to myself unless it was old news and Raff had already told SQ.

Still, I said, "The night when the Hôtel du Passé burned, I think someone was after Vittoria. We found her outside the building, burning. Someone had dragged her out, set her on fire, and left a note to us."

"Someone's after Vittoria?" He laughed, unable to believe it. "Do they have a death wish?"

If Raff had told SQ about the note, my father wouldn't have reacted like that. Maybe I could trust Raff after all.

"Are you going to do something about it?" he asked.

"I don't know," I admitted. "If I took action, where would I even start? Considering Vittoria's less-than-friendly character, everyone could be her enemy. Can I even do anything about it when I have the evaluation awaiting me?"

He stroked his chin thoughtfully. "If you look for the evildoer, would you like my help?"

I never considered it, but my father was more reputable among SQ than me. He could have access to information I couldn't. But I didn't see a reason to search for the bad guy. If Vittoria remembered, she would find the person and deal with them herself.

"If I do, I'll think about it," I promised.

But I wouldn't. Asking for help was foreign to me, and I would prefer to avoid it rather than deal with the discomfort.

My father sighed, as though he had read my mind. "It's okay to ask for help."

I knew that, but . . . he was not only my father, but Sybille's husband. I couldn't trust him even if I wanted to. "I will ask for your help if I need it," I said confidently. "But until I do, I would appreciate it if you tell nothing about our conversation to Mother."

"Why would I tell her? She never cared about Vittoria."

I snorted.

If she never cared about Vittoria, why visit her and ask about her well-being?

Father gave me a curious look. "Is there something you would like to share with me?"

If he believed Sybille didn't care about Vittoria, he might not know about her visit yesterday. I didn't want to interfere with my parents' relationship, but perhaps Mother didn't care after all. Maybe he could explain why she had been so eager to see Vittoria.

"She visited Vittoria yesterday."

The lines on his face deepened. My father rarely hid his emotions in front of me, and his expression now made me suspect Sybille hadn't told him.

"Why?" he asked.

"Funny," I said. "I was hoping you could tell me."

10
Jealousy

Teodora

THE NEXT WEEK, DR ZUNINO ENTERED THE HOSPITAL ROOM, HOLDING HER NOTEBOOK. I was sitting on the examination table, and Ettore was leaning against the wall. She greeted us with a smile. "How are you?"

Ettore and I exchanged glances, both uncertain about whom she was addressing. Since I was the one here for a check-up, I replied, "Good. I'm walking now."

"That's good." She noted something in her notebook and glanced at Ettore. "How about you?"

Ettore scratched his temple. "Good. I'm good. Mostly healthy, except for, you know." He pointed at his hearing aid.

Dr Zunino chuckled, a happy sparkle in her eyes. "You look better too."

Tension froze my shoulders, and a sick feeling twisted my stomach. I looked down, fearing I might give away my emotions.

Ettore did look better. Since Dr Zunino's visit last week, he had improved his appearance by shaving his stubble, cutting his overgrown hair, and the dark circles under his eyes were less visible. It felt weird that she noticed these changes. But it could mean nothing.

At least I hoped it didn't.

"I have your blood results." She waved the papers as she approached me. "I found nothing unusual, but your behaviour suggests you may have post-traumatic amnesia."

"Is it permanent?" Ettore asked.

Once again, a smile graced Dr Zunino's lips. "It hardly ever is, Mr Morrano. Amnesia can be short-term or long-term. If it's long-term, it might take weeks or months for Vittoria to remember everything before the accident."

"It's not the worst news," Ettore said. "Time will pass. At least it's not permanent."

"It's true," Dr Zunino agreed. "Apart from the memory loss, Vittoria, your body suffered third-degree burns," she explained. "You've undergone many surgeries. To avoid further damage, I'll need you to take precautions. No intense activities for at least a month. No sex, but if it's not possible, take it slow and be gentle."

The mention of sex warmed my cheeks. The thought of Ettore and me being intimate sounded dreamlike, despite him being my husband. I considered making a joke about there being no issues, but I hesitated. Was it appropriate to share that with my doctor? And if Dr Zunino had any interest in him . . . While it might sound selfish, I wasn't eager to give her any encouragement.

But what if she knew about our situation and didn't mean sex with Ettore specifically but sex in general?

Dr Zunino made a note in her notebook before suddenly lifting her head, as though she had a lightbulb moment. "Aren't you into acrobatics?"

I had never heard of such a thing. "Am I?"

Ettore stepped closer, and I caught a whiff of his cologne. Now, after he showered and applied that addictive smell, it became even more challenging to battle my growing feelings for him. More than ever, I craved his closeness.

"I'll make sure she doesn't do any physical activities," he promised. "Is that everything?"

"Yes." Dr Zunino smiled. "Take care of each other."

As she turned to leave, I quickly said, "Wait, I have a question."

Dr Zunino turned back. "Yes?"

"Am I supposed to remember everything myself, or can I ask questions about my past and expect answers?"

I felt Ettore's incredulous stare. I hoped Dr Zunino would tell me I was allowed to know about my past. It would show Ettore that he wasn't a doctor and shouldn't assume things.

"It's best if you remember on your own," Dr Zunino answered, disappointing me. "You don't want to confuse your memories with what others tell you. But you should surround yourself with familiar places, smells, sounds, and people. Does that answer your question?"

I nodded. "Yes."

"Is that everything?"

"Yes," I said.

"Are you sure?"

I chuckled. "Yes, I'm sure. Thank you."

With a faint smile, she left.

"See?" Ettore said with pride, "I know what I'm talking about."

He was clearly teasing me.

I hopped off the examination table. "I'm sure you do, but you're not a doctor. You can't know everything."

"But I knew this, didn't I?"

Suppressing a smile, I let out an annoyed sigh. When we left the hospital, I remembered to ask, "Why didn't you tell me I did acrobatics?"

We headed towards Ettore's convertible. The first time I saw it this morning, the claret-red sheen of his well-polished car dazzled me. It was almost blinding.

"You never asked about your hobbies."

"Why would I, when you made it clear you want me to remember everything myself?" I didn't hide the annoyance dripping from my words.

I had every right to feel frustrated. It could be months before I recalled everything.

As he said nothing, I spun on my heel and walked around the car. He followed suit immediately. When I reached for the handle, his hand brushed against mine, sending pleasant shivers across my skin. I looked up, meeting his eyes.

"Allow me," he said softly.

I hesitated for a moment but then withdrew my hand. As he opened the door for me, warmth flooded my cheeks. I thanked him, casting my eyes downward. Once he was sure I was settled inside, he closed the door and joined me in the car.

"Was I good at it?" I asked.

"I suppose so." He started the engine. "I was never an expert to judge."

He manoeuvred out of the parking lot, and I relaxed into my seat. "What about Dr Zunino?"

With his attention fully focused on traffic, he took some time to reply. "Are you asking if Dr Zunino is good at gymnastics?"

I snorted, sounding like a pig. Warmth flooded my cheeks. "Sorry."

"What are you sorry for?"

I shook my head. "Nothing. I didn't mean her gymnastic skills." Unsure how to ask without making it awkward, I hesitated. "Do you like her?"

The dimple in his right cheek made an appearance as he half-smiled. I was tempted to poke at it with my finger, but I folded my hands in my lap, keeping my fingers in place.

"What makes you think that?"

I shrugged, pretending it didn't matter, as if I was just asking to keep the conversation going. "I think she likes you."

His lips curled into a faint smile. "You know, when we got married, we agreed on some things. Sleeping in separate rooms was one, but we also agreed we could sleep with anyone *except* each other's relatives."

Relief filled me, but I didn't give in to it just yet. "Dr Zunino is my relative?"

"Your distant cousin."

My once heavy chest lightened. I couldn't describe how much I appreciated that he had told me instead of insisting I remembered, but . . .

"Wasn't I supposed to remember that?" I teased.

"You'll see Dr Zunino sometimes. It's best if you know she's not only your doctor. But that is the only exception. Everything else, you'll have to remember yourself."

I rolled my eyes, a smile dancing on my lips. But it dropped at the thought of Dr Zunino possibly being interested in Ettore. He could have lied about our pact not to pursue each other's relatives, and if Dr Zunino chose to romance him, it could lead to something. Of course, Ettore might already be involved with someone else, and

I wouldn't have a clue. If he was, there was nothing I could do. For now, though, the reassurance that our agreement prevented him from pursuing anything with her calmed me.

As we entered a more open road, Ettore sped up. The wind hit my face, and I held onto my wig, afraid it might blow away, while trying to see the sea. Ettore must have noticed my struggle because he slowed down.

"Sorry," he said.

"It's okay."

I slowly lowered my hand and, once certain the wig wouldn't slip away, turned my head towards the window. When the tops of the trees no longer obstructed the sea, an idyllic view opened up.

Buildings and vegetation stretched from the crescent-shaped coastline to the hills. The sun ruled the cloudless sky, casting a shimmer on the blue sea that invited for a dip. I hesitated to ask Ettore if I could. Even if I did, I doubted he would let me, especially after Dr Zunino advised against too much movement. Besides, he had been busy all week.

I only saw him at dinners. When I asked what he was doing all day, he answered *work* without elaborating. When I asked about what kind of work, he said this was one of the things I should remember myself. One of the many, endless things.

The buildings gradually moved into view, blocking the sea, and eventually, we ended up on the same street we had taken to the hospital.

Ettore turned the car, bringing it to a stop in front of a black gate. He got out to push it open wide, then drove inside. Afterwards, he left the car again to close the gates. When he returned, we continued down the tree-lined path that hid the garden, and our small, two-floor white-washed villa came into view. Earlier, when we had left for the appointment, the front of the villa was empty. Now a bright yellow convertible was parked there.

Ettore mumbled something, and I turned to him. "What did you say?"

He brought the car to a full stop and turned off the engine. "My brother is here."

"You have a brother?"

I shouldn't be surprised, as I knew little about Ettore, yet I had assumed he only had one sibling.

He let out a sigh. "Apparently, I do."

He stepped out of the car, and I unbuckled my seat belt. As I was about to open the door, Ettore was faster once again.

"You know I can open the door, right?" I stepped out. "I'm not disabled."

"I'm aware." He shut the door behind me. "But my grandmother would appear and smack my hand if she saw my wife opening the door when I was around."

Flushing, I turned my head away, wishing he would stop his chivalrous gestures. I felt like I owed him. To avoid that feeling, I'd rather open the door by myself.

He even opened the door to the villa for me.

"Thank you," I said quietly, mindful that he might not have heard it. Before I could repeat it louder, I saw a stranger sitting on the stairs inside. He got up, revealing his tall height. I stepped back, bumping into Ettore.

I glanced at him. "I'm sorry."

But Ettore's attention was on the man. "Antoine."

Antoine nodded his head to him. "Ettore."

He descended a step, and as he stood in front of us, he appeared less tall than at first sight. Yet, I stood stiff as he took my hand, pressing his lips to it while staring at me, his blue eyes sending a chill through my body. "No matter how long I stare, I see no signs of the incident. I must say, you look even more beautiful than before, Vittoria."

If he was trying to charm me with flattery, I was too busy staring at the place where his lips had been a moment ago. Despite the need to shake off the lingering shadow of his touch, I controlled myself, gently pulling my hand away and mustering a friendly smile. "I don't remember you."

He straightened. "According to my sources, you don't remember anything."

"Not entirely true," I corrected him, trying not to show my annoyance. "I mostly don't remember people."

"You don't remember your—"

"What brings you here?" Ettore interrupted him, rescuing me from further conversation with his brother.

Antoine chuckled, but Ettore's stern expression made him stop. "Am I not wanted here?"

"That's not what I said," Ettore said. "I asked, why are you here?"

"Not to cause trouble, if that's what you suspect." He scanned his surroundings. "Not much has changed here since I left. I didn't realise our parents would give you the traitor's villa as a wedding gift."

I felt a touch against my waist. Before I could jump away, Ettore's hand circled around me, pulling me against him. Regardless of the unexpectedness of his movement, I quickly composed myself, hiding my surprise.

"Perks of marriage," Ettore said without humour.

Antoine's eyes shifted to Ettore's hand around my waist. "I'm happy you're happy, *fratellino*," he said, and Ettore's fingers tightened on my side. "To answer your question, I'm planning to stick around for a while. Unless, of course, you're not okay with that?"

I raised my head, curious to see Ettore's reaction, but his face gave nothing away. Finally, he smiled.

Over the past week, I had come to recognise many of his smiles— amused, uncertain, teasing . . . But this one had nothing. It felt forced.

"No," he said, "not at all."

"Great." Antoine checked his wristwatch. "I'm afraid I must go." He looked back at his brother. "I can't wait to catch up with you later. I've left something outside your office, and I would love it if you checked it out. See you later, lovebirds."

He brushed past Ettore, and once Antoine closed the door, Ettore let go of me, his face etched in hard lines.

"You don't like him," I concluded.

I waited for an instant denial, but silence followed, speaking for itself.

The sensation of Antoine's lips pressed against the top of my hand burned. I wanted to wash it away, but I felt obliged to stay with Ettore. He appeared troubled.

I had only exchanged a few words with Antoine, but if Ettore didn't like his own brother, there must have been a good reason.

I hugged myself. "I don't like him either."

Ettore jerked his chin forward, amazement evident on his face. "*Really?*"

His question dripped with heavy sarcasm, causing frustration to build inside of me. But before it became too much, I realised why he wouldn't believe me. "What did I do now that I don't remember?"

"It doesn't matter."

He turned towards the stairs and began ascending. I stood still, puzzled by his behaviour, but soon after, I followed him. "Ettore."

He stopped midway and hesitated before turning to me. "I believe you've slept with him."

My mouth formed an *o*.

"You didn't tell me, of course," he went on. "I didn't stumble upon you two either. He *bragged* about it."

Nausea twisted my stomach.

I couldn't wrap my mind around it, searching for a reason why I would be attracted to Antoine when my first impression of him was nothing like that. Sure, the man was attractive, but as a person he was . . .

First impressions could be deceptive, and I might have known him better before the Fire.

Still, I couldn't believe it.

"But how could I breach our agreement?"

If neither of us could sleep with each other's relatives, why would I go for his brother? Was I that careless?

Ettore rested his arm on the balustrade, clasping his hands together. "Only you can answer that."

I searched his face for any sign of pain, but found nothing. Did he even care? Or did it not matter to him with whom I slept, whether it was his brother or some random stranger?

"You're okay with it?"

He took some time to answer. "I wish it didn't happen. When we agreed on something, I thought it was sacred, but you're not the kind of person to care, I guess."

Guilt pierced me, and I broke our eye contact.

If only I could go back in time . . . If only I'd had the mindset I had now . . .

"But he's . . ." I leant against the wall. ". . . not my type."

"He could have been your type before."

"Not anymore."

The silence enveloped us, and I raised my eyes, catching the curiosity in his. "What *is* your type then?" he asked.

You, I thought.

The longer we stared at each other, the faster my heart pumped. While he waited for me to describe my ideal person, I was searching my brain, unable to understand why my past self had chosen Ettore's brother instead of him. Was it because of our situation, and I didn't want to complicate it more? Or was it because I wasn't attracted to Ettore?

It was different now though.

I swallowed.

"I don't know," I said into the silence, my voice edging on frustration. "But it's not your brother."

I went past him, climbing the rest of the stairs. Once I reached the top, I glanced over my shoulder, expecting to catch his gaze. But he was going down instead of up, unlike before.

And I had a feeling he was avoiding me on purpose.

I was admiring my perfume collection when a knock sounded. Suspecting it was Ettore, I checked myself in the mirror, even if nothing had changed about my appearance since the last time I saw him. I stood and went to open the door, finding Natalie standing on the other side.

She raised her hand in an awkward hello. "By the look on your face, I can tell you were expecting someone else."

I hadn't realised my disappointment was so obvious, and I immediately felt a pang of guilt. "I'm sorry."

"Don't worry about it." She waved it off. "But if you were expecting my brother, I'd think you've got a concussion."

I stepped aside, letting Natalie in. "Did I hate him that much?"

Natalie grimaced. "Not *hate* him. He was like a brother you liked to annoy," she said before adding, "Like Raff."

Gathering Natalie would stay for some time, I closed the door. "How about you? Did you like me?"

"Nobody liked you." Natalie headed for the door leading to my wardrobe and swung it open, mindless of the pain her words brought me.

I followed her inside. "Why? What did I—"

"Let's see what you could wear for the dinner party," she said.

Dinner party?

It threw me off balance, erasing the fact that she had interrupted me. "What dinner party?"

"At my parents' place." She glanced around the wardrobe. "It's a fancy room you have here. Oh . . ." She put her finger up, remembering something. "Your parents will be there too, so you'll finally be able to see them. Or well, re-meet them."

My body went numb at the thought of meeting new people—my parents—whom I was supposed to remember. I bit my thumb's nail as my heartbeat went frantic.

They will expect me to remember them, and once they realise I can't, they will be disappointed. They might try to convince me it's okay, sharing memories I can't—

"Hello?"

I snapped back to the present and saw Natalie staring at me with concern. She must have been trying to get my attention for a while.

"Are you okay?" she asked.

Realising my nail was still in my mouth, I pulled it away and awkwardly lowered my hand. "I think so."

She took a step forward. "I was asking what you were going to wear."

Imagining going there, meeting Ettore's parents *and* mine, awakened anxious thoughts. I didn't want to go, but it didn't seem like I had a choice. I didn't feel safe telling that to Natalie. If Ettore was here . . .

"Will Ettore be there?"

"He will."

The knowledge eased my anxiety a bit. "Will you help me pick an outfit?" I asked. "I'm not sure what would be appropriate for a dinner party," I half-lied.

I might be able to pick an outfit suitable for a dinner party under normal circumstances, but I was feeling too anxious about meeting my parents to do it myself. I wanted everything to be perfect, and so far, I hadn't been able to do much of that yet.

She smiled. "It would be my pleasure."

11
La Niña

Ettore

ANTOINE LEFT A MODEL KIT OF THE NIÑA. The mere sight of the box outside my office boiled my blood. Did he really think a ship model of one of Christopher Columbus' vessels would make me forgive him?

I didn't know what to do with it.

Keeping it would make him think I forgave him, and we would be back to how things were. But if I threw it out, I would never forgive myself. The Niña was the final piece needed to complete my collection of Columbus' ships. This specific model was hard to come by. It took me five years to obtain the other two ships, and I didn't know if I could get this one once again anytime soon.

Would I let my pride win and return it to him?

I lifted the box and turned to move it, but Natalie was standing in my way, scaring the devil out of me. "You must be joking," I said.

She smiled ruefully. "What is this?" Inspecting the box with interest, she read, "*La Niña*. Did you get another model? Where are you even putting them?"

"I did not." I walked past her. "It's a gift from Antoine."

I carried it to the exit and placed it by the door. *Let him have it.* I would find my own someday. Hopefully.

"That's kind of him," she said.

I scoffed. "Right."

Natalie eyed me curiously. I hadn't shared what happened before the car accident with anyone. But when they found Antoine's car smashed into a tree, they must have had their suspicions. Natalie specialised in investigating murder cases. She could easily guess, even without directly asking me anything. Perhaps Antoine had already told her, but that was doubtful. My brother was a coward, and no Swiss rehab program could change that.

"What are you going to do with it?" she asked. "Throw it out?"

"It's a funny thing." I wagged my finger at her, impersonating an old man. "I don't remember inviting you here today."

Her eyebrows drew together. "I'm just curious, but if you don't want to talk, I won't force you to. I'm here to tell you our parents invited you and Vittoria for dinner. You're expected in an hour."

"You could have called instead of driving here."

"No, I couldn't. You never pick up the phone, and I had to come anyway to help Vittoria find something to wear."

"Help Vittoria? Why are you suddenly being so friendly to her?"

As far as I knew, Natalie had always been indifferent towards Vittoria. They acknowledged each other's presence but weren't friends. From what I had seen, they only talked about work and nothing beyond that.

"Why shouldn't I be?" She raised her eyebrows, as if my question was absurd. "She's been through a lot and barely survived. Also, she seems nicer now. I might actually become friends with my sister-in-law."

I regarded her with suspicion. It might just be curiosity. We had never dealt with someone with amnesia before. Even if Natalie had other reasons for helping Vittoria with her outfit and befriending her, she was harmless. I wasn't concerned.

"Fair enough, but did Vittoria even ask for your help?"

She turned to the stairs dismissively, her chin held high. "I will be a great help to her."

As she put her foot on the first step, I said, "Don't waste your time. I'm not going."

She stopped, turning to me with a scowl. "You have to. The Gallettis will be there."

"They're already back from Italy?"

I thought they weren't coming back until the evaluation. My heart raced. I wasn't prepared to meet Lorence Galletti today. He was overly serious and cold.

"It's been two weeks. It's not like they were going to stay there forever."

"I wish Antoine had stayed in rehab forever," I mumbled.

"Antoine will be at the dinner too," she said. I hadn't expected her to hear that, but I often forgot that not everyone had problems with hearing. "Try to play nice and don't bite."

"I'm always playing nice."

Her raised eyebrows suggested otherwise. "Will you be there?"

"Hmm . . ." I tilted my head in thought. "Will I be attending the dinner celebrating my dear brother's release from rehab, even though he was the one who got me into drugs?"

Natalie gave me an unimpressed look. "It was a conscious choice you made. You were an adult, and you can't blame Antoine for it. You would have joined him if you hadn't been in the car accident."

Guilt swept over me.

"That's right," she said, reading my guilt-drenched face. "You're the last person who should judge him."

I was about to explain that I didn't judge him for his drug abuse, but for letting me drive his car a year ago. If he hadn't, I wouldn't be struggling to hear people and wouldn't have constant ringing in my ears when it got too quiet. But I changed my mind.

Natalie watched me, and I realised it was exactly what she waited for. She wanted to know what had happened before the car accident, unaware that Antoine had let me drive while I was completely wasted.

I flashed her a sarcastic smile. "You're so right, Nat. I shouldn't judge him."

She rolled her eyes. "Will you come to the dinner party?"

I pretended to think about it, despite already knowing my answer. If Vittoria's parents were going to be there, I couldn't keep her away from her family. Seeing them might help her remember.

"I will," I reassured.

"Perfect."

As she disappeared upstairs, I cast one last glance at the box.

"One day I will have you," I whispered. "But today, I can't accept you as a bribe for forgiveness."

12
The Dinner

Teodora

OF ALL THE PLACES WHERE ETTORE'S PARENTS COULD LIVE, THE LAST THING I WOULD HAVE EXPECTED WAS A CASTLE. Yet, a castle wouldn't have been a far guess. As we drove up the hill, an enormous house came into view, rising like a pink dream with white accents.

At first, I was certain that Ettore was driving the wrong way. Or maybe he was taking me somewhere else entirely. The estate couldn't possibly be where his parents lived. I scanned the surroundings, searching for a smaller, more modest building, despite the people opening the gate for us. But the house, with its view of the sea and hills, was undoubtedly his parents' property.

The car moved, and I couldn't take my eyes off the estate as Ettore parked next to the others. It was only when my door opened that I realised he was no longer in the car. He offered his hand to me, but I hesitated to accept it, not wanting to make physical contact with him.

The mere touch of his skin against mine suffused me with a

warmth that felt too thrilling to be real. With every touch, it was harder to fend off my growing feelings towards him. I wished they would disappear once and for all. Not seeing him often and avoiding his touches helped with that.

Yet, I gave him my hand. There was no need to cause a scene.

He helped me out of the car. I looked around the area, noting three parked cars, but my attention was drawn to the pathway nestled between the bushes. It looked intriguing. I wanted to explore it, but I couldn't leave Ettore.

A harsh smell tickled my nostrils. I turned my head to Ettore, who had a lit cigarette poking out of his mouth. Frowning, I stepped away, waving my hand in front of my face to chase away the awful odour.

His expression tightened at my reaction. He opened his mouth, but his words were cut off by a familiar yellow convertible driving in. I tensed, watching the car park next to Ettore's, and soon after, Antoine stepped out.

Antoine tucked his sunglasses into his shirt collar while approaching us. "Haven't you heard of the studies?" He slapped Ettore's back. The force of the slap almost sent the cigarette flying out of his mouth. "Smoking kills."

"Yes, but it kills slowly," Ettore replied. "I'm in no rush."

Antoine shot a *Can you believe him?* look at me before offering his arm. "Should we go inside while my brother soothes his nerves with a smoke?"

Go with him and do what exactly?

Waiting for Ettore wasn't ideal, but joining Antoine, whom I had just met *and* didn't like, sounded even worse. I would rather wait for Ettore to finish his cigarette while catching the nasty smell every once in a while.

"Thanks for the offer, but I'll wait for my husband," I said.

From the corner of my eye, I noticed Ettore glance away when I referred to him as my husband. Despite our loveless marriage, he was still my husband, whether he liked it or not.

"You sure?" Antoine pressed, refusing to relent. "He's probably going to take a long time, *micetta*."

Disgust churned in the pit of my stomach at his endearment. "I'm no kitten to you."

He took a step closer, the expensive scent of his cologne catching me off guard by how similar it was to Ettore's. "Let's go inside," he coaxed. "The wind will surely ruin the hours you must have spent on your hair."

The hair I had spent 'hours' on was actually a wig—short, red curls just above my shoulders.

"No, thank you." I smiled with my teeth and controlled my voice, assuming a polite tone. "I'll wait for my husband."

"A woman shouldn't wait for a man to finish his cigarette," he said. "It's beneath her. Beneath *you*."

Still better than going with you, I wanted to say, but instead I looked over at Ettore, begging for help. He watched us as he exhaled a cloud of smoke, too intrigued by the scene to intervene.

Anger surged within me.

I'm on my own, then.

I fixed Antoine with a serious look, abandoning my polite tone. "If you were genuinely considerate instead of pretending, you wouldn't flirt with your brother's wife right in front of him."

"Since when do you care what he thinks? We've always enjoyed flirting with each other."

In what kind of delusional world was the man living? I did nothing but decline him, but he—

"At least you used to," he whispered, his tone carrying sadness.

My anger diminished, but before I could fully soften and apologise, Ettore cleared his throat, bringing me back to my senses. Why would I feel bad for the man who refused to leave me alone despite me saying no?

Antoine stepped away, avoiding eye contact with anyone as he turned and walked away. It wasn't until he disappeared inside that I realised I was gripping my skirt.

Ettore raised an eyebrow at me. "You okay?"

Tears burned the back of my eyes in anger. He *knew* how I felt about his brother, and whether I'd slept with him or not, it didn't matter. The past was in the past. The present was what mattered. I didn't like Antoine, and I wished to avoid any contact with him, but

Ettore did nothing. He stood, dragging on his cigarette and watching us as if my discomfort was the most entertaining show in the world.

I spun on my heel and strode towards the entrance.

"Okay . . ." He followed me. "What's wrong?"

I balled my hands into fists, ascended the three stairs, and whirled to face him, tears blurring my vision. "You were standing right there!" I pointed accusingly at the place where he was smoking and observing us a minute ago. "You could have interrupted us sooner. Your dearest brother doesn't know the definition of the word *no*, and it would have helped if you had intervened."

His face clouded with guilt.

Good. That was the least he should feel.

"I'm sorry," he said, and even if he was three steps down, I still had to tilt my head back to meet his gaze. "You're right. I should have intervened, and no excuse of mine is valid. All I can do is apologise and do better next time."

My bottom lip quivered.

I'm pathetic.

At the thought, I brushed the tears from my eyes with the back of my hand.

He gave me an apologetic look. "I didn't mean to make you cry."

I shook my head, inhaling the snot as I had nothing to wipe it with. Ettore pulled out a tissue from inside his jacket and handed it to me. Thanking him, I took it and turned away to blow my nose. Unsure where to dispose of the tissue, I carefully folded it. Seeing my hesitation, Ettore offered his hand. "I can take that."

I looked at him like he was out of his mind. "It's full of my snot."

"I don't care. Just give it to me."

Reluctantly, I handed him the tissue, and he tucked it into his pocket. I winced but didn't say anything. We were probably already late.

As we entered the estate, I was surprised by its emptiness. Moving through the entrance hall into the main hall, my gaze fell upon a dozen statues of naked women standing between the columns. A quiet conversation drifted from one of the statues, and as we drew closer, we discovered Antoine and Sybille.

Ettore cleared his throat, and the conversation fell silent. Sybille's lips curved into a small smile at the sight of us. She approached, her heels clicking in an echo.

"You've made it," she said, as if she hadn't expected to see us, wrapping her arm around mine. "Come, Vittoria. I'll escort you to the dining room."

I glanced at Ettore for comfort, and he responded with a reassuring smile. Encouraged, I let Sybille guide us forward.

"How are you today?" she asked.

"Uh . . . good?" It came out as a question, and I hastened to correct myself. "Today has been good to me, miss. Thank you for inviting me."

I squeezed my skirt, feeling sweat coating my hands. *Today has been good to me, miss? She's your mother-in-law, not Elizabeth II!*

My heart froze in my chest. *Elizabeth II . . .*

I remember the Queen of England, but I can't remember my own name?

Sybille laughed delicately. "No need for *thank yous*. You're like family to me."

Feeling someone's gaze on my back, I looked back and caught Ettore looking puzzled. When he noticed me staring, his confusion disappeared, replaced by a soft smile. It was like a mask he put on to convince me that everything was perfectly fine.

She put her hand on the handle of a large, white door and pushed it open. We entered first into a brightly-lit room with a table set with tableware. Natalie waved at us from the alcove, and an old woman sitting next to her joined her.

Sybille slipped her arm out. "Your parents will be here soon." She clasped her hands together. "Now, excuse me, but I have to find my husband. He's late. *Again.*"

She turned around with grace and left, closing the door behind her.

Natalie approached me. "Come." She grasped my arm and led me towards the old lady. "Grand-Maman wants to see you."

The old woman nodded her head in greeting. "Please, take a

seat."

Before I could, Natalie pulled me to sit next to her. The lady picked up a half-full glass of red liquid from the nearby table and offered it to me. "Drink this. It will benefit you."

Seeking reassurance, I glanced at Ettore standing in the closest corner. I didn't catch his eyes. He was too busy stealing a glance at his brother, who stood on the opposite end of the room, gazing out of the window.

I accepted the glass hesitantly. "How will it benefit me?"

Her faint smile touched her eyes, reminding me of a wise owl. "You entered the room like a cat brought home for the first time. It must be intimidating to walk into a room with faces that know you, but you don't know them."

Something cracked inside of me, making me speechless.

"But she's among family," Natalie said. "Here, there are no strangers."

Her grandmother issued a restrained chuckle. "To her, we are." She stuck out her hand. "I'm Reine Cosette, Sybille's mother and Grand-Maman of her three minions. And who are *you*, my dear?"

Who are you, my dear? The question reverberated in my mind, elusive to grasp.

She was the first one to ask me who I was, instead of assuming I would remember her. My heart swelled with joy. I struggled to find the right words to express my gratitude for offering me something

I didn't know I needed.

"I . . ." I lowered my eyes to her proffered hand. *Oh, if I could answer her question . . .*

She rested her hand on my knee. "What's on your mind?"

My every instinct resisted voicing my thoughts, but it was the least I could do. Reine had been so kind to me. "I don't know myself. I don't know who I am."

"You must feel pressured to remember, but remember . . ." She covered her mouth as if she had cursed. "Pardon my play of words. What I mean is, the more you force yourself to remember, the less likely you will. I'm no medic, but my advice has never disappointed people before."

Natalie rolled her eyes. "Always the one to brag, Grand-Maman."

"Bragging isn't bragging when it's the truth." Yet the glint in her eyes revealed her humour. "Now, go, you two. I need to talk to my grandsons before your mother walks in and tries to steal the show." She raised her hand to beckon them over, earning an uncertain look from the pair. "Oh, you two! Do you think time is all I have?"

Natalie laughed. "Let's go before her mood turns sour."

Reine reached over, poised to slap Natalie's hand, but Natalie sprang up fast enough to avoid it. I followed Natalie to the windows, offering a lovely view of the expansive garden.

"You haven't even tried it," she said.

I gave her a confused look, and she gestured at the glass I'd forgotten I was holding. I examined the claret-red liquid, swirling it gently.

Natalie's gaze narrowed on me. "You do know it's wine, right?"

I chuckled. "Of course."

I hadn't. Not before she mentioned it. But the moment she did, I knew.

I took a sip, and an unexpected sensation of silk caressed my mouth. As I swallowed, the fruity taste tinged with earth lingered on my tongue.

Natalie chuckled. "Good, huh?"

"It's absolutely delicious." I raised the glass, studying it as if searching for the magic that made the wine so tasty. "Wow."

"As it should be," she remarked, a hint of pride in her voice. "It cost my father five thousand francs."

I choked on the sip, hammering my chest. "Five thousand?"

What did they do for a living that allowed them to spend this much money on a bottle of wine?

But I shouldn't be surprised. They owned a property that could have once belonged to royalty over a hundred years ago.

I froze.

Where did I get that information from?

"Believe it or not, this isn't the most expensive wine," Natalie interrupted my thoughts. "You should try that one."

"How much does that one cost?"

She pouted, tilting her head from side to side as if weighing the price. "It could start at ten thousand, if you're lucky."

My eyes widened, making her laugh. "I'm surprised you like this one. Your tastes sure do seem to have changed. It's like you're a different person."

Discomfort crept over me at her comment. I glanced at my husband, who was leaning against the wall listening to his Grand-Maman tell him and Antoine, "Of course, I told him to stick his cigarette right back in his . . ."

For a mere second, our eyes locked before I looked away, as if he had caught me doing something wrong.

"Why does it surprise you that I like this wine?" I asked Natalie.

"You would never have any wine costing less than ten thousand. You always said it was beneath your taste."

Not sure what to say, I took another sip. It took three more to empty the glass. Natalie offered me more, and I extended my glass, letting her pour the amount she wanted. I didn't stop her.

Drinking before meeting my parents might not be wise, but the wine's warmth easing into my chest helped relax my nerves.

"Here are my partners in crime!" Raffaele dropped his hands around Natalie and me, and I flinched, his weight pressing uncomfortably on my shoulders. "But where are all the old people?"

"Thinking being late is stylish," Natalie mumbled.

"Is it not anymore?"

Natalie let out a dramatic sigh. "Of course, the same doesn't apply to you. When *you* are late, it's stylish."

Raffaele laughed and raised his hand towards Natalie's hair, but she drew back, her eyes wide as she put up a warning finger. "Don't even."

His smile grew into a grin, and he withdrew his hand, choosing not to risk tousling Natalie's hair.

"After this boring gathering, we should have some real fun. How about a bar?" he suggested, turning his head toward the Morrano brothers before Natalie could respond. "We should hit a bar after this!"

"We certainly should!" Reine pumped her fist into the air.

I raised my eyebrows, taken aback by Reine's behaviour, though no one else seemed surprised. Maybe this was just her usual way of expressing enthusiasm.

Ettore frowned, not sharing her excitement. "I have to work."

Reine waved him off as if he were talking nonsense. "Work will not run away. You're going, and so is Antoine."

The brothers opened their mouths. "But—"

"No *buts*," their grandma interjected before they could finish, "and no *double entendre* intended. Maybe you two will reconnect in the bar. It gets boring doing all the talking alone."

"It does sound more fun than having dinner with parents," Natalie agreed. "We're not sixteen anymore."

I'd choose dinner with parents over a bar, but it seemed like I was the only one in the room with such a preference.

"Just to be clear . . ." Raffaele said. "You're not coming with us, are you, Reine?"

"Am I excluded?" Offended, she placed her hand on her chest.

"I . . ." Raffaele fumbled for words.

Reine laughed. "No, I'm not going. You can all relax. Grand-Maman won't ruin your fun."

All eyes turned to me, awaiting my response.

Crap.

"Are you coming, sis?" Raffaele prompted, his tone slightly irritated, or maybe I just imagined it.

I didn't want to go anywhere. I hadn't even wanted to attend the dinner party, but I forced myself—for the sake of my parents and me. After all, they must be excited to see me after a two-month coma. Maybe socialising more instead of staying in the villa could even benefit my memory.

But going to a bar after this . . .

I looked at Ettore. Despite the earlier incident, he remained the only person in the room and beyond I felt safest with. If he was going to the bar, it shouldn't be so bad, right?

Maybe in a lively setting like a bar, he would see me as more than a wife in—

Gosh, I shouldn't go if I expect something to happen between me and Ettore. I really shouldn't–

"Yes," I said, "it sounds fun."

The moment I spoke, I felt instant regret. Before I could decline Raffaele's offer, the door swung open, and a couple in their forties entered. Despite the gradual effect of the wine seeping into my blood, my heart quickened.

"Finally," Raffaele mumbled. "We can eat."

The woman gave Raffaele a smile, while the man's eyes were fixated on me. I felt sweat on my armpits, hoping the roll-on I had used was strong enough to ward off any unpleasant odour.

"Vittoria!" The woman approached me with extended hands and hugged me in a way no one had before—tightly. "How's my gorgeous girl? Is she healthy and vigorous?"

I chuckled, confused why she referred to me in the third person, but I played along. "She's just about alright."

A laugh bubbled out of her. I supposed that when she was with me, we spoke in the third person. It was weird, yet kind of adorable.

"I'm Marie Galletti." She pressed her hand to her chest. "If you aren't comfortable calling me Mum, you can address me by my name instead."

I had forgotten I was feeling nervous until she mentioned the word *comfortable*. Marie's welcoming presence chased away my worries, erasing everyone else in the room. Only now did I remember we weren't alone, and everyone was watching us, including the man who had come with her. Sybille was also there, with a man wearing a hat beside her. He could be Ettore's father.

"Come here!" Marie beckoned the man. "Introduce yourself to your daughter."

The man hesitated before taking a step forward. A joke teasingly danced on my tongue about how alike we were, but I chose to keep it to myself.

He extended his hand to me. "Lorence Galletti."

His unease and formality brought back the discomfort that his partner had dispelled. Before I took his hand, Marie put a hand on his back, urging him towards me. "*Hug* her."

Lorence attempted a smile.

"I'm okay without a hug," I said, sparing him from the discomfort, as it was painful to watch. "I think we should eat before Raffaele dies of starvation."

Laughter echoed, lifting the heaviness that had settled upon the room like a fog.

"I think I speak for everyone when I say that, since it's a dinner party," Raffaele remarked, "we're *supposed* to eat."

"Yes." Lorence put his hand in his pocket. "Raffaele is right. We'll have plenty of time to catch up, but only after we satisfy our stomachs."

Unsure of which seat to take, I waited for everyone else to choose theirs first. But Ettore pulled back a chair, staring at me expectantly. As warmth tingled my cheeks, I approached him, silently thanking him before settling into the chair. To my relief, Ettore sat next to me, but that relief was short-lived because Antoine also took a seat beside me.

He couldn't even let me relax while eating, could he?

The servants entered the room, serving us food and pouring wine into our glasses. They placed a plate in front of me and uncovered four small but elegant bites that looked like bread. Each was topped with a creamy mixture flecked with green herbs and a slice of salmon.

I was a bit disappointed, having expected something more filling. My stomach growled, ready to eat, but I waited for someone else to start first.

As everyone else dug into their ridiculously tiny portions, I picked up one of the dainty pieces. Lorence Galletti remained still and said, "I talked to Evelina Zunino about Vittoria's condition. She said it could help her remember if she . . ."

Lorence's voice faded into the background as I tasted the first bite, which melted in my mouth. Resisting the urge to moan at its deliciousness was the most challenging thing I had to do.

"No." Ettore's voice brought me out of heaven. "Not yet."

Not yet what?

Lorence's eyes zeroed in on me. "Since you moved into the villa only four months ago, I believe spending more time in the home you grew up in might help jog your memory."

Marie offered a warm smile. "Would you like to move back home to Monte Carlo?"

13
Her Deadly Beauty

Ettore

***I* WATCHED VITTORIA, CURIOUS TO HEAR HER ANSWER.**

Lorence and Marie's suggestion was something I had expected during the dinner. Vittoria was their child, and they loved her deeply. I wasn't there when they learnt Vittoria had lost her memory. I could only imagine how they felt, not having a child of my own.

Even though I saw it coming and understood that it might be better for Vittoria to move out, I didn't want her to go. Every day over the past three days, I looked forward to returning home from work to have dinner with her. Even if we barely talked, her company was . . . comforting.

Vittoria dabbed her lips with a napkin before asking, "Can I think about it?"

Lorence opened his mouth, but Marie beat him to it. "Of course. Take as much time as you need to consider what's best for *you*."

Although Lorence showed no emotion, I could sense he didn't appreciate Marie's response. I'd bet that if Marie weren't here,

Lorence would have convinced Vittoria to leave with him right after dinner. He wouldn't be a superior if he weren't persuasive.

Marie was the opposite: warm and selfless. Despite years together, I still couldn't fathom how she endured his cruelty. He wasn't the family-oriented type to make up for it, either.

"Let's toast to Vittoria surviving that fire," Antoine suggested.

"Good idea." My father raised his glass. "To Vittoria's luck."

As everyone raised their glasses, Vittoria's grip around the fork tightened. "To Vittoria's luck," our dining companions echoed.

While searching for the reason behind her strange behaviour, I noticed Antoine's right hand positioned oddly beneath the table. It seemed to stray too far from his own lap as he held a glass with his left.

Antoine was right-handed.

I glanced at Vittoria to see if she was uncomfortable. She appeared tense, her body rigid with unease. My blood stirred, but I knew any intervention would only cause a scene.

After dinner, our parents stayed behind, likely discussing work. None of us had informed them about our plan to go to the bar, and knowing Grand-Maman, she wouldn't tell them. Even though we were adults and didn't need to hide such information, none of us felt compelled to share. If no one asked, why bother?

I opened the car door for Vittoria, and a whistle came. "Always a gentleman." Raff clasped his hands together, batting his eyelashes. "Ah, to find a man like him." He sighed dreamily, attempting to embarrass me.

Natalie swatted his arm. "You should learn from him instead of acting like a child all the time."

Vittoria's lips hinted at a smile before she settled into the car. After shutting her door, I circled around the vehicle, opened mine, and waved at the others before joining her inside. "See you soon."

Natalie waved back. "See you!"

As I closed the door and started reversing the car, I saw Raff hurrying to the passenger's side of his car. With a flourish, he opened the door for Natalie. He did it to mock me, no doubt.

Vittoria giggled.

"So you find chivalry amusing?" I teased.

"No," she denied. "I appreciate it. I'm always surprised in a good way. Makes me feel like a princess."

As I glanced at her, an unexpected and unconscious thought struck me.

She looks like a princess.

Startled, I dismissed the thought, chalking it up to her outfit choice for the evening. She wore a short, curly wig and a scarlet dress that fell to her knees, accentuated by a matching bow tied around her waist. All she was missing was a tiara.

Although I had seen her in red countless times, something about her tonight was—

"What?" She jerked me out of my musings.

Realising she had caught me observing her, I focused back on the road. *I wouldn't want to repeat the car accident . . .* "If I'd known you were going to dress up like a rose, I would have stepped up my dressing game."

She chuckled, pressing her hand to her chest. "Are you calling me pretty, Mr Morrano?"

"You *are* pretty." I met her eyes. "In fact, you're the most beautiful woman I've ever seen."

A rosy tint spread across her freckled cheeks.

After the Fire, her freckles had vanished, erased by the flames. Despite many surgeries, her skin healed, but the freckles hadn't returned. But whenever I stepped out onto the veranda for a break from work, I often saw her sitting on the rocks by the sea with a book, soaking in the sunlight. Sometimes Regina would approach her, and Vittoria would stop reading to give the cat attention. The sun must have given her back—

"Ettore!"

The car veered right, and I swiftly steered the wheel left. Luckily, no other cars were around us. Once I resumed driving in a straight line, I exhaled, calming my rapidly beating heart.

Getting lost in Vittoria's beauty would kill me quicker than the cigarettes. It had already nearly cost us both our lives.

"Are you even allowed to drive when we've had alcohol?" she asked.

A laugh escaped me. Did she think the car veered off because I might be drunk?

"I only had one glass," I said, instead of admitting that, no, I shouldn't be driving even after just one glass of wine. But I wasn't intoxicated, and the police couldn't stop me since SQ had waved money at them long ago. Now the police existed around us, but they were unable to do much.

I turned on the radio, and Édith Piaf's 'La foule' began to play. Vittoria glanced at it with interest.

"Do you know the song?" I asked.

Even though it was popular, I didn't expect her to know it, but I hoped it might ring a bell.

"No, I don't think so."

Despite her answer, she kept staring at the radio. Perhaps she was trying to recognise the song?

"You don't think so?"

"It sounds familiar," she admitted. "Maybe I heard it in the kitchen."

Her uncertainty coloured her words. I wondered why I hadn't played music for her sooner. Music had a mysterious way of evoking memories. Perhaps if I played her favourite song, it could jog her memory. The problem was, I didn't know what her favourite song was.

As we arrived at the bar, I quickly unbuckled my seat belt and moved to open the door for her. She stayed seated, giggling, amused by my persistent gesture of courtesy. When I opened the door, she stepped out without meeting my eyes, giving a shy *thank you*, as she always did when I held the door open for her.

Was it wrong if I found it endearing?

I closed the door, and when I turned around, she was gazing at me with a pleading look that rendered me still.

"Would you stay by my side tonight?" She fidgeted with her fingers. "Please?"

Her request puzzled me. "Why?"

"Please?"

Was this some sort of manipulation, or was she genuinely alarmed by something?

And that *something* might be *someone,* and his name was Antoine.

I felt terrible for watching Antoine harass her instead of stepping in. As I had told her, no excuse of mine was valid, but I hadn't realised how uncomfortable he made her until the tears welled up in her eyes.

"I saw you squeezing your fork at the dinner," I said, and she paled. "Did Antoine do something?"

Her eyes went distant before she parted her lips—

"What did I do?" Antoine asked.

I glanced over at him and noticed Natalie and Raff approaching. Raff beamed. "Why such serious faces?"

I pulled out a pack of cigarettes and drew one out. "Raff, Nat, would you mind escorting Vittoria inside?"

Natalie's eyes darted between Antoine and me, probably wondering what it was about. Raff's smile waned.

Natalie moved towards Vittoria. "Shall we go?"

I could feel Vittoria's disbelief piercing through me as she stared at me as though I had betrayed her. I never promised to stay by her side, but I hoped she would understand that I was acting in her best interest. If she wanted Antoine to stop troubling her, I needed to speak to him. Alone.

Yet, I couldn't shake off the guilt for not staying with her when she had specifically asked me to.

As Natalie led a speechless Vittoria to the bar, Raff hesitated briefly before following them.

I pushed the cigarette back into the box and returned it to my pocket. The temptation to light one up was strong, but I hadn't abandoned Vittoria to indulge in my bad habit.

I stepped closer to Antoine. He didn't move, raising his eyes to meet my stare. Antoine was destined to be a superior one day, being the oldest among the three of us, but I had the advantage of my height. Even though height didn't measure the lengths of one's power, towering over him certainly helped with my confidence.

"I'll say this once." I dropped my tone. "Stay away from Vittoria. You might be my brother, but she is my wife."

He laughed, not taking me seriously, but I kept my face still. "Is that what *she* wants?"

"Yes."

He inspected my face before stepping back, his tone lacking its usual amusement. "I never meant to harm you or her. If you want me to, I'll stay away from her."

He stepped aside, ready to leave.

Was this it? I had expected more resistance from him.

"No," I said, and he stopped. "You will stay away because *she* wants you to, not me."

"All right."

But something about his tone didn't sit well with me. I knew my brother, and I didn't believe him. He had a tendency to say things he didn't mean. Not truly. His actions were what counted.

"I'll believe it when I see it!" I tossed at him before he walked away.

14
Dance Like Nobody's Watching

Teodora

When Ettore entered the bar, I was worried he would continue where we left off. But to my surprise, he smiled as he sat beside me, casually draping his hand over my shoulders as if he had done so many times before.

I started to wonder if this was his typical behaviour in the bar, or if he became a different person outside—

The silence as his friends stared at us confirmed it was unlike him.

"What?" Ettore looked around bewilderingly. "Did I murder someone?"

"No, nothing unusual," Natalie answered. But her words implied that something was indeed unusual—like his arm around my shoulders. "We've already ordered drinks. Do you two want something?" She then addressed the brothers.

Antoine subtly raised his hand to signal the bartender. The same woman in a white shirt from earlier approached us.

"I'll have a Chivas Regal on the rocks," he said.

The bartender's eyes shifted to Ettore, her expression giving the impression that she would prefer to be elsewhere.

"No drink for me," he declined. "I'm driving."

"Who cares?" Raff laughed, and his carelessness baffled me. "Everyone drives when drunk. It's part of the night's fun."

I felt Ettore tensing against me. "I'm not drinking. Not tonight."

"But—"

"Respect my decision, Raff."

An uncomfortable silence fell over us, interrupted by the bartender. "I'll come back when you decide."

As the bartender walked away, Antoine spoke, "Before we go at each other's throats, Ettore is right. He shouldn't be drinking before driving. Neither should we."

Raff laughed. "As if. I'm drinking whatever I want, and if I'm too drunk to drive, Natalie will, right, Nat?"

"Maybe," Natalie said. "Except that I'm not responsible for you. What if I refuse to drive you? What happens then?"

Raff's mouth fell open in disbelief, his jaw muscles working as if searching for words, but then his eyes shifted to Antoine. "Antoine always has my back. Am I right, man?" He balled his hand into a fist and offered it to Antoine for a fist bump, but Antoine didn't respond.

"You can always find a taxi," Antoine suggested carefully.

Raff withdrew his fist. "Have you all conspired against me? Or is this a joke? What happened to us? What happened to our fun group?"

No one said a word. Emotions flickered on Raff's face, deeper than sadness. It was as if he suddenly realised the life he once had was slipping away.

"Am I supposed to drink alone?" Raffaele's voice edged toward panic. "If so, what are we even doing here?"

The bartender returned with our drinks, placing them in front of Natalie, Raff, and me. "Have you decided?" she asked.

"No," Raff muttered. "They will not have—"

"Chivas Regal on the rocks," Antoine cut in.

Raff raised his eyes at Antoine, hope shining in them, his sad mood gone like it had never existed.

The bartender looked at Ettore. "You?"

"Water," he said.

As I observed the scene, I wondered if Antoine had relented because he felt bad for Raff. Or maybe he secretly wanted a drink and saw giving in to Raff as the perfect excuse.

I sipped on the Margarita that Natalie had ordered for me, claiming it was the best cocktail at the bar. Trusting her judgement, I went along with it. It was better than relying on my own, as I didn't know any better. To me they were all alcoholic drinks, designed for relaxation and a confidence boost.

The bartender brought Antoine's drink. As he took his first sip, Raff asked, "Is this your first proper drink since your trip to Switzerland?"

"It is," Antoine admitted.

"Maybe I shouldn't let you drink then?" Raff laughed. "It would be a shame to waste a year by going back to old habits."

I gave Ettore an inquiring look, curious to understand what they were talking about. He leant closer, bringing our mouths dangerously close. "Antoine was in rehab for a year," he whispered. I expected to catch a whiff of cigarettes on his breath, but there was no bad smell at all.

I glanced at the laughing Antoine, impeccably dressed in a suit, projecting an image of having his life together. He didn't seem like someone who struggled with a drug addiction. If Ettore hadn't told me, I would have never guessed that he used to do drugs.

"Is that why you don't like him?" I whispered back.

Next to Ettore, Natalie leant forward, trying to eavesdrop on our quiet conversation in our private nook.

"No," he answered, unaware of his sister. "I'm relieved he faced his addiction, but . . ." He turned his head to Natalie. "A bit nosy, aren't we?"

Natalie took a drag on the straw. "Just curious." She pushed her empty glass aside. *Has she finished it already*? "I want to dance. Vittoria, would you join me?"

Crap.

While dancing didn't sound like a bad idea, I liked Ettore's possessive arm around my shoulders and his closeness. A little too much. Maybe it was a good thing for me to leave instead of entertaining unrealistic thoughts that it meant something. I couldn't fall for him. Not if he wouldn't feel the same way, and considering he had known me since childhood, that was highly unlikely.

"Actually, yes, I would."

Ettore removed his hand, and the corner of his lips lifted. "Have fun for the both of us." He winked. At *me*.

His unexpected gesture left my legs weak as I stood. Before I could muster a witty reply, Natalie grabbed my hand, dragging me to the dance floor. As she danced, I hesitated, stealing a glance at Ettore, hoping to find the uncharacteristic confidence he had brought with him into the bar. I would appreciate it if he shared it with me.

He gave me a nod, which encouraged me to start moving my body to the jazz rhythm, though I felt a little uncertain at first.

"You're dancing like a tree," Natalie said. "More movement won't kill you."

Perhaps I had agreed to dance too early. I hadn't even finished my cocktail, and the effects of the wine from dinner had worn off the moment we arrived here. The thought of people watching and possibly judging my non-existent dance moves was unbearable. I thought about going back to the bar, but I'd feel guilty for leaving Natalie alone.

The only solution was to pretend no one was around, imagining I was dancing alone in my room.

Closing my eyes, I swung my hips to the left, then to the right.

"Yes, Vittoria!" Natalie cheered. "You're a natural."

I blushed, wishing she wouldn't make a big deal about it, drawing attention to us. But I tried to ignore it, swinging my hips and adding more movements. As the tension eased from my body, I opened my eyes to avoid accidentally bumping into someone. The more I danced, the easier it became to ignore the people around me, even if some of them were watching. But as more people joined, I became just another person on the dance floor.

We danced a few songs, and my gaze wandered to Ettore every now and then. A part of me wished he would join us. Some couples were holding each other as they danced, and it sparked a fantasy in my mind. I imagined Ettore coming over, putting his hands on my waist, our eyes locking as the crowd faded away while we danced alone.

I spun and spun, finding dancing more enjoyable than when I first stepped onto the dance floor. Dizziness set in, and I giggled at the misshapen silhouettes twirling around me.

What if I could fly? A thought crossed my mind. It felt strangely possible.

My spinning came to a sudden halt as someone touched my hand. A man's voice called my name, his face blurry at first but gradually sharpening into the familiar features of my husband.

A smile lit up my face, fuelled by excitement. "Did you come to dance with us?"

With me? I almost asked.

But his serious expression didn't match my mood.

I stepped towards him but tripped over my foot, stumbling forward. My hands pressed against his chest, unexpectedly firm beneath my touch. I raised my head to look at him, meeting his gaze as he peered down at me. "Sorry," I whispered with a sheepish smile, my fingers lingering on his chest. "Gosh, you're so hard."

A few lines creased his forehead, partly covered by his messy hair. Tempted, I buried my fingers in his curls as I'd always wanted. "*J'aime tes cheveux, mon mari*," I said.

He grasped my wrists, guiding my hands away from his hair. "Let's get you out of here."

My smile fell. "But we just came!"

"*Came*," a voice laughed.

Ettore dragged me outside, and a cold brush of wind caressed my face. I craned my neck to gaze at the starry sky and smiled, even as Ettore kept pulling me forward. I didn't care much about the destination, and I wasn't worried. He was my safety.

"You know I trust you, right?" I asked as he carefully assisted me into the car seat.

"I . . . Let's get you home."

As the car moved, I watched the streetlights glide past with my chin in my hand. Once the view of the sea unfolded, I banged on the door. "Stop here!"

"Don't pound on my door."

"Then stop here!"

He leant over me, peeling my hand off the door. Once his hand was back on the steering wheel, I resumed pounding on it. Words, in another language—French?—poured out of my mouth in a stream, making no sense to me. Suddenly, the car jerked to a halt, and I lurched forward, held back by the seat belt. Ettore left the car, but before he could play the gentleman, I pushed the door open and leaped out.

The waves called my name as I ran towards the sea.

Vittoria! Vittoria!

For once, I felt free—like a bird released from a cage, learning to—

I tumbled over and rolled down the steep hill until my body collided with a hard object. Every inch of my body seared in pain, and I let out a moan.

A blurry face appeared over me, and I was lifted off the ground. "Let's hope you don't have a concussion. You only just started to remember things. We don't want you forgetting everything all over."

I looked over his shoulder at the sea moving farther and farther away. I was so close. I didn't reach it this time, but I knew I would someday.

15

Brotherly Threats

Ettore

"YOU WERE RIGHT, MR MORRANO," THE DOCTOR SAID. "We found something unusual in Miss Galletti's blood. Likely a sedative drug, but we can't identify it."

I assumed calmness, despite the intense urge to drive back to the bar and set Antoine's car on fire. I knew Vittoria's drunken behaviour couldn't be from the wine she had hours ago or the cocktail she barely touched. The fact that she suddenly fell asleep on the way to the hospital erased any doubts. There had to be another reason, which led me to ask the doctor to test her blood. If he couldn't identify the drug, it only meant one thing—it came from SQ's science lab. Few had access to it, and even fewer had a motive. It had to have been him. Antoine.

"No broken bones," he continued. "She has some wounds, but nothing that requires stitches."

Stopping the car was a foolish move on my part, but I hadn't anticipated Vittoria to jump out like a zoo monkey tasting freedom for the first time. In hindsight, I should have seen the signs. Her behaviour had been peculiar all along. She spoke French as though she were fluent, even though it was her third language. Italian was her first. Her eagerness to go to the sea also seemed odd, considering she already lived close to it.

"No concussion?" I asked.

"No."

"Can I see her?"

"She's currently asleep, and we don't expect her to wake up until the morning. I suggest you go home, rest, and come back to pick her up tomorrow."

That wasn't what I asked, but I didn't have the energy to repeat myself. I resigned with a simple *thank you* before making my way towards the stairs.

I glanced back. The doctor was gone. Ignoring his advice, I proceeded to Vittoria's room. There, she lay peacefully in bed, sedated by whatever Antoine had slipped to her. An IV was attached to her inner elbow, providing necessary fluids.

My mind raced, attempting to pinpoint when Antoine could have given her drugs. The only plausible time was during dinner. He sat close to her, and her glass of wine was within his reach. Yet, it seemed unlikely. If he had tampered with her wine, the effects would have manifested sooner. But if not then, when? After that, Vittoria drove with me, and Antoine went with me to the bar.

I would have stayed to ensure she wouldn't wake up alone and confused, since she might not remember why she was here. But I had a pressing matter to deal with first. Vittoria was safe here. If she awoke, no one would disturb her because I hadn't told anyone about the accident.

I exited the ward and headed for the stairs. A wince contorted my face as I saw my car parked haphazardly in front of the hospital. Vittoria's well-being had been my main concern, not parking.

While driving, all I could think about was Antoine and what he had done.

What was he thinking? Did he truly believe it would work with me nearby, watching her every step?

My brother wasn't a saint, and neither was I, but trying to assault someone when they were too high to resist? I thought our parents had raised us better.

The idea of setting his car on fire crossed my mind. I had a tank of gasoline in the trunk, prepared for any scenario. It would anger him to see another one of his cars destroyed, but if I did it, Antoine would retaliate even more in the future. Eventually, when our mother retired, he would step into her role as a superior, becoming one of those responsible for assigning me cases.

And he could *really* make me miserable then.

Some might call me a coward, but I cared about my future and didn't want to watch my back more than I already did.

I stopped by the bar with a plan. My anger had calmed, allowing me to think more rationally rather than impulsively.

Before the Fire, Vittoria would be disappointed in me. Instead of burning his car, I had come up with a more mature way to address the situation. It may not have been as thrilling, but my brother and I were adults now. There was no need to add more fuel to the fire.

I entered the bar, finding Antoine with my eyes. As I moved towards him, Natalie appeared in my view.

"You're back?" She swayed to the side, and I caught her arm to prevent her from falling. An obviously drunk smile tugged at her mouth. "Is Vittoria with you?"

How many drinks has she had since I left?

I led her to the nearest seat, and she happily complied. "Stay here. I'll drive you back home. But first, I need to speak to Antoine."

"Why?" she asked, but I was already striding towards Antoine.

He was in the company of a stranger and Raff, who had his tongue deep in a blonde girl's mouth. My brother didn't notice me until I grabbed him by his shirt, dragging him away.

"What are you doing?" He grabbed my hand, forcing it away.

Heads turned our way as I stepped closer to Antoine, for the first time not caring about causing a scene. "What the hell were you thinking?" I hissed.

Antoine played clueless. "What do you mean?"

"You *dosed* her."

"I dosed who? Natalie?"

"No, Vittoria."

"*I* dosed Vittoria?"

Wasn't that what I meant?

"You spiked her drink."

"How do you know? Did something happen to her?"

His responses triggered a stream of questions in my mind, adding to my confusion. Was he trying to manipulate me into thinking he didn't do it? After he harassed her and touched her under the table when she clearly was uncomfortable?

I carefully chose my next words. "Don't play the fool. You drugged Vittoria. The results came back unclear, and you and I both know that it means it was a narcotic from SQ's lab."

He furrowed one eyebrow and raised the other. "The results? What—"

"Just admit you drugged her."

He hesitated, as if pondering. "Let's say I did drug her. Would you believe I hadn't done it to harm her?"

"Why else would you drug her?"

"Maybe to help her loosen up?"

"Loosen up?"

"Haven't you noticed?" he asked. "She was tense. The old Vittoria wasn't like that."

I closed my hand into a fist, my resolution to handle this maturely faltering.

His response shouldn't have surprised me. My brother was a drug addict, and no time in rehabilitation could change that. Over the years, he had dragged many people, including me, into the deep hole of drug abuse. It was his thing—to help people loosen up with narcotics, family or not.

"She has amnesia. And you *drugged* her because she's so tense? She's undergone more surgeries in one month than one person should experience in their entire life. Or hell, maybe she's so tense because, in her eyes, everyone's a fucking *stranger*?"

"One pill when she was with her family wouldn't hurt her."

"She fell off a hill!"

Antoine frowned. "How did she end up on the hill?"

Feeling eyes on us, I unclenched my fist. "We should talk somewhere more private."

"I agree."

As we walked towards the exit, I discreetly retrieved a pocket knife. Once we were outside and away from prying eyes, all thoughts of reason and consequence fled my mind. I grabbed his shoulder and delivered a powerful punch to his stomach, causing him to double over and grunt in pain.

"You're not the one to decide what's best for her," I hissed in his ear. "If I ever see or hear you touching her again . . ." I pressed the knife against his stomach. He held his breath, afraid that exhaling might cause the blade to cut him. ". . . consider yourself dead."

"You can't kill me. I'm your brother and your future superior. Familia. Officium. Honos. Remember?"

"Vittoria *is* my family."

"You never cared about her as much as you do now. What changed?"

I hesitated before releasing him, pocketing my knife. "Before the Fire, she could fend for herself and protect others at the same time, but not anymore."

"So you're playing her knight in shining armour?"

"No." I levelled my gaze at his eyes. "I'm trying to protect her from you vipers until she remembers."

He laughed, clutching at his stomach. "Isn't *she* the most venomous of vipers?"

Refusing to entertain him, I turned away, ready to return to the bar and find Natalie. But then he said, "I know you didn't abandon your work for two months just to take care of her."

I stopped. Despite my hatred for Antoine, we were once close, and I had confided in him about how certain cases affected me. While high, I must have confessed things I had never shared with anyone before—about how I truly felt about working for SQ.

Honest truths that no one should know about, or else SQ would punish me severely, if not kill me.

I glanced back at him. "You're grasping at straws, brother."

"Maybe." He shrugged. "But you never once mentioned Vittoria. However, you did talk about how being responsible for finding people haunted you. The thought of SQ ending their lives kept you up at night."

Threatening him with a knife was a mistake, but would he really tell on his brother, knowing it could cost him our relationship forever?

What was his goal? If he wanted me to admit it and beg him not to tell anyone, he could keep dreaming.

"Maybe you should voice your suspicions tomorrow," I advised before walking away. I pretended to be brave, but secretly, I feared he might do just that during tomorrow's evaluation, which could doom me.

I wouldn't be surprised.

I was the one standing in the way between him and Vittoria.

And I was the reason he was sent to Switzerland after I crashed his car.

16
The Velvet Discoveries

Teodora

*W*hen I opened my eyes, I didn't expect sunlight to be pouring into the room already. Normally, I woke up when the sun was just peeking over the horizon.

After what felt like the deepest sleep since my coma, I struggled to sit up, every part of my body burning in pain. As I raised my hands to stretch, I noticed a familiar tube connected to my inner elbow.

My heart sped up and then dropped as I saw Ettore sleeping on the couch across from me.

Before panic could fully set in, fearing I was in the same situation as over a week ago, I realised the room was different. The walls were white, not dark, and the windows were empty of curtains. Despite that, I couldn't remember how I ended up here.

While I tried to recall the events after Natalie dragged me onto the dance floor, Ettore's eyes fluttered open.

He greeted me with a warm smile. "Good morning."

I smiled back. "Good morning."

I wished we could start every day like this. But instead of waking up with him across the room, I would find him next to me after falling asleep in the same bed.

"What am I doing here?" I asked.

Ettore stood and approached me. "You drank a bit too much. On our way home, you insisted on seeing the sea. You were so determined that you banged on the door, and I had to stop the car. Next thing I knew, you were rolling down a hill. I was worried about a possible concussion, so I rushed you to the hospital."

I waited for his words to trigger my memory but nothing came. "Did I drink that much?"

All I could recall was having three glasses of wine at dinner and a bit of a cocktail at the bar. I didn't even drink the whole thing. Could the expensive wine and Margarita have been strong enough to erase my memory?

"I have no idea," he said.

It had to be the drinks, because what else?

I promised myself to never drink that much again, if ever.

"Did I get a concussion?"

"Luckily, no. We can leave now if you want and have breakfast at home."

My chest felt lighter at the suggestion, and I couldn't reply fast enough. "Yes, please."

After spending a day stuck in my room with a headache and an aching body, I realised how much I despised it. Usually, I dressed in the morning and only returned at bedtime, so I didn't have time to notice the room's gloomy darkness and lack of personality.

As the next day dawned, my headache was gone and my body felt less sore. Marie called to ask if I had thought about moving back to my parents' place. I was too nervous during dinner to decline their offer with all those watchful eyes, but I assured her I was content here. While returning home might have been better for my memory, I knew I would have felt even more uncomfortable there than I did here.

Later on, I began my project to rid my room of things that weren't *me* anymore which, as it turned out, was almost everything.

When I asked Sofia for something to collect the items I would either donate or discard, she was hesitant. She suggested reconsidering, in case I remembered and wished to keep everything as it was. But I remained determined, and eventually she relented, providing me with bags.

Even if I did remember, I doubted I'd come back to my old self as if nothing had happened. I had changed and now my own room felt like a stranger's.

The first thing I threw out was the cat's skull. Even if I hadn't experienced a single nightmare about it, I couldn't have it around me.

As I walked into my wardrobe, the sight of hundreds of items of clothing instantly made me feel tired. Sorting through them would take forever. Despite disliking most of the clothes, I began sorting meticulously, making sure I didn't part with anything I might want to wear someday.

The door was open, and Regina wandered in, sniffing every corner before settling on the pile of tops I wanted to keep.

I tsked. "That's not okay, Regina."

But as she lay there, curled up in a ball, it was hard to resist the urge to sink my fingers into her fluffy fur. While I took a break to pet her, my gaze wandered to the top shelves. My extensive collection of wigs never ceased to amaze me, but why did I need so many? Either I dressed up for balls or collected things. But wigs didn't occupy all the top shelves. Amongst them were several black and red boxes.

I guessed they were shoeboxes, but that didn't stop me from bringing a stool from my bedroom. Despite the pain in my legs I carefully climbed onto it, wincing as I steadied myself on wobbly legs.

"If I fall, go get someone, okay, Regina?"

She barely cracked open her eyes before lazily shutting them again. If I were to fall from the stool, she would hardly spare me a glance before drifting back to sleep. I couldn't blame her. Cats might be cute, but they weren't as caring as some humans.

The boxes had no labels, offering no clue to what was inside. I reached for the closest one and opened it, finding what seemed like hundreds of dark red lipsticks.

I chuckled. "Am I obsessed with dark red lipsticks?"

Or maybe someone had given them to me as a gift and instead of getting rid of them, I kept them in a box.

After closing the box and returning it to its place, I pulled out another one—a square, velvet red box. I lifted the lid, and my hands nearly slipped at the sight of a pistol.

I carefully stepped down and placed the box on the island with drawers. Then, I raised the pistol, careful not to touch the trigger.

Why would I need it?

For safety, it occurred to me.

When I was about to return the pistol to the box, I noticed a red book nestled inside. It had been hiding beneath the pistol. Setting the pistol beside the box, I picked up the book and opened it. Inside, I found pages and pages of handwritten text, marked with dates.

Excited, I flipped back to the first page.

August 5, 1965

I shut the journal quickly, not quite ready to delve into it. My first thought was to share it with Ettore. Driven by the excitement of my discovery, I rushed towards his room with the journal.

My journal.

My journal that might answer my questions and help me remember.

As I reached for his door, my hand paused, clenched into a fist, ready to knock. But I couldn't bring myself to do it.

It was *my* journal. Why would I share it with him? He shouldn't know about it. It was a secret. *My* secret.

I lowered my hand, turned around, and was walking away when I heard the door open behind me. Clutching my journal to my chest, I hoped he wouldn't call out to me and ask what I was doing here.

But instead, I heard a female voice. "Vee?"

My heart went still.

It wasn't Sofia's voice. It wasn't Natalie's voice.

I turned around with hesitation. A beautiful woman stood in the doorway, her chocolate curls tousled and brown skin flushed.

I thought I was about to pass out.

The woman approached with the biggest and brightest smile, enveloping me in a hug. "It's been so long," she said. "We should catch up."

I couldn't speak. I couldn't *make* myself speak.

She left Ettore's bedroom.

A woman left Ettore's bedroom.

"Unfortunately, not today." She offered me a sad smile. "I have to leave, but soon." Walking backward, she pointed a finger at me. "I promise."

And she was gone.

Emotions battled within me as I stood, frozen in disbelief. But as the shock dissipated, giving way to a surge of anger, I screamed and flung the journal against the wall.

The journal landed on its back, its pages splayed open as if beckoning me to read it.

I grabbed it and hurried back to my room, eager to immerse myself in it and forget about the woman and her connection to my husband.

August 5, 1965

Dear... me, I suppose.
I've heard people write in journals to help sort out their feelings.
But that's not why you're here.
It was never my thing to write down every single messed-up thought. Maybe that's the reason why I'm so... the way I am.
But here you are, and I'll try.
It's time to let go and...
Maybe I'll finally feel right?
Or at least better.
Maybe.

17
The Evaluation

Ettore

AS I STOOD BEFORE THE TOWERING TABLE OF THE SUPERIORS, I FELT INSIGNIFICANT. They exuded authority and power, akin to Kings and Queens seated on thrones. Among them was my own mother. Their gazes were icy and impersonal as they looked down upon me.

The members, including Raff, Natalie, and Antoine, watched me as I pretended to appear calm despite the sweat coating my skin and my heart threatening to burst from my chest. Perhaps if I lost my heart, I could avoid the evaluation where my punishment had already been decided. The evaluation was just a show, meant to prove to the members that everyone was subject to the same rules regardless of their background. Everyone, except for the superiors.

They were our gods.

"Ettore Cosette Morrano." Lorence's voice rang out through the hall. "You have been invited to testify for neglecting your duties. Let's begin your evaluation."

Invited.

I *had* to attend, unless I wished for death.

"Please." Lorence made a motion with his hand. "Tell us why you have abandoned your work for two months, Mr Morrano."

I resisted the urge to slip my hands into my pockets, unsure where else to put them. Such a gesture might be perceived as careless and could worsen my punishment. I couldn't take that risk.

"As some of you may already know," I began slowly, ensuring my voice was steady, "Lorence's daughter, Vittoria Galletti, who is also my wife, was in a coma. I couldn't bear the thought of leaving her alone in the room, in case she woke up confused. I could have hired someone to take care of her, but I thought waking up to a familiar face would be less shocking for her."

"Is that the whole truth?" he pressed, his tone tinged with scepticism. "Remember, lying to us could result in severe consequences for your punishment."

"Yes," I lied. "She is my wife, and I care for her."

I was treading on thin ice with my lie. Antoine might have already shared his suspicions with them long before the evaluation. If he had, this meeting wasn't only a spectacle but also a way to determine if my punishment should be made worse.

"Even if you married her out of duty to SQ rather than love?" Lorence asked.

Perhaps it was futile to touch his heart, knowing it to be cold and limited, but it was worth the attempt. "Yes. I've known her since childhood. I might not be in love with her, but I care deeply for your daughter, sir. She is my friend."

Lorence made a note, as did several of the other superiors. Then he inquired, "Do you confirm you stayed in her room day and night?"

"Yes, sir. I left only for bathroom breaks, showers, and the occasional smoke."

Lorence motioned to the guard stationed by the door on his left. "Please, allow the witness to enter."

The guard opened the door, and Sofia stepped in. I kept my emotions in check, careful not to give away anything to the superiors, who probably mastered reading body language before they could walk. I had suspected they would involve Sofia in this, and I had told her if they do, she shouldn't cover for me. If she lied and they discovered it . . . I didn't even want to think about what they might do to her.

Sofia stood a few steps away, facing the superiors.

"Sofia De Luca," Mia addressed, lifting her chin. "Is it true that you work for Mr Morrano as his housekeeper?"

Mia's ridiculously tiny nose distracted me, making it difficult to focus on her words. Why would anyone choose to go under the knife to change something already perfect? Could she even breathe with her new nose?

"Yes," Sofia replied.

"Do you work every day?"

"Yes, miss. I start at six in the morning and finish at six in the evening, every day."

"Have you been at his house in the last two months?"

"Yes, miss."

"Where was your employer when Vittoria Galletti was in a coma?"

"At home, miss."

"What was he doing?"

"He was taking care of Vittoria, miss."

"What was he doing to take care of her? Can you describe it to me?"

"He stayed in her room, sometimes even slept there. He let in the nurse to check on her pulse and move her muscles. He also brought her flowers from his garden."

"Did he do anything more than that?"

"Not that I know of, miss."

"I have no more questions."

Silence settled before they all stood, collecting their notebooks. "Very well, Mr Morrano," Lorence concluded. "We will deliberate on your situation and return with an appropriate punishment. You may sit, and so may you, Miss De Luca."

The superiors left, and I sat on the bench, tension weighing on every inch of my body. Even though my shoulders and head felt heavy, I made sure not to slouch, sensing curious eyes on me.

Raff slipped in next to me. "What do you think your punishment will be?"

"I can't think about that."

"You should. I wanna bet."

I shot him a glare. "You want to profit off my impending doom?"

His smirk faltered, morphing into a sheepish expression. "Whoops, my bad. That was insensitive. Sorry, man." He offered a half-hearted pat on my shoulder.

I let the discomfort simmer before I said, "I bet a hundred they'll stop my pay for a bit."

Raff eyed me sceptically, then wagged his finger. "Impressive move. I bet they'll go straight for your fingernails."

A shiver skittered down my spine.

"Are you betting?" Natalie settled in next to Raff.

"Yes," Raff confirmed. "We're betting on Ettore's punishment."

"Oh! How much?"

"One hundred."

"That's nothing." Natalie scoffed. "How about five hundred?"

Raff arched an eyebrow. "Are you that confident?"

"I'm just good at betting."

"No," I interjected. "We're sticking with one hundred. Take it or leave it."

Natalie laughed. "You're so cheap." She pulled out her wallet from her tiny purse and peered inside, her lips pursed in thought. "Fine. One hundred. So, what are your guesses?"

"He thinks they'll suspend his earnings," Raff said. "And I think they'll remove his fingernails."

"Ew." Natalie grimaced. "Sorry, not sorry, Raff, but that sounds like a loser's bet. It's too extreme for someone neglecting their duties."

But Raff wasn't deterred. "You might be surprised."

"Well, I think he will have to work without pay and rely on other sources of income."

"So the same as Ettore's."

"It's not the *same*."

"It—"

The return of the superiors cut short their impending bickering. As everyone rose, I returned to stand in front of them.

"Ettore Cosette Morrano," Lorence began. "We have reached our decision."

I kept my hands to my sides, my shirt clinging against my back.

"Your first punishment will be . . ."

More than one?!

". . . the next four missions are to be completed without compensation. Failure to do so will result in further evaluation. No financial assistance will be provided under any circumstances. Anyone who does so will also face evaluation regardless of their position. However, you may have another job if it doesn't interrupt your work for SQ."

Fuck.

Not receiving payment for four missions meant no income for possibly a year. Typically, I completed four to six missions every year. If I had another job, it would consume what little free time I had left. I could rely on my savings, but they wouldn't last for a year if I spent as much as I did now.

"Do you understand, Ettore?" Lorence asked.

I concealed my frustration as I answered, "Yes, sir."

"For your second and final punishment," he went on, "to ensure your loyalty and remind you of your duties, you will bear our symbol on your chest."

Vivienne stood up and came out from behind a table, holding a branding iron with the letters *SQ* engraved on it.

My heart dropped.

Vivienne's hand rested on my arm, gentle yet firm. "Let's get you seated," she said, her voice surprisingly tender, given what she was about to do to me.

She guided me towards the solitary chair against the wall. I tried to look anywhere but at the branding iron in her hand.

Despite every instinct urging me to protest or flee, I knew it would be futile. Accepting it seemed to be the wisest option, preventing trouble for everyone and sparing me from further punishment.

I lowered myself into the chair, willing myself to sit straight and composed. If I wanted them to respect me and prove my loyalty, I had to appear fearless.

Last night as I lay awake worrying about my punishment, the idea of branding didn't even cross my mind. It was usually reserved for treason, not for those who simply neglected their duties. And it had only been two months.

As Vivienne plugged it in, I saw Natalie's shocked look, reflecting my own surprise. Neither of us had expected this, because it made no sense. Not receiving payments was bad enough, but being branded . . . unless they knew the truth. Perhaps Antoine had shared his suspicions to prove his loyalty and to show the leaders that he was still worthy of becoming a superior. Yet, I couldn't believe my brother would betray me like that. He wasn't a snitch.

It didn't have to make sense, really. SQ didn't exist to follow logic. It existed to wield power and incite fear.

SQ must have escalated punishments to prevent another betrayal like Maxime's.

They were determined not to let history repeat itself after my uncle's betrayal, which nearly caused the downfall of SQ when he shared confidential information with foreign authorities. If such a treason were to occur again, SQ might not survive. Those witnessing this today would undoubtedly spread fear among others. If even the son of a superior could be branded, what fate awaited those who dared to misbehave?

It was a calculated strategy, instilling fear to maintain control.

It was brilliant.

"Where would you like the symbol on your chest, Mr Morrano?" Lorence inquired. "Or should we decide?"

I glanced at the letters growing redder on the iron, their size akin to a pinball. Not too large, not too small, but unwanted regardless.

"Above my heart," I muttered.

"Our apologies," Lorence said, "but we couldn't hear you."

Because he's *the one with hearing—*

"Above my heart," I repeated louder, this time with a hint of anger slipping through.

But it appeared that no one noticed as their focus was on the iron heating up—

"It's ready," Vivienne announced, lifting it.

My fingers trembled as I unbuttoned my shirt, taking longer than usual. Finally, as I removed my top, I pointed to the left side of my chest. "Here."

A brand over my heart would symbolise loyalty, a testament to my unwavering devotion to SQ.

There was a time when my loyalty was unbreakable, and I considered myself fortunate to be born in SQ. But as I grew older, my devotion waned as my nightmares grew stronger.

Gripping the chair, I braced myself for the intense pain, locking my eyes with my mother. She had been there when they had made the decision. She could have intervened. She could have stopped this.

She was my mother, for heaven's sake.

As the iron seared the letters into my skin, I gritted my teeth, refusing to make the slightest sound. I dug my fingers into the chair's arms, forcing myself to maintain eye contact with her.

She had to witness this.

She had to see her son in excruciating pain.

Perhaps this time she would realise what she could have stopped instead of always going along with the other superiors.

Yet, she looked down at the table.

I kept my eyes locked on her, refusing to look away, as the letters branded themselves onto my skin. The pain paled compared to the knowledge that I didn't have a mother who could protect her child. Even if those letters stayed with me forever, they could never beat the betrayal from the woman who had given me life.

18
The Girl I've Been Looking For

Teodora

I WOKE UP WITH AN URGENT NEED TO GO TO THE BATHROOM. Comfortable in my bed, I didn't want to leave it. But the urgent need to relieve myself forced me to get up. Once done, I emerged from the bathroom and glanced at the clock.

5:33

I would wake up in thirty minutes anyway, as I always did at six o'clock sharp. There was no point in returning to bed and trying to sleep again.

Was I always an early riser before the Fire, or was it a recent change? Ettore typically woke up late, and we never had breakfast together. While he worked all day I usually spent my time watching Sofia cook, reading by the sea, playing with Regina, or brainstorming room renovation ideas.

When I suggested redecorating my rooms to Ettore, he was sceptical. He worried I might regret the changes. While I understood his concern, I couldn't live in a place where I didn't feel comfortable. In the end, he relented and told me I should do what was best for me.

While getting dressed, I thought about what to eat. With Sofia still thirty minutes away, this was the perfect opportunity to make breakfast for myself.

What about some freshly squeezed orange juice?

My mouth watered at the thought.

Giving in to the craving, despite the early hour, I headed for the kitchen. I switched on the lights, startling at the sight of someone slumped across the kitchen island.

My heart raced, afraid it was Antoine. But the man had messy curls.

Feeling more secure knowing the man in our kitchen was my husband, I approached quietly, only to find his head resting on an open folder.

Ettore had never told me what his job was. Whenever I asked, he would repeat the same old phrase, 'It's best if you remember.' He used this response for other things as well, but whenever I mentioned his work, his entire behaviour shifted. His tone would sharpen, and he became less friendly.

I couldn't resist taking a peek, but he was covering most of the text, leaving only the big, bold letters of *JULIEN MARTIN* visible.

Ettore's eyes snapped open suddenly, as though in a horror film. I stepped back, but he seemed unfocused, as if he were staring right through me. Like he wasn't here. His eyes closed again, and he raised his head, rubbing his eyes with the heels of his hands.

Unaware of my presence, he closed the folder and took it in his hand. He stood, and only then did his eyes land on me. He froze, his eyes widening. "How long have you been standing here?"

"Not long," I squeaked.

He sat back down, rubbing his temples.

I moved closer. "Are you okay?"

"Yes," he said. "I came for a snack and fell asleep. Why aren't you in bed?"

I smiled faintly. "It's almost 6 o'clock in the morning."

The shock was evident on his face.

I clasped my hands in front of me, unsure if I should bring it up and risk changing his mood. But in the end, I asked, "Don't you think you should take a break from work?"

"I was on a break for two months," he said. "But yes, you're right. I'm overworked and exhausted, but I have so much to do and so little time. I don't have a choice."

It was the most he had spoken about his job, which encouraged me to press further. Maybe he would reveal his profession. "Can't you quit your job?"

He laughed as if I had told the most hilarious joke. Still laughing, he stood and approached the kitchen cabinets, leaving the folder behind. He poured water into a glass and paused his laughter to drink.

I glanced at the folder, wondering what secrets it held.

"Why can't you leave your work?" I prodded.

He set down an empty glass. "Because."

"That's not an answer."

He stared at the glass, lost in thought. I had a feeling he was thinking something I wanted to know. Then he groaned. "I completely forgot."

"Forgot what?"

"Your friends are coming over to take you out tomo—today."

A chill ran through me. "I have friends?"

"You don't see me as a friend?"

His eyebrows lowered and his lips formed a pout, but I was too stressed about the upcoming meeting to engage with his joke. Part of me was mad at him for not warning me earlier, depriving me of at least a day to mentally prepare myself.

"What are their names?"

Perhaps if I heard their names, it would trigger my memory.

"Barbara, Jacques, and that other girl . . . I think her name starts with *E*?"

No, those names didn't trigger any memories. "You don't know all my friends' names?"

"It's not like you ever told me about them."

Fair point.

I crossed my arms. "It's been two weeks since I woke up. Why am I only now hearing about these *friends* of mine?"

Wasn't I deemed so unlikable that nobody bothered to befriend me?

"Because you should remember them yourself. But I also forgot, and Barbara just contacted me about her idea."

My anger diminished. I understood why he hadn't mentioned my friends earlier. But he could have at least warned me a day before. I decided to let it go. I hadn't come here to fight him. I came here to make myself some orange juice, but he had distracted me.

As I approached the counters, I reached out for a cutting board and grabbed an orange from the nearby basket. "If you think you're doing me a favour by keeping your profession a secret from me, you're mistaken," I said. "I wonder about it every day, and it's causing me headaches."

Not quite true. It didn't cause me headaches, but it did bother me. Why was he keeping his job a secret from me? It couldn't be because he wanted me to remember. There were things before that he hesitated to discuss but still shared with me. The only plausible reason left was that he was involved in something I wouldn't approve of, and he didn't want to tell me because if we worked together, it would imply I was involved in something bad too.

I was probably overthinking it.

"I'm sorry, but it's best if you remember."

I pulled out a knife, stifling a groan as I heard the same old tune again. "I sense a secret." I cut the orange in half. "Do you think you can keep your secrets from me until my memory returns?"

A smirk tugged at the corner of his mouth. "Absolutely."

But I wasn't amused. What was he hiding?

"There's something you should know about me, *husband*." I took another orange. "I can be very persistent. I survived a fire, I'm sure I can find out your secrets."

"You wouldn't have survived it if it weren't for me."

"Hmm." I sliced the orange in half. "You're a tracker, maybe?"

It was a shot in the dark, yet his smile faded. Could it be that I struck close to gold if not right *at* gold?

"I'm not," he replied weakly at first, then cleared his throat and repeated with a more confident and deeper tone, "I'm not."

I regarded him suspiciously, but I couldn't concern myself with this. I could pester him forever, but if he hadn't revealed his job before, I doubted he would now. Giving up, I opened a drawer to search for the tool Sofia used to squeeze juice. Meanwhile, Ettore turned and opened a drawer nearby, retrieving the orange squeezer I was looking for and handed it to me. I took it and thanked him, narrowing my eyes in suspicion, wondering if he could read my mind.

But why else would I be cutting oranges if not to squeeze juice from them?

I pressed down half of the orange, twisting it to extract juice, but it was harder than it seemed when Sofia did it. Maybe I couldn't squeeze out all the juice because I wasn't strong enough. Or maybe I was being clumsy because Ettore was watching.

"Do you want help?" he asked.

"No, it's okay."

I pushed the orange harder, twisting it with determination while trying to hide any signs of struggle.

"But I can help," he said.

"It's—"

He put his hand on my shoulder, and I paused, hesitating before looking up at him.

"It's okay," he said gently. "I can help."

I wasn't sure why I had surrendered and stepped aside, letting him take over. Perhaps Ettore was convincing, making it hard to say no, or I simply lacked the strength to resist him. That seemed far more likely.

He gestured towards the chairs. "You can go sit."

But I wasn't going to. Instead, I stood a step away from him, staring at my uneven nails. "You're not very good at hiding your emotions."

"Really? I thought I'd got better at it. Or maybe I just can't hide my emotions when I'm with you." He shot me a lazy smile as he squeezed the last drops from the orange.

And God, was his smile attractive, revealing a small indentation on his right cheek.

Refusing to entertain my futile feelings, I focused on watching the orange juice drip into the bowl below through the little holes. Ettore didn't seem to exert any effort, squeezing the juice as if it were nothing.

"Either something is holding you back from expressing your emotions, or you're flirting with me," I noted.

"What if I was flirting with you? Would you flirt back?"

My cheeks blushed fiercely. "I don't think I'm as skilled as you are in the flirting game."

I don't have beautiful women leaving my bedroom, at least.

"I'm flattered you think that, but I get shy when I'm in the company of a pretty girl."

The girl who left his room yesterday made it clear he was anything but shy. I felt tempted to bring it up, but I knew I shouldn't. If he hadn't lied, we agreed before getting married that we could sleep with whomever we wanted.

"Thanks," I said with clear sarcasm. "I've never heard a kinder way to tell someone they're ugly."

His amusement faded. "No, you're . . ." He set the used orange aside and turned to me. "*You're* the pretty girl."

I could have melted, but I told myself I wasn't this stupid. Yet my lips betrayed me, forming a faint smile.

A shadow fell over his features. "You're messing with me. Is the Vittoria I knew back?"

Since he had finished squeezing the oranges, I pointed at the glass he had used earlier. "Are you going to use it?"

"Right," he sighed, grabbed it, and headed to the sink.

I rushed after him. "No, don't. Give it to me. I'll use it."

He hesitated before passing it to me, but once he did, I placed it down and poured the juice into the glass. "Thank you for squeezing the juice," I said before taking my first sip.

"No problem."

Yet, he stared at me like he couldn't believe I was drinking orange juice.

"What?"

Could it be that I used to dislike orange juice before the Fire, but now I enjoyed it? Just like how I used to like tomato juice but now found it repulsive?

"It's unusual to see you drink from the same glass as me," he explained. "You have your own marked glasses that, if someone touched them, they would risk losing their fingers. But here you are, drinking from an unmarked one. Most importantly, from the one touched by *my saliva*."

The way he stressed *my saliva* made both my cheeks and neck burn. "Why waste time and energy cleaning two glasses when you can use one?"

His intense stare felt hotter than the sun in the middle of the day. I wished he would stop looking at me like that, especially when he was so close, making the room feel warmer than usual.

"If I didn't know better, I'd think I had saved the wrong person."

I clutched the fabric of my nightwear as I licked the juice off my lips. "Could it be possible?"

His eyes drifted to my lips. "No," he said, "but . . . not entirely impossible."

When had he got so close? Only moments ago, he stood three steps away, far enough that I couldn't even catch his scent. Now, I could reach out and lay my hand on his tempting chest and feel it against my fingertips. But the sudden image of a woman with perfect brown curls shattered my delusion.

I set my glass down, the heavy thud rupturing the tension between us. "Is it possible that I'm not who I should be?"

My heart raced as I awaited his response.

"No." He took my glass, pressing his lips to where mine had been moments earlier. His sharp, electric gaze locked onto mine, holding me captive. "But it's possible that I've found the girl who should have been my wife all along. Or perhaps, she found me?"

August 6, 1965

Dear me,

I don't think I should say this, but I'm thinking about ending it.
Ending what? I won't specify. It's my journal, and I know what I'm talking about. And that's what matters, isn't it?
No one else will see this. If I do decide to end it, this journal will disappear with me.
But the thought of it doesn't sit well with me.
Not even after what happened.
It's time for a story. I mean...

that's why you're here, my journal of secrets. It's probably stupid to think this little journal could help me after I reveal everything. Whether it does or not, it's time to give you a proper chance.

But I don't know what exactly happened that night. I doubt I will ever be able to remember.

Maybe it's for the best that I will never remember what happened before I woke up alone in a room I'd never seen before. I will never remember how I ended up in the hotel until I walked out of the room and recognised where I was. But I will always remember

leaving my cocktail unattended as I went to dance with Eleonore. And I will always remember Antoine Morrano being around me right until I forgot.

At the very least, I hope he used protection.

19
In Monte Carlo

Ettore

I'VE FOUND THE GIRL WHO SHOULD HAVE BEEN MY WIFE ALL ALONG.

The words had haunted me since I left the kitchen. I wished I could reach into my head, tear out my brain, and throw it away, just to escape them.

What had I even meant? What girl should have been my wife all along, exactly?

My words made no sense. *I* made no sense. The only way I could explain my behaviour was that sleep deprivation had clouded my thoughts.

After I said that, I fled the kitchen like a coward, leaving Vittoria alone with no explanation. It wasn't until I was on my way to the bedroom that I realised I had left her with the folder. Returning to the kitchen made it even more awkward. I hoped she hadn't peeked at it, for her own sake.

She couldn't find out about my job before her memory returned. It might shock her, even if her guess was uncannily accurate.

Perhaps she remembered everything but pretended not to.

I've found the girl who should have been my wife all along.

But what could I have really said? She had drunk from the same glass as me. Vittoria before would have puked if her lips touched the same spot mine had. And yet, she did it while gazing at me as if I were the most fascinating person in the world. No one had ever looked at me like that before. It unsettled me, but at the same time, it felt . . . good?

What if she learnt about all the terrible things I had done, continued to do, and would do until I was dead in my grave? Would she still gaze at me with such admiration? Would she still share the same glass as—

I was so lost in thought that I barely noticed I had parked my car outside Raff's house. The door opened, and Raff slid into the passenger's seat.

"Julien is a smart guy," Raff remarked. "Should we bet we won't find anything in his house? Oh, wait, I can't pay you if you win." He grinned at me shamelessly.

Ignoring his attempt to provoke me, I reversed onto the road. But Raff might be wrong.

If Julien was rushing to leave his home, he might have left behind an important clue. Julien Martin was not just a scientist but also a human, prone to making mistakes despite his intelligence.

He had stolen our supplies of the Cure and other drugs. By the time SQ discovered it, he had already vanished. For months, he had been pilfering from us, but in the last two weeks, he focused on the Cure. To cover his tracks, he pretended to discard them, claiming they were 'failed.' While occasional failures were expected, their frequency spiked significantly in the last two weeks.

Julien had been working for SQ for five years, and he might have been doing this for a while but less often. What was his plan? Was he intending to sell the Cure for profit, or distribute it for free, risking his life for the sake of his kindness?

In any case, we had to find him, extract information, and hand it over to the superiors, who would decide what to do with him.

Yesterday, I spent most of the day mapping out potential locations where he might have fled. My plan was to start with his apartment and gather clues, possibly by interviewing neighbours.

"How's your . . ." Raff shifted uncomfortably in his seat. "Chest?"

I gave him a strange glance. It was unlike him to express concern for anyone besides himself.

"It's healing."

I didn't mention the constant pain it caused, unlike anything I had ever felt before. The burn required frequent care to prevent infection. But bearing the pain couldn't compare knowing that the letters would stay on my body forever, and my mother could have prevented it.

"That's good," he said, the discomfort in the air thickening. "I've been training hard lately, especially with the championship coming up, and I was thinking . . . It's been a while since I saw Ettore train. What happened to you, man?"

Suspicion crept into my mind. Raff's sudden interest in my absence from training was odd. He wasn't the type to notice or ask about others. "Have you talked to my father lately?"

"No." His snort sounded off. "I just figured you might like to join me for a training session sometime?"

It couldn't be his idea. Raff had never cared about my physical health before. My father would, but he might not tell me that to my face. "I don't have time for it."

That wasn't the whole truth. I prioritised other tasks over training, especially after the evaluation. Devoting most of my time to an unpaid job for a year left me with little time for anything else. Once my savings ran out, I'd have to find a side job.

I felt Raff's scrutinising stare. "If I didn't know you, I'd think you wanted out. You've become lazy in the last few months." Before I could react, his hand was on my bicep, squeezing it. "Not even a marshmallow is as soft as you."

With a sudden manoeuvre of my arm, I freed myself from Raff's grasp. "Vittoria lost her memory, and I've been the only one there for her."

I knew I shouldn't judge after lying about taking care of her for two months in front of the SQ audience. But Raff was worse than me. At least I was around, visiting her every day. Raff hadn't bothered to see her once during those two months. Her father didn't visit either, but I suspected Lorence avoided the villa because of its previous owner, Maxime. The only family members who visited her were Marie and Dr Zunino, who came for check-ups.

"To be fair, it's a relief when she's not around," Raff said, pretending not to hear my accusation. "I enjoy my work more without her."

Now that Antoine and I weren't on good terms, I should understand Raff's feelings towards Vittoria better, but I still couldn't. No matter what happened between me and my siblings, I could never speak about them as if I hated them.

"She's still your sister, Raff."

"*My* sister?" He laughed bitterly. "She killed my dog for biting her. It was a little, harmless wound. Then, when my parents got me a cat, she slit its throat and left it to bleed to death in our garden. Her excuse? The cat scratched her when she tried to pick it up." Tears welled in his eyes, filling me with discomfort. "These are just two of the many awful things she's done. Do you honestly expect me to look at her and see my sister? To treat her as one?"

I swallowed hard, unsure of how to respond.

"Did I mention she kept the cat's head as a trophy?" He wiped away a tear. "Vittoria is a monster. I'm surprised *your* cat is still alive."

Regina did once return home with a limp. The vet diagnosed a broken rear leg. Many reasons could have caused it to break, but I hadn't seen Vittoria around that day.

Vittoria was capable of many things, but harming an animal? She wasn't particularly fond of them, and Regina didn't seem to like her either. But was it because Regina could sense Vittoria was dangerous?

"You should be grateful for what happened to her," Raff said. "Vittoria is the worst. I feel sorry for you that you married her. And since it's going to be the two of us for a while, let me tell you something. If you ever decide to . . . get rid of her, I'm a call away."

Despite his accusations against Vittoria, I still couldn't believe him. Since childhood, my mother drilled into me that family always came first, no matter how awful they might be. And Vittoria was my family. So was Raff.

"She's not the same as she used to be," I defended, refusing she was capable of such stuff. I did believe Raff, but . . . Vittoria had changed.

"Of course she's not." He huffed out a laugh. "But once she remembers, the Vittoria we dislike will come back."

I opened my mouth, ready to disagree, but I couldn't. I couldn't be certain of what would happen when she remembered. "But how could someone's personality change so drastically because of memory loss?" I said instead. "Vittoria cares and doesn't pretend now. Not to mention, Regina likes her. She rejected Antoine, she—"

"No way!" Raff exclaimed in surprise. "She rejected Antoine? Is that even possible?"

"Is that even possible?" I frowned. "Do you think Antoine is so irresistible?"

Raff gave me a knowing look. "You're related to him and don't see him that way, but yes."

"Have you slept with him or something?"

"Not yet."

I pouted. "I thought I was your one true love." I feigned wiping away a tear. "You wound me, Mr Galletti."

"Don't be jealous, handsome. I may be a snack, but many can share me. Including you." He winked.

Instead of playing along, I focused on the road as we drove into the Monte Carlo area. The traffic slowed down here, with more road signs to keep track of.

I would always choose Nice over Monte Carlo. Despite their similarities, SQ spoiled Monte Carlo's beauty. In Monte Carlo, crime thrived, and I felt more watched. Even if my work often took me here, I refused to let SQ define me. Yet, the burning letters on my chest begged to differ.

The streets grew narrow as we approached Julien's apartment. I parked half on the pavement to avoid obstructing traffic.

"Okay, it's time to get to work," I said, killing the engine and unbuckling my seat belt.

"Look at you, turning into your mother just like that." He

snapped his fingers, stepping out of the car. "It's scary, but it is a turn-on."

"You have a thing for my mother as well?"

Raff closed the door and raised his hands in surrender. "Can't say I'm entirely innocent, baby."

After locking the car, we strode into the apartment building and ascended the stairs. When we reached Julien's door, Raff crouched down to pick the lock.

"Shouldn't you check if it's locked first?" I asked.

"Why bother?" He jiggled the handle, but the door didn't budge. "See? They always are."

I leant against the wall, waiting for him to finish. It took him a minute before he opened the door, and I followed him inside. Unwashed dishes, mugs, and papers littered the table. Paint tubes lay discarded in the corner, and clothes were strewn across the couch. I hadn't expected such a disorder from a once reputable scientist. But strangely enough, even with food still on the plates, the place didn't smell.

"He seriously made it hard for us to find something." Raff inspected the living room as he walked around.

I headed to the kitchen, leaving Raff to search the living room. This room was less chaotic, with books cluttering the counters and the table instead of dishes. I flipped through them, finding nothing noteworthy.

"Look at this." Raff appeared in the doorway, waving a book. He opened it and turned it to me. "Do you see what I see?"

I took it and examined the sketch of a woman by the sea, engrossed in a book. Turning the page, I found another sketch of the same woman. This time she was reclining on the bench, her head tilted back and her curly hair cascading nearly to the floor. More sketches of her followed until halfway through the book, where the rest of the pages were blank.

The woman looked strangely like Vittoria.

"You think it's Vittoria?" I asked.

Raff shrugged. "Could be."

It made no sense. I had never seen them interact. Julien was mainly in the lab, and Vittoria . . . I wasn't exactly sure what she did when she wasn't with us, aside from practising acrobatics.

"It could also be someone else." I gave the sketchbook back to Raff. "They're sketches, not photographs."

Raff looked at it again. "It could be, but it could also be her. We shouldn't rule it out."

He left the room, and I spent another ten minutes scouring the kitchen to no avail. Next, I checked the bathroom, finding nothing there. Feeling the need for a break, I stepped onto the balcony for a smoke, watching Raff search the mess in the living room.

Something didn't add up.

Julien had paint tubes scattered around, but where were his

canvases? Did he bring them with him? It would be too much of a hassle if he did.

He might have put them somewhere else because the apartment was smaller than I had anticipated. The blueprints I checked yesterday showed the living room should extend farther to my left, where only a single bookshelf stood.

I stubbed out my cigarette and returned to the living room. As I stepped closer to the bookshelf, I was disappointed to find that the cream wall behind it matched the colour next to it. I knocked on the wall beside the bookshelf, then on the one behind it. The sound echoed behind the wall.

Grasping the shelf, I first pulled it towards me, but nothing happened. I tried pushing it.

It swung open slightly.

"Sneaky," Raff whispered from behind.

The room was dark, with only a faint light trickling in from the living room, but not enough to see. I pulled out a flashlight and turned it on. My gaze first fell on an easel with a canvas, then on paintings leaning against the walls.

Raff's hand rested on my shoulder. "Well, well, well. Won't you look at that?"

I already was.

My flashlight shone on a bearded man crouched in the corner, his eyes wide with fear.

20
Shopping Troubles

Teodora

I HAD ONLY TEN MINUTES BEFORE THEY—MY *FRIENDS*, SUPPOSEDLY—WOULD SHOW UP, AND I WASN'T READY.

Dressed in a corduroy skirt and a white top, I paced nervously in front of the window, knowing they could arrive any minute.

I needed a day, preferably two, to prepare myself for meeting more people who were strangers to me. I was not even given half a day.

As I caught myself chewing on my nail, I pulled my hand away. It was time to control this bad habit of mine.

The gates opened, and I stopped pacing. A vibrant blue convertible drove in with three people inside. Worried they might see me staring out the window like a creep, I hurried to the door just as Sofia walked in with a basket of clothes.

She smiled warmly. "Have a good time, Vittoria."

I felt my cheeks redden. "Thank you, Sofia."

As she ascended the stairs, I left the villa just as my two friends were getting out of the car. One of them wore sunglasses that reminded me of mine somewhere in my room. Even though the sun was glaringly bright, I hesitated to go back for them, not wanting to keep everyone waiting.

The brunette woman in the driver's seat stepped out of the car wearing knee-high boots and a short yellow dress with white patterns, looking as if she had walked out of an *Elle* magazine. She took off her round glasses and flashed me a radiant smile I had seen before.

My heart sank.

It was *her*.

"Vee!" She extended her hands, walking towards me. "I told you I'd see you soon."

I stood frozen, my stomach twisting with each step she took closer. She hugged me gently, as if I were a delicate vase, and I forced myself to reciprocate instead of wrapping my hands around her neck for sleeping with my husband.

She pulled away. "Do you remember me?"

I would never forget her leaving Ettore's room, but that wasn't what she meant.

"No," I said.

"Weird. It's hard to forget me."

"But I lost my memory?"

She laughed. "I'm only joking!" She gestured towards the petite girl with a chic bob and a beret. "She's Eleonore."

So she was the Eleonore I had read about in the diary.

I gave a hesitant wave, but Eleonore remained still. With her large brown eyes, unshielded by sunglasses, she seemed lost in her own world.

"Don't mind her," Barbara said. "That's just Eleonore being Eleonore. And over there is Jacques."

Jacques stood out in his red pants, yellow shirt, and a loosely tied red scarf around his neck. He was the most flamboyantly dressed man I had ever seen.

"The names would do for now, I'm sure. You'll get to know them better today, and maybe you'll remember something. Who knows?" She put her glasses back on, then spun elegantly towards the car.

Now that I had learnt the girl who had left Ettore's room was one of my friends, I felt even less inclined to go. But since they were already here, I made my way to Barbara's car.

"What are you doing?" Barbara asked, staring at Eleonore as if she had caught her stealing her favourite blouse.

Eleonore carefully pulled her hand back from the passenger's door.

Barbara hummed in approval, her serious expression turning into a smile as she looked at me. "Go ahead, Vee. You sit here."

I hesitated, not particularly eager to sit next to her. But instead of outright rejecting her offer, I responded, "It's okay. I can sit in the back, and Eleonore can have the passenger's seat."

"No, Vee." Barbara opened the door and settled into the driver's seat. "If you're not the one driving, your spot is always next to me. Eleonore and Jacques sit in the back. That's how it's always been."

It doesn't mean it should stay like that, I thought.

It was just a seat. Why make such a big deal?

But I was silent, not wanting to be the one who spoiled everyone's mood for the entire day.

"Sit down, Vittoria," Jacques said, peering over his sunglasses. "I want to grab the macarons before they sell out again."

I relented, switching places with Eleonore. When everyone was in the car, Barbara drove out. She tossed her hair aside. "Have you been to Monte Carlo yet, Vee?"

"Not since I woke up, no."

"You'll like it there," Jacques interjected. "It has *the best* stores."

The drive to Monte Carlo felt excruciatingly long. Even when Barbara was driving, she didn't stop talking, bombarding us with stories of her holiday in Sicily. She claimed to have met a man so attractive that her entire body was on fire.

"Your body or your lady parts?" Jacques commented.

"*Everything,*" Barbara responded.

Eleonore snorted while I managed an awkward smile, feeling uncomfortable. If it weren't for the pressure to please people by making an effort to remember something, I wouldn't be here. Instead, I'd be listening to Sofia complain about her kids, which was one hundred times better than being here.

"It's a shame you couldn't come with me, Vee." Barbara pouted. "Rocco had a friend who would have been the *perfect* match for you. His tongue was so . . ." A telling smile graced her lips. "But I'm getting ahead of myself. You will have to judge it for yourself."

Suddenly, the collar on my shirt felt extremely tight around my neck. I tugged at it, wishing I could disappear.

The ride eventually ended, but my day with them had only begun. I didn't need to worry much, though, as Barbara did all the talking during our trip to the stores, whether we were inside or out.

"My vacation might have been eventful, but I also read five books in a single month."

"Rocco was great fun, but sometimes I wonder if I should find someone more permanent? Like a husband?"

Before anyone could respond, she answered her own question. "No." She laughed. "He would only be a burden."

Was she even aware we were also here?

"Wow!" Barbara exclaimed, stopping to admire an avocado-green short-sleeved dress on a mannequin. "This dress is so mod. I *need* it."

She hurried into the store, and we followed closely behind.

"May I help you?" A girl working in the store appeared out of nowhere, startling me.

"Yes." Barbara gestured towards the dress. "I want this in size thirty-four, coral blue. I'll pick it up on Wednesday."

"I'm afraid—"

"Where is it?" Barbara rummaged through her purse. "Aha!" She pulled out a card and stuck it out to the girl.

The girl glanced down at it, hesitating to take it. "I'm afraid the colour you want isn't available, Miss Nino. We only have it in green and white."

"Then make it available." She grabbed the girl's hand and pressed the card into her palm.

I watched in shock as Barbara released the girl's hand, spun on her heel, and marched towards the exit. "The audacity of some people," she muttered, leaving both the girl and me frozen in place.

"Vee!" Barbara called.

"I'm sorry," I said to the girl before hurrying after my friends, who were waiting for me by the exit.

As if nothing had happened, Jacques delved into his adventures in a casino. Nobody mentioned the incident, treating it as if it were nothing out of the ordinary. I contemplated whether I should let it slide, but since they were my friends, shouldn't I be honest with them? Why pretend everything was normal when it clearly wasn't?

But it wasn't until we were sitting at the cafe, waiting for our drinks and desserts, that I found the courage to speak up.

"How can she get the dress in coral blue when she's not the one who made it?"

Barbara furrowed her brow. "What are you talking about?"

"Remember when you asked the girl for a dress in coral blue earlier? And you pushed your card into her hand?"

Barbara stared at me as if she had no idea what I was talking about. Had she already forgotten? Was it that insignificant to her?

"She's talking about the girl in the La Belle store," Jacques clarified.

"Ah!" Her face lit up with recognition, but then she frowned. "Why does that matter?"

"Why does that matter?" I repeated, astounded.

I felt anger rushing through me. As if sensing it, Eleonore placed a hand on my thigh, shaking her head. Did she want me to be silent about this? Because I wasn't going to.

"Okay," I tried to speak in a calm and steady voice. "If she doesn't get that dress in coral blue, what are you going to do?"

Barbara laughed, prompting a smile from Jacques. But I found nothing funny about it, staring her dead in the face.

Her laugh faltered. "You're joking, aren't you?" She leant in, resting her arms on the table. "I get it. You have amnesia. Ettore told me I shouldn't explain too much so you'd remember on your own," she said, and I tensed at the mention of his name, "but I'll make an exception. I don't want to fight you. I've invested in various brands, including La Belle. If they want my support, they will do whatever I please. Do you still see a problem in that, Vee?"

As far as I knew, investing didn't work like that. Investing in a brand might grow her wealth, but brands didn't make custom clothes for investors for free.

I was about to disagree when the waitress brought desserts, interrupting the tension between Barbara and me. We both looked away from each other as the waitress set a chocolate fondant in front of Barbara and a *crème brûlée* in front of me.

"I'll bring your drinks out soon," the waitress announced before hurrying off.

"I'm going for a smoke," Barbara declared, rising from her seat and grabbing her purse. She turned to Jacques. "Care to join me?"

Jacques was too busy drooling over the macarons in front of him to hear her.

"Jacques?" she prompted.

"I—Oh." He raised his head to look at her. "I'm trying to quit."

Her smile wavered, betraying her frustration that she tried her best to hide. "You must have misheard me. Are you coming with me, Jacques?"

"I would, but I'm trying to—Right." Jacques promptly shot to his feet, putting on a broad smile. "Of course, I'll come with you, Barbs."

Her smile widened, curving at the edges like a crescent moon, similar to a content cat from a cartoon I vaguely remembered. It was about some girl, maybe a princess?

They strolled away, leaving me alone with Eleonore. Why hadn't Barbara insisted on her joining as well?

"I suppose you don't smoke?" I ventured to start a conversation.

The side of her lip lifted, bordering on creepy.

"Is something wrong?" I asked.

She scrutinised my face, and my unease deepened under her perusal. "You look like her, but the more I look, the more I can see the differences between you and her," she said.

"Between me and who?"

She held her smile, not saying a word. As the waitress returned with our drinks, I thanked her while Eleonore watched me instead. This was becoming too eerie for my liking.

I pushed my chair back. "Excuse me, but I need to use the restroom."

Even though I had been in the city for two hours, I didn't need to go. But to avoid Eleonore and the awkward wait for Barbara and Jacques, I took the opportunity to freshen up. As I washed my hands, I braced myself for the uncomfortable situation awaiting me at the table. If I had the choice, I would walk out the door, but how would I get home?

I could try calling home and hope Ettore was there, but I couldn't ask him to drive to another city just to pick me up. Besides, he was probably still at work.

My time with 'my friends' would eventually end. I had already endured the drive here and another two hours of shopping. I could handle the rest of the day. And after today, I would never have to see them again.

On my way out of the restroom, a man emerged from the balcony, almost bumping into me. We exchanged apologies, and he walked away. As I turned to return to the table, Barbara's voice halted my steps.

"She has always been . . . you know. But now she's absolutely insufferable. All these questions . . ."

I glanced back, finding the door slightly ajar. Curious, I approached it to hear better.

"Look at the bright side," Jacques suggested. "She can't remember. You can manipulate your friendship with her more easily now."

"Not with that personality. Did you see the way she was staring at me? She disagreed with me, and the worst part is, she can. Being a Galletti and married into Morrano's family, on top of that."

"Are you dreaming about stealing her life?" Jacques joked.

"She has everything I want . . ." Barbara whined.

"You should be the last one to complain. You have your own money, but what about me and Eleonore? We have more at stake. Be a team player and don't jeopardise us. What if we need the Cure someday? How will we get it without Vittoria?"

The Cure, the Cure . . . Why does it sound so familiar?

"If those stupid scientists had been more careful, we wouldn't have to stoop so low and lick her feet."

"What's done is done. We have to do what we have to do."

The voices grew louder, and I hurried away before they saw me. I returned to the table where Eleonore was sipping her latte and staring at . . . nothing. Uncertain, I took my seat, and her unsettling stare shifted to me, sending shivers down my spine.

I focused on my dessert, hoping Barbara and Jacques would return soon to rescue me from Eleonore's weirdness and the awkward silence.

Barbara dropped her purse onto the table and fell into her seat. "What have you two been up to? Gossiping about us?"

Like you were gossiping about me?

I forced a smile.

I had questions, but these fake people wouldn't provide me with any answers. I couldn't wait to return home and ask Ettore about the Cure and what it meant to be both a Galletti and his wife. Hopefully, he wouldn't avoid my questions and give me the answers.

"Actually, Eleonore was telling me how gorgeous you look today," I said. "I couldn't help but agree."

Barbara laid her hand on her chest, flattered. "Thanks, Vee. But let's not forget about you. How can one survive a fire and still look stunning?"

Before, I would have blushed and believed her compliment was genuine, but not after hearing their conversation. They were only pretending to be my friends to gain unlimited access to some cure. *Did I know about this before my memory loss and let them use me?* Regardless, being used felt awful. I was no longer willing to be their pawn.

"What was that saying in English?" Jacques pondered, then snapped his fingers. "Rose like a phoenix from the ashes? But quite literally, in your case."

Rose like a phoenix from the ashes . . . I kind of liked it, but I felt more like a baby learning its first steps, and that did not feel good.

Barbara's eyes widened at the sight of something behind me. I turned to see a dozen people bursting into the cafe, their faces and exposed skin marked with red dots.

Before I could react, one of them—a woman—sprinted towards me, grabbed me, and coughed directly at my face. I recoiled, trying to break free, but her grip was unnaturally strong.

"Enjoy it, you spoiled brat," she spat before letting go of me and running away.

The red-dotted people left as quickly as they had come. A long silence enveloped the cafe until I snapped out of my stupor and grabbed a napkin, wiping my face. "What the hell was that?"

"The sick," Barbara muttered, her face twisted in disgust. "Selfish people who spread the Rash by infecting innocent people."

"The Rash?" I asked. "What is the Rash?"

Barbara and Jacques exchanged wary glances.

Eleonore slurped her latte loudly, as if the red-dotted people infecting others was another ordinary day for her. "If you don't know, you'll find out sooner than you think, *Vee*."

"What's the Cure?"

Sofia stopped chopping an onion. "Why?" She swept a lock away from her face. "The Cure can mean anything."

I refused to accept vague responses any longer. "I'm aware, but what is *the Cure*?"

"Isn't it something you should remember rather than me telling you?"

Had Ettore told that to every single person in the world?

"What *is* the Cure, really?" Antoine asked, leaning against the doorframe. "I can give you answers. All you have to do is ask."

After what I'd read in my journal, the mere sight of him sickened me. I wished he didn't live under the same roof as me. But he was Ettore's brother. What choice did I have?

"Ettore said she should remember things instead of learning them," Sofia remarked.

"Is Ettore suddenly an expert on amnesia?" Antoine stood

straight and walked over to the kitchen island. "I highly doubt it."

As Antoine approached, my first instinct was to run and lock myself in my room. But I stayed, determined to learn the truth. I would not let it slide. Not this time.

"Are *you* an expert then?" Sofia asked, but received no answer from Antoine. "Just as I thought."

"I'm not an expert, but it's been at least two weeks. She doesn't remember anything, and I think she's been kept in the dark long enough." His eyes locked on me. "You don't even know your true identity, do you?"

"What do you mean?" I asked.

His lips curled into an amused smile. "You—"

"Don't involve yourself in their relationship," Sofia interrupted him. "It's between the husband and wife. You're just a guest here, not the owner."

"And Ettore is?" He leant closer to me, and I pulled back, causing his smile to fade. "The true owner is a traitor. Technically, this house belongs to SQ." There was a flicker of anger in his eyes.

A traitor . . . SQ . . . What made it so special, and what did those letters signify?

"This is Ettore and Vittoria's house. It was their wedding gift," Sofia said, holding the knife in a menacing manner. "*You*, mister, are their guest. Show some respect."

"Ettore is also my little brother, and since you don't—"

"Enough." I rose to my feet, tired of listening to them disrespecting each other. "Could someone please enlighten me about the Cure?"

Antoine's smile widened. "I swear your hair becomes more fiery when you're demanding things."

"You disgust me."

Antoine recoiled at the impact of my words. "My brother isn't here. Why pretend you don't like me?"

"Because I *don't* like you, Antoine!" I clenched my fists in frustration.

"Don't you?" He stepped closer, his tone suggestive. "Do you truly dislike me?"

I was on the verge of saying yes when I realised he wasn't worth the effort. Antoine was someone who didn't take no for an answer. Why waste energy on someone who had hurt me in the past, even if I couldn't remember it?

I relaxed my fists. "What is the Cure?"

"Oh, goodness gracious . . ." Sofia slammed a cabinet shut with a bang. "It's a remedy for . . ."

A door slammed shut behind me. I spun around but saw no one, only a closed door. I tried the handle, but the door didn't open.

My heartbeat quickened.

"Guys," I called, "I think you locked me in."

Silence.

Panic rose in my throat. Did they actually lock me in? Why? Did they want to steal the Cure from—

A laugh sounded. "You're a hypocrite, Sofia," Antoine said.

I blinked, bringing my focus back to the present. Sofia was glaring at Antoine, but then her eyes shifted to me and softened. "I shouldn't have told you that."

Told me what? I couldn't remember because of a strange . . . memory? I was trapped in a room by two men who wanted to steal the Cure from me. Who were they? No matter how hard I tried, their names eluded me.

"Vittoria?" Sofia asked, worry in her tone. "Is everything okay?"

"I . . ." I winced. "What did you tell me about the Cure? I didn't hear."

She frowned. "You didn't hear?" Then realisation dawned on her face. "Did you remember?"

I felt Antoine's curious eyes on me.

I might have remembered, but I didn't want to say anything until I understood the memory. It confused me. Maybe Ettore would know and could explain it to me.

"What's the Cure for?" I asked again, more confidently.

Sofia pressed her lips together, refusing to speak.

"It's to heal a disease called the Rash," Antoine explained.

"Sanctus Quinque created it to manipulate people."

An illness to manipulate people? I hadn't expected that. Yet, it sounded oddly familiar.

"What is Sanctus Quinque?" I asked.

"The Holy Five." Antoine grabbed an apple and tossed it from one hand to another. "They do very dangerous things."

I wouldn't have felt safe around him if Sofia wasn't in the same room. Although Antoine was unpredictable, he wouldn't dare to do anything with her around.

Or so I hoped.

"So it's a criminal organisation," I concluded.

"Not only is she beautiful but smart." He sank his teeth into the apple.

It all began to make sense.

It made sense why Barbara and Jacques were using me. It made sense why the people surrounding me were prosperous, including myself.

I turned and left without a word like Ettore this morning. I wanted to run away, but I didn't know where.

If SQ was a criminal organisation, and according to Barbara and Jacques, I was part of it . . .

Then I, too, was a criminal.

August 7, 1965

I feel like I'm going crazy.
I haven't told anyone what happened. If I don't remember most of the night, it doesn't mean anything, right?
Then why can't I stop fucking thinking about it?
Every time I think about it, which happens a lot, I want to throw up. Sometimes I do. The day after it happened, I threw up three times.
I didn't leave my room. No one noticed a thing.
No one cared.
Not even our housekeeper.

It awakened memories I thought I'd buried long ago. I'm scared. Scared of the men around me.
Scared of everyone but Ettore.
I know I should have told him. We promised each other no secrets. We might not be lovers, but we are friends. Just because the superiors forced us into marriage, it doesn't mean we have to hate each other. We are partners.
But Antoine is his brother. A future superior. I am just his wife, married to him out of duty. And his loyalty is to his family above all else.

I can't risk it.
Some secrets are better left unspoken than risking death because of them.
But would death really be that terrible?

21
The Secrets of the Painter

Ettore

"**Well, well, well . . .**" Raff approached Julien with deliberate slowness, aiming to intimidate him further. "An artist disguised as a painter. And a traitor, too."

In the middle of the room stood a lamp. I walked over, switched it on, and tucked the flashlight back into my pocket.

Wide-eyed, Julien watched him, appearing too scared to utter a word.

"We'd like to speak with you." Raff pulled out a pocket knife. "If you answer our questions without causing any trouble, I won't use this. Got it?"

Julien nodded shakily. Raff stepped away, gesturing towards me with a nod. "He's all yours," he said before casually leaning against the wall.

Julien's eyes drifted to me. "H-how did you k-know about t-the s-secret room?"

As I surveyed the paintings, one caught my eye: a red-haired woman by the sea, smiling softly as she read a book. It was like the sketch from his sketchbook, transformed into a painting, and it was beautiful.

"You and I have different gifts," I replied, meeting Julien's gaze. "You're good at science and painting, while I have a knack for finding things that are hidden."

"Painting is just a hobby."

"A wasteful one," Raff interjected. "You shouldn't have betrayed us."

Julien glanced downward, laden with guilt.

"Why did you steal those batches?" I asked.

"W-Why do you t-think?" Julien replied. "You're t-he brains, right? After searching my apartment, you s-should have your suspicions."

I did, but I needed concrete proof, not merely my speculations. It wouldn't be enough for SQ, and I hoped his theft had nothing to do with his unexplained obsession with Vittoria.

"Why did you steal those batches?" I repeated, my tone stricter than before.

"F-For the money, of course."

"Is more money worth risking your life?" I stepped closer to the painting to study it better.

Julien was undoubtedly a talented artist, but the more I examined the painting, the less I saw Vittoria in it. Not only was she reading a book, which was unlike her, but the girl in the painting exuded a dreamy nature. Perhaps Julien portrayed her the way he wanted to see her. Or perhaps it wasn't Vittoria at all. But who else could it be?

"No," he said.

"You did it not only because of the money?"

"No, m-money is the only reason."

I turned to Julien. Though he held my eyes, I had a strong feeling he was hiding something important.

"How do you know Vittoria?" I studied his reaction closely, but his face didn't betray any recognition of her name.

"W-Who's Vittoria?"

I inclined my head towards the painting. "The girl in the painting."

"That girl?" He laughed, but it came out strained. "It's a r-random girl I painted from my imagination."

While I had doubted it could be Vittoria, Julien had just confirmed it. But why was he trying to hide it? Since he wasn't willing to admit it, there was only one way to find out.

I nodded to Raff, who quickly grabbed Julien's wrists, pulling them behind his back. As he pressed the knife against his neck, Julien tensed, fear flooding back into his face.

"How do you know Vittoria, Julien?" I repeated.

His Adam's apple quivered as he swallowed carefully. "O-one

day, I-I heard a k-knock on my d-door. I-I didn't expect anyone because I'm a l-loner, so i-imagine my surprise when I opened the d-door and saw a b-beautiful girl. She was like an angel, with hair as the s-sun up close—"

"Booooring," Raff sang out, tracing the knife along Julien's chin. "Get to the point already."

His fascination waned. "S-She entered my apartment. I didn't know who she w-was. She saw my p-paintings and complimented them, and it felt g-good. A beautiful girl c-complimenting my work? One c-could only dream of that." A dreamy grin spread across his face, forgetting about the knife against his neck. "S-she introduced herself as Vittoria Galletti. Vittoria Galletti, the d-daughter of Lorence Galletti in my apartment? It was h-hard to believe. Then she asked me for a f-favour. She wanted me to falsify r-records for drugs so I could p-provide them to her. When I asked w-why she needed them, she n-never gave me an answer."

It sounded like Vittoria. She would ask questions but never answer them.

"What drugs?"

As he hesitated, Raff pressed the knife harder against his throat, causing Julien to blurt out, "A-Anaesthetics."

His decision to apply more pressure to the knife concerned me, especially when I hadn't told him to.

Raff grimaced. "What is that?"

"They're drugs that can n-numb a specific part of your b-body or induce a state of u-unconsciousness."

Why would Vittoria need them? I couldn't think of any situation where she might have used them. None of our missions could have benefitted from anaesthetics.

"I suppose you agreed?" I asked.

"Not at first," Julien said. "She might have been Vittoria Galletti, but her f-favour came with a price. I wanted to p-paint her. One painting for seven vials. We reached the agreement."

"How long ago was that?"

"About f-five months ago."

Vittoria had no clear reason to need anaesthetics, but if this happened five months ago, Julien might be telling the truth.

"What about the recent batches of the Cure?"

"Three weeks ago, I received an a-anonymous letter asking me to d-deliver them to the harbour. It s-smelled of cherries, and I knew it was her."

"Have you met the person who sent you the letter?"

"No. I delivered the b-batches at five in the morning as instructed and left."

"You didn't stay to make sure it was Vittoria?"

"I couldn't. I would have broken her trust."

"You're so full of shit." Raff laughed, and I noticed blood seeping from the tip of the knife. "Vittoria was in a coma when you got the letter. How could she—"

"Umm, Raff?" I interrupted, noticing the pure fear in Julien's eyes.

"Let him answer," Raff insisted while blood trickled down Julien's neck.

"I . . ." Julien began. "Maybe she was f-faking it, I don't know, but I k-know it was Vittoria. She needed those b-batches for a reason. You s-should ask her about that." Julien's response was so rushed that it was surprising I caught his words at all.

But I was more worried about Raff harming Julien than whether he was telling the truth or not. "We want to bring him to SQ alive, Raff."

He didn't retract the knife. If anything, his grip tightened on the handle. I fought to stay calm, though my heart thumped against my ribcage. I didn't know what to do. Walking to him and trying to wrestle the knife out of his hand would risk Raff slicing Julien's throat. If Raff killed him, we would learn nothing. Even worse, SQ would punish both of us, despite Raff being the one who killed him.

"Raff?" I tried again.

Raff's face darkened with an unsettling intensity, verging on madness. I had never seen him like that before. Fear clenched my heart as I braced for the worst. Yet, he withdrew the knife. His features softened back to their usual self as he laughed it off like it was just another one of his jokes.

Despite the shock of what I had witnessed, I relaxed a little once I saw him pocket the knife.

"Whatever." Raff grabbed Julien's arm, hauling him upright. "You're in the superiors' hands now. They'll know what to do with you."

I stepped in Raff's way. "I'm not done questioning him yet."

Perhaps it was a terrible idea to test Raff after seeing a side of him that could turn against me at any moment. But it was my last chance to gather all possible information from Julien. Once he fell into the hands of SQ, I would never be able to talk to him again. And I needed answers. This situation made little sense.

"Didn't you ask enough?"

"Two more questions," I insisted.

He let out an exasperated sigh. "Fine, but be quick. I have a massage in two hours."

A massage?!

I hid my surprise at how certain he was that we would finish his work in three hours to schedule a massage. It was beyond me how he could even attend it after almost ending someone's life. It was as if he didn't care.

But I focused on what was important right now, and it was getting answers. "Where's the letter?"

"I burned it," he admitted. "I couldn't leave any evidence."

"Where did you deliver the batches?"

"As I said, to the harbour."

"Any specific place?"

"That's three questions—"

I put up a hand, silencing Raff.

"To the boat called *Ele*," Julien answered.

"That's it," Raff announced, dragging him out.

I stayed behind.

It couldn't be real. Vittoria had been in a coma when this took place. It wasn't possible. Also, Julien's willingness to risk his career *and* his life for a letter from a stranger was illogical.

But Julien could be too infatuated with Vittoria to see logic. If the letter was real, perhaps her scent clouded his common sense. But he was also a scientist. He had time to think before making those batches, smuggling them out, and delivering them. He must have known he was risking his life for a mere letter, most likely aware that Vittoria was in a coma.

Men might become stupid when smitten by women, but not *that* stupid.

Maybe she's faking it, I thought.

If Vittoria had woken up with the same personality, I wouldn't have even entertained the idea of believing him. But now I didn't know what to believe, except that I needed to dig deeper and hope to find everything out.

Starting with the place where Julien had delivered the batches.

After dropping off Raff and Julien at SQ, I drove to investigate the harbour. As I walked among the boats, I didn't expect to actually find one named *Ele*. Yet a wave of disappointment engulfed me when I arrived at the end of the pier, not finding it.

Julien lied, and the boat probably never existed. SQ might investigate this further, but for me, it was a dead end.

I turned on my heel when I heard a whistle.

Glancing over, I spotted a man sitting at the edge of the pier, drinking from a bottle.

"You one of those saints?" He surveyed me from head to toe. "Gotta be. You dress so fancy."

Normally, I would have ignored him and carried on with my day, but the man was hanging out by the boats. He could know something valuable.

I turned to him fully. "Isn't it early for a drink?"

"Taking break from work, saint." He nodded towards the boat in front of him.

Did I actually come across a man who made a living working with boats? He seemed like one of the lonely souls who spent afternoons at the harbour drinking alone with no one to return to. He didn't have a wedding ring, and he looked to be in his late forties.

"What's your name?"

The man let out a laugh, taking a sip. "If you not want boat ride, maybe you go back where you come from."

"Oh, my apologies. I thought you were trying to get my attention by whistling."

"You lost or something, saint?"

The man was either bold or incredibly stupid to keep calling me *saint*. He clearly knew the insult it carried for anyone associated with SQ. Or he might have underestimated the threat I posed. I had no desire to prove him wrong, but I was curious. Besides, his trustworthiness might be an issue. The only way to find out was to intimidate him.

"You fix boats?"

He went still for a split second, then tipped back his bottle and swallowed, refusing to answer.

I took it as a yes and continued, "I see no ring on your finger. Either you're not married, or your marriage isn't important to you. You think it can't get better, and working with boats is the one thing you feel capable of fixing," I observed casually, shrugging. "But I could be mistaken."

Amusement drained from his face. "What do you want?"

"If I asked you questions and received honest answers, what would be your price?"

He curled his lip in disgust. "I take nothing from your people."

"Doesn't choosing to get paid instead of ending up beaten to near death sound like a much better option?"

"You against me?" He snorted. "You won't beat me to near death. I'll be one to beat *you*, *saint*."

I might be lean and lack the muscle mass to intimidate a man, but it didn't matter. He posed no threat to me, not even with the glass bottle. Unlike me, he wasn't trained to kill a man within seconds when he was fifteen. It didn't require big muscles to do it.

"Maybe I won't beat you," I said. "But Raffaele Galletti definitely will."

He halted, his bottle midway to his lips before he lowered it, frowning. "You're spitting names."

"I might, but are you willing to risk your life because you refuse to name your price for some harmless questions?"

He set his bottle aside. "I want Cure for five people."

"Tell me your name, and consider it done."

The man regarded me sceptically. I didn't blame him. Trusting anyone from SQ was a gamble. He probably feared that instead of getting the Cure, I might kill him. We were that unpredictable. I could bet all my savings that was exactly what he was thinking.

"Sacha."

"And your last name?"

He grimaced as he hesitated to respond, "Dryomov."

"We have a deal, Sacha Dryomov." I slipped my hands into my pockets. "Tell me, do you know anything about the boat named *Ele*?"

He didn't rush to answer. "I can know, and I can't know."

"Do you or don't you?"

"It's boat that's unpredictable," he said. "It comes and goes."

I squatted next to him, noting the flicker of alarm in his eyes. "Do you know who drives it?"

"No," he replied. "I saw boat only when it was here, and when it was gone. I never saw it come and leave. Maybe someone steers it at night."

"You've never seen anyone getting onto the boat?"

"Oh, yes, I did," he admitted. "One man with beard came early morning, put box on the boat many times, but he always left. Never drove it."

"Is that all the information you have about the boat?"

"Sorry to disappoint, saint."

I observed him, looking for any signs of lying in his facial expressions and body language. He stayed still, giving away nothing. Despite working for SQ since such a young age, I still had room to improve my ability to read people.

Discreetly, I pulled out a gun and leant in, pressing it against his side so that passersby couldn't see.

"I'll ask once more," I said calmly. "Is that all the information you have?"

The tough façade crumbled like a wall as the reality of the threat to his life sank in, and he shook his head.

"I'm listening."

"I saw the boat in early morning, and when I came back, it was gone. But right there, where boat was, I found ticket," he said. "Maybe someone else dropped it, not driver. Many things get lost here, and—"

"What ticket?"

He reached into his pocket and pulled it out, handing it to me.

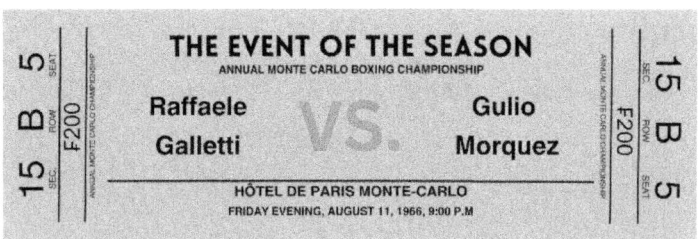

The ticket could belong to anyone. The boxing match was one of the most anticipated events of the year. But Sacha might still be onto something. There was a possibility that it could be connected to the boat driver.

I returned the ticket to his pocket and gave it a reassuring pat. "I'll see you there if you decide to come."

But after everything, I doubted he would risk his life by showing up.

22
The Deadly Truth

Teodora

THE SUN BEAMED DOWN AT ME AS IF ATTEMPTING TO CHEER ME UP WITH ITS WARMTH, BUT WITHOUT SUCCESS. It couldn't lift my spirits, not after discovering I was a criminal.

Hunched over the flowers, Ettore tended to them while I lingered on the stairs, holding the box I had found in my wardrobe days ago. I needed answers. After recalling a fragment of my past, I tried to remember more, but nothing came to me, even after a day. I couldn't keep waiting to remember everything. I wasn't even sure if I wanted to remember anymore.

Unbeknownst to him, I watched, mustering up courage to approach and confront him. It seemed that taking care of flowers was his hobby, while he made money from his criminal activities. His parents must also work in the organisation. How else could they afford an estate that cost the same as ending famine in several countries?

I drew in a deep breath before taking a step further. And another, and another, until I stopped behind him. He was lost in his own world, whistling a familiar tune, oblivious to my presence. It gave me time to think about how to address the topic. Should I take it slow, or jump right in?

He stopped whistling. "Good morning to you as well, Vittoria."

"How long have you known I've been here?"

"A while."

I doubted it.

He chuckled. "Alright, not long, but I heard you moving through the grass."

It was rare to find him in a good mood. Usually, a sense of sadness emanated from him. But not today. Once I shared my discoveries with him, I knew I would ruin his mood. As much as I hated to, I couldn't delay it any longer.

He gestured with his gloved hand, motioning for me to draw near. I leant in, searching for a reason why he wanted me closer.

"Look over there." He pointed at something in the bushes.

I carefully squatted down in my long white dress to see what he was pointing at. Then I froze, a wide smile spreading across my face.

Nestled in the indentation under the bush was a litter of five hedgehogs.

"They've been keeping me company," Ettore said, resuming to pluck out the weeds around the flowers. "Even though they've been asleep and completely unaware."

Something soft brushed against my leg, and I looked down to see Regina nuzzling up against me. I gently scratched her neck, to which she responded by sitting and extending it further. Was she aware of the hedgehogs?

"She smelled them earlier in the morning," Ettore said, almost as if he had read my mind. It wasn't the first time he had surprised me like that.

As he turned to face me, we spoke simultaneously.

"You look less tired today," I noted.

"Since when do you wear long white dresses?" he asked.

We shared a laugh.

"I slept through the entire night this time without waking up once," Ettore explained. "Today is my day off."

I lowered my eyes at the box, remembering the reason I was here. If only I could avoid the topic and pretend I knew nothing . . .

He pulled off his gloves. "What's in the box?"

There was no avoiding it now.

I slid my fingers under the lid. *Now or never*. But I couldn't make myself open it. Not yet.

I looked back at Ettore. "You said you have a day off?"

He raised his curious eyes from the box, appearing uncertain. "Yes?"

"Yes or no?"

"Yes," he said, more certain this time.

"Could you take me somewhere? Maybe to a place that could help me remember?"

I could also share the memory with him. Maybe he could provide answers about that as well.

He pondered for a moment. "I might have something in mind but—"

"Perfect!" I rose to my feet. "I'll start getting ready!"

"Vittoria, wait!"

I kept going, confident he was going to ask what was in the box, and I wanted to avoid it.

"Vittoria!"

I halted, hesitating before turning around. He stood with Regina sitting by his side. "Yes?"

Please, don't ask about what's in the box. Please, don't ask—

"If you want to remember, we have to go there in the evening."

"Oh?"

"Be ready at nine."

Ettore parked his car in front of a six-floor building. As he exited the vehicle, he quickly came to my side, opening the door before I could even touch the handle. Anxiously, I forced a smile and accepted his offered hand. He assisted me onto the empty street.

Ever since I had left him in the garden, I hadn't been able to sit still. I felt even more nervous now. I should have shared my discoveries with him right away.

He closed the door behind me. "Does anything here stir your memory?"

I glanced around the buildings with a creamy texture. It was another typical yet beautiful city street, softly lit up by the cosy light of the streetlights. But nothing stood out that would trigger my memory.

"No."

He locked the car and marched towards the building. With a confident pull, he opened the door that I didn't expect to be unlocked.

I hastened to catch up with him. "Are we allowed to go in here?"

"Do you think I would make you do something illegal?"

Yes, I wanted to say, *because we are criminals.* But I hesitated to admit that I knew that, at least for now.

Before I could answer with a *no*, we entered the building. The door closed, trapping us in the darkness. Shivers ran down my spine. It was just Ettore and me in this dark, unfamiliar space, with an unsettling feeling that we shouldn't be here.

"Are you going to kill me?" I attempted to joke, but as my voice echoed in the darkness it didn't sound funny at all. I wrapped my arms around myself, seeking comfort from the uncertainty lurking in the shadows.

Where was the light?

"Is that a genuine question?" His voice sounded in the dark.

A yellow glow appeared, illuminating the staircase in front of us. Ettore proceeded up the stairs holding a flashlight, and I followed closely behind.

"To me, you're a stranger," I said. "You know my favourite colour, but I don't know yours."

"What makes you think I know your favourite colour?" He turned to ascend another flight of stairs. "Maybe I don't."

"Tell me, and I'll tell you if you're correct or not."

"Is it red?"

I smiled, unsurprised. When red and black clothes filled my wardrobe, it was no wonder he thought that way.

"No."

After climbing only four flights of stairs, I was already out of breath. No wonder. My feet were already sore from hours of walking yesterday, and my body was still adjusting to being active after two months of sleeping.

"Is it black?"

"No."

A pause followed. "What is it, then?"

"I can't pick one. I like green, like freshly cut grass, but I . . ." Pausing at the landing, I took a deep breath before continuing, "I also like blue, like the sea outside our villa."

At last, we ascended the final flight of stairs and stood before the door. Catching my breath, I leant against the cool wall. *Water would be so good right now.*

"Can you hold this?" He handed me the flashlight.

I accepted it, uncertain of what to do with it.

"Can you point it at the handle?" he asked, and I complied. "Thank you."

I watched him work on the lock using sharp tools with a frown. "Isn't that illegal?"

The corner of his lips lifted, but he said nothing. This couldn't be his first time doing this. Before, I would have been suspicious, but now I knew it was a part of his criminal lifestyle.

He opened the door and took his flashlight back. "Ladies first," he said, gesturing for me to enter.

I gave him a suspicious look before stepping out reluctantly. A soft wind brushed against me, and I tucked my hands into my coat pockets as I surveyed the emptiness around me.

"Does anything look familiar yet?" he asked.

I didn't answer him, moving closer to the edge with cautious steps. When I reached the low wall, I rested my hands on it and leant over, peering down at the street below. A lump formed in my throat as I realised how high we were from the ground.

I drew back. "Why would I come here?"

Standing atop the five-floor building was a bit scary, yet it offered a lovely view of the sea. Did I use to break in for this view alone?

He stepped next to me. "You liked putting yourself in dangerous situations. At night, when visibility was poor, you would stand on the edge and perform acrobatics."

"I love danger?"

"You did."

I put my hands on the low wall, using it for support as I climbed up. As I cautiously rose to my feet, my legs trembled. The thought of being just one step away from a fatal fall made me quickly crouch down. As I sat, I brought my legs from underneath me, letting them dangle in the air.

"You never told me what your favourite colour is," I said.

He executed a similar manoeuvre, settling beside me. "It depends on which flower I like that day."

I stared at him expectantly, waiting for him to elaborate.

"For instance," he began, "one day I am drawn to the allure of red roses. But the next day, I prefer the delicate charm of pink tulips."

"What flower do you like today?"

He smiled dreamily. "Gardenias. My favourite colour is white today."

"How many flowers do you know?"

"A lot." His eyes sparkled with enthusiasm. "My dream is to have a garden with every type of flower. I know I'll need to tailor the conditions for each one, but I'm not afraid of—" He paused, a furrow appearing on his brow. "I'm sorry." His gaze lowered suddenly as if he became shy. "I forgot you don't like listening to my ramblings about flowers."

"I don't?"

It made no sense. Who wouldn't want to listen to someone talking about something they loved? Especially when witnessing someone like Ettore become excited about anything was rare. His enthusiasm was magnetic. I felt eager to hear more about flowers. Goodness, I'd even be eager to listen to him talk about something as mundane as peeling potatoes if he was passionate about it.

"Not before the Fire. You said it bored you to death."

I frowned. "That was in the past. It doesn't bore me now, and I want to hear more, please. About flowers. If you don't mind."

He closed his eyes, appearing annoyed.

I looked down, plucking at my skirt. "Am I annoying you? Because if you don't want to tell—"

"No." His eyes snapped open. "It's just . . . nobody has shown an interest in my hobby before." A tentative smile tugged at his lips.

"Of course, not many know about it."

I placed my hand next to his, feeling a flutter in my chest as our fingers lightly grazed each other. Meeting his gaze, I offered an encouraging smile, despite my heart pounding so fast I could faint.

"But I am interested," I assured softly. "So please, tell me."

His eyes lit up with renewed passion, and once he opened his mouth, the words flowed without pause. He explained the differences between flowers and what they needed to thrive. He shared how some were poisonous while others could heal. With every word, his eyes shimmered with fervour. Watching him come alive with enthusiasm for the first time entranced me. I hung onto his every word while our pinky fingers brushed against each other. I ached to touch more than his finger, but I wasn't brave enough to hold his hand, even if he hadn't rejected me so far.

"How long has it been your hobby?" I asked.

He made a pensive face. "I'm not sure. It has to be over a decade. I remember how it all started."

"Am I going to hear an interesting story?"

He leant back on his other hand. "You're actually involved in it."

I inclined my head towards him curiously.

"When we were kids, you always received flowers for your birthday. I never received a single one. I asked my mother why I couldn't get one, and my father overheard. He told me before my mother could say a word that flowers were for girls, not boys."

I twisted my lips. I disagreed with his father, but I stayed silent so he would continue his story.

"My next birthday came," he went on. "I received a bouquet of pink carnations from my mother. She wished me to continue blooming like a flower and to fight for what I want, despite what people might think."

"Do you?"

"Excuse me?"

"Fight for what you want?"

He straightened, rubbing his temple with two fingers. "I don't recall the last time I wanted something so much that I couldn't relax until I got it," he admitted. "You see, why fight for something when everything I want is handed to me on a silver platter? It kind of defeats the purpose, doesn't it?"

"Mmm . . ." I pondered. "The downsides of being born a rich kid."

"You're mocking me."

I scoffed. "It wouldn't be fair of me if I did. I also come from a wealthy family, Ettore."

"And yet you're still mocking me."

The corner of my lips turned up. "I indeed am."

He snickered, but it abruptly faded. "How do you know your family is wealthy?"

My smile dropped as his question reminded me why I had asked him to bring me here. Nervousness surged back, and I withdrew my hand. "I remembered something yesterday. Or at least I think I did."

He went stiff. "What did you remember?"

"Two men locked me in a room, and I was thinking about the Cure they were going to steal from me."

A crease appeared between his eyebrows. "The Cure? Why would they steal it from you?"

I shrugged. "Maybe I had some and they wanted it." It made sense since my friends were only pretending to be my friends because of it. If the Cure was such a precious drug, why wouldn't two men lock me in a room to get it? "I don't know. Maybe you know which memory I'm talking about?"

I looked at him hopefully, but he only gave me a sad smile. "No, I have no clue what you're talking about."

Disappointed, I looked down. Maybe he knew but didn't want to tell me because he thought I wasn't aware of SQ.

I chewed on my lip. "I know about Sanctus Quinque."

Deadly silence fell over us, punctuated by the distant hum of passing cars. Despite expecting his shock, my heartbeat quickened with each excruciatingly silent second.

"You remembered that too?" he spoke at last, his voice uncertain yet hopeful.

"No."

"Who told you that?"

"It doesn't matter. I know you're a criminal, and so am I."

I waited for his denial, but none came, dispelling any doubts I had.

I wrung my hands in my lap. "Was I happy being a criminal?"

He opened his mouth, but I anticipated his response. "And don't you dare tell me I should remember it."

His mouth closed, and he stared deadly serious into my eyes as he said, "You were a natural, Vittoria."

I pulled away as though his words had a physical impact on me. "What was my role in this criminal organisation?"

The image of me doing paperwork at a desk flashed in my mind, but I quickly dismissed it. I had found a pistol in my wardrobe, and Ettore said I loved danger. It was unlikely that my job involved mundane, innocent paperwork.

Ettore offered me an apologetic look. "You were an assassin."

I stood, the impulse to run coursing through me. But I had nowhere to go. Running away without knowing the way back, especially at night, would be foolish.

"But if it makes you feel better, you were a damn good one," he added.

"I was good at killing people?" My hands shook with anger. I was angry at him. Angry at myself. I pushed them into the pockets of my coat, clenching them tightly. "What did you do? Cleaned up after my mess?"

"Why do you think that?"

I shrugged, pretending to not know.

Since the moment I woke up and saw him enter my room, I had felt safe around him. In the past week, I had encountered many people, but none of them made me feel this way, not even close. With Ettore, I felt like myself, not the spoiled, horrible girl others told me I was before the Fire. Maybe this feeling meant that I also felt safe with him before my memory loss. If so, it wouldn't come as a surprise if he used to clean up after my . . . assassinations.

He stood and offered me his hand. "Let's go home?"

"Only if you tell me something."

His expression betrayed his reluctance, yet he complied. "Okay."

"Am I allowed to leave Sanctus Quinque?"

His facial expression spoke volumes before he shook his head.

"Can *you*?"

"No," he said, dismissing the idea as if it were absurd. "Unless you die, then you're free of all the responsibility you've pledged to SQ."

"So it's a cult, not an organisation," I blurted out, startled at my own words. For the first time, I hadn't shied away from voicing exactly what was on my mind.

He looked at me like I was a madwoman spouting crazy theories. "I'm sorry?"

"You don't swear loyalty to someone, believe in their created rules, and remain loyal to their beliefs?"

He stepped down from the barrier. "We're going home," he stated, extending his hand to me. "It's getting late."

I didn't move.

He waited for me to take his hand, but I held my ground. I would not leave before he answered my questions. I was tired of getting a headache from trying to remember.

Realising I wouldn't back down, he lowered his hand. "Yes, *we* swear loyalty, but not to someone. *We* swear it to our superiors. *We* believe in the rules passed down for generations, yet *we* also have our own beliefs, like every human does. But it's not you or I in SQ. It's *we*, Vittoria. And whether you like it or not, you're a part of us."

Denial was on the tip of my tongue, but I bit it back. I didn't know enough to deny his words. Not yet.

"Fine. We're part of a cult. Fucking fabulous," I spat out.

"It's not a cult!"

"If it's not, then I'm not a girl with amnesia who married some guy because probably some superiors said so."

"How do you . . . It's not even the same. SQ isn't a cult."

"It sounds crazy when you say it, but it doesn't make it any less real."

"Vittoria . . ." He pressed his hands together in a praying position. "You can complain about SQ all you want to me, but remember, if you disrespect SQ in front of others, they can punish you."

"What are they going to do?" I scoffed. "Spank me?"

"No, they're going to hurt the people you love most."

"Good thing that I don't love anyone then."

His eyebrows shot up, and his mouth parted ever so slightly. Guilt crossed my heart as I realised the cruelty of my words.

"You don't remember anyone." His tone softened, and I detected a faint shadow of sadness, but I could be mistaken. "You don't remember anything. But once you do, you'll regret everything you said about your family."

"My family? The cult is not my—"

As I spoke, I stepped back, forgetting I was on the edge of the building.

My foot teetered halfway over the edge. As I thought this was it, a firm hand gripped my wrist, yanking me forward. Another arm encircled my waist, preventing me from falling.

Blinking in astonishment, I locked eyes with my saviour.

"Careful, flower," he said, his voice tinged with concern.

He helped me down to the ground, my body numb, his gentle caress lingering on my waist. I couldn't find the words, still affected by the near-death experience. I couldn't stop reliving the terrifying situation of being on the brink of—

"Do you need to sit?" he offered.

I managed a nod, and he eased me to the ground. He crouched in front of me, tucking my hair behind my ear. "Nothing happened, okay? You're here."

I'm here.

I closed my eyes and exhaled before reopening them. "Continue," I uttered. "Continue the conversation we had."

"Are you sure?"

"Please."

I needed something else to focus on.

With an unsure expression, he resumed, "You accused your family of being a cult, but what I meant were your parents. Lorence is one of the superiors."

If I wasn't sitting, I would have fallen. *Is my entire family in the cult?* I wouldn't be surprised anymore if they were. "But . . ." A lightbulb went off in my head. "That's good! If I deny the cult, no one will hurt me because Lorence is a part of dictating the rules!"

His face, however, remained serious. "He swore to be unbiased. When any member, including their loved ones, sins, they vote, and the majority of the votes wins. Do you think my mother wanted me to be sworn to marry you before I was even born?"

My eyes went wide. "You weren't even born?"

"Neither were you."

I wrapped my arms around myself, feeling like I was on the brink of madness. This was too much. As I was convinced I knew everything, there was more.

"That's why you should have remembered it all," he said quietly.

For once, I wasn't annoyed, finding some truth in his words. If I hadn't felt the need to seek answers and remembered instead, I wouldn't be feeling so shocked and miserable.

"Home?" he offered.

I smiled, though it might have appeared unhinged. "Tell me, Ettore. What exactly is home?"

With his hands on his knees, he stood up and offered his hand. "The villa by the sea?"

"Then let's call it that." I took his hand, and he pulled me to my feet. "The villa by the sea because I'm pretty sure it's not my home."

I wished I had burned down in the Fire.

Ettore and I returned home in silence and exchanged our goodnights before he disappeared into his room. With a heavy ball of sadness in my chest, I trudged towards my bedroom.

I didn't want to remember anymore. I didn't want to return to my criminal activities. With no safe way out of SQ, I clung to the hope that if I didn't remember, I could retire.

But hopes were just that—mere hopes. Even if I couldn't remember a thing, they would force me back into the life of crime. SQ was more than a crime organisation. It was a cult. There was no escaping its grasp.

I stopped at the sight of Regina sleeping on the windowsill. A smile spread across my lips on its own, and I approached her, careful not to disturb her sleep. As I gently touched her fluffy fur, she released a soft cooing sound that almost sounded like a pigeon, easing my worries and melting my heart.

"Aren't you a cute one?" I whispered.

Regina rose and stretched her front legs before moving to face the window. I felt guilty for waking her, but maybe I shouldn't. Didn't cats spend most of their lives sleeping and had no problem going back to sleep?

"Okay, gorgeous creature." Leaning towards her, I rested my hands on my knees. "Good night." I planted a gentle kiss on her snoot, but she pulled away, ignoring me.

I resumed walking to my room, but as soon as I opened the door, something soft brushed against my legs. I looked down to see Regina entering with her elegant, effortless stride. My first instinct was to pick her up and let her out, but that thought vanished once she hopped onto my bed and settled down.

I turned on the switch. Her blue eyes narrowed, but despite her dissatisfaction with the bright light, she didn't move. With a sigh, I closed the door behind me. "I suppose you're sleeping with me tonight."

After changing into my pyjamas and finishing my nightly routine, I carefully lifted the blanket, making sure not to disturb her. As I settled in, I switched off the night lamp and nestled under the covers, feeling a weight pressing against my chest.

Smiling, I sank my fingers into her fur. She began purring. Her comforting presence calmed my concerns about SQ, but it didn't stop my nightmares. I was burning again.

August 10, 1965

I kissed a girl today.
I've kissed girls before, but this time it was different. It was her.
I feel so giddy, I can't stay still. I can't sleep. I want to see her again, but it's not possible.
She's married, but her marriage isn't like mine with Ettore. If her husband found out... let's say it's better if he doesn't.

23
Burning Ghosts

Ettore

"**HELP!**"

The relentless pounding reverberated against the door.

"Help me!"

Smoke billowed from the roof. I gripped the door handle, ready to open it, but a hand landed on my shoulder, sending a jolt through me.

I glanced back at Raff in the passenger seat.

"You can't save them," he said.

"Of course I—" My response caught in my throat as half of his face melted, like wax dripping down a candle.

"Help!" voices cried out in agony. "We're burning!"

I pulled the handle, but the door didn't budge. I attempted to stand to leap out of the car, but I couldn't move.

Raff's laughter echoed, his taunting words repeating, "You can't help them. You can't help them. You can't—"

I shot upwards in the darkness, greeted by an eerie silence.

Panic gripped me.

Where am I? Where are the screams? Why is it so—

I found the bedside lamp and flicked the switch, filling the room with light. *My bedroom.* I exhaled in relief. It was only a nightmare. *Another* nightmare like that.

The ghosts from the Fire didn't stop haunting me. I wasn't even there when they burned. I didn't hear them scream. I didn't hear the pounding on the doors. Yet, I dreamed as if I was there and heard everything.

But I couldn't blame them for plaguing my sleep. I deserved it. I had let them burn, doing nothing to save them. I couldn't. It was my duty to ensure that everyone who entered the abandoned hotel never left it, except for Vittoria.

Vittoria . . .

I scrubbed my face with my hands and slid out of bed. As I exited the room, I let my legs lead the way, taking me to her bedroom door.

I paused in front of it, minutes drifting by as I remained motionless.

She had remembered something. Not much, but it was a start. Her memory puzzled me as much as it did her. I didn't know Vittoria well. Perhaps she really had been locked in a room by men who wanted the Cure. I wouldn't be surprised if she often found herself in dangerous situations and never told anyone.

One thing was certain: I shouldn't have left her alone to deal with the heavy, shocking news. It had only been two weeks since she woke up from a coma. She should have remembered everything, and I should have kept my mouth shut. But I was too weak.

At last, I managed to move, turning away from her room. I went downstairs and stepped outside. The conservatory beckoned me, and I strode to it with purpose. I usually came here for comfort when I couldn't sleep or woke up from a nightmare. But not today. Vittoria was an early riser, and she could awaken any minute. Before that happened, I had something to do.

I grabbed the scissors and approached the gardenias. Carefully, I snipped seven blossoms, along with some leaves. As I returned to the table, I arranged them into a bouquet and bound the stems together with a string.

Back in the villa, I wrote a letter in my office.

I placed the bouquet and the letter by her door, picturing her reaction when she woke up and found them. Imagining her smiling brought a smile to my face. I hoped they would bring her some joy and provide a brief reprieve from the harsh reality awaiting her once she remembered, even if only for a moment.

24
The Audacity of Gardenias

Teodora

I WOKE UP SWEATY WITH THE LINGERING SENSATION OF THE FLAMES LICKING AT MY SKIN. If it weren't for the urge to pee, I would have returned to sleep. Regina remained unmoving at the foot of the bed as I returned from the bathroom.

The next time I awoke it was to Regina's insistent meows, demanding to be let out. With my eyes barely open, I struggled to get out of bed and stumbled to the door. As I opened it, Regina slipped out through a small gap, pausing in the doorway.

"Regina, go," I mumbled, about to nudge her, but she seemed distracted, sniffing at something. Curious, I pushed the door open wider, revealing a bouquet of white flowers on the floor. Regina lost interest and walked away.

As I picked up the flowers, I noticed something fall—a letter. I reached for it and unfolded it.

Dear Vittoria,

I know what you learned yesterday was heavy news, but I promise once you remember, it will get easier.
You, or Vittoria before the Fire, adored this life. The danger. The adrenaline. You were addicted.
I fully understand the point you made, and I admit it. It's a cult, but it's a cult that could get you killed if you don't follow the rules. It may be forgiving at times, but it won't last if you continue speaking ill of it.
Remember, even if you're an

assassin, you don't have to kill anyone until your memories return. Your cousin said it could take months. There's some comfort in that, isn't there?

Did you know that gardenias symbolise love and respect for the receiver?

Consider this an open invitation to tell me anything that's on your mind. You're free of responsibility. As temporary as it is, treat it like a holiday.

        Ettore

I crumpled the letter, my drowsiness stolen away by its words.

Free of responsibility? Treat it like a holiday?

How dare he? How could I consider my amnesia as a break from killing people? It was infuriating. If I had blood on my hands, I didn't want to continue ending lives. I wanted to escape the life waiting for me. Not his nonsensical comfort.

I stomped towards his room, but I refrained from barging in, choosing to knock on the door instead. As I waited, the handle remained still. I considered letting it be and ignoring the audacity of his letter—

No.

I couldn't, actually.

I lowered the handle and pushed the door open. As expected, he was sleeping, oblivious to my knocking. Sleeping *and* drooling over the pillow.

I marched to his bed and flung the bouquet at his face, startling him awake. His eyes snapped open, clouded with haze. It took a moment for the fog of sleep to clear, and for him to register his surroundings.

"Vittoria?" he asked uncertainly and pinched himself in the arm for whatever reason, staring at me as if expecting something. Suddenly, he snapped out of it, pushing his hair away from his face. His hand froze mid-motion as he noticed the bouquet. "What's this?"

I threw the crumpled letter at him. "I don't have to kill anyone until my memories return? Treat it like a holiday? I finally understand why we don't sleep in the same room. You, Ettore, are a complete moron."

He slipped out of bed. "I understand you're angry, but . . ."

The rest of his words went in one ear and out the other as my attention shifted to his white boxer shorts. His dick protruded through the fabric, long and proud, with a wet spot—

He quickly snatched up a nearby pillow to cover himself, his cheeks flushing with embarrassment. "Fuck, I'm sorry," he said.

A rush of heat crawled up my neck, and I took a step back, my eyes darting everywhere but him. "No, it's me who should be sorry. I was the one who barged into your room. It's fine, honestly. It's completely normal."

Even if it was normal, we both avoided looking at each other.

"You probably were in the middle of some hot and steamy dream, and I came and ruined it, right?" I tried to joke, but the awkward silence that followed only made the air more uncomfortable. "I'm sorry," I mumbled, spinning on my heel towards the door.

"Vittoria, I—"

"No need to explain," I interrupted quickly, eager to remove myself from the situation. "I . . . I'll see myself out."

I rushed out of the room, mortified. I should have respected his privacy and waited to confront him when he was awake. It was incredibly rude and stupid of me to barge into his bedroom.

Throughout the day, I couldn't force the image of his erection from my mind. I wondered if it was simply a morning arousal, or if that wet spot was something else. Maybe my joke was spot on, and he had actually been dreaming of someone.

I was overthinking, but if it was true . . . What was he dreaming of? Or *whom* was he dreaming of?

Was it Barbara?

Or another girl I had no idea about?

August 25, 1965

It's my birthday, and I'm going to celebrate it. I know, I know, I have work tomorrow, but you can't pause having fun because of work. Tonight, I will have the best time of my life because I deserve it, dammit.

25
An Appropriate Distraction?

⋯❋⋯

Ettore

***I* FUCKED VITTORIA.**

In my dream.

It was the current Vittoria. She even had the same voice and way of speaking as after she woke up from the coma.

It was the first dream I'd had in the last two months that wasn't a nightmare. As she glanced at me, her hair tangled in my grip, I suddenly woke up. The real Vittoria stood in front of my bed, dressed in her pyjamas, glaring at me. Then she saw my erection.

I exhaled and refocused on my bicep curls, but I couldn't remember which one I was on.

Goddammit.

I resumed from the beginning, determined to concentrate this time.

The mere thought of this morning made me uncomfortable, but dwelling on it was futile. Working out offered a great distraction. Sort of.

When Raff called this morning, inviting me to a gym session, I didn't decline. I could have stayed at home and prepared to return to work when SQ called, but Vittoria was at the villa. I knew I couldn't avoid her forever, but for now, I did.

But Raff failed to mention that he was boxing someone to prepare for the championship next week. I suspected Raff had invited me solely to watch him fight. He was one of those weird people who performed better with an audience.

Counting my reps helped to distract me from this morning. Ideally, I wanted to forget it all, but that would mean hitting my head really, *really* hard against the wall.

"I can't believe this." Natalie jolted me out of my thoughts. "You, training? What happened?"

I lowered the dumbbells to the floor. "What are you doing here?"

Natalie didn't train here, at least not when I used to come regularly. Unless something had changed, since she wore her sportswear.

She put her hands on her hips. "Raff asked me to come and cheer him on. I was jogging past this place so I thought, why not?" She turned to look at Raff in the ring.

"Have you heard about my case?"

Since she was here, I might as well ask for her input. Natalie was smarter than me. A year ago, SQ had promoted her to handle not only interrogations but also cases of betrayal and murder mysteries, although they were rare.

"Which one exactly?"

"Julien Martin stealing the batches of the Cure."

Raff's opponent hit the floor, and the trainer's voice boomed through the silent gym as he began to count. Everyone had stopped what they were doing, their full attention fixed on the ring. Raff's opponent lay motionless on the ground for the entire ten seconds, earning Raff a point.

Natalie threw her hands in the air. "Woohoo!"

"Nat?" I prompted.

"Oh." She lowered her hands. "Of course I heard about it."

"Did you interrogate him?"

"No, why?"

I wasn't sure about the extent of Natalie's knowledge regarding the case. We rarely discussed work. For all I knew, she knew nothing. Or perhaps she was among the first to learn about Julien's betrayal.

"Isn't it strange that he believes it was Vittoria, despite knowing she was in a coma?"

As Raff punched the other guy, causing him to spit blood on the floor, everyone cheered. Except for me.

"I wouldn't think too deeply about it," Natalie said as the cheering ended. "Julien is a scientist. They tend to be mad. Plus, he's a man, clearly infatuated with her. It's not Vittoria."

"I don't think it's her either, but after I dropped him and Raff off at SQ, I went to the harbour."

She glanced at me, surprise apparent on her face. "You did something beyond your job?"

I had expected her to be surprised. It was the first time I had gone beyond the cases provided by SQ. Usually, once I found the people I was assigned to, I left the rest to them. But my cases had never involved my family before.

"When a scientist claims he delivered the Cure batches to my wife, of course I dig deeper."

"Your wife?" She raised her eyebrows. "You never referred to Vittoria as your wife before."

As she analysed me, my sex dream resurfaced in my thoughts. I worried that she might somehow read my mind and expose me, even though it was impossible.

"I don't know why you find it surprising. She's my wife," I stated calmly, forcing the memories of the dream away. "You know what I found at the harbour?"

"The boat named *Ele*?" she mocked.

"The man who found a ticket to Raff's show right where the boat parked."

She stared at me, unimpressed. "That man found a ticket to Raff's show, the most anticipated of the year? Well, Ettore, you struck a gold mine," she said sarcastically before turning her head back to watch Raff.

"I know the ticket could belong to anyone, but what if the person who contacted Julien shows up?"

"First of all, we don't know if the letter is real. Second, why would the person want to attend Raff's show in the city they stole from? And finally, even if they do, there will be hundreds of people, and we have no information about them except that they drive the boat *Ele*."

I had already considered everything she said, but hearing it spoken aloud made me realise how absurd I was. The only way to track the thief was to find them by their boat, not by hoping they would show up at Raff's show. And even if they did, I wouldn't know who they were.

"Has SQ tracked the boat?" I asked.

"I guess not, since I'm interrogating Julien tomorrow."

I frowned. "And you didn't tell me?"

"Why? Is there something you want to ask him?"

I was certain I had asked him all I needed to know, but now that I had another opportunity, I wondered if there was something more. While I was lost in thought, Raff punched his opponent to the ground once more, and he didn't stand up. Raff's trainer raised his hand in victory, and I joined the applause.

Raff stepped out of the ring and headed towards us. I tensed up as a vivid image of his sister on all fours flashed before me.

Natalie whistled. "Do I smell a four-year winner in a row?"

He laughed and flexed his biceps, emphasising his strength.

I used to envy his physique, but the effort required to achieve it discouraged me. I couldn't complain about my body. I was lucky to have a naturally slim frame with some defined muscles. Instead of striving to sculpt myself into a Greek god, I preferred to exercise my brain. The power of knowledge sounded far more exciting than the power of muscle strength.

"I would hug you," Raff said, "but I'm all sweaty right now."

Natalie scrunched up her face playfully. "Yes, me too, so we better not."

Raff grabbed some water and gulped it down, then capped the bottle and set it back on the windowsill. "Did you see, Nat? Our brain is back at the gym."

"Don't pressure him," she cautioned, leaning towards Raff and whispering loud enough for me to hear, "You might scare him away."

"Ha ha," I laughed without humour.

Setting jokes aside, while I wasn't obsessed with working out, it was beneficial for both my body and mind. When anger clouded my thoughts, I would put on my shoes and go for a run. The fresh air and increased heartbeat helped dispel the feeling. Although it had been a while since I had felt intense anger, I could feel it slowly returning. I chose to channel it into something healthy, rather than falling back into drugs.

"I see you're doing amazing," Natalie noted. "You don't need my cheering when all the gym is cheering for you. Is it fine if I return to my jog?"

"You go, Nat. And thanks for wasting your time to come here for me."

"Are you kidding me? How could I possibly miss cheering on my favourite boy?" She tousled his hair then pulled away, wincing. "That's sweaty. Do you have a towel?" She turned to me.

I gestured towards the windowsill. "Feel free to use it."

She grabbed my towel and wiped her hand.

"Okay, I'll head out now. Bye." She waved as she jogged away.

I lifted the dumbbells and started another set of twelve reps, expecting Raff to leave, but he stayed. After five reps, I put down my dumbbells and turned to face him, extending my hand. "I charge a hundred for every minute you stare at me."

He raised his hands in surrender, laughing. "Okay, okay, hint taken."

He walked away.

Unlike him, I wasn't comfortable with someone watching me as I worked out. It felt weird.

Also, I had a sex dream about his sister.

I winced at the intrusive thought.

The longer I was around Vittoria, the harder it became to ignore my attraction. The worst part was, it wasn't her looks that captivated me, though she was an undeniably beautiful woman. Instead, it was her intellect and personality. But those things were temporary. Once she regained her memory, she would revert to her old, careless, narcissistic self.

If I had told Raff about the sex dream, I doubted he would care. Despite knowing each other since childhood, Raff and I weren't close enough to talk about our personal lives.

But if I did tell him, he wouldn't say anything new. He would tell me to get over the crush and bury it deep down because nothing good would ever come of it, only trouble.

The memory of the pain in her eyes when I told her she was an assassin sprang to mind. How could a girl like her cause trouble when all I wanted was to embrace her and shield her from her past sins? Part of me craved to express anger and deny my whole life, just as she had. But agreeing with her would mean betraying my own family.

After returning the dumbbells to their place, I grabbed my towel and approached Raff. "Good luck with your training," I said before I turned and walked away to avoid saying something I'd regret.

26
At Natalie's

Teodora

THE NEXT MORNING, WHEN I LET REGINA OUT OF MY ROOM, I FOUND A SINGLE WHITE GARDENIA, A SQUARE BOX, AND A NOTE SAYING *SORRY*.

I continued to receive flowers every morning, each time a single one of a different kind, yet always white. But I never saw Ettore leave them, as though he was deliberately avoiding me.

And maybe he was.

I flinched at the sudden sound of the phone ringing. With neither of the Morrano brothers in the villa today, I had the place to myself. Normally, Sofia would handle calls, but it was her day off.

What if it was Barbara calling to invite me for another shopping trip? But what if it wasn't her?

I placed my book upside down on the couch before reluctantly walking over to the phone and picking it up. "Hello?"

"Vittoria?" a woman's voice greeted me.

My heart dropped. I couldn't tell if it was Barbara or not. I had no idea how her voice sounded on the phone. She had already tried to reach me before, but Sofia was always the one who answered the calls.

"Who's calling?" I tried as I pleaded in my mind. *Please not Barbara. Please not—*

"Natalie, of course!" Her melodic laugh sounded. "But it's Vittoria, right?"

I relaxed, relieved that it wasn't her or one of my other 'friends'. "Yes, it is."

"Perfect! I reached you right away!" she exclaimed. "I'm not sure if Ettore mentioned it, but I recently bought a house. I spent my first night here yesterday and was hoping you and Ettore could join for dinner tonight. He already said yes."

"Oh, I . . ." I hesitated, unsure of how to respond. While I didn't have any plans for the day, I didn't want to be a nuisance and tag along if Ettore didn't invite me to join him.

But I couldn't remain silent for too long.

"Congratulations on your new house!" I said.

"Thank you!" Her voice bubbled with joy. "So, will you come?"

"I . . . I don't know." I twirled the cable around my finger. "I'll have to ask Ettore."

"Nonsense," she dismissed. "It's your decision. Do *you* want to come or not?"

I wasn't so sure.

Ever since the incident in Ettore's bedroom, I'd been avoiding him. I spent most of my time alone. When I felt like socialising, I went to the kitchen where I talked to Sofia. Sometimes, I insisted on helping her with meals, despite her protests. And every night, Regina kept me company.

Other than working on my room renovation project, I didn't have any other major activities. While I could handle redecorating my rooms alone, I needed help to change the wall colour. I had to talk to Ettore about it.

And attending Natalie's dinner offered the perfect opportunity. But . . .

"Who else, apart from Ettore and you, will be there?" I asked.

If Antoine was also invited, I would have to decline. I avoided him at all costs. Sofia always kept me informed if he was in the villa or not, and whenever he was around, I locked myself in the room.

"Only the three of us," she said. "If you decide to come, of course. I really hope you do."

I hated disappointing people, especially when Natalie sounded so excited. Saying no to her didn't feel like an option, unless I wanted to feel like the worst human alive afterwards.

"You didn't invite Antoine?"

There was a brief pause before she spoke again. "Do you want him to come?"

"No," I said, but I was too quick. Hastily, I searched my mind for the right response. "I mean, it's fine if he's there. He's your brother. He's Ettore's brother. He's—"

"It's okay, Vittoria," she interrupted with a laugh. "Antoine won't be joining us. But will *you*? That's what I want to know."

I took a deep breath before responding. "I'll be there."

"Wonderful!" she exclaimed. "I'll prepare dinner for three. I hope you like beef stew!"

I had no idea if I did, but I was already looking forward to it.

"You should stop leaving flowers," I said, breaking the silence in the car.

I felt Ettore's eyes on me as I stared out of the window, avoiding looking at him. It had been five days since the morning incident, and today was the first time I had seen him since then. I missed him, but I was also angry about the letter and how he left me a flower every day instead of simply saying *I'm sorry*.

Yet it was hard to stay mad at him when his intoxicating cologne hung in the air, teasing more than just my nostrils. As if that wasn't torturous enough, seeing him behind the wheel, steering it with one hand, was deadly. In the worst possible, yet best way imaginable.

The only way to stay mad at him was not to look at him. At all.

"You don't like them?"

"No, I do. I . . ." I drew in a breath.

I needed to focus, but he was making me nervous.

His entire presence was making me nervous!

"I like flowers," I managed, staring at my folded hands in my lap. "But I want you to apologise to me in person instead of leaving me flowers, expecting them to suffice. It doesn't feel mature."

He didn't respond, letting the silence linger as we drove. It felt even more uncomfortable than the silence that was before I had spoken. It stretched on for so long that I didn't expect him to say anything—

"I'm sorry."

My breath caught in my throat. "For what?"

"For assuming I know better what's best for you, but . . ." He scratched his head. "I'm worried about you. I don't want you to get in trouble with SQ. No one should know that you hate it and call it a cult. Not even your parents."

I hadn't planned to share my thoughts with anyone else. I knew my words were risky. Talking about SQ in the way I did was dangerous. The last thing I wanted was to risk my life. To risk *Ettore's* life.

"But what if I don't remember?" I asked a question I must have asked a hundred times before. "Will I be spared from my life before the Fire?"

"You will remember," he replied with certainty, as though there were no other option.

"You can't be sure. I might be a new person, learning things as I go."

"Dr Zunino said you would remember." His tone grew stricter. "And I believe her. The chances of you not remembering anything at all are out of the question."

"But what if—"

"Vittoria." He fixed me with his gaze. "You will remember."

I went stiff. Why was this topic so sensitive to him? I would have asked, but he seemed on edge, and I didn't want him to become even more annoyed with me.

Crossing my arms, I turned to the window, watching the mountains and sea pass by.

"Are you mad at me?" he asked, his tone quiet and gentle, unlike before.

I wasn't mad at him, but I was upset. I wished he hadn't spoken to me the way he had.

"Vittoria?"

I shifted my knees closer to the door when he suddenly gripped my left knee and yanked it towards him. I looked at him, but he kept his eyes on the road, tightening his grip on my bare knee.

It was a hot day, and it intensified the warmth of his touch, making the discomfort almost unbearable. Yet, despite this, I made no move to remove his hand, staying still. I liked it there. I wanted it to stay there for the entire ride.

I felt . . . owned. By *him*. And the feeling . . . excited me.

"Are you mad at me?" he repeated.

If I answered, would he remove his hand?

Not willing to risk it, I covered his hand with mine, making sure he couldn't pull it away unless needed.

"No," I said. "I'm not."

His hand stayed on my knee, moving only to change gears until we reached our destination. Natalie's navy-blue house, small and nestled near the sea with no neighbouring houses in sight, looked more like a cabin than a typical house.

Ettore opened the door for me and offered his hand. As our fingers touched, he helped me out. His touch lingered for a moment before releasing my hand to close and lock the car.

Come on, I urged. *Hold my hand.*

Or maybe it was my turn now? I was the first to brush my finger against his when we were on the roof. Then he placed his hand on my knee, keeping it there for the rest of the ride. It seemed only fair if I made the next move, like holding hands. Yet, I hesitated.

"Natalie lives here alone?" I asked, tentatively moving my fingers towards his. I still wasn't sure about any of this, but since it was my turn to make a move . . . As I looked down, I saw him doing the same, and for a second our fingers brushed.

Before he could answer, the front door flung open, and Natalie came running towards us. We withdrew our hands at the same time.

"I'm so glad you didn't get lost on the way!" She hugged Ettore first before turning to me for a quick embrace. "So?" With her hands on her hips, she stood proudly in front of the house. "What do you think?"

I glanced back at the strikingly blue sea metres away from us, much like at our place. But her house was smaller than our villa, with a cosier vibe and it was more secluded.

"I think it's amazing, Nat," Ettore said.

"Vittoria?" Natalie's hopeful gaze turned to me. "What do you think?"

I smiled. "Can we trade houses?"

She laughed as a faint smile touched Ettore's lips.

"Don't expect much from the inside." Natalie led the way as we followed her. "I've just moved in and I'm too busy to decorate it properly, but I will someday."

As we approached the stairs, Ettore paused and offered his hand to help me up the three steps to her porch. Going up, I unintentionally met Natalie's gaze. There was something in her expression that unsettled me, but I brushed it off. It was probably nothing.

"Dinner will be served soon," she announced. "But first, please remove your shoes. This isn't your villa. I don't have a housekeeper, and I didn't buy this house to clean the floor every day."

She disappeared to the right, leaving us to take off our shoes. I unclasped my Mary Janes, slipped them off my feet, and neatly placed them by the wall. Ettore took longer to remove his shoes. Out of politeness, and not wanting to be alone with Natalie, I waited for him.

"I miss the villa already," he joked.

As I clasped my hands in front of me, I surveyed the navy-blue hallway. "The villa is a bit too big for me." I smiled at the sight of two paintings of a white and a ginger cat on the wall across from me. "I like it here better."

The villa had more rooms than two people needed, and I never felt completely safe, not even in my own room. Only a week ago, a cat's skull had been standing in my bathroom, like a haunting nightmare.

Ettore opened his mouth to speak, but before he could, Natalie shouted, "Are you two coming or not?"

I followed Ettore into the living room. A blue couch sat in the centre, with a brown table in front of it. Next to a long square window was a table with three yellow chairs and two plants in the corners.

When Natalie warned us not to expect anything from the inside, I didn't expect it to be completely furnished.

"Please." Natalie appeared from the other room, gesturing towards the table. "Take a seat."

"Okay." Ettore approached the table set with three plates and neatly arranged cutlery. He lifted a chair. "Thank you."

He pretended to leave, and a chuckle escaped me. Natalie rolled her eyes. "So dad of you," she muttered as she disappeared into the kitchen.

Smiling, Ettore put the chair back. I settled into my seat and gazed through the window, taking in the picturesque view of the beach. They might have thought my suggestion to switch houses was a joke, but . . . I truly wished it could happen.

"It's so beautiful here," I thought aloud, and Natalie poked her head out of the doorway. Seizing the opportunity, I couldn't resist asking, "How much did it cost?"

"My year's worth of salary," she answered. "I've been saving up ever since I started my interior design business."

Interior design business?

If Ettore's mother was in SQ, did Natalie also work for it? She might have used her interior design business to cover her real job. I could be wrong, and Natalie might actually be a designer, but if her brother worked for SQ, why wouldn't she? Their entire family was likely part of the organisation. It would make sense if Natalie was also involved.

"Liar," Ettore accused. "You've been travelling more than saving up."

Natalie's eyes narrowed. "What if I was? I still got my own place, didn't I?"

I held back a smile, pressing my lips together.

Ettore sighed in resignation. "Yes, you did."

"And now I'll be serving beef stew to my first ever guests!" she announced cheerfully. "You should feel honoured." With that, she disappeared back into the kitchen and returned with a pot a minute later.

I stood. "Do you need help?"

"Absolutely not." She placed the pot on the wooden coaster, and I took my seat again. "You're my guests, and today, I shall serve you." Speaking in a posh British accent, she playfully bowed before heading back to the kitchen. She returned with a plate of bread and set it down. With a flourish, she uncovered the pot. "Voila!"

A rich aroma wafted out, and I breathed in deeply, savouring the scent. My taste buds tingled in anticipation. I couldn't wait to taste it.

"Vittoria." She motioned towards the pot. "Please."

I preferred not to serve myself first with them watching, but their expectant gazes gave me no choice. Hesitating slightly, I scooped some of the hot stew onto my plate.

"Get some bread as well," Natalie encouraged.

As I added a piece to my plate, they didn't hesitate to fill their own plates with food.

"If it's bad, kindly keep it to yourself," Natalie quipped, holding her spoon near her lips. "I'd much rather live in the illusion that it's the most delicious dish on earth."

I blew on my spoon before bringing it to my mouth. As it touched my tongue, eliciting unexpected pleasure, I closed my eyes in delight. A quiet moan escaped before I could stop it. I covered my mouth, my cheeks burning with embarrassment as their laughter filled the room.

"Is it that good?" Ettore asked.

I swallowed before answering. "It's amazing."

Sofia's cooking was still the best, but Natalie's beef stew exceeded all my expectations. It was perfect.

"Are you a chef at a restaurant, by any chance?" I asked Natalie.

"Oh, stop it." Natalie waved it off. "You're making me blush."

"But it's amazing." I took a sip of water. "This beef stew deserves five stars, if not more."

The answering smile didn't leave Natalie's face as she ate. After finishing, I savoured the lingering taste of the meal in my mouth, not wanting it to ever go away. Natalie leant back, hand on her stomach, while Ettore seemed content sipping his water.

Sensing it was a good time to discuss changing the colour of my rooms, I prepared to speak, but Natalie was faster.

"Ah!" She raised her finger, as if recalling something important. "Have you chosen your outfit for tomorrow?"

She stared at me expectantly, but I had no clue what she meant.

I glanced at Ettore for help, but he was giving Natalie a subtle warning look, though she appeared unaware.

What was that about?

I let out an awkward chuckle. "Do I have to be somewhere?"

"You don't know about Raff's show?" she said incredulously, as if expecting me to know, but my obvious cluelessness made it clear I didn't. "Please, don't tell me this is news to you."

"What show are we talking about?"

She swatted Ettore's arm. "Why didn't you tell her?"

He said nothing.

"Such idiots," Natalie muttered as she leant forward to grab a bottle of wine. She offered to pour it into my glass, but I declined. After rolling down the hill and ending up in the hospital, I was done with drinking.

She poured it into her glass instead. "Every year, there is a boxing match where Raff competes against one of the world's most renowned boxers. So far, he's won three times in a row," she explained. "Do you know what you're going to wear?"

Boxing didn't interest me, but that wasn't the only reason why I didn't want to go. It was Raffaele's show, and we didn't really get along. But did I have a choice not to go?

"No."

"Perfect, because neither do I." She stood with her glass of wine. "Let's go, Vittoria. Maybe we'll find something for you in my wardrobe. Ettore can do the dishes while we're at it."

Ettore frowned. "Didn't you say we were—"

"Na-ah," she interjected, putting up her finger. "*Vittoria* is my guest. You're my brother, who failed to inform your wife about her brother's most anticipated day of the year."

"But if they don't want me there . . ." I started, earning a warning look from Natalie, as if asking what nonsense I was spouting. "If they don't want me there, maybe I shouldn't go."

"Nonsense." She walked towards the hallway and paused by the door, waiting for me to follow. "You have to get out of the villa more often. You need to see new places that could help your memory," she said as I stood to join her. "Ettore should have said something. You've never missed the show before. It's our tradition. We go to the casino after. You've always enjoyed it, and I'm sure you'll like it this year too."

The more I hung out with people, the stronger the pressure to remember my past life became. After everything I had learnt, I didn't want to remember at all, but again, that wasn't an option.

Unease gnawed at me at the thought of going where I wasn't invited. Raffaele might be my brother, but we didn't speak, and he had made it clear he didn't like me. Why would he want to see me on his special day? Wouldn't it ruin his mood if I came?

"I don't think I should go if I wasn't invited."

"No one is invited." Natalie laughed as we climbed the stairs.

"We're all expected to come, but I'm surprised no one even mentioned it to you. They could have forgotten, I suppose. You know how men are."

She opened the single door on the second floor, and I followed her inside. Her bedroom radiated with brightness, dominated by shades of blue and yellow. It was much smaller than mine, with furniture almost touching, but it felt cosier.

She opened the wardrobe. "Do you think you'll find something to wear in your wardrobe?"

I remembered the few clothes I had left after disposing of most, especially the dark ones I'd never wear. I couldn't understand why I had accumulated so many of them. We lived in sunny and vibrant Nice. Why would I dress as if going to a funeral?

It also didn't help that I disliked dark colours. With such limited options, finding something to wear every day was a struggle. Today, as usual, I settled for a simple white shirt and a red dress.

At least Sofia did laundry often, and I could wear the same clothes many times a week.

"I don't think so," I replied. "I don't have many clothes I would like to wear."

She eyed me. "I assume you're extra small. I'm a bit taller than you, and most of my clothes are tailored for me, but let's see . . . Maybe we'll find something for you in my donation bag."

She squatted down and brought out a bag, unzipping it. From

inside, she pulled out a wrinkled white shirt.

"Ah! This has a few creases, but maybe you'd like it?"

I regarded it with doubt. I already owned several white shirts and wore them often, like now.

She took note of my shirt. "One more to add to your collection?" she suggested jokingly.

I responded with a small smile.

She tossed it aside. "Let's see if there are more formal clothes here."

As she rummaged through the bag, tossing clothes onto the floor, I felt awkward standing there doing nothing. Wanting to be helpful, I picked up the clothes and neatly folded them on the bed.

A long silence settled in the room. Suddenly, I became aware of Natalie staring at me, confusion written all over her face. "Are you cleaning up after me?"

I released the jeans, bringing my hands behind my back. "I'm sorry."

She burst out laughing. "That's interesting. But don't be sorry. Do whatever you want."

I hesitated before sitting on the edge of the bed, where I continued to fold the jeans.

"I'm redecorating my room," I admitted at last.

She turned her head away from the red polka-dot skirt dangling between her hands. Although the skirt caught my attention, I stayed silent. Natalie most likely wouldn't have minded if I showed some excitement, but I found myself holding back, even if she was nothing but kind to me.

"That's awesome!" She handed me the skirt. "You can take this."

I accepted it from her, hiding my joy.

"What are you changing in your room?" she asked.

I ran my hands over the skirt. Its colour matched my wig perfectly. This might be the first piece of clothing I was excited to try on and possibly wear.

"Almost everything."

She stopped going through the bag. "Almost everything?"

"I would like to, at least. I don't like the bathroom. It's too dark for me. I'd like to change the walls and maybe the floor, but Ettore is sceptical. I'm sure I want the changes because I feel awful every time I enter it. I want to get out of there as soon as I step inside."

"That's no problem."

I watched her, not sure what she meant.

She proceeded to explain. "It's just a bathroom. You don't lack money. If you remember and end up regretting the changes, you can always do another renovation. It's no big deal."

But I wasn't convinced. "Do you think you can convince Ettore to be more open to the idea?"

"I'll try, and if he doesn't agree, we will change your bathroom anyway. I'll make sure of it." She offered me a smile, and I couldn't help but reciprocate it. "Do you like the skirt?"

"I love it."

"You're in luck then." She reached into the bag. "I used to adore polka patterns and had a closet full of polka dot clothes." She pulled out something green, letting the clothing sway between her hands as she held it out for me to see. "I think you'll love this. It's perfect for the casino. What do you think?"

It was a long, dark green dress dotted in white. It might not fit me perfectly, but I liked what I saw.

"What if I told you I also want to repaint my bedroom?"

Her smile widened. "I would say, hand me the paint and the brush, and I'll do it for you. The grey depresses me. I'm surprised you can still smile."

A genuine laugh escaped me for the first time in a while.

"Hmm . . ." She stood. "Why don't you try on the clothes you like while I go talk to Ettore about your project?"

"Really? You would do that for me?"

"Of course. You're my sister-in-law."

My heart warmed at her words. *Her sister-in-law.* Maybe my family wasn't as bad as I thought. I could see why Ettore hesitated to call his family as part of the cult when they were all so loving and caring with one another.

Maybe it was only a matter of time before I would feel comfortable among them and consider myself one of them.

"I'll be back in a few minutes," she said before she left.

In the quiet of the room, I slid into the red skirt and twirled in front of the mirror. The fabric spun with me, and I felt a rush of affection for it. I *loved* it. Then, I slipped into the dress, and to my surprise, it hugged me like a second skin. The short sleeves draped over my shoulders, and as I spun, half of the skirt swirled around me while the other half clung to my hips. I had never worn a dress that bared my shoulders, but it was beautiful. I didn't want to take it off.

And I didn't, hoping for Natalie to return and see me in it, but she was taking longer than a few minutes. After waiting a bit longer, I gave up and went downstairs. I searched the living room and the kitchen, but no one was there. As I continued exploring, I came across a door with a window. Peeking outside, I saw Natalie and Ettore smoking on the veranda.

"Are you sure?" Ettore asked, the cigarette burning between his fingers.

"Yes, expect the call in the next two days," Natalie replied.

They were discussing something else, not my project. But I didn't want to eavesdrop on anything I shouldn't. The last time I had, my whole perspective on life changed, making me never want to remember anything from my past.

I turned on my heel and returned to Natalie's bedroom, deciding to keep waiting for her there.

August 26, 1965

I missed work today.
I overslept.
When I woke up in the hotel room with a hangover, I realised my mistake. I knew I shouldn't have partied, or if I did, I should have been more responsible.
But there is nothing I can do now.
I'm afraid of the consequences. I can pretend that I forgot, but I will get punished either way. But I'm Vittoria Galletti, and Lorence Galletti is my father.
Nothing bad will happen to me.
Or at least, I hope not.

27
The Missing Scientist

Ettore

THE LAST TIME I STOOD IN THE SAME ROOM WITH THE SUPERIORS, IT WAS WHEN I RECEIVED THE SCAR THAT WOULD LAST FOR A LIFETIME. This time, Mother called me early in the morning, telling me to be in Monte Carlo for their meeting.

I hadn't felt excited about a meeting in a long time. The last time was when I was fifteen and didn't fully understand what my first mission would cost me.

Unexpected as it was, the call came as a relief. If I hadn't got it before Raff's show, I couldn't have relaxed, always thinking about what Natalie had shared with me.

As the superiors gathered around a large round table, Natalie, Raff, and I took seats along the wall.

Lorence and Mother entered last. Mother settled into her seat, while Lorence stood in front of the table and placed the folder he had brought. "Now that we're all here, thank you for coming on such short notice," he began. "As some of you may know, Julien Martin's case has taken an unexpected turn. Our crime investigator,

Natalie Cosette, uncovered shocking evidence suggesting that one of the scientists may have survived the Fire."

No one reacted, perhaps because everyone already knew the meeting's agenda. As far as I was aware, the superiors always had some information beforehand.

Lorence opened the folder and withdrew a picture. "Please, take a closer look at this." He passed it to Mia.

Mia leant in, inspecting it closely. "This can't be real," she said, her voice filled with wonder.

She handed it to Vivianne, who snorted at the sight before passing it to Bastien. He stayed impassive and silent, handing it to Mother.

"What do you see, Sybille?" Lorence inquired.

She stared at the picture for a few seconds longer before placing it on the table. "A girl shyly smiling at the camera as she holds her graduation certificate."

"Does she look like someone you know?" Lorence pressed further.

After another long look at the picture, Mother leant back, her expression revealing nothing. "No," she replied calmly, "this is my first time seeing her."

I was curious to see the picture. But I needed to be patient. If everything went as planned and they assigned me a new case, then I could look at the picture as much as I wished.

Lorence extended his hand towards her. "May I?"

Mother handed him the picture, and he pushed it in front of Mia with two fingers. "What do you see, Mia?"

"I see a girl who looks just like Vittoria Galletti."

A significant silence fell over the room until Lorence gestured towards Natalie. "Natalie, could you please stand up and present your case?"

"With pleasure." Natalie stood, and Lorence sat down. "Yesterday, I spoke with Julien Martin. Prior to that, I reviewed the information obtained from him when Raffaele Galletti and Ettore Cosette Morrano found him in his apartment. Julien claimed he received a letter from Vittoria. She requested him to deliver the batches of the Cure to the harbour. However, we know that couldn't have happened. Vittoria was in a coma when he supposedly received the letter, and she has remembered nothing since waking up. Additionally, we know he was obsessed with Vittoria from his paintings of a red-haired girl. But what if it was never Vittoria, but someone who looked like her?"

Bastien's eyebrows rose in curiosity, while Mia leant in, eager to hear more. The rest of the room showed no emotion.

Natalie continued, "I recalled the photos we took of every alleged scientist who worked in the abandoned hotel, and I remembered this one girl who looked like my sister-in-law. When I showed the picture to Julien Martin, I asked him if perhaps it wasn't Vittoria who had visited him but Teodora Sauvage?"

"Teodora Sauvage?" Bastien echoed.

"Sauvage?" Mia said. "Isn't that . . . ?"

"Yes," Lorence confirmed. "Teodora Sauvage is believed to be Morgana's niece."

"*Merde*," Vivienne laughed, both in disbelief and amusement.

Morgana's name was rarely spoken, and when it was, it was on special occasions. I had never met her face-to-face, only heard stories. Morgana Sauvage was a formidable woman whom no one dared to cross. Yet, she played a key role in rebuilding SQ after my uncle Maxime's betrayal. If she hadn't given us the name of the scientist who created the disease known as the Rash, SQ might not even exist today.

If Teodora Sauvage turned out to be Morgana's niece *and* a scientist who contributed to an alternative version of the Cure, we wouldn't know what to do if we found her. Killing her seemed like the obvious choice, but if Morgana found out that we had taken her niece's life, SQ would lose its most crucial ally and informant.

"What did Julien say?" Mia prompted.

"If you look at the picture and compare it with Vittoria," Natalie said, moving closer and placing Vittoria's picture in front of her, "you'll see they're not exactly the same. But at first glance, they look like they are."

Mia inspected the pictures, comparing them. "Yes, I see. Teodora's eyes are slightly bigger, and Vittoria has more freckles on her face."

"Two of the distinct differences, yes," Natalie said, straightening up. "After staring at the picture for a while, Julien confirmed she might be the woman who entered his apartment and introduced herself as Vittoria Galletti."

Mia clapped her hands excitedly. "Isn't that something?"

Natalie half-smiled. "Quite indeed, Miss Quintana."

"Is that everything, Natalie?" Lorence inquired.

"Yes, sir."

"Thank you for the impeccably delivered information," Lorence acknowledged. "You may return to your seat now."

She lowered her head in a reverent nod. "Always at your service, sir."

As Natalie returned to her seat, Lorence stood up. "Given the new evidence and suspicions that one of the scientists might still be alive, I believe we can all agree that we need to find her."

"Are you suggesting she's out there making the Cure from the batches she received?" Sybille asked in disbelief.

"We don't know," Lorence replied. "We can't be certain if she's alive. If we were, that would mean trusting Julien Martin, who betrayed us. However, we can't dismiss the possibility entirely. It would cost us dearly in the future if we didn't take action to find her now."

"She might also be one of the scientists who discovered the

alternative version of the Cure," Vivienne suggested, as she analysed the contents of the folder. "According to this, Teodora Sauvage was born to a drug addict, Lizette Sauvage. The father is unknown. She also has a nine-year-old sister, Lilou Sauvage. They could be half-sisters if their mother had multiple partners," she remarked. "Teodora left France at the age of fifteen and went to study medical science at Oxford University. She graduated four years later, despite the usual six-year duration of the program."

"A wunderkind," Mia remarked, her tone impressed.

"She was spotted in Monte Carlo a few days before the Fire," Vivienne went on. "But it's because we were looking into who would be at the hotel that night. It says she had long, curly red hair, hazel eyes, and freckles, like Vittoria Galletti."

"But she's just a twenty-one-year-old girl," said Mother. "Is she really capable of everything we accuse her of?"

It was unusual for Mother to doubt someone's crimes just because they were young. I was yet to see Teodora Sauvage's picture, but I believed she was capable of manipulating our scientist into committing treason. Growing up among cunning, powerful women, I never doubted their potential. Women could start wars as easily as they could end them.

"As Mia pointed out, the girl is a wunderkind," Vivienne asserted. "I wouldn't underestimate her. She seems harmless, but she was one of the scientists involved in creating the Cure. We can't allow her to roam freely with information that could destroy us—

for good this time."

She paused, giving everyone a moment to recall Maxime's betrayal, the one no one had spoken about since it happened. No wonder. My uncle had sold every well-guarded secret to foreign authorities and was now living comfortably somewhere under a false name. He was our family's greatest shame and SQ's most notorious back-stabber. If anyone ever saw him again, he would be killed.

Vivienne rose to her feet. "We should vote. Those in favour of looking for her, please stand."

Lorence remained standing. Mia and Bastien joined him, and Mother hesitated before standing as well.

"It's settled," Vivienne declared, then directed her attention to me and Raff. "Welcome to your new mission, boys."

28
Raff's Show

Teodora

THE VENUE BUZZED WITH SUCH COMMOTION THAT IT FELT AS THOUGH MY HEAD MIGHT IMPLODE.

This morning, I found another gardenia waiting for me. Ettore was nowhere to be found, and neither was Sofia. Later in the day, Natalie called to inform me she would drive me to Raff's show.

Once we arrived, I felt out of place among the crowd dressed in leather jackets and casual clothes—the complete opposite of Natalie and me. Natalie looked stunning in a black short dress layered over a transparent black-dotted shirt with puffy sleeves, while I felt better suited for a classy restaurant in the dark green dress she had given me.

Natalie tugged at my wrist, urging me forward. I glanced up at the rows of seats and the stairs, hoping that was where we were going. Being too close to the boxing ring made me uneasy. As we pressed on past the stairs, pushing through the crowd towards the first row, tension settled in my body.

"It's okay," Natalie reassured me. "You're not the one fighting tonight. But I suppose it's more of a misfortune than a blessing for you."

Imagining fighting someone for the sake of enjoyment made my skin crawl. How could anyone derive pleasure from participating in or even witnessing such brutality?

But I was being stupid. The crowded venue was the perfect example that anything could be entertainment, even watching people fight until they bled.

"Aren't we overdressed?" I asked.

Natalie's lips curved into a faint smile. "No, we're dressed the way we should. Most people here are less fortunate than us. Dressing up asserts our authority and status."

A wave of discomfort swept through me.

I didn't like it. I didn't like the idea of people thinking I was better than them and resenting me for it. We weren't royals. We weren't more special than anyone else. Yet, here we were, feeling the need to prove our superiority through playing dress-up?

Suddenly, I felt a deliberate pinch on my bottom. I glanced back, locking eyes with the bald man. Disgust churned in my stomach as he smirked. Then he turned away and proceeded up the stairs, leaving me feeling both immensely disgusted and embarrassed.

"Here we are," Natalie said, settling into her seat gracefully, clueless of what had happened to me. "If you want, you can sit next to me," she added with a hint of humour, clearly aware that it was the only available seat.

I sat down reluctantly, clutching my purse in my lap, still shaken. I wanted to punch the man and cry at the same time. But the latter urge proved stronger as I battled back tears. I killed people for a living, yet here I was, struggling not to cry over a stranger grabbing my behind.

If I were the Vittoria everyone claimed I was, I would have hit him when I had the chance, but I didn't. Why didn't I?

"Vee!"

I was still in my chair when Barbara hugged me, catching me off guard. I failed to respond, but she didn't seem to notice as she pulled away and took a seat beside me, much to my dismay.

Kill me already.

"I thought I'd find you here," she said, sweeping her hair away from her shoulder. "Didn't you receive my calls?"

I couldn't stand being around Barbara right now. I needed a moment to compose myself. The only place I could go to without raising suspicion was the restroom, but I had no idea where it was. Even if I did, I would have had to push through the crowd again. And if someone had grabbed my butt, what would stop someone else from trying something worse when I was all alone?

I had no choice but to stay and act like I hadn't been ignoring Barbara's calls to avoid meeting her. I could ask Sofia not to pass on her calls, but dodging her at social events was impossible, wasn't it?

"No," I replied with a forced smile. "I didn't."

Natalie shot me a suspicious glance, aware of my lie. She of all people knew it wasn't easy to pry me away from the villa.

"That's unfortunate," Barbara said, feigning disappointment. "It seems you're as healthy and well as I am." She leant in and whispered in my ear, "We were lucky to avoid catching the Rash."

I stiffened, sensing Natalie's curiosity. I hadn't told anyone about the sick people ambushing the cafe. Partly because if they were keeping secrets from me, why shouldn't I keep secrets from them? And partly because I expected to get infected.

SQ spread a dangerous disease, and it appeared they were the only ones who could cure it. I wanted to experience the illness myself to understand how bad it was and what drove people to intentionally infect others.

"Anyway, we should make plans," Barbara continued, her face brightening. "I have this charity event coming up—"

"Ettore!" Natalie interrupted, standing up and raising her hand. "Over here!"

Once my eyes found Ettore making his way towards us, I lost all sense of my surroundings. A lock of his untamed hair fell over his eye—a sight that never failed to make me smile.

He never failed to make me smile.

His presence alone melted away my tension, and suddenly,

nothing else mattered. Not the man who had grabbed my butt and got away with it. Not our proximity to the boxing ring. Not even the possibility of Barbara being his lover while pretending to be my friend. When he was around, I felt safest.

As he stopped in front of us I snapped back to reality, noticing his attire: a white jacket and shirt paired with a green waistcoat that perfectly matched my dress. Could he have known what I was wearing? If so, why would he choose to match me if our marriage existed solely to please SQ?

He acknowledged us with a nod. "Hello, ladies."

Barbara giggled, extending her hand as if she expected him to bow and kiss it.

My tension returned as I waited for his reaction, but he either didn't notice her hand or pretended not to.

"This event has been unusual so far, don't you think?" he remarked, looking around.

Barbara awkwardly withdrew her hand and looked away, trying to act as if nothing had happened. I caught myself feeling a little sorry for her, even if I shouldn't. Awkward encounters happened to everyone, but finding out that your friend befriended you only for your title was much worse. She could deal with this.

Natalie furrowed her eyebrows. "The match hasn't even started."

"I know, but . . ." He flashed a dimple as he shrugged his shoulders. "It feels different tonight."

A sense of foreboding crept into my chest, but I pushed it aside. Ettore could be messing with us, speculating, or he might know something we didn't. But one thing was certain—he was in an unusually good mood.

"Ladies and gentlemen!" A voice boomed over the crowd, drawing my attention to the boxing ring. A man stood in the centre, speaking into a microphone he was holding. "Are you ready for our annual boxing event?"

The crowd erupted in cheers and whistles as Natalie and Ettore took their seats. I winced, not used to such deafening noise.

"The enthusiasm is through the roof!" the announcer exclaimed. "Shall we begin?"

People yelled in response, their loud voices making me wish I had worn something to cancel out the noise.

"Alright, alright. I feel your excitement." The announcer chuckled. "Ladies and gentlemen, introducing first, weighing in at ninety-five kilograms, with an impressive record of ten wins and three losses, Giulio Morquez from Italy!" He extended his hand to his left.

Lights shone on the bulky man as he approached the ring with his entourage. Giulio climbed into the ring, raising his hands in the air and prompting even more applause from the crowd. As he took his place in the left corner, the excitement in the venue barely subsided.

"Yes, we *all* love Giulio," said the announcer. "Coming to the ring now is Monaco's favourite, weighing in at ninety kilograms, with a record of three consecutive wins and only one loss. Give it up for Raffaele Galletti, also known as Brutal Raff!"

The crowd went wild.

The sudden uproar hurt my eardrums, and I pressed my hands against my ears. Raff emerged from the opposite side and made his way towards the ring, moving slower than Giulio. Along the way he paused to sign autographs for fans, on paper or their body parts. Barbara laughed, finding it amusing, but Natalie shook her head in disapproval.

"Typical Raff," she mumbled, though a hint of amusement tinged her tone.

Everyone adored Raff, but they despised me. What made us so different?

A man behind Raff nudged him forward. As Raff entered the ring and beamed, the audience erupted with even more enthusiasm. Among them, female fans screamed declarations like, 'I'll be your wife, Raff!' and 'I'll give you children, Raff!'

They made *me* blush, but Raff revelled in them, basking in the adoration of his fans.

Would it last if he lost? Didn't it put more pressure on him? Or maybe it was the opposite, fuelling him with more motivation to win?

As Raff settled into the opposite corner, preparing for the fight,

I studied the two men.

Giulio had a strong, muscular body, with veins visible on his arms, while Raff, although fit, didn't have as large muscles. Raff's three victories and only one loss must have earned him his fans' love. Or it was his charm that stole their hearts. But in this male-dominated audience, I doubted they would cheer for him just because of his charm. Not in a sport like this. After all, people called him Brutal Raff for a reason.

I leant closer to Natalie and asked, "Is there a place where I can make a bet?"

Before the fight, I overheard people bragging about how much money they'd bet without saying who they were betting on.

Natalie narrowed her eyes. "Are you going to bet against Raff?"

Bet against Raff? "No, I wouldn't bet against my brother."

Natalie waved it off as if it didn't matter. "We don't bet on or against our family. It's off-limits."

"Why?"

"It could cause unnecessary conflict, and the last thing we need is tension within our circle."

I suspected she was referring to SQ, not our family. More than ever, I was convinced Natalie was also involved with SQ. She was born into the cult, with Ettore as her brother and her parents being criminals. But if she was indeed involved and didn't lie about her career as a designer, how did she juggle it with her criminal life and also travelled?

If she *was* working for the organisation, it couldn't entail killing people. I couldn't imagine her doing that. But I could be mistaken.

"Why are you staring at me like you're trying to read my mind?" she asked, snapping me out of my speculations.

Instead of immediately looking away to avoid suspicion, I responded with a warm smile. "You look gorgeous, Natalie."

Natalie laughed as if I had told the funniest joke, but her laughter quickly faded when she saw I wasn't laughing along.

"You're serious?" She pressed her hand to her chest. "Whoa. Who are you, and what have you done to Vittoria Galletti?"

I chuckled softly. While I might have complimented her to distract her from the real reason I had been staring at her, I hadn't lied. Natalie truly was the most beautiful woman in the venue, and it wasn't because she had dressed up. She didn't have to try. Even in casual clothes with no makeup, she would have been the prettiest woman here.

Giulio and Raff met in the middle of the ring, tapping their gloves together. The gesture looked familiar. I tried to recall if I had ever seen a boxing match before.

Natalie lightly touched my arm. "Thank you," she said.

Before I could say anything, the voice came through the speakers. "First round begins . . ."

"*. . . now!*"

The crowd roared in response, and a hand slipped away from mine. I looked up at the woman with flowing red hair.

"Can you stay here for a bit, Dora?" she asked. "Mommy will be back soon."

Completely captivated by her beauty, I couldn't look away. I believed in my heart that she would return soon, reassuring myself that I would be fine. I would watch the two men fight while covering my ears from the head-splitting shouts.

"Okay," I said.

She smiled at me before turning away and disappearing into the crowd. I hugged myself, already missing her and wishing she would come back now.

As time passed, people began to notice me. Without parental supervision and all alone. A man not too far away kept his gaze fixated on me, refusing to look away. I avoided meeting his eyes, focusing instead on the fighting men. But I couldn't help but glance at the man every once in a while, checking if he was still staring.

He was.

He smirked.

He started to move in my direction.

My heart raced as I scanned the crowd, desperately searching for Mommy, but she was gone. Panic set in as I debated whether I should wait for her or flee. If I left, she might never find me again. The thought of losing her forever scared me. I loved my mum. She was the most beautiful woman. I wanted to look just like her when I grew up.

Someone grabbed my hand, and I froze in place.

"Dora?"

My aunt's voice cut through my panic, and I almost melted from the surge of relief that flooded over me.

I lifted my head at my aunt, but before I could utter a word, she spoke, "Let's go."

With determined steps, she pulled me away from the spot where Mommy had told me to stay.

"I can't leave," I protested. "Mummy won't find me."

"It's okay. She told me to come and get you."

Come and get me? *Mommy had told me to stay here. "But—"*

"I'll get you ice-cream. Do you want ice-cream?"

I threw a glance back, searching for Mommy, but she was nowhere in sight. Defeated and with a weeping heart, I reluctantly looked away. "Yes, I want ice-cream."

I wanted Mommy more, but something inside me whispered it wasn't—

"Someone help!"

I zoomed back to the present, recognising the familiar yet different surroundings. My face felt damp, and when I touched it, my fingers came away wet. *Tears.*

"Please!" came a desperate cry.

I whipped my head around, searching for the source of the voice. And there she was, the woman from upstairs, frantically waving her hands. "I think this man is dead!"

August 30, 1965

I faced the consequences.
One month of house arrest. What am I supposed to do here for so long, confined within these four walls?
At first, I thought it wasn't so bad. I could leave anytime and be careful without anyone seeing me, but then they assigned me a guard. Not even a sexy one, but a bald, beefy, and grumpy man who looked like life had hurt him.
That would make two of us.
He's standing outside my door. I feel like I have seen him before, but I'm not sure where.

Anyway, I thought about sneaking out of the window, but men came earlier today and made sure my windows couldn't be opened. Am I supposed to suffocate in my own air?

At least I could leave for work related matters, if they appeared, of course.

But a month stuck in the house with my own thoughts?

People already called me crazy, and I never disagreed. Do they want to drive me even crazier, to the point where I can't be saved?

29

A Dead Man

Ettore

THE VENUE ERUPTED INTO CHAOS—SHOUTS AND GASPS FILLED THE AIR AS PANIC SPREAD LIKE WILDFIRE. I scanned the venue for anyone suspicious, but with the crowd freaking out, spotting the murderer was impossible.

I powered through the crowd to get a closer look.

People were shoving and trampling each other in their frantic attempts to flee, while others stayed, paralysed with shock, unsure if the match had ended or if they were still in danger.

Some backed away from the body in horror, while others gaped at it, frozen with morbid curiosity. When I finally saw the man the girl was screaming about, a chill ran through me. It was Victor, a member of SQ and one of Raff's friends.

I knelt beside the body, inspecting it for any injuries. Apart from the wound bleeding from his side, there was nothing else. Swallowing hard, I stood and carefully descended the stairs.

"What's going on?" Raff's voice broke through the chaos as he jumped down in front of me. "Is someone actually dead?"

I didn't know Victor well. Over the years, I had seen Raff and him together a few times. Once, Victor was stationed outside Vittoria's room when I arrived to collect her for one of our missions. But apart from exchanging greetings, we had never spoken.

Raff hadn't lost a friend before, at least not that I knew of. I wasn't sure how to break the news to him.

"It's Victor," I said quietly, the words catching in my throat like gravel.

I expected him not to hear it over the chaos, but his face drained of colour. "Are you sure?"

I nodded, unable to say it out loud again.

His eyes travelled to where Victor's body lay, his expression a blend of confusion and uncertainty. "How?"

"Someone stabbed him."

"What's happening?" Natalie appeared.

Raff let out a bitter chuckle as if he didn't believe what was happening, raking his fingers through his wet hair. "My friend is dead."

Natalie's eyes widened. "Who?"

"Victor Silveria," I answered.

I didn't see Vittoria right away. She stood behind Natalie, hugging herself as if seeking protection in her own embrace. Suddenly, my jacket felt too hot and heavy. I removed it and gently draped it over her shoulders. As she raised her head, a myriad of emotions swam in her beautiful eyes—emotions I couldn't decipher. Had she been crying?

An intense urge to lift her in my arms and carry her out of here seized me.

She wasn't the Vittoria I'd grown to know, but a stranger who had no idea what was happening around her and why. A stranger who was gradually taking over my heart.

It made no sense.

She wasn't a stranger, of course. She was Vittoria. She looked too much like Vittoria to be someone else. But she also . . . didn't. I had seen the picture of Teodora Sauvage, and she could be standing right in front of me.

But it was absurd.

Or was it?

"People die every day," Raff remarked with a strange, renewed energy. "But this championship doesn't happen every day."

Natalie frowned. "Are you seriously going to continue fighting when your friend died minutes ago?"

"I'll mourn him later," Raff said, his voice hardening. He turned and climbed back into the ring. "I'm not waiting another year to prove my name."

I would have been lying if I said I hadn't expected it from him. Raff was unlike anyone I knew, and it was no surprise he dealt with death in his own mysterious way. If some people weren't fleeing for the exit, I might have agreed with him that death was a part of life and shouldn't stop you from having fun.

Natalie cupped her hands around her mouth and shouted, "You're an idiot, Raff!"

He disregarded her, heading for the announcer. I glanced back towards Victor's body, but two men in black suits were already carrying him out—members of SQ. I would have liked to investigate the body for clues, but it wasn't my job. Even if I did, I doubted it would tell me anything. I already suspected the owner of the *Ele* boat, Teodora Sauvage, was behind this.

But how?

Teodora Sauvage was a scientist who aimed to eradicate SQ, not kill random and insignificant followers.

"Alright, ladies and gentlemen," said the announcer into the microphone, causing some to pause near the exit. "Please return to your seats. We're about to resume the fight!"

Vittoria's eyes widened as she watched people return to their seats as if nothing had happened. It was unsettling, yet sadly normal. In Monte Carlo, public death like this was not uncommon. Although some people left, not everyone could afford to waste their money on a show that had yet to end. They had paid for their tickets, and no death would deter them from staying to witness the rest of the match.

And that was the sad reality we lived in.

Despite Victor's sudden death, it didn't affect Raff's performance. He won, securing nine victories out of twelve rounds.

"He crushed him," Barbara said, wrapping her hand around Vittoria's. "Are you proud of your brother, Vee?"

Vittoria tensed at Barbara's touch, reminding me I had never asked her about her shopping trip with her friends. She hadn't mentioned it either, leading me to assume it hadn't gone well.

"Yes," she answered monotonously. "I'm very proud of him."

She was an awful liar, which was strange. Before the Fire, it was almost impossible to tell when she was lying and when she was telling the truth. Now, it was so easy, one might believe she was a different person.

Natalie walked uncharacteristically silent beside me. I nudged her arm, drawing her attention. "Are you okay?"

She gave me a weak smile. "I was thinking about what Vittoria told me before the first round."

Fear and hope stirred inside me. "What did she say?"

It was typical for Vittoria to be rude to people, but if she was now . . . it was a good sign, right? It would mean Vittoria was coming back, and my absurd suspicion that she was the missing scientist would no longer be valid.

"She complimented me," she said, shattering my hopes. "She

told me I look gorgeous. It's so . . . unlike her."

Everything about Vittoria was unlike her, except for her appearance. But even that changed the more I looked at her. If Teodora Sauvage did walk in front of us, nodding absentmindedly at Barbara's prattle as we inched towards the exit, it wouldn't make much sense. Why would Vittoria abandon the life she cherished and steal the Cure from her own family?

Once we stepped outside, I slipped away to smoke behind a corner. Rubbing my temples, I felt a headache coming on.

Before Raff's show, I had thought deeply about the case. Finding Teodora was nearly impossible without locating her family and threatening them. But how could I get to them when the infamous Morgana Sauvage could be Teodora's aunt?

Morgana was a smart woman, possessing the kind of knowledge SQ could only dream of. Anyone needing detailed information turned to her and paid big money. She had spies everywhere, probably even within SQ. That was why it was crucial that only superiors and those involved knew about this case.

She might be the only one who knew where Teodora was, besides her mother. But before I contacted her, I had to find other ways to locate Teodora without Morgana finding out our plans. SQ would never forgive me if she did.

I had to find her. I would not rest until I did. Teodora Sauvage posed a great threat to us all. If she was creating her own cure and distributing it to other people and countries, no one would fear us as they did now. SQ would be weak again, and it might not recover this time.

I crushed the cigarette butt under my shoe before walking to join the girls on the pavement.

"It will be the most wonderful event of the year," Barbara boasted, "except for my Christmas party, of course."

"Four wins in a row, baby!" Raff exclaimed, appearing out of nowhere and pulling me into a tight hug.

Taken by surprise, I awkwardly patted his back. I couldn't recall if we had ever hugged, but that wasn't what unsettled me the most. Raff might have won another championship, but his elation was alarming. Had he forgotten that someone had killed his friend?

Yet, I still said, "Congratulations, man."

Vittoria's eyes narrowed with disapproval at the scene.

"You kicked Jay's ass!" Barbara punched the air playfully. "And the way you did it was so fucking hot."

Raff pulled away, forgetting about my existence as soon as he laid his eyes on Barbara. "Barbara," he said, his voice smooth as velvet, as he took her hand and kissed it. "I didn't know you were coming. If I had, I'd have put on a better show. Just for you," he drawled with a playful wink.

Natalie rolled her eyes. "Oh my gosh."

It wasn't the first time Raff had used those exact words with a girl. Internally, I also rolled my eyes, but I knew I shouldn't judge.

I had done similar things for the current Vittoria, although it was different. My intentions never involved seducing her into sleeping with me.

Vittoria's disapproving expression morphed into one of confusion. Despite her silence, her emotions were loud and clear. As she noticed me watching her, she glanced down, and I could discern a faint rosiness blooming on her cheeks.

A smile tugged at the corner of my lips.

She's so cute, I want to squeeze her.

"You never stop being a player." Barbara playfully pushed Raff in the chest. "And I love that about you."

"If you spend the night with me, you'll find there's more to love about me," Raff said.

Barbara giggled, and I shook my head. This was nothing new—Raff always charmed women with his smooth words. If only she knew she wasn't so special, she wouldn't be won over so easily.

"So, Vittoria," Raff addressed her.

Vittoria looked at him, uncertainty flickering in her wide eyes.

Were they always this big?

"Did anything jog your memory?" Raff asked.

"Wait until we get to the casino," Natalie interjected. "I can drive you there if you'd like."

But Raff stared at Vittoria, waiting for her answer.

Before the Fire, Vittoria had attended matches, but I didn't think she enjoyed them as much as what came after. She seemed to prefer gambling, despite losing money more often than winning it.

After our visit to her favourite spot, I hadn't expected the boxing match to trigger her memory. Why would she remember something from the boxing match if she couldn't remember her favourite place?

"No," Vittoria replied, wrinkling her nose. "Nothing."

Her tone sounded uncertain. If she had remembered something, why would she lie about it now, especially after already sharing her first and only memory with me?

Raff shrugged and turned to me. "Let's go to the casino?"

I wasn't particularly enthusiastic about the idea. Unlike my friends, I no longer found pleasure in the casino as I once had when life was simpler. Now, I was too stressed to enjoy such things, knowing that a small mistake could lead to severe punishment.

I flashed a fake smile. "Do I have a choice?"

"You don't," he quipped.

Vittoria grimaced.

I could only imagine her silent thoughts as she stood further away, watching instead of joining us, ever since I returned from my smoke break. It seemed as though she didn't feel like she belonged, or perhaps she didn't want to. Either way, it was clear she felt uncomfortable.

If I cared less about what people thought, I would have walked to her, taken her hand, looked into her eyes, and whispered, *"You don't have to worry about a thing as long as you're with me."*

I wanted her to feel at ease or less discomfort because, unfortunately, I cared about her. I always had, but now my feelings were so strong that when work wasn't on my mind, she was all I could think about.

"Did you come here by car, Barbara?" Raff asked.

"No, I took a taxi," she replied. "Are you offering me a ride?"

"Of course, *bella*," he said, placing a hand on the small of her back before casting a glance in my direction. "Are you coming, Ettore?"

"You all go," I said. "I'll take Vittoria with me."

As they sat in their cars and drove away, I took two steps towards Vittoria. She tugged my jacket around herself, avoiding my gaze as she said, "Thank you for the jacket."

I tucked her hair behind her ear, gently brushing my fingers against her cheek. As she looked up at me, I noticed a hint of resigned hopelessness dancing in her eyes.

"Are you upset because of the man who died?" I asked.

"No." She blinked, and when her eyelids opened again, her eyes had glossed over. "But I don't think I am who you think I am."

30

Blackjack

Teodora

"**W**HAT MAKES YOU THINK THAT?" HE ASKED.

I should not have said that.

I shouldn't have brought it up, but ever since the sudden memory—or whatever it was—I'd been struggling with my own thoughts. But what else could it be if not a memory?

"I'm not quite sure," I replied with a faint smile. "It's been a hectic day."

He withdrew his hand from my cheek, and the absence of his touch left me cold. "Are you hiding something?"

Without thinking, I shot him an accusing look. "It's only fair."

He arched his eyebrow. "Why did you say you're not who you think you are? Did you remember something?"

I felt sweat trickle down my armpits. I wanted to share my memory with him, but I was afraid. What if . . .

No, I couldn't think about the *what if*.

"No, I didn't," I said. "It was the match and the death that shook me." I frowned, remembering two men carrying away the body. From what I had seen, it was the same man who had groped me. I could be wrong, but if it was him, I felt less sorry. "I don't think I enjoy watching boxing. It looks so cruel. Did I enjoy it before the Fire?"

His eyebrows drew together thoughtfully. "I'm not sure. I know you definitely enjoyed the casino more. Maybe we should go there before they start without us? What do you think?"

A distraction from the last hour seemed like a good idea. "Yes, I would like that."

As we walked towards his car, I was surprised he believed my half-lie. I didn't consider myself a good liar. Maybe he just didn't want to probe further.

When we were in his car, I asked, "Is Sofia not working for us anymore?"

"I gave her a holiday."

"How long?"

"As long as she needs it."

An unlimited holiday for a housekeeper who kept our house clean and our stomachs full? It didn't sound like a sensible idea unless there was more to it.

"Are you planning to hire someone else to fill in for her in the meantime?" I speculated.

"Do you think there's anyone half as good as Sofia?"

I had a feeling Ettore was hiding something, but I didn't press him further. I now had some secrets of my own, beginning with the diary and ending with the sudden memory.

As we arrived at the impressive white building with its greenish copper roof, unease settled within me. Many expensive cars were parked around the square, their owners most likely inside the building. If it were up to me I would have gone home instead of joining them at the casino, filled with unfamiliar faces.

The door swung open, and Ettore gallantly extended his hand to me. I placed mine in his, and with his help, I stepped out of the car. After he closed and locked the car, he offered his arm, and I looped mine through his.

"This," he whispered close to my ear as we slowly made our way to the casino, "is the gem of Monte Carlo."

I could understand why. The building was the grandest one I had seen in Monte Carlo so far, but it had a clear purpose. I felt uneasy around establishments designed to attract the wealthy, and I wasn't sure why. I was born into a rich family. Being among luxurious structures should feel like–

Can you stay here for a bit, Dora? The woman's voice from the memory echoed. *Mommy will be back soon.*

Why did she call me Dora? Was that a short name for Vittoria? If she was my mum, why did she look nothing like Marie? Why had I never met my aunt? Why had no one mentioned her to me? Was she dead? Nothing made sense.

The only logical explanation was that I wasn't who everyone believed me to be. But how could they confuse me with someone else?

We ascended the stairs and entered the grand hallway through the large doors. Each click of my heels echoed on the polished floor until we stopped at the centre. Tall golden marble columns rose to support the second floor, where elegantly dressed people chatted by the balustrade. As I craned my head at the skylight, the shifting clouds in the night sky created the illusion that I was spinning.

"Anything?" Ettore asked.

A little dizzy, I looked at him, finding his gaze on me instead of the interior.

I gave him a sad smile. "It rings no bell."

A soft smile graced his lips. "It's okay. I didn't expect you to remember."

I scowled. "Your lack of faith in me is comforting."

"I have faith in you, but I try not to expect anything. So that I don't pressure you," he explained, and I couldn't help but feel warmth at his thoughtfulness.

"Should we proceed?" He motioned towards another room.

"Lead the way."

We entered the bustling room, alive with the sounds of clinking coins and laughter. Tables filled the space where people gambled away their money, surrounded by the elegant white and golden decor.

"Don't let your eyes deceive you," Ettore warned, noting my impressed expression. "The place is our family's ruin."

"Or it's where we thrive." Another voice chimed in behind us.

As we turned, Raff stood there, arm-in-arm with Barbara, followed by Natalie. I felt relieved now that Barbara was Raff's problem. Hopefully she would remain so, sparing me from enduring her tedious stories.

"This feels like old times again," Raff said nostalgically, glancing around the tables. "Should we start with blackjack?"

"Yes," Natalie agreed. "It's perfect for warming up."

As we walked, Natalie asked me, "Do you know how to play blackjack?"

If I did, I had no memory of it.

"No," I replied.

"It's simple," Raff said, stopping at a table where people were playing. He cleared his throat, and they hastily rose, scooping up their coins and scurrying away like startled mice. I wanted to reassure them that there was no need to leave, but I held back.

With each encounter like this, I grew more used to our lifestyle. It didn't mean I accepted it, but it was a reality I couldn't change. I heeded Ettore's words, knowing that standing up for my beliefs could be dangerous not only to me but also to him. And the last thing I wanted was to expose him to unnecessary danger.

Raff took a seat at the table. "You get two random cards and decide whether to hit and draw more cards, or stand and keep your current hand. The goal is to get a score of twenty-one or less. If you exceed twenty-one, it's a bust. If your total is twenty-one or less, you hope the dealer's total is lower or above twenty-one. Understand?"

I didn't, not after Raff's explanation.

"I think I should watch you play before I join," I said carefully.

Raff shrugged. "Suit yourself." He slapped four hundred francs on the table. "Barbara, are you going to play?"

"I'll be your cheerleader," she said.

"I don't expect any less from you." He winked at her.

Natalie settled in beside him, pulling out a wallet from her purse. She retrieved two hundred francs and placed it in front of the dealer, who then dealt the cards to them.

Still arm-to-arm with Ettore, I turned my head to him. "You're not playing?"

"Not today."

Raff snorted as he received his two cards. "Not in a year, probably."

"Why?" I asked. "Do you have a gambling problem?"

"No," Ettore answered. "It's related to SQ."

Raff mimed zipping his lips shut, leaving me to guess that it was something I shouldn't be privy to. Once, I might have been displeased, but now . . . maybe it was for the better if I didn't know.

Natalie was dealt two cards, while the dealer had one card face up and one face down.

"Why isn't he showing both of his cards?" I asked.

"To add complexity to the game," Ettore whispered close to my ear, sending a wave of goosebumps across my skin. "Do you know the names of their cards?"

Despite his distracting closeness, I tried to focus on the cards. They all looked familiar, but I couldn't remember their names.

"No," I replied, my voice coming out so quiet, I thought he–

"The dealer has the four of spades," he explained, remaining close as the warmth of his breath spread through every inch of my body. "Raff holds the three of diamonds and the queen of hearts."

"Hit," Raff ordered, and the dealer provided him with the seven of . . .

"The seven of diamonds," Ettore finished for me, "bringing his total to twenty."

Natalie seemed to hesitate, unsure what to do with her five of diamonds and ten of . . . I couldn't remember the names of the black symbols.

I felt a touch against my earlobe, causing me to go still. Realising it was Ettore's lips, my breath hitched. Was it intentional or—

"With the five of diamonds and ten of clubs, she should hit," he whispered.

But she said, "Stand."

Ettore leant away from me, grimacing. Although I could breathe normally again, I still felt the shadow of his lips so close to my ear that he could bite it. Maybe I wouldn't have minded it if he did.

My cheeks warmed at the thought, and I pressed my lips together to hide a smile, hoping once again that no one in the room was a mind-reader.

The dealer's gaze shifted to Raff.

"Stand," Raff declared.

The dealer revealed his card, showing the two of hearts.

"Two of hearts," Ettore said.

"Thank you for your help." I offered him a smile. "But I think I've got the hang of it now."

The dealer drew another card, the king of hearts, then another, which was the four of hearts.

"A push," Ettore mumbled.

I inclined my head towards him. "What's a push?"

"It's when the player and the dealer have the same total. In this case, Raff gets his bet back."

The dealer returned Raff's bet, but Natalie lost hers.

"Didn't you say you were good at betting?" Raff teased.

"*Betting*, not *gambling*." Natalie rolled her eyes. "While I have my lucky days, today might not be one of them. But I do have an idea." She pulled out another two hundred francs, but instead of putting it on the table, she offered it to Ettore.

"I can't," Ettore said.

"Obviously, but if you win, you give the money to me."

Was he forbidden from gambling or something?

Raff laughed. "Are you doing that just so you have a higher chance of winning?"

"No, you idiot. We came here to have fun," she pointed out, "and no one's going to if we don't all play together."

Ettore pulled his hand back from my arm, seeming somewhat reluctant, but I might have imagined that. He accepted the money and joined them at the table, where they each placed their two hundred francs down.

Feeling alone and missing Ettore's warmth, I hugged myself, but my arms couldn't replace the void he left.

Barbara slid closer to me. "I guess we're both going to be their cheerleaders."

Before she could wrap her arms around me and trap me, I plopped onto the seat next to Natalie. "I'm playing too," I declared.

"Your bet?" the dealer inquired.

I hesitated, realising I had left my purse in the car. "I . . . I don't have anything."

Raff threw his head back with a laugh. "You can't play if you have nothing to—"

"It's okay," Natalie interrupted him, reaching for her wallet. "I've got her."

She placed two hundred francs on the table, and I quietly thanked her.

The dealer's hands moved swiftly, distributing cards around the table. Ettore received the ten of diamonds and the queen of clubs, totalling twenty. Raff was dealt a pair of sixes—clubs and diamonds. Natalie's hand consisted of the eight of hearts and the ten of spades, adding up to eighteen. I glanced at my cards: clubs and diamonds. Thirteen. The dealer added a concealed card to his four of clubs.

Ettore chose to stand, while Raff said with a laugh, "Oh, I'm splitting."

My body tensed. *Splitting?* I didn't know about splitting. I should have observed the game a little longer before diving in, just to avoid Barbara's clinginess.

"Stand," Natalie declared firmly.

The dealer's expression remained neutral as his eyes focused on me. I quickly calculated the odds, my heart speeding up with each passing second. But it couldn't have been more than a few seconds before I blurted out, "Hit."

He dealt me the five of hearts, and my total was eighteen.

Not ideal.

Raff hit, adding the jack of hearts to his six of clubs and the king of diamonds to his six of diamonds, resulting in a total of sixteen.

Everyone waited for my decision as I nervously chewed my lip. With the dealer showing the four of clubs, he had a high chance he would get a total between nineteen and twenty-one, meaning I would lose. But if luck was on my side and he went over twenty-one, I would win.

The odds were slim, but the chance of the dealer dealing me less than four was even slimmer.

Steadying my breath, I uttered, "Stand."

Raff stood with his king but persisted in hitting with his jack. He drew the ace of spades and then the three of clubs before he finally decided to stand. His total was twenty.

It was the moment of truth.

The dealer turned over his card, revealing the queen of hearts. Drawing another one, he revealed the queen of diamonds. It was a bust. Everyone ended up winning, and I understood the concept of splitting.

In the following game, I triumphed, doubling my winnings to eight hundred. Perhaps overconfident, I continued betting everything, but I hadn't regretted it yet as I won ten rounds in a row.

As Raff had said, the game was fairly easy. My first win was pure luck, but with each successful play, I gained a better understanding of the game. I even developed a counting system, which had yet to fail me.

"Must be beginner's luck," Raff remarked, sounding a little on edge, which made me smile. "Barbara, come over here for good luck."

Barbara approached him, and Raff's lips curved into a broad smile in anticipation. But she settled on Ettore's knee, wrapping her arms around his neck. Both mine and Raff's smiles dropped.

Ettore drew back in surprise, but his expression quickly became neutral.

My stomach twisted with nausea, and I lost all desire to continue playing. As I contemplated excusing myself to find a restroom, Raff asked, "Another game?"

"I'll pass on this one and grab a drink," Natalie announced as she stood up. "Does anyone need one?"

"Water, if you can," Ettore said.

"Water?" Barbara brushed aside the lock of hair that was covering his face, bringing his attention to her. "Why not go for something a bit . . . stronger?"

I clenched the fabric of my dress tightly, grinding my teeth together.

"He's driving," Raff noted with a hint of annoyance. "I'll have a gin."

"Vittoria?" Natalie asked.

Releasing my grip on my dress, I forced myself to meet her gaze, pretending like nothing was wrong. "Nothing, thank you."

"You sure?" Her eyebrows knitted. "It's been a while since you drank something."

I didn't want anything. Not water. Not food. The mere thought of consuming anything filled me with nausea.

"Yes," I said firmly. "I'm sure."

Natalie regarded me with concern before turning and walking away. I realised too late I should have joined her to spare myself the pain of watching Ettore and Barbara together.

Tears burned at the back of my eyes.

Don't cry, don't cry, don't cry—

"We can start," Raff informed the dealer.

I bet all my money, and everyone except Barbara received new cards. Trying to ignore Barbara in my husband's lap, I couldn't fully focus on the game. The worst part was he didn't seem to care. But his face showed no signs of enjoyment either.

I gave myself a mental shake. I was being naive, grasping at false hope. If he didn't like her in his lap, he would have pushed her away. No matter the pain it brought me, that was the reality.

It was time to give all my focus to the game.

The dealer dealt me the queen of clubs and the nine of diamonds. *Nineteen.* It could have been better. I considered standing, but as I surveyed everyone's cards, trying to count, I lost track. I had lost my focus. I had no clue if I should stand or hit.

I shouldn't have continued playing.

Panic threatened to take over, but I held onto my self-control, knowing that giving in to it would only make things worse.

I couldn't afford to make a wrong decision. Stupidly, I had bet all the money and now I risked losing everything I had earned in the last thirty minutes.

But did I have anything to lose when I had already lost someone no amount of money could replace?

I swallowed, finding my throat dry. *I shouldn't have declined that drink.*

Everyone's stares weighed on me, but I finally made my decision. "Hit," I announced.

Raff snickered before he sang, "Looks like someone's finally losing."

The dealer drew a card from the deck, and I held my breath. If my calculations were correct, I would receive a card valued below three. But if I was mistaken and received a card valued at three or more, it would be a bust.

He flipped over the card, placing it before me.

The two of spades.

Raff's jaw dropped. "What the fuck?"

I should have felt relieved, but it felt like the world was collapsing around me instead. My vision blurred, but it cleared as I blinked.

Everyone else stood with scores below twenty-one. But the dealer scored exactly twenty-one, causing the men to lose. I ended up with a push and received my entire bet back.

Raff clicked his tongue. "Does amnesia come with a talent in blackjack? If so, maybe I should run into a wall with my head?"

"You'd risk a concussion too if you tried," Ettore pointed out.

"Is this a quartet of gamblers I see?" A man's voice sounded behind me.

A cold shudder went through me. *No, not him.*

"What else?" Raff stood, and he and Antoine hugged in the way I typically saw among men. "Why so late? You've missed witnessing my fourth victory. You've missed witnessing me making history!"

Antoine let out a light chuckle. "Work doesn't care about my personal schedule, unfortunately. But congratulations on your victory."

Taking a quiet breath, I placed two hundred francs down for another game.

"Why just two hundred, Vittoria?" Antoine asked with a hint of teasing. "Afraid to lose it all?"

"*Actually*," I replied, my tone sharp, "I haven't lost a single game."

I bit my tongue, refraining from adding the word *prick*.

"*Yet*," Raff emphasised.

"How many games have you played?" Antoine leant forward, a smirk playing on his lips. "Two?"

I tensed as his face came inches away from mine, giving me an uncomfortably close view of his jawline. The scent of his perfume enveloped me like a cloud, once again reminding me of the one Ettore used. By now, I was certain they used the same cologne, but I liked it better on Ettore.

"Fifteen," Ettore interjected. "She played fifteen hands and didn't lose a single one."

I glanced at him for the first time since Barbara had cosied up in his lap. A fluttering feeling burst through me, only to vanish as Barbara affectionately patted his chest. "If you win the next one, I'll . . ." she whispered the rest into his ear.

All the possibilities of what she might have said raced through my mind, sparking my anger. I couldn't keep playing while pretending that it didn't bother me to see my husband being intimate with her in front of everyone. In front of *me*.

I stood up and threw my arms around Antoine, pressing myself against him. "Oh, Antoine . . . you look so handsome tonight."

I felt Ettore's eyes on me.

Confusion flickered across Antoine's face, but soon his charm returned, along with his smirk. "You don't look too bad yourself." He pinched my chin between his fingers. "What do you say if we get out of here?"

I felt sick to my stomach. This was so unlike me.

What was I trying to prove? Antoine could have done terrible things to me while I was unconscious, and yet here I was, throwing myself at him? I was giving him the wrong idea, and he wasn't the type of guy to handle rejection graciously.

"Now?" I asked. "I still have an unfinished game, and I'm very lucky tonight."

Antoine's smirk widened into a grin, taking my words the wrong way. "I have another game in mind for us. You won't get any luckier than that."

I forced a smile. "I'll go to the restroom first," I said, extracting myself from him. "Excuse me."

Pretending to look for the bathroom, I wandered around the casino. Once I was sure they weren't paying attention, I made a beeline for the exit. Never in my life would I go anywhere alone with Antoine. That man was trouble, and not in a charming way.

Since I didn't have a car, and I wasn't sure if I had a driving license, I couldn't leave. Frustration and anger boiled inside me, and the urge to kick something was tempting. But instead, I collapsed onto the fountain's edge, sucking in a sharp breath.

Did I know about Barbara and Ettore before the Fire, or was it a brand new affair? It was one thing seeing her leave his room, but seeing them together and this close . . .

I hated her. I hated *him*.

Tears gathered in my eyes, and I gazed skyward, willing them away.

"That's not the restroom."

I froze. Ettore stood a few steps away with an almost imperceptible smile on his lips. I wanted to slap it away. There was nothing amusing about this.

"Is that who you dreamed of?" My voice came out bitter. "Of *her*?"

His smile faltered, a flicker of recognition passing through his eyes. He knew precisely what I was talking about.

Ever since I had stormed into his bedroom, the memory haunted me, refusing to leave me alone. I doubted it ever would, not as long as my feelings for Ettore existed. But could they ever be gone when we lived under the same roof?

"Barbara is temporary. You yourself once said . . ." He scratched at his nape. "You said before the Fire she and I wouldn't last. If I planned to fall in love, I should pick someone else as she'd move on to the next one before I knew it, leaving me heartbroken. Those were your words."

"Why are you telling me this?"

He knew I couldn't remember a thing. What was the point?

"I . . ." He swallowed, his Adam's apple bobbing. "I'm not sure myself."

If he wasn't lying, and there was nothing serious between him and Barbara, the thought of them together, tangled in bed, still stung. It was almost as painful as my mother abandoning me in the crowd of strangers as a child.

"Are you in love with her?" I asked, my heart pounding as I awaited his response.

"No," he answered, though it provided little relief. "In truth, I've never been in love before."

"Never?" I echoed, incredulous.

He gave me a sad smile. "Never."

The heavy silence hung between us, weighing down on me. Should I say something? Do something? As panic began to rise, he broke the quiet.

"What was that scene with Antoine about?"

"What scene?" I pretended to play dumb.

"Don't play coy. Are you and Antoine a thing?"

"Would it matter to you if we were?"

"Hmm . . ." He tapped his chin thoughtfully. "Would it matter to me if my brother was fucking my wife? It's happened once, maybe even more than once. I should be used to it by now."

Should. "But you're not?"

He was silent, his lips pressed into a thin line and one eyebrow raised, as if mocking.

There was no point in continuing the conversation. I might as well return inside and focus on the game. It was the only thing that could distract my mind.

I stood up, but my vision darkened, and I swayed to the side.

He gripped my arm. "Vittoria?" he asked, his voice tinged with concern. "Are you okay?"

No was on the tip of my tongue, but my vision cleared, and I forcefully yanked my arm from his grasp. I strode towards the casino, determined to get away from him.

"Vittoria!" he called, but I pressed on, ignoring his pleas.

Yet, with each call, my resolve faltered, and my steps slowed. When he added *please* to my name, I finally gave in, halting before I reached the steps.

I had never felt this lost, unsure of where to go. Despite my good luck, I didn't want to return to the casino. All I truly wanted was to go home, crawl into bed, and cry myself to sleep, maybe with Regina in my arms. She might not like it, but she would understand.

Slowly, I turned to him.

"What are you doing?" he asked, his voice echoing the bewilderment in my mind. "I don't understand. Are you truly planning to fuck my brother again?"

My hands clenched at my sides, and I stomped towards him, halting when our feet were mere inches apart. I tilted my head at him. "You're fucking *her*. Why can't I fuck *him*?"

"You absolutely can," he said, but his frustrated tone

contradicted his words. "Go ahead. Do it now. You are, after all, your own woman, capable of making your own choices and doing whatever you want. I can't stop you from anything, and I should not."

My fingers twitched with the urge to grab him by his shirt and shake him. Shake him until he understood how much I liked him—so much that it hurt every day to know someone else could freely touch him in places I could only dream of. Maybe then he would finally see my pain.

Yet, I did nothing, resigning with a curt, "Fine."

As I turned to leave, his hand closed around the nape of my neck, yanking me back towards him. Caught by surprise, he robbed me of my breath. My eyes widened as my heart quickened, thudding against my ribcage.

He had never been this rough before.

I didn't even know he could be.

His lips pressed against mine, and his tongue swept between my lips, demanding entry. Still taken aback by how unexpected it all was, I hesitated at first. But afraid he might pull away, I surrendered, parting my lips for him. As our tongues met for the first time, all my anger and frustration melted away, replaced by fireworks setting off inside me.

I heard explosions booming behind me as I drew nearer to him, sinking my fingers into his hair, just as I had always craved to do. His hand found my waist, bringing me closer.

Was it crazy for me to like his possessive grip on me as he kissed me like I belonged to him? Was it crazy to let him explore my mouth after another woman had sat in his lap, whispering seductive words to him just minutes ago?

His lips lingered against mine as he murmured, "I was dreaming—"

"I . . ." I gripped his shirt, struggling to stay on my feet as sudden lightheadedness hit me.

My vision fogged again, and this time, it didn't reappear.

"Vittoria?" His grip on my arms tightened. "What's wrong?"

"I . . . don't feel well."

I felt a gentle touch against my forehead, and his voice, filled with worry, reached me through the haze. "You're burning up."

The world spun, and my head grew heavier. I rested it against his chest.

"Are you . . ." he uttered, sounding a little uncertain. "Sick?"

a_i

31
The Cure

Ettore

VITTORIA MOVED HER HEAD AGAINST MY CHEST, LIKELY NODDING. "I . . . I think so."

Has she caught the Rash? I wondered. But I wasn't a doctor. It could be any virus or just a cold.

I wrapped my arms around her and swept her up. She clung to my neck, resting her head on my chest. I had expected her to be heavier, but I lifted her effortlessly. Perhaps the gym sessions were paying off.

"Should we go to a hospital or drive back home and call Dr Zunino?" I asked as I carried her towards the car.

"To the villa, please."

"Are you sure? It's a thirty to forty-five minute drive, and Dr Zunino might not even come."

It was close to midnight, after all.

"Yes," she said. "I'll be fine."

I wanted to take her straight to a hospital, but I hesitated. This was Monte Carlo. I didn't trust anything or anyone here. If her parents and I had a better relationship, I would have felt more confident about that route. Hopefully whatever she had wasn't too serious.

I carefully settled her in the passenger seat and secured her with a seat belt. "If you change your mind and want to go to a hospital instead, don't hesitate to tell me, okay?"

Her eyes were closed as she softly replied, "Okay."

I closed the door and got into my seat. The ride home was quiet and mostly free of cars. I kept checking on Vittoria, asking her questions to make sure she remained conscious and didn't need a hospital.

Once we arrived home, I carried her to her room and immediately called Dr Zunino.

I didn't expect her to answer, but to my surprise, she picked up and agreed to come see Vittoria.

While waiting for her, I brought a glass of water to Vittoria, but she shook her head. "No, I don't want anything."

"Not even me?" I half-joked.

Her eyes cracked open, and a faint smile touched her lips. "No." She reached out, lightly brushing her fingers against my arm. A warm sensation blossomed in my chest. "Please, stay with me." Her fingers curled around my arm, weakly pulling me towards the bed. "Next to me," she whispered, her voice barely audible.

I couldn't say no even if I wanted to.

I placed the glass on the bedside table and settled beside her. She tugged me closer, more urgently this time. "Can you hold me, please?"

I glanced at the narrow space beside her. The only way I could lie next to her was to move behind her.

"Okay," I agreed, carefully manoeuvring to her other side, my heart thumping with uncertainty.

I had never been in this position before, never cuddled with any of the women I had slept with. I hadn't even slept with Vittoria.

Not that I expected to.

I hesitantly draped my hand over her body. "Is this okay?"

"Mm-hmm," she hummed in approval.

We lay in silence. The soft glow of the night lamp enveloped us in a warm light. Thoughts of the kiss we had shared crossed my mind. I had never kissed anyone like that before. I wondered if she had. Most likely, yes.

"Do you want to talk?" I ventured.

She murmured something indecipherable, and I knew I shouldn't press her. She wasn't feeling well. I would talk to her when she was ready.

She shifted closer, nestling her butt against my crotch. It felt warm. It felt good. The tension in my body slowly eased. I closed my eyes, savouring the moment.

Someone cleared their throat.

I opened my eyes to see Dr Zunino standing in front of us. I must have drifted off to sleep because I hadn't heard her entering the room. It was a good thing I had left the front door unlocked, or I might not have heard the doorbell.

I withdrew my hand and stood, letting Dr Zunino examine Vittoria. I watched as she checked her eyes, pulse, mouth, and temperature.

"It's the Rash," Dr Zunino said, peeling off her gloves. "You know the drill. If you've had close contact in the last week, quarantine and take the Cure before any symptoms appear. There's a high chance that you've been infected too."

Vittoria's eyes were barely open. Her skin showed no rash, but faintness typically was the first symptom before red spots appeared.

I nodded to Dr Zunino. "Thank you for coming here regardless of the hour."

"Don't worry," she said, grabbing her bag. "I'll see you if something else comes up."

As she left us in silence, many questions swarmed in my mind, but I chose not to overwhelm Vittoria with them. Not when she was in such a state, her eyes drooping as she fought to stay conscious. I couldn't start her on treatment either, as it was too late to contact work to request the Cure.

It was time to leave her alone. "Sleep well, my flower," I

whispered as I switched off the light and slipped out of her room.

After making a call in the morning, a package arrived on my porch an hour later. I didn't rush to give Vittoria the medication. First, she needed to eat. Since I had fired Sofia due to financial reasons, I had to put something together myself.

I wasn't a skilled cook, but breakfast was the easiest meal of the day. It didn't have to be anything grand. I could manage.

After feeding Regina, I checked the croissants I had bought yesterday and was relieved they weren't dry. Then I poured two glasses of orange juice, intending to have breakfast with Vittoria if she was awake. As I gathered everything onto one tray, I carefully walked down the hallway to her room. There, I found Regina waiting at her door, but before opening it, I knocked.

"Yes?" responded the most adorable morning voice from inside.

I lowered the handle and pushed the door open with my shoulder. Regina slipped through the crack before it fully opened. Vittoria smiled at the sight of me, or the food, or perhaps Regina—likely Regina.

"Good morning," I greeted.

She sat up, and I placed the tray over her.

"Good morning." She surveyed the food. "That looks amazing."

"There's a pill you need to take after you're done eating," I informed her, taking my plate and sitting on the edge of her bed.

She picked up the white pill, turning it between her fingers as if searching for hidden secrets. "How many of these do I have to take?" She set it back down.

"Three pills every day for the next six days."

As we delved into our breakfast, a calmness settled over us. My gaze wandered around the room, landing on the vase filled with various types of white flowers.

I stopped eating.

"Is something wrong?" she asked.

Those flowers shouldn't be in the same vase. Those flowers shouldn't be in the same—

But she kept the flowers you gave her, a rational voice pointed out, dampening the rising panic.

I focused on the positive aspect. "You kept the flowers?"

"Of course."

A smile tugged at my lips as I whispered, "Unbelievable."

"What?"

I cleared my throat. "I thought you threw them away."

After all, she had made it clear she didn't like them and that I should stop leaving them outside her door.

"Why?" She sounded clueless. "They're pretty."

"It's just . . ." I started, but didn't know how to finish it. "No, nothing." I shook my head and whispered, "It's nothing."

I felt her curious stare as I returned to my meal. She savoured each bite at a slower pace. By the time she was on her second croissant, I had already finished and taken my pill.

I waited for her to finish eating and take hers. Eventually, she lifted the glass of juice, but as she brought it to her lips, she accidentally spilled it. The juice cascaded onto her chest, staining her dress.

"Oh." She lifted her gaze from the stain, her expression apologetic. "I'm sorry."

"Don't worry about it." I rose and fetched some tissue from her bathroom. As I returned, I handed her the papers, and she used them to dab her chest.

She managed a sad smile. "Poor dress."

She was still in the same green dress from yesterday. I could have offered to help her change into something else, but if I were to see her naked, I wanted it to be under different circumstances.

"You should take your pill," I reminded her.

"I already did."

"You . . ." I searched for the pill on the tray, but it was gone. "You did?"

"Yes, while you were in the bathroom."

She was quick.

Since she wasn't using the tray anymore, leisurely sipping her juice, I gestured towards it. "May I?"

She giggled. "Yes, you *may*."

After removing the tray and setting it aside, I settled back on the edge of the bed. Regina rose to her feet and approached Vittoria. With graceful steps, she positioned herself on Vittoria's lap and kneaded it as if making dough.

"You never told me what happened when you were out with your friends," I said.

"I didn't think you'd be interested," she replied with a humourless smile. "And the fact that you're asking me a week later proves it."

"I was . . ." I rubbed my forehead with my fingers before realising I was searching for a non-existent excuse. "I'm interested now."

She stroked Regina, curled up in her lap. "We drove to Monte Carlo and did some shopping before we went to a cafe, where a group of people stormed in and coughed at us."

The infectors, spreading the Rash among the wealthy. They were not uncommon in Monte Carlo. I was surprised Barbara didn't mention it or ask for the Cure.

"Why didn't you tell me about them?"

"Because I learnt about the Rash and the Cure after I returned. I believed I was infected, and I didn't want to be treated too soon. I wanted to experience what people have to go through because of

SQ."

"I thought you were smarter than that," I muttered.

She scrunched up her nose. "What did you just say?"

Realising my mistake, I hurried to clarify. "Sorry, I didn't mean to insinuate that . . ." But her stern expression unnerved me, and I shook my head. "What I meant is, the Rash is harmless if treated, but if not, it can cause long-term complications that could affect your entire life."

Her face softened. "Okay, I didn't know that, but if I did, I wouldn't have said a word about it anyway."

I raised my eyebrows but said nothing.

She looked down as she mumbled, "You shouldn't have kissed me."

It was like a knife piercing my heart. "I shouldn't have?"

But as she kept her gaze down, I realised she had no regrets. She felt shy and perhaps guilty because she had the Rash when I had kissed her.

I wasn't entirely sure what had compelled me to pull her close and force my lips against hers. Yet she had kissed me back just as passionately. If I had known she had the Rash, I might have refrained. Maybe.

Probably not.

"You should have told me about the infectors," I said before adding a hint of playfulness to my tone. "But if you had, we wouldn't be stuck here together for a week."

She lifted her eyes, and an uncertain giggle slipped through her lips. "You say it like it's a good thing."

"Do you think it's bad?"

"Why, Ettore Cossette Morrano, would I think being stuck at home with my husband for a week is bad?"

Resting my hands on the mattress, I leant in her direction. "I know you don't remember, but surely you can't believe that every married couple always gets along perfectly. Some couples want to throttle each other when they're alone."

"Are we *that* married couple?"

I shrugged. "It would certainly make things more exciting at home."

"So you're bored of home?"

"When you're not around, I am."

Our faces were so close that I could breathe in the lingering scent of her perfume and soap in her hair. She exuded the fragrance of a flower, unlike any I had encountered before—a unique bloom yet to be discovered and explored by someone.

I burned to be that someone.

I burned to explore her, from the inside out. From the softness of her lips to the smooth arch of her neck, the swell of her breasts, the curve of her belly, and finally, her most intimate places. But I knew it was wrong.

On paper, she was my wife, but we never felt that way about each other, and now she didn't have her memory. If she remembered who she used to be . . . she would break my heart. *I don't think I am who you think I am.*

Or perhaps she wasn't Vittoria at all, but someone who looked uncannily like her. Like Teodora Sauvage, the scientist capable of creating something that could threaten my life. Imagine that: Teodora Sauvage, the thief not only of the Cure but of my heart.

I was being silly.

"What's so exciting about me?" she breathed out, suddenly short of breath. "I don't even remember you."

"You . . ." I struggled to form words, feeling as if my mind was wrapped in a fog, either from the medication or her mere presence. "You challenge me."

"I challenge you?" She chuckled as she pressed her hand to my chest, stopping me from going further but not pushing me away either. "Is that all?"

"No," I whispered, my fingers closing around her warm wrist. "But do I need a reason to feel at home every time you're around? Do I need a reason for my heart to race with excitement when you enter a room? Do I need a reason to—"

She silenced me with a finger against my lips, a smile dancing at the edge of her mouth. She leant in, replacing her finger with her lips. I couldn't help but grin, feeling her smile as our tongues reunited in a delicate dance.

I couldn't remember the last time I had smiled like it was the simplest thing in the world. I wasn't even sure if anyone had ever made me smile like that before. Perhaps she was the first.

As her fingers roamed through my hair, I eased her against the bed, careful not to hurt her. But Regina made a sound, and I paused. I had completely forgotten about her. When I looked at her, she was already off the bed.

I winced. "My apologies, Regina."

"She forgives you," Vittoria said, gripping my shirt and tugging me closer, finding my lips again.

As I lay on top of her, I slipped my legs under the blanket and pulled my lips away from hers to kiss her neck. I was tempted to remove her dress, but I wanted this moment to last. I didn't want to rush into anything—not this time. I had rushed too many times before, simply because I didn't care. But now, things were different.

Now, I cared.

But the pill was making me feel tired.

"Maybe . . ." I pulled away, gazing into her sparkling hazel eyes. "Maybe we should sleep."

She frowned in confusion. "Sleep?"

I settled in beside her, my eyelids growing heavy. "Yes," I murmured. "Sleep."

As I rested my head on the pillow, I closed my eyes just for a second. Just for a . . .

32
Fear of Rejection

Teodora

***E**TTORE FELL ASLEEP.*
Ettore was *asleep*.

Regina's meow echoed my frustration, though she was annoyed because she couldn't go out. I slipped out of bed, being careful not to disturb Ettore, and opened the door for her.

After closing the door, I peeled off my stained dress. Now that Sofia didn't work here, I would have to find a way to remove the stain myself. It was my own fault anyways.

As I was about to put on my pyjama pants, my legs began to itch insufferably. Stopping to scratch, I noticed red dots covering my thighs.

Maybe I should have taken the pill.

I slipped into my pyjama pants, put on a top, and approached the bedside table. Quietly, I opened the drawer and picked up the pill I had stashed there while Ettore was in the bathroom.

I didn't want to take it. But what if I could get worse? If Ettore hadn't lied to scare me into taking the Cure, I didn't want to risk the complications. They could threaten my life.

And why did I have to experience something with my own body to understand the cruelty of SQ?

With the last drops of my orange juice, I swallowed the pill.

I settled next to Ettore. His hair fell over his eyes and I was tempted to brush it aside, but I refrained. I feared the slightest touch might disturb his sleep.

The Rash drained most of my energy and although I could easily surrender to sleep, I wished he hadn't stopped. I wished his lips had lingered on my neck and maybe ventured lower. My body ached with heat. While I might have blamed it on the fever, I felt intense discomfort in my core, yearning for attention. Maybe it was for the best that he fell asleep instead. Maybe the sickness clouded my judgement—

No, it didn't. I had desired him since the moment I first saw him.

I wanted him. I wanted him all to myself.

Smiling at the thought, I rested my head close to his chest, closed my eyes, and soon drifted off to sleep.

When I awoke I felt a hand on my lower abdomen, its pinky finger positioned just above the edge of my pyjama pants. It took a moment before I realised a man was behind me in my bed, holding me. Not just any man. Ettore.

I smiled contentedly in my dream and closed my eyes—

They flew open, my smile wavering. No, it wasn't a dream. Ettore had fallen asleep in *my* bed.

As I turned my head, I hadn't expected to find his eyes already open.

A mischievous smile curved his lips. "You snore when you sleep."

Heat flooded my cheeks. "No, I don't."

He shrugged his one shoulder. "You would know," he said. "After all, who else hears you snore at night but yourself?"

Annoyed, I turned away, trying to break free, but he held me tight against him. His hand edged lower, turning me still.

I swallowed. "How long have we been asleep?"

"A few hours." His breath ghosted over my ear, sending heat down to my core. "Not nearly enough."

He pulled my hips to him, and I felt his erection pressing hard against me. Or so I thought.

Glancing back, I met his eyes. "Did you have another *special* dream or . . . ?"

He chuckled, recognising the reference. "Not this time." His fingers toyed with the ties of my pyjama pants. "This time, I woke up next to a girl, and it wasn't a dream."

"Who was the girl you dreamed of last time?"

He slowly pulled on a tie, loosening the knot. "Didn't I tell you?"

"No."

His hand slid beneath my pyjama pants, meeting yet another obstacle—my underwear.

"You know her," he murmured, his fingers slipping beneath the elastic.

My heartbeat quickened.

"Barbara?" I teased.

His fingers went still.

"Naughty girl," he whispered before withdrawing his hand, leaving me with immense disappointment.

I had made a mistake. Joking wasn't the way to go. What if I ruined the only chance we had? What if—

"Hey." He brushed my hair aside, finding my eyes. "Do you really think I dreamed of Barbara?"

I averted my gaze, not sure where to look. "I . . . I don't know. It makes sense. I saw her leaving your room once."

His brows furrowed. "You saw her leaving my room?"

"Uh-huh."

He rolled over on top of me, trapping me with his body. With his face mere inches from mine, it was almost impossible to avoid making eye contact. "When was that?"

It was difficult to keep from reacting as if I didn't feel his hardness pressing against my leg and stay focused. "Before I knew who Barbara was."

"That must have been the last time she left my bedroom." He paused. "The last day she entered it too."

"You don't sleep with her anymore?"

"No."

"Why?"

"Someone else caught my interest."

My heart quickened, but then it hit me . . . "Is she another one of your flings?"

"I hope not. She's the most interesting girl so far."

"So far?"

He groaned. "Why do you have to make this so hard? I dreamed of you. When you barged into my room and saw my erection, you woke me up from a sex dream about you, my flower."

Heat rushed from my neck to my cheeks.

It was a relief to know it wasn't Barbara or someone else. But if I was just another one of his conquests . . . I should put an end to this before I fell deeper for him and risked getting my heart broken.

"I'm flattered, but . . ." I chewed on my lip. "It's just sex."

And I needed more. I had no idea what sex felt like, but I knew physical intimacy wouldn't be enough for me.

His intense stare made me uneasy. "What do you mean?"

"I . . ." I began but faltered. Why was voicing my needs aloud so challenging? At least Ettore was patient with me.

"I don't want to have just . . ." I articulated slowly, ". . . *sex*."

"What do you want then?"

I hesitated. Did I really have to spell it out to him?

"I can't read your mind," he said.

"I know, but I'm afraid to be rejected," I mumbled.

"I can't hear you."

Right . . . the hearing aid.

"I said I'm afraid to be rejected," I repeated louder before adding, "If I say it."

"I don't think you should have anything to fear."

A laugh escaped me. "You said you've never loved anyone before."

"You want love?"

I nodded shyly.

He tucked the wig behind my ear. "Just because I've never loved anyone before doesn't mean I can't fall in love."

He could fall in love with me.

Butterflies fluttered in my chest, and I bit my bottom lip, containing my excitement. The thought made me feel giddy. I couldn't wait for it to—

"But what happens if you remember and reject *me*?" he asked.

The butterflies vanished.

I hadn't thought about that. I hadn't considered the risks he would face if he developed feelings for me.

So stupid.

If I truly was Vittoria and turned out to be as awful as everyone described me, I could crush his heart. I had been so absorbed in my own feelings that I had completely forgotten about his.

He knew who he was. He remembered his past. He knew what he could promise me, but I . . . I couldn't promise him anything despite my current feelings. I didn't know how I would feel about him once my memories returned.

"Are you willing to risk it?" I asked.

"I don't know." His lips revealed a slight smile. "But I've never felt this way about anyone before. Maybe you're everything I never knew I needed, and that's worth risking my heart for." He caressed my cheek with his knuckles. "*You*, my flower, are worth risking my heart for."

I melted. How could he think I would reject him? He was perfect.

Yes, he was a criminal, but it wasn't my fault he happened to be not only drop-dead gorgeous but also smart *and* suave.

"To answer your question," he continued, "yes, I'm willing to risk it, but are you?"

Yes, I wanted to scream, but instead, different words came out. "I don't want to hurt you."

"That's not an answer."

I raised my hand, grazing his hair with my fingertips. "When Barbara sat in your lap, I felt so . . ."

"Jealous?"

"In *pain*," I stressed, looking away.

"It made me jealous to see you press your body against Antoine and . . ." He shook his head, as if trying to rid himself of the memory.

"I don't want to feel in pain again," I confessed.

"Me neither."

The decision was mine to make.

When Ettore had kissed me, it felt better than winning in blackjack. A thousand times better. I yearned for that feeling to last. I yearned to wake up next to him, to kiss him, to feel his touch in the places that craved it. I wanted him to love *me*.

And I wanted to love *him*.

"Yes," I decided. "I want to risk it."

Feeling a little better, I relocated to the living room while Ettore prepared dinner. Red dots had appeared on my arms, and I fought the urge to scratch them, no matter how irritating they became.

Ettore returned with food half an hour later. "I made something easy," he said. "Let's hope it's edible."

He presented a plate of spaghetti with meatballs in red sauce. It looked delicious, but I wasn't that hungry. Yet, knowing the effort he had put into preparing it, I had to eat something. I didn't want to disappoint him.

I flashed him a smile. "I can't wait to try it."

We ate in silence, savouring each slurp of the spaghetti. The appearance hadn't deceived me, and I found myself enjoying every bite. In the end, I finished everything, thoroughly satisfied.

"Since we're stuck together for another six days," he said, rising from his seat. "I have an activity in mind."

I raised my eyebrows in question. "Oh?"

He took my plate and set it on the coffee table. I accepted the pill and the glass of water he offered.

"How do you feel about reading a book together?" he suggested.

Excitement rushed through me. I swallowed the pill, trying to temper my eagerness as I asked calmly. "What book do you have in mind?"

"Hmm . . ." He approached the bookshelf, scanning its contents. "Ah!" He pulled out a book and fell beside me. "Teddy's Secret. I've forgotten it exists."

The name sounded familiar, but I couldn't remember ever seeing it on the bookshelf, even if I had explored it countless times. Still, it should have been there, because why else would it ring a bell?

"I'll read the first chapter out loud," he proposed. "Then you'll read the second. Is that okay?"

I nodded, taking a sip of water.

He opened the book and cleared his throat before starting. "Teddy says the secret of happiness in life . . ."

The door opened, and a woman stumbled in, almost tripping over her own feet. She shut the door behind her, a smile spreading across her lips that didn't reach her eyes. Despite me sitting on the sofa, she didn't seem to see me.

She approached the sofa, dragging her feet. To avoid her body crashing into mine, I hastily jumped off. She collapsed onto it and laughed, while I hid behind, clutching the book.

Her laughter gradually turned into tears—a desperate, hopeless cry.

My heart ached, but I knew I could do nothing to help her. I opened the book and read the first page again.

Teddy says the secret of happiness in life is to love and be loved, but—

"What are you doing here?"

Ettore's voice startled me, bringing me back to . . . reality. I followed his gaze, finding Antoine leaning against the doorframe.

He smirked. "Staying here?"

"We're quarantined," Ettore said, his tone sharp. "Didn't they tell you?"

"You're not the only one," Antoine retorted. "I was also in contact with Vittoria."

Their eyes shifted to me.

"We had no contact," I defended myself. "All we did was hug."

"Still a contact," Antoine remarked, pushing off the door. "Don't get too cosy. I'll be joining your quarantine duo. Make it a trio now."

With that, he turned around and left the room.

August 31, 1965

I wish I could tell that to a living being and not some diary, but no one would believe me. No one ever did. Not my father. Not my stepmother. They always took his side over mine.

Eventually, I stopped trying.

One might be surprised how I've kept going. If someone were to ask, I wouldn't know how to answer. Some might call me strong, but is hiding the thing that traumatised me considered strength? When it is gradually taking over my well-being?

Not talking about it is the worst. And despite knowing that, I don't even try.
Is that strength? Because it sounds like a weakness to me.
I'm weak, and I'm not ashamed to admit it. I hate myself. I hate my body.
I just want to... disappear.
Do you understand?

33
Intriguing Similarities

Ettore

***T*EODORA *FUCKING* SAUVAGE.**

The mere thought of her sent a sharp pang through my already throbbing head.

I stood before the evidence board, chin on hand like *The Thinker*, as I studied the picture of Teodora Sauvage. No matter how long I stared, she hardly differed from Vittoria.

It intrigued me more than the case itself.

Both had strikingly red, curly hair and freckles dusting their noses, but . . .

Turning away, I walked to my desk and flipped open the folder containing Julien's case. I retrieved two sketches of Teodora—one the oldest, and the other the most recent. With these in hand, I also grabbed the picture of Vittoria and returned to the evidence board. I attached Vittoria's picture next to Teodora's and positioned one of Teodora's sketches on each side. Intrigued, I examined them closely.

I found no difference between Teodora's picture and the first sketch of her reading a book. But the sketch didn't provide a clear view of her face. In the second one, capturing her emerging from the sea, her face was more visible. Unlike the first sketch it didn't perfectly match Teodora's photo, but it matched Vittoria's.

As I compared Vittoria's picture to Teodora's . . .

Teodora did have bigger eyes, but the soul behind them was different. A gentle, almost apprehensive light glowed in Teodora's eyes, while a mischievous flame danced in Vittoria's. Even the sketches portrayed different individuals.

They were not the same person. Obviously.

I glanced at the picture of Teodora's mother, Lizette. It was old, likely taken when she was around twenty years old. I had no idea how SQ had got their hands on it. As far as I knew, the Sauvage family had no ties to SQ back then. Now Lizette was one of the many who bought our drugs, and Morgana occasionally sold us information. But they didn't work for—

"Jazz?" a voice interrupted, breaking my thoughts. "Why so quiet?"

I turned to find Antoine standing in the room.

Goddammit.

I had forgotten to lock the door. I had grown so used to being alone that I forgot two other people were here all day.

"What do you mean?" I asked.

He nodded towards the radio, looking away. Taking the chance,

I quickly removed Vittoria's picture and the sketches.

"You have jazz playing at such a low volume," he noted as I hurriedly stashed everything into my pockets.

Right. I had been so focused that I forgot about the jazz playing softly in the background. I had turned it on to drown out the persistent humming in my ears. It helped me concentrate on my work.

"Helps with the humming," I said.

"Humming? What—" He averted his gaze, visibly uneasy, and placed a folder on my desk. I half-expected an apology, but instead he said, "Here's the interrogation report from the time Natalie questioned Julien, as you requested."

I couldn't even be disappointed. Even if he apologised, it wouldn't mend our relationship. He was the reason I was partly deaf, and forgiving him wasn't easy. But the least he could do was apologise.

"Thank you."

I hoped he would leave, yet he stayed and asked, "How's the scientist's case? Any clue what your next step is?"

"It's interesting," I replied curtly, walking over to the table. "I'm thinking of starting with the obvious."

I opened the folder Antoine had brought. As requested, it contained the remaining information about Vittoria from the SQ archives.

"Her family?" Antoine guessed.

"Her mother, in particular."

Antoine furrowed his brow in thought. "Isn't she a drug addict?"

"Yes, but it's worth a try."

Antoine approached the board, narrowing his eyes as he scrutinised it. "Do you think the Sauvage girl is behind the creation of the new drug?"

I hesitated.

The scientists who created the drug remained unknown, and SQ didn't consider it important since they all perished in the Fire. If SQ knew their identities, perhaps they wouldn't be so fixated on finding the girl. They would have avoided wasting their time if she wasn't a threat.

"I wouldn't be surprised," I said. "She's smart."

"So her education says," he pointed out. "That doesn't prove much."

I hated to agree with Antoine, but he was right. Not everyone with a higher education was smarter than someone without it. But Teodora had started university at a younger age than most. If it wasn't her aunt who pulled some strings, it was likely due to her own intellect.

"I'll find her anyway," I promised. "I always find them."

He turned to me. "You do, but you still have two days left until your quarantine is over. Someone might find her for you."

I couldn't afford to let that happen, especially not in my current situation. If I failed this case, it could be a long time before I got another one, leaving me without income for even longer.

"So . . ." He put on a smile, but it was tinged with sadness. "Are you and Vittoria a thing now?"

I kept my expression guarded, hiding any suspicion even if the mere thought of her unleashed butterflies in my stomach.

Vittoria and I had spent her sick days together, watching movies, reading books, and honing my culinary skills. She seemed to enjoy my cooking, and her health was improving. Although her rash had disappeared, she still had a minor fever. If not tomorrow, then the day after, she would be healthy again.

I remained uncertain about where we stood since we hadn't made it official. I wasn't sure if I wanted to. We had kissed but never taken it further as Antoine was often around. Whenever he joined us for a movie, Vittoria would become uncomfortable and wouldn't say a word.

"She's my wife," I replied.

He let out a suppressed laugh. "You know what I mean."

"If we were a *thing*, wouldn't it be difficult for you to sleep with her?"

"No," he said with a pout. "I don't think she'll be able to resist me."

I offered a faint smile. "I don't doubt your seduction skills, brother, but why did it happen only once? Now she's avoiding you. Was the experience that bad for her?"

Antoine chuckled. "Your comebacks are improving," he said, though a hint of annoyance peeked through his words. "Keep—"

A scream echoed outside, plunging my heart into my gut.

Without a second thought, I bolted out of my office towards the source of the scream. In the hallway, I found Vittoria kneeling in front of an open door.

"What's . . ." I began, but my words trailed off as I saw *it*.

Regina limped towards her, and Vittoria scooped her up. While Regina was lying on her back, I noticed crimson-red stains smearing her snowy stomach.

It felt like the entire world stopped spinning as I saw the pure shock in the blue eyes of my beloved cat, pleading for help.

34
The Church

Teodora

"**I'M TAKING HER TO THE VET,**" **ETTORE ANNOUNCED.**

I looked up at him, tears flooding my eyes and blurring my view of him.

I had stumbled upon Regina by sheer coincidence. As the day progressed and darkness fell, I began to miss her. She had been outside since the morning. When I stepped out and called for her, she limped out from the shadows towards me. The horrific sight caused me to scream.

"Can I join?" I asked tentatively.

If I stayed behind, I would be overwhelmed with worry, but I would understand if he chose not to take me along. Despite feeling much better, I wasn't entirely healthy.

"She has a cage," Ettore replied, seemingly unaware of my question. "But I don't know where it is."

"I can hold her," I offered, standing up. "And I can stay in the car while you're at the vet."

For the first time since he had shown up, he met my gaze.

"Okay," he said, glancing back. "Could you open the gates for us?"

Only now did I notice Antoine standing a few steps behind me. And for the first time, I didn't care.

His forehead showed worry, but he didn't hesitate to reply, "Of course."

We rushed out of the house. Ettore unlocked the car, holding the passenger door for me. I eased myself in, being careful not to disturb Regina. Her head rested on my chest, her eyes lacking their usual spark that came with her purring and kneading, whether it was my legs or a blanket.

Such innocent creatures didn't deserve to suffer. Not like this. Not in any way.

"It'll be okay, baby girl," I whispered, pressing my lips to her head. "I know you're in pain, but you'll be okay."

If I lost her, it would tear my heart apart. I loved her too much.

Ettore slipped into the driver's seat and started the engine. As he approached the open gates, he gave a thumbs up to Antoine, who returned the gesture. I had never seen them exchange friendly gestures or be kind to each other before, but I couldn't think much about it. Instead, I focused on soothingly rubbing Regina's back, whispering that I was there for her. I had no idea whether she understood it or if it was helpful in any way. But Regina was a smart cat, and I wouldn't be surprised if she did.

Ettore drove faster than usual. Earlier, I might have mentioned it but now, I couldn't care less. Only a few cars were on the road, and as far as I knew, worrying about the police was pointless when SQ ruled the area.

He carelessly parked the car and quickly got out. After throwing open the door, he extended his hands, and I carefully passed Regina to him. As he rushed into the building, I closed my door, left with nothing to do but wait.

My first thought was to step out and explore, but was it worth risking complications just to satisfy my curiosity? I decided to sit and wait patiently instead. But time crawled by at an agonising pace. Restlessness gnawed at me as I wished to know what was happening, and whether Regina would live.

I suddenly realised I was biting my nails.

"Stop it," I scolded myself, forcing my hands into my lap.

As I glanced out of the window, I noticed someone leaning against the streetlight. I tensed, goosebumps popping on my skin at the unsettling feeling that I was being watched.

I exhaled slowly, trying to steady my racing heart. Maybe the figure wasn't watching me at all.

But why was their head turned towards me?

Hoping the stranger meant no harm, I leant in for a closer look. Dressed in black from head to toe, they lowered their hood, and red long curls spilled out.

Could it be—

The door opened, and I flinched.

Ettore settled into his seat. Relieved it was him and I wasn't in danger, I looked back to where the woman had stood, but she was gone. I searched around, but it was as if she had never been there.

Why had she been watching me? Who was—

"I'm sorry for leaving without a word," Ettore said.

"I—Oh . . ." I paused, pushing aside the mystery of the woman, and turned my attention to Ettore with a smile. "Nothing to be sorry for."

He stared down at his lap. "It was rude of me. I'm—"

I placed my hand on his and found his eyes. "How is she?"

He released a heavy sigh. "She's lost a lot of blood." He rubbed his forehead. "The vet is going to run some tests, but nothing is certain."

Tears welled up in my eyes. I tried to force them away, but then I saw a tear trickle down *his* cheek.

"She'll be okay," I whispered, trying to reassure us both.

More tears rolled down his face. "I can't lose her."

I squeezed his hand. "I know."

"Regina . . ." He paused, taking a moment to collect himself. "She appeared after the car accident."

The car accident . . . The first time I had asked him about it, he had grown tense and distant, his eyes haunted as if by ghosts. I hadn't brought it up since then, but it had been a while. Maybe now he would be willing to share more?

"Can you tell me more about the accident?" I asked gently.

His shoulders tensed, and I held my breath, expecting him to snap at me again. Instead, he scratched his head, and I quietly breathed a sigh of relief.

"I was in a car accident last year," he finally said. "I drove off a hill and crushed my car into a tree. Because of the adrenaline, I managed to stumble down and sit in the street. I only vaguely remember, but an ambulance found me there. While sitting, I heard a meow and turned my head. There she was, a white cat looking at me." A faint smile flickered on his lips. "She found me. Sometimes I think if not for her, the ambulance wouldn't have come. And I can't help but feel guilty that . . . that this happened to her."

"Have you told me about the accident before the Fire?"

He gave me a strange look. "No, why?"

"I don't know. It sounds familiar." I shrugged, trying to shake off the flashes of a white cat sitting on the pavement and a blurry image of a man who seemed unaware of her.

I felt Ettore's curious stare. "Did you remember something?"

I wasn't sure. It could be my imagination conjuring images of his car accident. "No, I don't think so." I met his eyes. "But you know what happened to Regina isn't your fault, right? You gave her home."

He frowned but said nothing.

I smiled, gently brushing the hanging lock away from his face. "She chose you. Do you have any idea how rare that is? If she's strong enough to help you, she's strong enough to survive this."

He gave me a look of uncertainty. "Are you sure?"

"Absolutely."

I wished it was only him I was trying to convince. But she had to survive. She had to.

As we drove through the quiet streets, taking a longer route, I found myself lost in the passing buildings. There was something cosy about navigating the city at night, bathed in the soft glow of streetlights.

We turned a corner, and before me rose a striking church made of white stone. An unexplainable desire to explore its interior swept over me, and before I knew it, I blurted out, "Stop over there."

Despite a glance in my direction, he didn't slow the car.

"Please, can we stop there?" I repeated, almost pleading, unsure of the reason myself.

This time, he relented and slowed down to find a parking spot. After he parked, I remained in the car, waiting for him to open the door. There was no reason for me to do it myself when he would do it anyway.

As he opened the door, I accepted his hand, meeting his gaze for the first time as I thanked him.

"What's the reason we're here?" he asked, locking the car.

I gestured towards the church. "It's the most beautiful church I have ever seen."

Once he looked at it, he visibly swallowed, awkwardly touching the back of his head. "It's beautiful, yes."

Was he . . . nervous?

I offered him my hand. He hesitated, and for a moment I feared he wouldn't accept it. But just as I was about to pull away, he took it, intertwining his fingers with mine. With a sense of relief, we proceeded towards the church, my steps more confident than his.

As we approached, I felt small in the face of its grandeur. The warm glow of the streetlights enveloped the white stone, and the yellow trims seemed to emit a gentle radiance. I didn't know if I was religious, but judging from my career as an assassin, I probably wasn't. Maybe it explained why Ettore appeared reluctant and nervous. Churches weren't his scene.

Yet, he grasped the handle and pulled the door open. The sound of a pipe organ drifted out, and he hastily shut it, as if frightened.

I tilted my head towards him. "What's wrong?"

"There are people inside," he whispered, despite us being alone.

I laughed. "I'm sure they won't attack us, but if they do . . ." I leant in closer to him. "I'll be the first to run and won't look back."

He gave me an unamused look. "Well, I'll make sure to trip you first."

I gasped. He chuckled and opened the door for me, but I tugged him inside. The pews were barely occupied, with most people sitting towards the front. Without knowing why, I gravitated towards the front benches, but Ettore stopped, tightening his grip on my hand. His weight and strength made it impossible for me to move any further.

I glanced back at him. "What are you doing?"

"We sit in the back," he whispered firmly.

When I opened my mouth to ask why, I paused, realising that sitting among the people was a bad idea. What was I thinking? I was still sick. I couldn't be selfish like those who spread the Rash to others.

As I complied, we settled in the last row. Holding Ettore's hand, I listened to the pastor quoting from the book in his hands. Ettore restlessly checked his watch almost every second. I could swear beads of sweat formed on his forehead. Guilt pricked at me for dragging him somewhere he wasn't comfortable. But before we left, I had to do something.

Clasping my hands together in prayer, I closed my eyes.

Dear God, if you exist, please help Regi—

Ettore grabbed my wrist, snapping my eyes open.

"What are you doing?" he asked in a low voice, cautious not to attract attention.

I jerked my hand away from his grasp. "Praying?"

He frowned. "You don't pray. And you never go to churches. You *hate* them."

"I *hated* them," I hissed, feeling anger flare within me. "In the *past*, I might have avoided churches, but things have changed. I don't remember who I was, but I know who I am now, and that's what matters. So stop trying to convince me of who I am. Even if I was like that before, I'm not anymore. Stop defining me by my past."

He drew back, silent.

I returned to praying for Regina to survive. I wasn't sure about my relationship with God or if I believed in His existence, but I believed in something greater than us—a power capable of miracles. If it didn't exist, I would be long dead.

Someone had dropped that note, informing Ettore about my location. The whole thing might have been orchestrated, but Ettore found me, and I survived.

Wasn't it a miracle?

Maybe if I prayed, Regina could survive too.

Ettore leant closer to me. "Can we go now?"

"No," I shot back.

It was good for him to step out of his comfort zone. Whether he believed in God or not didn't matter to me. All I wanted was for him to open his eyes a little more and see a life beyond the expensive and dangerous lifestyle. A life beyond SQ.

Ettore's hand suddenly rested on my thigh. I shot him a worried glance but didn't ask him to remove it. Not sure why. But displaying *that* kind of affection in a church couldn't be appropriate, right?

He slid his hand up slowly, without pause. Higher and—

I gripped his hand, halting his advance. "Not here," I uttered, meeting his gaze.

He didn't retract his hand, staring at me with uncertainty, as though he thought I didn't mean my words. As though I might change my mind.

I was about to repeat myself when he slipped his hand out from under mine. An unexpected disappointment descended upon me, catching me off guard. Did I secretly wish for him to continue, even if I had said no?

As I listened to the sermons, I couldn't focus anymore. My mind wandered away from the priest's words. I couldn't shake off the curiosity about what Ettore would have done if I hadn't stopped him. Maybe he would have teased me, leading to nothing, but maybe . . .

Shaking my head, I dismissed the pointless wonders.

Nothing inappropriate could happen here. We were in a church, a sacred place, and in a public space. The risk of getting caught was inevitable. If anyone saw us engaging in anything, I would have died from the embarrassment.

I felt warm air against my neck, causing my breath to catch in my throat. His lips hovered near, evoking shivers, and not just.

"Ettore," I whispered in warning, though a part of me hoped he didn't hear me.

And he might not have, as his hand returned to my thigh. He pressed a kiss to my neck, soft as a feather. My eyes fluttered closed, savouring the pleasure pulsing through my body.

"Ettore," I repeated, this time my voice lacked warning.

He pushed his hand down while his lips moved, pausing between my neck and my jaw. His teeth grazed my skin before gently nipping that *oh-so-sweet* spot. A moan threatened to come out but I held it back, still aware of the fact we were in *God's* house with the pastor preaching. Yet, his voice sounded far away and easily forgettable.

His hand paused as it reached my bare knee, the touch like the sun on a warm, pleasant day. With deliberate slowness, he slid his hand up behind my skirt, nearing the part that craved his touch, threatening to burn up without it.

Wasting no time with teasing, he pressed his finger against the centre of my underwear. I gripped his arm, shooting him a nervous glance. Holding my gaze, he watched me intently as he applied the perfect pressure, promising an exquisite sensation with even the slightest movement.

"Do you want me to stop?" he asked.

The answer should have been yes, but the anticipation was too great, and the opposite slipped from my lips. "No."

He moved his finger, and I bit my tongue to silence any sounds. As he kept up the slow, varied strokes, my muscles gradually relaxed, growing used to the pleasure. A minute later, he added another finger, hitting all the right spots in the right way. My nails dug into his skin, my eyes closing in delight. But he withdrew without a warning.

My eyes shot open, confused and—

"Don't worry, my flower," he said, fitting himself between me and the pew in front of us as he knelt down. "I'm only getting started."

My cheeks flushed. "Ettore . . ." I trailed off, unsure of where I was going with this.

"Should I stop?"

I glanced ahead at the priest, who was still delivering his sermon. Everyone remained turned towards him, listening eagerly. I had no idea what Ettore was planning, only able to guess. But whatever it was, I couldn't deny the flutter of excitement and nervousness in my stomach.

"No," I responded, giving him a warning look, "but please, be quiet."

A smile tugged at the corner of his lips, and I lowered my gaze, realising how dumb I had sounded.

Be quiet.

As if *he* were the one capable of making the most noise, drawing everyone's attention.

Hiking up my skirt, he dragged his lips along my thigh with purpose, inching upwards. Then he hooked his fingers under my underwear, tugged it down my legs, and stuffed it into his pocket. My eyes widened, and before I could speak, he gripped my thighs and abruptly pulled me closer, his head disappearing under my skirt.

He spread my legs wider. I could feel his fingers parting my lips, and I tried my best not to think of what he might see. I knew my intimate area wasn't pretty to look at. I hoped that it was dark enough—

I felt a soft brush of his lips against *the* spot before he replaced it with the wet warmth of his tongue. He flicked it against my clit, and my fingers tangled in his curls.

As I squeezed his hair tightly, he ignited sensations I hadn't felt before. I wished I could unleash my screams and moans to echo throughout the church. It was easy to forget our surroundings, with people mere steps away. Should they turn . . .

I kept my eyes open, fighting the temptation to give in to the pleasure of his tongue, performing things that no one should do in a church.

Sinful, dirty, but oh . . . so pleasing things.

He sucked my clit into his mouth, and I almost lost it. *Almost.* My grip on his hair tightened, and I half-worried I might yank some out. Yet my concerns faded as tension coiled inside me, darkening my vision and tensing my limbs.

"Stop," I whispered, loosening my grip on his hair.

But he didn't stop.

Whatever I was experiencing, it wouldn't last. I felt it coming. Something powerful and—

"*Stop*," I said louder, desperation rising in my tone.

He pulled back, confusion in his eyes. "Am I doing it wrong?"

"No," I managed to answer, trying to regain my breath.

That was close. Although still hungry and not fully satisfied, if I had let him continue, I doubted I could have controlled—

He buried his face between my legs again. Before I could protest, his mouth found the spot once more.

This time, I didn't stop him. I couldn't. The wave of the most intense pleasure crashed through me, fuelled by the unexpectedness of it all. A scream tore from my lips shamelessly.

I quickly covered my mouth, gripping the edge of the pew as waves of pleasure wrecked my body. When they eventually ebbed away, Ettore grabbed my wrists and pulled me upright before I could fully recover.

"I think it's time to go," he said.

But my legs felt weak and unsteady. "I . . ."

He scooped me up in his arms and carried me away from the pews. Suddenly, I became aware of complete silence in the church. The priest's voice had fallen silent, and no music played. Glancing back, I saw every head turned in our direction, casting what might be judgemental looks. I couldn't be sure. I couldn't see.

I flushed from my neck to my cheeks.

Ettore carried me out. Once he set me back on my feet, he helped me walk to the car. Still a bit dazed, I couldn't fully comprehend the severity of what we had done. But as soon as we were in the car, the realisation set in. I dropped my face into my hands, overcome with mortification.

"What have we done?" I whispered. "What have we done?"

"Do you regret it?" he asked.

I hesitated before uncovering my face. *Do I regret it?*

I grimaced. "Would it make me insane if I don't?"

He chuckled, starting the car and licking his lips. "Always at your service, my flower."

February 12, 1966

It's been a while without you.
I thought we were done after I revealed my biggest secret to you. I planned to burn you. But I didn't, and now I'm back. For a reason, of course.
Today, I saw someone who looked like me. Not exactly like me, but very similar.
I followed her. Following could be my second name. The girl had similar hair, face, even those annoying freckles. Who was she?
I couldn't ask her. If I had revealed myself, I might have

scared her. She was wearing glasses, so she might not have even noticed the similarity between us. She entered the apartment. I assumed she lived alone. It made me question things.

Who was the girl, and why did we look so much alike?

35

Starting on the Right Foot

Ettore

KNOWING REGINA WAS FIGHTING FOR HER LIFE KEPT ME AWAKE. I tossed and turned in bed, occasionally cracking my eye open to check the clock. Time ticked by fast. As I considered going to the conservatory, I felt someone slipping under the covers next to me.

"Is it okay if I sleep here tonight?" Vittoria asked softly.

"You can, but I might not be able to sleep."

"Is it because of Regina?"

"Yes."

All became quiet, and I could feel her gaze on me as I stared blankly at the ceiling.

She drew closer, nestling her head into my chest. "Can I ask you a question?"

"Go ahead."

She paused for a moment, then asked, "Are we together now? I mean, we do *things* when we're alone, but whenever your brother comes into the living room and we sit together, you instantly pull away. You touched me in front of him before. Why don't you do it now? Are you suddenly embarrassed of me?"

I turned on my side, propping my head on my hand and trying to find her eyes in the darkness, but it was futile. "I'm definitely not embarrassed of you."

"Then why are you afraid to show affection in front of others?"

I didn't know how to respond because I wasn't sure myself.

But I wasn't embarrassed of her. In the past, I didn't care about others' opinions and would touch her in front of them because I wasn't interested in her. Now that we were serious, I was worried that word would spread about our relationship and I'd never hear the end of it.

Or perhaps I felt guilty. When Vittoria remembered, she wouldn't believe I had taken care of her. She would see through my façade. Now she might have a different image of me, only seeing my good side. But what about my flaws? What about the time when I used her coma as an excuse to indulge in my hobbies?

"What if . . ." I began, biting the inside of my cheek, unsure whether I wanted to risk ruining our relationship.

What we had now was perfect. But did I really want to start off on the wrong foot? Besides, it was only a matter of time before the truth came out.

"What if what?" she asked.

Summoning my courage, I suggested, "What if I show you something?"

"Like what?"

"It's something we have to leave the bedroom to see."

"Is it far?"

"No." I rose from the bed. "It's in our house."

She slid off the bed. "Is it your office? I still haven't seen it."

"No." I opened the door and held it for her. "It's something even more interesting."

Once she walked out, I emerged from behind her, taking the lead. I descended the stairs, crossed the hallway, and entered the living room. With a flick of the light switch, the space brightened. Vittoria watched me with curiosity as I moved the coffee table aside, then tossed the carpet away, uncovering a secret door.

Vittoria gasped. "Is it actually . . . ?"

"A secret door?" I reached for the handle and lifted it, pulling the door towards me. "One might say so, yes."

She approached and peered into the stairs descending into darkness. Then, she looked at me. "Any light?"

"Not yet." Stepping down the first step, I flicked on the light. I flashed her a smile. "Now, yes."

As I descended the stairs, Vittoria followed behind, taking in the space. Shelves lined the walls. Two faced each other, each holding rows of books, while the third displayed ship models. In the centre stood a desk with my nearly finished Santa Maria ship. Had Vittoria woken up a week later, I would have completed it.

"Has this been under my feet this whole time?" she asked incredulously, stepping closer to the ship. "Is this yours?"

"Yes and yes."

Her lips quirked. "You like building ship models?"

I nodded slowly, pressing my lips together to hide my smile.

"That's amazing," she said.

I went still, unable to believe it. I had expected her to dismiss my hobby as foolish and a waste of time. Then again, she wasn't the same Vittoria I had grown to know.

She walked over to the shelves with the ships, surveying them with genuine curiosity. "But how is this related to our relationship?"

My heart sped up. Perhaps if I explained why I had used her, she wouldn't change her opinion of me. Perhaps she would still like me. But what if . . .

"This is a Santa Maria ship model." I gestured towards the ship on the table. "It took me five years to get it."

She approached it, tilting her head. "Isn't it one of Columbus's ships?"

I arched an eyebrow. "You remember that, but you don't remember your past?"

She shrugged. "It's weird, but I do remember some historical facts or random things. Like, who the Queen of England is."

"So you're not entirely hopeless."

She shot me an annoyed look.

"My apologies," I quickly added, remembering that this Vittoria might be more sensitive to jokes. "As I was trying to say, you can see the model isn't finished."

She nodded with the confidence of an expert, although it was difficult to see any missing parts aside from the unattached sails. Still, she was cute.

"As you know, I'm usually busy with work. I'm rarely home, and when I am, I'm confined to my office. But since I didn't go to work for two months . . ."

Her eyes widened with realisation. "You didn't."

"I didn't what?"

She burst into laughter, her hand coming to rest on the table. "Don't tell me you were building this while I was in a coma, pretending to take care of me just to get a break from work."

"I . . ." I was at a loss for words, stunned by her accurate and quick speculation. "That's not the only thing I did. I also took care of the flowers."

She laughed even harder, shaking her head. "You're such a nerd, I love it."

"Aren't you mad?"

"Mad? I was in a *coma*. I don't know what happened during that time, and frankly, I don't care. I think it's great you took advantage of my situation to take a break from work. You didn't waste the time, either." She looked meaningfully at the ship. "This is impressive."

A heavy weight lifted from my chest, and I had never felt lighter. "I thought you'd be angry, which is why it took me so long to tell you. But as something started to become of us, I felt it was necessary to share this so we could begin our romantic relationship with no secrets."

Her smile grew wider until she squealed, rushing towards me and leaping into my arms. I barely had time to brace myself as she enveloped me with her legs.

"Our romantic relationship?" She tossed her arms around my neck. "Are we officially a couple now? Can we sleep in the same bed?"

I chuckled. "I'm not sure if we'll share a bed, but we can kiss in public if you'd like."

Happiness beamed from her as she crushed her lips against mine. I spun her around, and our kiss turned sloppy, eliciting a giggle from her. It was hard not to smile. Impossible, actually. Smiling didn't come naturally for someone like me, but with her, it felt effortless.

Setting her back on her feet, I asked, "Should we go try to sleep?"

She clasped her hands behind her. "First, I have a question." She swung her leg towards the table and bent forward, forming an enticing curve of her backside.

I moved closer, nearly pinching those perfect cheeks, when she turned her head towards me. "Who is Maxime?"

My blood ran cold. "What?"

She pointed at the letters engraved on the side of the table. "It says here *A gift to Maxime*. Who is Maxime?"

I had been aware of the inscription, but with how often I used the table, it had completely slipped my mind. Vittoria knew about my uncle and his treason—everyone in SQ did—but she didn't remember. I could avoid the truth by claiming the table had already been here when we moved in, or that I found it in a used store, but . . .

"He's a traitor," I spat.

"You seem angry." She straightened up. "Isn't it common to have traitors? Especially in a line of work like yours?"

"He's different. He almost ended the existence of SQ."

Her eyebrows rose in interest. "Is that even possible?"

"Anything is."

"How did he do it? Maybe I'll jot some notes down and . . . I'm kidding!" she said, noticing my alarmed expression. "I was only kidding."

Perhaps she was, but I couldn't find any humour in it, not when SQ had been on the brink of collapsing twice.

"Can you tell me how he did it?" she asked, her tone more careful and less confident.

I wasn't too eager to recount the story. Maxime was my uncle, and his actions filled me with shame. Our entire family was ashamed of him. We avoided mentioning his name in our conversations, hoping to erase him from our lives.

Yet, despite my reluctance, my mouth moved on its own. "He betrayed us to the British authorities about five years ago. In exchange for a safe life, he traded the names of our superiors and details about drug exportation and importation. What was once a secret organisation became public knowledge, all thanks to Maxime.

"SQ workers were tracked down to testify against us. Drug manufacturers were either killed or banished. People fled and leaked more information. Everyone knew the faces behind the names and no longer feared us. We lost many members. SQ had to act fast to re-establish itself before it crumbled for good."

I regretted keeping the table. I should have thrown it away, along with the archives he stored in the basement.

When SQ searched the villa for clues, I doubted they found the basement, or they would have informed me. I stumbled upon it while rearranging the living room out of boredom. Inside, I discovered information that SQ would undoubtedly want if they knew it was here.

Keeping everything hidden from SQ felt like I was contributing to his treason. Why I still hadn't told them, I didn't know.

"I don't understand . . ." Vittoria said, puzzled. "If he caused so much damage, how did SQ recover from it?"

"We were desperate." I leant against the table. "We reached out to a notorious informant, paying a hefty sum for their advice."

"An informant?" She scrunched up her face. "Who are they?"

"Their name is irrelevant for this story," I said, avoiding talking about Morgana. "Now, where was I? Right. Their advice paid off. They informed us of a scientist experimenting with a new disease, now known as the Rash. By threatening them, we coerced them into working for us. Within a month, the disease spread, and people came crawling to us for the Cure. And we provided it in exchange for money or favours."

"What favours?"

I paused, pondering. "It depends on their societal role. It can be as minor as delivering a risky package abroad or as serious as carrying out a killing."

"How can they do that if they are sick?"

"When people's lives are at risk, they'll do anything, regardless of how they feel physically."

"That's manipulative," she remarked.

"That's the point."

She sighed heavily, burdened by the weight of it all.

"The Rash is why SQ came back stronger than ever. Even though we're no longer a secret organisation and the entire world knows about us, it can be seen as an advantage. Monaco is our kingdom. Every person who lives there has contributed to SQ in some way. They know that no mole can bring us down. We've grown too powerful for that."

"What if someone else had a more accessible cure?"

"It nearly happened," I admitted. "A group of scientists were secretly working on it on the fringes of Monte Carlo, but we stopped them before they released it. We might have avoided a big problem, but we also almost lost our greatest assassin." I gave her a meaningful look.

She looked away, crossing her arms over her chest. "I suppose SQ found Maxime and killed him?"

"No, actually. He's still out there somewhere."

She let out a short laugh. "You told me no one can escape SQ, yet he did."

"It's possible, but is it a life worth living if you have to be constantly vigilant, checking over your shoulder every minute?"

Her silence answered my question.

I knew she was against SQ, and I hoped her distaste for it wouldn't last once she remembered. SQ was many awful things, but if she chose to flee from it, I wouldn't follow. Working for it drained me mentally, but I dreaded even imagining being hunted by them if I left. It felt safer and much less stressful to stay and remain loyal.

"Why is his table here?" she asked. "Could it be that he used to live here?"

"Yes." I shifted uncomfortably and glanced down at my fingers. "He did . . . live here."

I sensed her suspicious gaze. "Why are we living in his house?"

"SQ gave it to us as a wedding present."

Her eyebrows furrowed. "And you accepted it? Even though it's the house of a traitor?"

When my mother offered the villa to me, she was certain I wouldn't accept it. But I had known Maxime before he betrayed us. I knew him as my uncle and more.

He was much younger than my mother, and during my teenage years, he was like my best friend. I used to spend a lot of time with him in this villa, where he introduced me to good literature. If I hadn't accepted the villa, it would have gone to someone else who I doubted would have valued it as much as I did.

"It is the house of a traitor." I sighed. "But unfortunately, the traitor is also my uncle."

Someone was shaking me.

"Ettore . . ." a woman's gentle voice called. "The phone is

ringing."

I slowly cracked my eyes open, her words taking a moment to register. When their meaning finally sank in, I sprang out of bed—a move I quickly regretted. My vision dimmed, and I staggered to the side.

"Ettore," Vittoria said with a concerned voice.

"I'm okay."

Through the remaining dark spots, I headed to the living room and answered the phone. "Hello?" I said, steadying myself with a hand on the bookshelf.

"It's Mariana from the vet clinic," she said. "Am I speaking to Ektor Marrano?"

Ektor Marrano?

"Yes, that's me," I confirmed, deciding not to waste time correcting her.

Vittoria emerged, dressed in a silk robe. She stopped a few steps away, watching me with concern.

"Regina's health is stable," the vet reported. "I've stitched the wound and taken X-rays. Her right front leg and both back legs are broken."

I closed my eyes briefly, relieved she was alive, before inquiring, "Do you know what happened to her?"

"About that . . ." The uncertainty in her voice sparked a sense of unease inside me. Perhaps the nightmare wasn't over. "When you brought her in, I thought an animal attacked her, but the wound looks . . . deliberate."

Vittoria stepped closer as I fell silent, the ringing in my ears growing louder and louder, and—

"Mr Marrano?" the vet prompted. "Are you still with me?"

"Yes," I replied, clearing my throat. "Are you . . . Are you certain it wasn't an animal attack?"

"Yes, Mr Marrano. I'm afraid someone intentionally cut her and broke her bones," she explained. "It's shocking to hear, but some people are monsters."

I tightened my grip on the shelf, trying to sound composed despite feeling anything but shocked. "Can I come and see her?"

"I'd prefer if you did. I have more information to share, but I think it's better to tell you in person."

"I'll be there," I promised, almost hanging up before remembering my manners. "Thank you for helping her."

"It's my job *and* my passion, Mr. Marrano. Please, don't thank me."

Regina's treatment would cost me a fortune, making it harder to survive on my savings. But there was nothing I wouldn't do to save her life. If giving up the luxuries I was used to meant giving her a chance, it was a sacrifice I was more than willing to make.

After ending the call, I headed for the front door.

"Where are you going?" Vittoria asked, hurrying after me. "Don't you need to change first?"

I stopped. She was right—I was still in my pyjamas. I turned around and returned to my bedroom.

"So?" Vittoria pressed. "What's the news?"

I opened the first drawer of my dresser and grabbed the first shirt I saw. "Three of her legs are broken, and the vet suspects the wound in her stomach was deliberate."

Leaving the shirt on the table, I moved to the wardrobe and randomly selected a pair of pants.

"A human attacked her?"

I ground my teeth. "Who else?"

As I unbuttoned my shirt, my fingers trembled with anger. I wouldn't rest until I found the monster responsible and made them suffer the same fate they inflicted on Regina. People like them shouldn't roam freely, harming innocent animals without consequence.

Such monsters didn't deserve to live, yet neither did they deserve a quick and painless death. They deserved to be tortured for the rest of their worthless—

Vittoria gasped, and I snapped my head in her direction. Her eyes were wide open, staring at the imprint of *SQ* on my chest. I had completely forgotten about it.

She started towards me. "What is—"

As she reached out to touch it, I grasped her wrist, meeting her startled eyes. "Don't."

"Why?" she asked, baffled. "Did SQ do this? Did they brand you? It's so—"

"*Stop*," I snapped.

Her small frame flinched, and I immediately regretted raising my voice at her.

Releasing her hand, I softened my tone. "You shouldn't have seen it. I'm sorry for raising my voice, but please . . . let's not talk about it. Pretend like you've never seen it, okay?"

She wrapped her fingers around the same wrist I had touched, gazing at me with pity. I hated it. I didn't want her to feel sorry for me. I didn't want any of it.

But she responded in a sad voice, "Okay." She began to turn away. "I'll leave you alone."

"Please, don't leave."

"No, I think I should. I think—"

"Bullshit," I interrupted, stepping in front of her. "I don't want you to leave sad."

"I'm not sad."

But the tears in her eyes betrayed her. Aware of it, she looked away.

Gently, I lifted her chin, guiding her gaze back to mine. "I'm sorry for raising my voice at you."

"That's not why I'm sad," she muttered.

I smiled slightly. "So you *are* sad."

She rolled her eyes. "Of course I am. They hurt you, leaving a scar on your body for—"

"Vittoria," I warned, mindful of my tone this time. "I don't want to talk about it."

She went quiet, clearly unhappy.

I released her chin. "Do you want to come with me to visit Regina?"

She crossed her arms over her chest, nodding stiffly.

"Could you please get dressed? And can you promise me you won't mention what you saw again?"

"I will get dressed, but I can't promise you that I won't mention it again."

With that, she stormed out.

36
Bad News

Teodora

***E**TTORE HAD BEEN *BRANDED*.** By *SQ*.

Anger coursed through my veins. If I could drive to SQ, I would have gone and unleashed exactly what I thought about them. But as I dressed and sat in Ettore's car, my anger began to fade. I chose not to bring it up with him, despite my curiosity about how and why he received the branding. Did SQ brand everyone? But if they did, I didn't have anything like that on me, unless it vanished in the fire when my body burned.

I shifted my focus to Regina and asked, "Who could have done that to her?"

It took someone truly evil to harm an innocent animal and leave her to suffer in agony until she bled to death. But I was happy she had persevered and returned home to seek help. She was alive, but at what cost?

"I don't know," he replied. "But I'll do anything to find them."

I hoped whatever the vet had to say wouldn't be anything bad.

"Is that possible?"

"I can track down anyone."

"Is tracking people your job?"

Could I have been right all along? The time in the kitchen, I was merely guessing, not seriously considering it. But it seemed I might have stumbled upon the truth.

"No," he said absentmindedly, making no effort to hide his job this time.

"How can you track someone knowing nothing about them?"

With one hand on the steering wheel, he reached towards the glove compartment. "I have no clue yet."

As he stretched out his hand, his sleeve rose, uncovering an inked stem winding up his forearm and disappearing beneath the fabric. Knowing his love for flowers, it had to be a flower. I didn't even know he had a tattoo. He always wore long sleeves, regardless of the weather.

He pulled out a tissue and dabbed it against his forehead, absorbing the sweat.

"Do you have a flower on your arm?" I asked.

He went still before answering hesitantly, "Yes."

"Can I see more of it?"

"I'm driving."

I nibbled on my lip. "Can you tell me what flower it is?"

"An iris," he said. "I got it when I turned eighteen."

"Does it have a special meaning?"

He frowned. "Why do people always assume tattoos must have meaning? Can't we get a tattoo just because?"

"Yes, but isn't it because tattoos are permanent? People might want something meaningful if it's going to last forever."

"Fair enough."

Silence fell.

"So your tattoo doesn't mean anything?" I pressed.

"No, it does."

I gave him an unimpressed look, but he ignored it, proceeding with, "Do you know what irises symbolise?"

"I thought you were the flower enthusiast among us."

A faint smile graced his lips. "Can you guess?"

I didn't like guessing games, but Ettore was going through a tough time. Regina's condition was uncertain. As much as it pained me to think about her, I could only imagine how he felt.

The least I could do was humour him.

"Hmm . . ." I pressed my lips together thoughtfully. "Does it symbolise a strong and handsome man?"

He let out a laugh. "Pardon?"

I shrugged. "It would suit you."

He lowered his head slightly, his lips closed in a shy smile. His awkwardness brought a smile to my face, not because I enjoyed his discomfort, but because I found him endearing.

"Should I keep guessing?" I asked.

"No," he said hastily. "If your guesses are anything like the first one, I'd die from your compliments."

"That's precisely my plan."

He shot me a playful glance. "Evil."

I could come up with plenty more compliments, but if they had such an impact on him, I didn't mind saving them for later.

"So what does it mean?" I asked.

"Loyalty."

I stifled a laugh. "To whom? The cu—I mean, the organisation?"

He shot me a pointed look, causing me to bite back a smile. "SQ is my home. I don't know life beyond it. My entire family is part of it. Well . . . almost."

He meant his uncle—the traitor.

When I saw Maxime's name on the table, it was the first name that rang a bell since I had woken up. Maybe it had nothing to do with my past. Maybe I had just heard it before. It was strange how I knew his uncle's name better than my husband's.

Ettore parked the car outside the clinic and opened the door for me. As we walked towards the entrance, he hurried ahead to hold another door open. I thanked him and entered the clinic, where a lanky man with glasses slipping down his nose stood behind the counter.

"Good morning," Ettore greeted. "We're here for Regina."

"Good morning." The man glanced up, pushing his glasses back up. "Please, wait a moment."

He turned around and disappeared through the open doors. After a short while, he returned with a woman half his height, dressed in a white lab coat, her black hair styled in a pixie cut. She must be a veterinarian.

"Mr Marrano," she addressed him, "please, come with me."

We followed her as she led us through the doors and down the hallway into a room with cages. We passed row after row of empty cages until we came to the end.

The vet turned to face us. "I'm sure you want to see her." She inclined her head towards the cage on her right.

I turned to look and saw Regina lying there with a cone around her neck. A tube connected to her front leg, while bandages wrapped her presumably broken legs.

It felt like my heart was being squeezed.

Poor baby.

"When can we take her home?" Ettore voiced what was on my mind.

"About that . . ." She let out a heavy sigh. "Since Regina lost a lot of blood, I had to transfer some. But while running tests, I found something."

In the deafening silence of the room, I could only hear the pounding of my heart.

She drew in a deep breath. "I'm afraid Regina has contracted bubonic plague."

Ettore stormed out without waiting to hear the rest. Despite my urge to go after him and comfort him, I remained behind. Someone needed to stay to get more information.

"How serious is it?" I asked.

"I can't say for certain. I've given her antibiotics, but it will be three days before we know if her condition improves. But given how weakened her body is after the incident, it may impact the healing process."

We could do nothing but wait.

"Is there anything else we need to know?"

She offered me a sad smile. "No, that's it."

I glanced at poor Regina. At least she was in good hands and well cared for. Ettore, however . . .

"I'll go check on Ettore," I said before hurrying out.

I found him leaning against the building, a cigarette between his fingers. As soon as he saw me approaching, he quickly dropped it and extinguished it with his foot.

I looked at him, puzzled. Did he think I wouldn't notice? And why would he care if I saw him smoking now when he hadn't before?

"She's in good hands," I tried to reassure him.

He shook his head, his expression heavy with worry. "I have no doubt about that. It's just . . ."

"Just what?" I prompted gently.

"It's bad news after bad news. When is it going to stop? For all I know, they're going to find a tumour the next day."

Crossing my arms over my chest, I stepped towards him. "I don't believe in God."

Confusion flashed across his face, and he opened his mouth, but I pressed my finger against his lips.

"I'm not finished."

As I withdrew my finger, he mimed zipping his lips shut.

"I know I asked you to stop by the church and forced you to stay there. But if I truly believed in God, do you think I would have allowed what you did?" The memory resurfaced of his head disappearing under my skirt, and his skilled tongue . . . I wished to experience it at least once more.

"But you . . . *prayed*," he whispered the last word as if it were taboo.

"I did," I agreed. "But not to God. I believe in a higher power than us. I believe in miracles. But I also believe in medicine. I believe the veterinarian will do everything possible to treat her. She'll live. And they won't find any tumours."

I might be lying.

But I was telling him what he wanted to hear. What *I* wanted to hear. As if knowing that someone intentionally hurt Regina wasn't enough, we received more terrible news.

It wasn't fair.

"But come to think of it . . ." I pondered aloud. "If not for the evildoer who attacked her, we might have never learnt about the plague, or learnt about it too late."

He frowned. "Those are cruel words, Vittoria."

"They're cruel, but they're no less true."

"You don't know," he objected. "Maybe the same monster injected her with the plague."

I opened my mouth to dismiss the possibility but stopped, realising I could be wrong. If the evildoer was from SQ, anything was possible. They had already coerced a scientist into unleashing a disease. Who knew what other secrets they were hiding?

We stood in silence until he tenderly lifted my chin with his fingers, drawing my gaze towards his own. "Thank you for caring," he murmured softly. "It feels less lonely now that I know I'm not alone."

I smiled, covering his wrist with my hand. "We'll get through this. We'll fight with her. Together."

His lips lifted slightly—a glimpse of sunlight amidst the uncertainty and chaos of the past twenty-four hours. "Together," he promised.

We held each other's gaze for a long moment. The desire to draw closer and kiss him surged inside me, yet I remained rooted in place.

He didn't make a move either.

Maybe later.

February 15, 1966

Our mystery girl gets picked up early in the morning and taken to a secluded building outside the city. The building was new to me, but it looked like an abandoned hotel.

Some shady stuff was definitely going on, but I wasn't there to snitch. I was there to find out who the girl was.

They would kill me if they learned I had suspicions about this place without telling them. But they're going to find out eventually. They always do.

Unless, of course, nothing shady is

going on.
She left late, when the sky was dark, and someone drove her to her apartment. It's the same routine every day. I think it's time to ask questions instead of just observing.

37
Off To Paris

Ettore

AS FAR AS I KNEW, TEODORA SAUVAGE HAD NO FRIENDS. Morgana was my best lead, but getting in contact with her wasn't so easy. Her drug-addicted sister, however . . .

As a former drug addict, tricking other addicts was hardly a challenge. But, in the large city where Lizette Sauvage lived, locating the places where drugs were sold was much more difficult.

I narrowed my search to the bars and nightclubs near her apartment, excluding those that only sold soft drugs. She was too deeply involved for those to have any effect on her.

I called Raff, hoping he was home, although he rarely was.

To my relief, he answered. "Yes?"

"I need to check out some locations where Teodora's mother might be," I said. "I'll need you to gather a team of four people who can travel to Paris and keep an eye on these spots."

"Already on it, *boss*," he responded, causing me to grimace at the word *boss*. "Anything else?"

"Yes." I glanced at the map of Paris pinned to the evidence

board. "Pack the essentials. We're also going to Paris."

We drove all night and arrived in the morning. It had been a while since I had last ventured outside Monaco and Nice. While five men watched the spots where most drug deals appeared to happen, we kept an eye on Lizette's apartment. I had chosen not to risk breaking into it.

This wasn't Monte Carlo. Any suspicions could lead to police involvement, forcing us to leave to avoid trouble. The French police didn't scare us, but their interference could slow us down. We couldn't afford to waste any more time when Teodora might be out there, working on an alternative cure.

We might be wrong and she might not know the recipe for the Cure, but it was better to be safe than sorry. Even if it turned out she wasn't involved, she still had to be found, then imprisoned and killed. She was meant to die in the fire alongside the other scientists.

Raff opened the door, about to leave the car.

"What are you doing?" I asked.

He gave me a puzzled look. "Going to check the apartment?"

I grabbed his sleeve and pulled him back into the car. "Someone might see you and alert the police."

He worked his jaw before closing the door with reluctance. Raff had no patience to wait and watch, but it was inevitable in our work.

We spent an hour observing the building, but none of the people who came and went had red hair.

Raff's stomach growled in the silence.

I gave him a pointed glance. "Tell me you brought something to eat."

We didn't know how long it would take to find her, and there was always the risk of something going wrong. Although I had told Raff to pack the essentials, I didn't specifically mention food, assuming it was obvious. Now, I was worried it wasn't. You could never be sure with Raff.

"Of course." He leant over to grab his backpack from the back seat. Sitting back down, he unzipped it and took out a box of crackers.

"Don't you have something more filling?"

"Why? This is plenty." He tore open the box and offered it to me. "Want some?"

I declined, preferring to stay focused.

He shrugged, grabbed a handful of crackers, and stuffed them into his mouth, chewing with his mouth open. Was he deliberately trying to annoy me out of boredom? If so, it was working.

"Could you *be* any louder?" I asked.

He grinned. "Of course!"

His chewing intensified, the rhythmic sound growing increasingly irritating. *Chew, chew, chew, chew—*

I snatched the box from him. "You should eat proper food, not this junk."

"I deserve it," he declared. "I won the championship."

"Lost your friend too."

The words slipped out faster than I could think. My chest felt heavy with regret as an uncomfortable silence filled the car. But in my defence, every time Raff won he wouldn't stop bragging for weeks. He rarely lost, and when he did, he fell silent. Only Vittoria dared to tease him about losing, often leading to a fight between the two.

But Vittoria usually quickly put an end to it with a kick to his groin. Raff was terrible at defending his weakest spot. If hitting your opponent in their private area wasn't against the rules, he wouldn't win as often.

This would have been more lively if Vittoria was here. She and Raff would bicker endlessly, but at least I'd be left in peace with my thoughts. Now, Raff had only me to annoy, and my patience didn't last long.

Sighing, I handed the crackers back to Raff. His face lit up as he took it, and he batted his eyelashes, adopting a childish tone. "Thank you, daddy."

This was going to be a long wait.

After he finished the crackers, he pulled out a bottle of soda.

"Don't drink too much, or you'll need a restroom," I warned.

"I won't."

He gulped down the entire contents of the bottle.

Raff was the epitome of a child. Working with him was a constant reminder that I wasn't cut out for fatherhood. I was easily annoyed, cherished silence, and valued my alone time. Having children would take all of that away.

And if the doctors were right, having children wasn't an option for me anyways, not after the car crash. At least it was something I could thank Antoine for.

"Can you keep watch while I find a peeing place?" Raff asked.

I looked at him unbelievingly. "And what if Lizette shows up? I leave you behind and follow her?"

"You'll manage." He opened the door. "But I really need to pee."

As he left, I sank deeper into my seat, watching, watching, and . . .

Despite feeling less annoyed when alone, I hoped Raff would return soon. I was a tracker and a driver, but dealing with people was best left to him.

As I reached into my pocket for a cigarette, my fingertips brushed against something soft. Confused, I pulled it out. It was a white lacy underwear, a memento from when I had taken it off Vittoria in the church. I smiled at the memory.

The crackle of the walkie-talkie startled me, breaking the moment.

"Ettore, are you here?" Raff's voice crackled through the device.

I hadn't realised he had taken his walkie-talkie with him. I pushed the underwear back into my pocket. My own walkie-talkie lay at the far end of the back seat. As I reached for it, my fingers couldn't grasp it.

"Ettore?" Raff asked.

I stretched as far as I could, finally grabbing it. Back in my seat, I pressed the button and asked, "Did you contact me to tell me you found a *peeing place*?"

I released the button, and his distorted laugh came through. "I did, but that's not why," he said. "One of my men contacted me. They spotted our redhead at a nightclub."

38

Teodora Sauvage

Teodora

THE SOUND OF WAVES CRASHING ON THE SHINGLE BROUGHT PEACE TO MY MIND AS I STOOD ON THE ROCK IN FRONT OF THE SEA. It offered a much-needed break from constant worry about Regina's condition.

Just in case, I had put on a swimsuit beneath my dress. The cloudless sky offered no protection from the blazing sun, tempting me to take off the dress and dive into the water. It would have been a true blessing, but I remained rooted in place.

I couldn't bring myself to dip even my toes into the water, and I never knew why. It was just water—something I felt drawn to, yet every time I neared it, I didn't dare to touch it. *Strange.*

"Natalie is asking for you on the phone."

I startled, hesitating to turn to him. Being alone with Antoine always sent uncomfortable chills down my spine.

I tore my gaze away from the sea and made my way up the stony stairs back to the backyard, avoiding looking at him.

Part of me felt relieved that Natalie's call interrupted my

internal dilemma about whether to go for a swim. But another part of me wondered if I would have mustered the courage to do so if she hadn't called.

"Why do you act so strange every time I'm around?" Antoine asked.

He knew perfectly well why. I had no reason to say it.

Ignoring him, I hastened towards the villa.

"It's rude coming from my sister-in-law," he said. The word *sister-in-law* sounded completely wrong after learning about the sexual assault. "You're treating me as if I've committed murder. The least you could do is explain, so I can avoid making the same mistake again."

He followed me into the villa and straight into the living room. Despite the tension in my body and my shaky fingers, I found Natalie's number in the phone book. As I lifted the handset, it almost slipped from my grasp, but I managed to dial the number before bringing it to my ear.

"Vittoria?" she guessed.

I managed a smile, even with Antoine in my peripheral vision, waiting for an explanation. "Yes, that's me."

"I have good news," she said. "I talked Ettore into letting you repaint your room."

Even though I had slept in my own room every night, except for the one time I slept in Ettore's bedroom, I hadn't thought about our conversation about repainting. But ever since returning from the vet, I rarely spent my days indoors. The dark bathroom and the depressing bedroom no longer occupied my thoughts. Suddenly, caring about renovation seemed trivial.

"That's *great*," I replied, unintentionally emphasising *great*.

Hopefully, Natalie wouldn't ask if something was wrong.

"I heard about Regina." Her voice lowered, less enthusiastic. "But she's a strong girl. I'm positive the plague has no chances against her."

I sensed Antoine's eyes on me, intense and unwavering. Why couldn't he let it go and leave me be?

"Yeah, I agree." I pursed my lips together, not sure what else to add.

A pause hung between us. If she expected more from me, she would be disappointed. It was a sensitive topic, and I didn't want to delve deeper into it.

"I think a little distraction will do you good," she suggested finally, her tone lightening up. "I'll swing by later today, and you will tell me what changes you want in your room. Then, I'll organise a renovation team to start. Does that plan sound good to you, or have you changed your mind?"

I considered not renovating my room, but Natalie was right—I needed a distraction. Waiting for news about Regina's condition was torture, and it hadn't even been a day.

"No, I . . ." I took a deep breath. "That sounds good."

"Great! See you soon!"

As she ended the call, I hesitated to return the handset and face Antoine. I clutched it tighter, then relaxed my grip and put it down.

"I believe it's best if you respect my wishes and keep your distance, Antoine," I said, hiding my surprise from my own sudden courage. "The why doesn't matter. All that matters is what I want." Turning to him, I forced myself to meet his gaze. "You will respect that. Do you understand?"

My heart raced. I hoped I hadn't made a mistake. It might have been foolish to talk to him like this while we were alone. There would be no one to help me if he attempted something.

He chuckled, but his amusement faded when he noticed my serious expression. "Is this about the drugs I gave you according to my brother?"

I frowned. "Drugs?"

He stepped back. "Never mind."

As he turned to leave, I stepped forward. "No," I said firmly. "You will tell me exactly what you meant."

"If Ettore didn't tell you, I shouldn't meddle."

"You're already meddling," I retorted. "You mentioned it; you might as well finish explaining."

I knew I should stop now. If the diary was right . . . this could end badly for me.

He turned to me slowly. "Remember the night we had dinner with our parents and then went to the bar? You ended up in the hospital, and . . ." He paused, furrowing his brow. "Is it even relevant? You don't remember."

"I do," I assured him, though I couldn't recall how I ended up in the hospital. But now I had an idea why. "My guess is you're the reason why I was there."

"So Ettore thinks."

His response left me puzzled. "Is that not what you think?"

"I'm not the bad guy here, Vittoria," he said. "But I have a history of drug abuse, and sometimes I'm in the wrong place at the wrong time."

Even though he sounded sincere, I couldn't bring myself to believe him. Not because of what the diary said, but because I didn't remember Antoine. To me, he was a stranger with drug issues. Could I really trust someone like that?

"If you're not the one who drugged me, who was it?"

He looked down, and I could tell he knew who had done it, or at least suspected. But he wouldn't tell. Maybe there was nothing to tell after all. I couldn't be sure if he had drugged me, but one thing was clear: he was a big liar, and not very good at it. If someone else had drugged me, he would have told me. Why hide it unless there was nothing to hide in the first place?

"Just stay away from me," I said before making my way to leave.

Once again, Antoine couldn't take the hint and followed me. I quickly opened the first door I saw, entered the room, and slammed the door shut, locking it before he could enter.

His footsteps quieted. He stood outside the door, silent. I listened intently, waiting for him to say or do something. Finally, I heard him walking away. As his footsteps faded into the distance, I hesitated to leave.

I didn't want to.

Not after I had entered the one room that had always been locked. Until now.

I turned around, taking in Ettore's office. I was seeing it for the first time. I had always respected his space, never entering while he worked. But in his absence, I attempted to get inside only to find it locked. He must have forgotten to lock it this time.

Ettore's office had a veranda, which he likely used for breaks to enjoy some fresh air or smoke a cigarette. Papers cluttered his desk, tempting me to tidy them up. But as I moved closer, I stopped myself. I couldn't risk him finding out, even if Antoine knew I was here and could snitch on me anyway.

My eyes caught on the photo amidst the mess. A woman in a bikini stood with the sea behind her, her curly red hair flowing. She wore a slight smile, with a playful twinkle in her eyes. She looked like me, and yet not quite.

Was that me before the accident?

I swallowed hard.

I shouldn't be here.

I looked away, noticing a large board with notes, photos, and red threads forming straight lines. They all led to the picture at the centre, barely visible from where I stood. Intrigued, I stepped closer.

Another picture of a girl with long, curly hair who closely resembled me. But her glasses appeared too big for her face, and her eyes lacked emotion. There were red threads stretched from the image to different locations—an apartment building, a house, a map of Paris. If Ettore was a tracker, he must have been searching for her.

In the corner, a stunning woman smiled in the picture. She looked incredibly familiar. I moved closer, studying the photo. Above it, a note read *Lizette Sauvage*.

I glanced at the name below the girl's picture.

Teodora Sauvage.

They were related.

We—

I staggered back, a sinking feeling settling deep in my stomach, constricting my chest. Each name echoed in my mind, like the beat of my racing heart.

Morgana . . . *Beat.* Lizette . . . *Beat, beat.* Lilou . . . *Beat, beat, beat.*

My head spun, and I stumbled backward, the back of my legs hitting the edge of the desk.

Teodora Sauvage. Teodora Sauvage. Teodora Sauvage.

Falling to my knees, I pressed my hand to my head, looking up at her picture on the board.

I knew *her*. I knew Teodora Sauvage.

Because Teodora is me.

February 26, 1966

Lorence caved in.

I had him cornered. He tried to dodge my questions, but I was done accepting things as they were. He was clearly hiding something, and I was going to find out what it was, no matter what.

The mystery girl I've been following wasn't a waste of time. He told me everything. If he had told me that three years ago, I might have been surprised, thrown a tantrum, and rejected him as a father. But I didn't have that in me anymore. I cared less.

The girl is my twin sister, who was fortunate enough to escape my crappy life.

Acknowledgments

I feel like no one reads the acknowledgments (I rarely do), but I have people to thank, okay. They deserve it.

First, a huge thank you to my Beta Readers—Marta, Britt, Hanae, Jasmine, Mystique, Bianca, Molly, Anmol, and Magdalena. You have all been absolute angels, and I don't know what I would have done without you. This book certainly wouldn't have been as good without your feedback, that's for sure! And a special thanks to Nale, the follower who suggested the perfect name for this duology!

I'm incredibly grateful to my parents. Without their sacrifices, which allowed me to live rather than exist, this book wouldn't have been possible. I also want to thank my partner's parents and grandparents for giving me the freedom to focus on writing without worry.

To my partner: you have been the most supportive. Even when it was hard for me to find time to write without feeling guilty about not spending it with you, you always understood. The desktop computer you gave me helped immensely with my motivation. The big screen! You also helped me figure out the first chapter when I was rewriting the book in Autumn, 2023. We had our arguments about what's real and what's fiction. Fiction doesn't always have to be perfectly logical, but I still wanted it to make sense. You helped me achieve that.

I must also acknowledge my precious cats. Without Mice, whom I thought was a girl until he got sick, Regina wouldn't exist. And without my five-year-old cat, Night, who survived a horrifying 24 hours, nearly bleeding to death, and returned home on two bent legs—a haunting image that will stay with me forever—Regina wouldn't exist either. Mice and Night, without you, Regina wouldn't be possible. Night, my dear dark beauty, I love you so much. I'm beyond grateful that you persevered like Regina and returned home to get help. You deserve to live, my gentle creature.

To my need to experience new things. If I hadn't applied to the European Leadership School in Nice in 2022, the events would have only taken place in Monte Carlo. Nice is beautiful, and I hope to return someday. I want to see the locations I've included in this book in real life (like the church). And since this story isn't over, I already have another story planned in this universe.

Thank you for reading!

Love,
Austea

Currently, Austea lives in Norway with her partner, writing books and creating silly videos on social media. She has three cats in Lithuania and misses them every day. Staying in one place, whether physically or mentally, doesn't work for her, and this affects her writing. She can write in any genre but promises that there will always be romance.

Follow her journey on Instagram! @austea.kette

Printed in Great Britain
by Amazon